I0594917

ISBN 979-8-9922586-3-9

THE
KEY
TO THE
CUBIC
CONUNDRUM

By

Steve Rundle

PROLOGUE

1

The giant accusatory finger of the smokestack stabbed upwards through the falling rain towards the roiling night above. From Richard's perspective, blinking back raindrops as he peered upwards, his objective at the top of the stack appeared impossibly out of reach. His eyes followed the twin lines of thin cord appearing out of the mists above down the curved concrete face of the smokestack to where he held them in his hand. They ran down to one side of thick cable that when the mists cleared could just be glimpsed running up to a metal box near the top of the stack. Satisfied that the lines were not caught on any of the brackets holding the thick cable to the stack, he lowered his head allowing the brim of his western hat to shed the rain down the back of the long leather coat that was keeping the rest of him mostly dry.

Richard had flown the cord with a top pulley and climbing hook up to the top of the stack in the last rays of sunset using one of his work drones. Now securely hooked on to the top of the stack, the cord was ready to lift the carefully laid out coil of climbing rope that lay at his feet. Richard glanced out towards the guard shack at the construction site entry.

He reached inside the long leather coat and keyed the transmit button on the radio. "Everything's ready here at the stack. As soon as the night shift guards complete their patrol and are back inside the guard shack, I'll start my ascent."

As he waited for the guard patrol to pass, Richard took a moment to look around. He was standing on the roof of a single-story extension running from the newly built power plant building out to the smokestack. The newly built coal fired power plant was lit up brightly against the misty night sky behind him, but the roof area, where he was standing, was lost in the shadows at the foot of the towering smokestack.

The thick cable he had to deal with this evening came off the bottom of the concrete smokestack onto a curving cable tray. The cable tray held the cable in gentle right angle turn until it was running horizontally across the roof toward the plant building.

Behind him was the brightly lit turbine building and the steam plant wing where coal was burned. He followed the steel structure of the coal conveyor out from the power plant building until it was lost in the darkness of the massive coal yard beyond. Only the first few coal cars of the long trains of waiting coal were visible at one side of the yard. Shorter coal ash conveyors angled down from the steam plant building towards the waiting ash containment lagoons that would soon start to fill with the massive quantities of burnt coal ash.

Richard recalled how the power plant had been built over the objections, protests, and even arrests of members of the environmental and social justice groups that he had first become involved with during his college years. The power plant was huge - oversized in fact for the regional power needs. The monopoly utility company, constrained to low profit margins for the electricity it produced, was allowed to make a generous profit on any newly built power plants. This meant the larger and more expensive the plant, the larger the profit margin that could be raked in from the associated customer electric bill increases.

The problem for the utility managers was that distributed clean renewable alternatives like solar panels were plunging in cost and were now making traditional centralized fossil fuel generation look expensive by comparison. To maintain the generous profits that kept shareholders happy paying their generous salaries, the utility management needed new plant projects. New projects for which the costs plus a healthy profit could be fully passed on to thier customers. The prospect of more and more of their bill paying customers independently, being able to generate their own electric needs with free sunlight during the day and stored battery power at night would mean their electric bills would fall to nothing.

Growing numbers of energy-independent customers, with low or no power bills, would push electric bills for those customers left holding the coal-fired bag into double-digit territory. Steep electric bill increases would drive even more customers to adopt solar/renewables to avoid paying the coal-fired "tab". This "death spiral" cycle of fewer and fewer customers left to pay a higher and higher percentage of the new coal plant "tab", was a nightmare scenario for utility management.

It had led utility management to spend millions in customer dollars lobbying legislators to slow and undermine renewable adoption and had achieved getting the most utility-friendly public utility commission regulators appointed. While the utility management saw the proverbial writing on the solar panels for their generous profits, their lobbying investment provided this last chance. Getting a new coal-fired plant of this size built would lock in their monopoly control over power generation. This would ensure the decades of generous profits needed to prop up their salaries for the remainder of their careers.

Activists and community groups had mobilized early in opposition to the utility management's initial proposal for the huge coal-fired power plant. The utility-friendly regulators had received an earful about how clean renewable technologies were now the best "least cost" option for power generation. It was argued by these groups that rooftop solar distributed across home and business rooftops, when paired with batteries and demand response controls, made communities more resilient and healthier.

The groups felt it was a mistake for regulators to even consider building this fossil-fuel dinosaur of a power plant. The megatons of greenhouse gases, heavy metals emitted and local pollution that would be generated would increase asthma and shorten lives in the region. The "cozy" relationship with the utility-friendly regulators, that the years of lobbying had achieved, paid off with deaf ears and a vote to allow the utility to proceed with construction.

So, construction of the plant began along with increased rallies and actions by Richard's activist friends and organizations in protest. The size of the power plant would require endless trainloads of coal to be burned, producing hundreds of thousands of tons of smokestack emissions and nearly half a million pounds of coal ash every year. Due to the size of the plant, these stack emissions would make the plant a major emitter of mercury and other harmful pollutants.

Pressure by environmental organizations produced changes to environmental law that now required major emitters of hazardous emissions, such as the coal-fired plant, to install the best available pollution control technology. This would at least "scrub" most of the harmful pollutants out of the coal-fired power plant emissions before they were sent out the smokestack. This scrubbing process came at a cost, so utilities had been known to disable the scrubbers to avoid the cost when they could get away with it.

A requirement for the latest on-stack emissions monitoring equipment and independent third-party monitoring of its data was also included, so the utility could no longer get away with shutting off or bypassing the pollution control scrubbers. Additional efforts at the national level by a coalition of non-governmental environmental and social justice organizations looked likely to achieve even further emissions limiting rules for fossil fuel plants. The proposed rules this NGO coalition was advocating for would require, not just the present day removal of the most harmful pollutants, but also the phased in future capture of the millions of tons of climate-warming carbon emissions produced over the life of the power plant.

The plant manager, used to the old coal fired plants he had

operated that were able pollute without limits, had resisted the expense of the pollution scrubbers and was loudly opposed to the carbon capture and sequestration rulemaking that the NGO coalition was pushing for at the federal level. When the federal rules came out that functionally mandated the coal-fired plant to install carbon capture equipment and to sequester the train loads of captured carbon emissions in offsite permanent storage locations, the plant manager was irate. Richard had seen him on the local news railing against the new rules and the added expense that might "bankrupt" the utility. Word from the NGO coalition was that there was no danger of bankruptcy. There was only the danger that the overpaid utility management salaries might have to be trimmed back and the plant becoming an expensive stranded asset if renewable energy prices continued to plummet.

Once the ruling had been issued and it was clear there would be no avoiding the expense of carbon capture, the plant manager decided the "cozy" relationship with the utility-friendly regulators had to be leveraged. Even though he had no influence over the respected third-party monitoring group that had installed the smokestack pollution monitoring system, he had managed to repeatedly delay the system's final check out. He intentionally rescheduled the plant startup test runs to a weekend when the third-party group would not have the pollution monitoring system running.

A utility-friendly testing company was brought in to do only spot pollution sampling in the area surrounding the plant during the startup tests. As the plant manager expected, only favorably low emissions were included in the sampling report. At the next utility commission hearing, the plant manager was able to produce the gamed low emission reports, saying they showed concerns voiced by the community and environmental expert speakers were overblown. He said the results of the spot test reports were clear enough that the power plant could be reclassified as a minor emitter that would not be required to have any pollution or carbon capture equipment installed.

A woman from one of the national NGOs, pointed out the

potential errors in the spot pollution testing methodology used in the report and noted the previously delayed smokestack emissions monitoring system was scheduled to be fully working in time for the upcoming final commissioning tests of the power plant. She said with all the expert opinion concerns voiced and the testimony of hundreds that had turned up to the hearing in opposition, holding off any decision until the monitoring system installed in the smokestack could give provide them more accurate data was surely warranted.

The cozy relationship with the regulators paid off with a vote at the end of the hearing in favor of reclassifying the plant as a minor emitter and not requiring any pollution controls or stack emissions monitoring at all. To the visible chagrin of the plant manager, one of the regulators bucked the majority and said they would revisit the issue if data from the smokestack monitoring during the final tests varied significantly from the reports the plant manager had submitted.

After the surprise ruling and the resulting community uproar, regulators quickly moved to end the hearing, leaving out the back so they could avoid the press. As Richard and his friends had come out of the hearing room, he saw a huddle of the local community leaders and non-governmental organization experts gathered at the far end of the lobby. One of the regional environmental leaders, who knew Richard, waved for him to wait up and walked quickly over. He thanked Richard's friends for speaking out against the reclassification at the hearing, but said he needed to nab Richard.

He ushered Richard over to the huddle where a couple of the leaders nodded at him as joined. A discussion was going on around the importance of setting a precedent with this power plant that would head off utilities across the country from similarly attempting to flout the new emissions laws. It appeared to Richard that the leaders were counting on the continuous emissions monitoring system installed on the smokestack to provide data from the final commissioning testing that would contradict the spot testing reports. By proving their point about the plant being a major hazardous emitter, they could then have the minor emitter permit revoked, and the utility would be forced to install the emission control equipment to remove the pollution and train cars of carbon.

One of the NGO leaders said that the fully installed continuous emissions monitoring system had reported a serious error that morning. He said that the tubes in the cable that brought emission samples from the probe at the top of the stack down to the analyzing equipment on ground level appeared to have been cut. The error had occurred before dawn that morning just ahead of the scaffolding contractor unexpectedly showing up early to take down the scaffolding surrounding the smokestack. By the time a service technician could get out to the site, the scaffolding had already been taken down and the probe box at the very top of the smokestack was left inaccessible. This seeming sabotage would make any data worthless in their effort to overturn the minor emitter decision.

A debate about the need to bring in a very large crane with a work bucket to make the repair had started up, but the woman from national that Richard had seen testify, interrupted the discussion. She suggested to the group that the utility representative that had sauntered over to listen in on their conversation, was surely being too polite to verbally ask them to leave. She said they could take a hint and would do their part to help clear out the lobby of the building. The NGO leaders announced the lobby was closing and for those remaining to please take their conversations outside.

They all headed out the doors into the night, but the regional environmental leader that had called Richard aside, steered him towards a church bus at the far end of the parking lot. As they climbed onto the bus and took seats at the back, the regional leader showed Richard some photos of the tall smokestack with the probe box looking tiny near the top and the thick cable containing the sampling tubes that ran vertically up the stack. They talked over ideas amid the increasing buzz of surrounding conversations as the gathering from the lobby reconvened in the bus seats.

Silence fell over the bus when the woman from national ushered a man Richard had not seen, into the bus. There was only room left for her to stand in the front stairwell as the person in the driver's seat closed the door. The woman introduced the man as being from the respected third-party emission sampling company that had installed the monitoring system. She said that the man was someone she had worked with over the years who could be trusted. She asked the man to give the group an overview of the problem and what it would take to get it fixed.

The man outlined the probable cutting of the "umbilical" cable sampling tubes inside of the probe box a hundred feet in the air near the top of the smokestack. The tubes could not simply be spliced and still meet code, so any repair would involve dealing with the entire length of the "umbilical" cable, as he called it. The man faced a flurry of questions about; how fast could another umbilical be ordered in? – would the scaffold need to be erected again? – could a new umbilical be installed with just a crane and a single man bucket? - could the system be back working in only a couple of days in time for the commissioning tests? The woman from national let the group run on for minute before asking for them to pause their discussions to let the man speak.

"No, No", he said, "You don't understand. There is additional umbilical cable length down in the analyzer room behind the equipment racks. We do not need to replace the entire "umbilical". We just need to loosen the clamps spaced up the smokestack and scoot the cable up a couple of feet through the strain relief mesh grips and we will wind up with plenty of length at the top to reattach the sampling tubes to the probe. It all comes down to how to make that happen hundreds of feet in the air now that there is no scaffold to get up there."

One of the leaders said he had checked on a crane and the few that were tall enough were not available for weeks. Another leader said that a scaffold approach, unless the exact same configuration was used could take days to engineer and days to set up. Either way they would miss repairing the monitoring system before the final commissioning tests of the plant took place in a couple of days. Because the utility could again game the spot testing without the continuous stack monitoring system working, the minor emitter ruling would stand, and the plant would be able to start up without pollution controls.

The group again broke into simultaneous discussion that after a moment was cut through by the loud voice of the regional environmental leader who had brought Richard out.

"Folks, may I introduce you to Richard, a member of our organization that has taught rock climbing and who is working his way through engineering school doing specialty climbing repairs for an antenna tower service company."

He asked Richard to tell the group what they had been talking over while looking through photos. Richard outlined how he was brought in to use climber's ascent gear to get up to cell phone transceivers mounted on tall water towers and grain silos to troubleshoot and make needed repairs. If the necessary "umbilical" cable length could be pulled out of the analyzer room out to the base of the smokestack, Richard said he could ascend on his climbing gear, pull up the needed cable length to the probe box and make the repair.

There were some interested murmurs from the gathering and the woman from national spoke up saying, "To clarify, the utility officers and plant manager have not yet heard from your company that there is a problem with the stack monitoring system, correct?"

The man nodded and the woman continued, "Good, whoever is behind cutting the sampling tubes cannot acknowledge they did it. They are probably relying on the inaccessibility and short time window to keep the monitoring system from being repaired ahead of the commissioning. I would suggest Richard be hired to make the repair using his climbing skills. To avoid any further chance of sabotage, I would suggest the work be done in relative secrecy to keep the restoration of the cable tube connections concealed. We know the plant manager had a role in the ongoing delays and likely had a hand in causing this incident, so we need to be sure he and any utility personnel that could report back to him are not aware of the repair. It's my understanding we can restore the umbilical connections but keep the smokestack sampling offline until the regulators are onsite for the emissions tests?"

The man from the monitoring company nodded his assent. She checked with the leaders and after some discussion there seemed to be agreement on the plan. Having consensus, she looked back his way and said, "So, Richard, do you have any problem climbing at night?"

And so it was that Richard found himself on the roof huddled in the rain waiting for the guard changeover. He kept back out of sight as the guard patrol passed and soon the radio in his ear crackled with an all clear once the guard changeover had occurred.

Richard pulled on the lifting cord hoisting the end of the rope quickly up, through the pulley at the top of the stack, and then down until he could securely tie off the end of the rope to the heavy cable tray supports. He then opened the front of his long leather coat to feed the rope through the ascender rig attached to his climbing harness. He felt behind him to see that the small block and tackle was securely clipped onto the back of his harness belt and then double checked all the knots and ascender rigging. Satisfied, he took off his long coat and western hat to hang on the curved cable tray and strapped his climbing helmet on.

His black skintight climbing wear, that had been kept dry by the coat, was now getting wet. His climbing shoes were soaked and soon the rest of him would be soon as well, so he started the deliberate ascent, loosening the clamps holding the umbilical on the side of the stack as he went. Using the mechanical advantage of the block and tackle, he soon had the slack pulled up through the lowest mesh strain relief grip and was on his way ascending from clamp to clamp up the side of the stack.

He was entirely soaked an hour later when he had worked the umbilical slack all the way up to just under the probe enclosure box near the top of the stack. From this height he could look down on the entire expanse of the power plant appearing ghostly in the blowing mists far below. The tinge of fear that always came when working at height was a familiar reminder to take things slowly and carefully. It was those who lost their fear and focus while working at heights that made for unfortunate statistics.

He carefully removed the screws from the one side of the probe enclosure door, pocketed them and zipped the pocket of his climbing jersey closed. He pushed his body out to one side so he could swing the hinged door of the heavy metal enclosure open. Using slings from his harness belt, he worked up a tie back for the door so it could not blow shut on him. He turned on his helmet headlamp on low to examine the damage and was relieved to see only the sampling tubes had been cut through while all the wiring appeared unharmed. Using the block and fall, clamped to the top of the box enclosure he pulled the umbilical slack up through the mesh strain relief just below the box until the slack was all inside the box enclosure.

He carefully cut back the sheathing and insulation surrounding the center sampling tubes to free the length needed for reattachment. He reported in over the radio to say he was ready to reattach the sampling tubes and the voice of the man from the monitoring system company came on to talk him through the steps they had practiced that afternoon.

With the sampling tubes reattached, Richard did some clean up with cable ties to neaten up the installation and then turned off his headlamp to wait in the dark, while the man ran through the calibration tests.

As he hung there on the side of the stack waiting, Richard warmed his hands in the front pockets of his jersey and noticed the familiar soreness that came from hanging in a climbing harness for this long. The radio at last crackled with the acknowledgement that all was back in working order and he was clear to button up the box and come down. Richard made sure his hands were warmed up before carefully taking out the screws one by one to seal up the enclosure. Fumbling a screw at this height, meant it was gone for good.

He again checked his hands and arms to make sure his grip was strong, before changing over from the ascent rigging to rappelling configuration. He kicked back gently and lowered himself to the first umbilical clamp below. Keeping a hold on the rope with one hand, he reached out to tighten the clamp with his other hand. Kicking off repeatedly he made his way down tightening clamps and checking the mesh strain relief grips were properly holding up each section of umbilical.

The tiredness did not hit him until his climbing shoes had firmly landed back in the puddle on the roof. He quickly unclipped from the rope, stripped off the climbing harness, and then using the thin cord, he lowered and coiled the rope. With the rope coiled and the cord detached from the end, he stepped back and yanked on the cord to cause the end to zip up out of sight, come out of the pulley at the top and start the long fall back from the top of the stack.

Richard traded his soaked climbing helmet for the warm felt of the western hat and wrapped himself back in the long coat. As he closed the front, the gusty mists were fended off and warmth started to spread back through his limbs. He took a last look up at the repaired umbilical cable running up the smokestack, gathered up the coils of rope and cord, and then headed down off the roof.

The next day Richard was in the conference room at the monitoring company facility with many of the NGO coalition leaders to watch the commissioning tests. One of the monitoring company techs had set up a camera in the control room and everyone was gathered in the conference room to watch the feed on the large screen at the end of the room. They watched as the plant manager ordered the coal-fired power plant to start up and run at a low level. The regulatory agency inspectors were watching the banks of readouts in the control room expecting them to spring to life.

One of the inspectors noticed that the continuous emissions monitoring system was not showing the stack sampling analysis and mentioned it. The plant manager said that stack sampling had unexpectedly failed, and they would regretfully have to go back to spot sampling for the commissioning test. They watched the man from the emissions sampling company enter the control room and ask the plant manager what the problem was. He nodded at his explanation that the emission samples just weren't coming in from his worthless monitoring system. They saw the plant manager turn away to hide a self-satisfied grin as the man walked over to the analyzer rack and flipped a switch. The smokestack emission sample readings magically started appearing in front of the widening eyes of the plant manager and the inspectors. The inspectors looked more closely at the readouts and then their eyes narrowed. Even at this low level of plant operation, the hazardous emission readings from the huge plant were clearly showing up in the stack analysis as anything but "minor" and the inspectors told the plant manager so.

Just then a utility employee came running into the room, to hand the plant manager a press release, hurriedly saying the protest groups were going to be holding a press conference out front regarding the upcoming pollution and carbon emissions capture equipment the utility would be responsibly installing.

The plant manager sputtered as he glanced down at the press release saying, "They'll get emissions captured over my dead body."

Richard had read a draft of the release earlier which outlined the major emissions the plant was discovered to be producing in this morning's commissioning tests. The plant manager was listed as one of those invited to speak on behalf of the utility to the press regarding the newfound concern the utility had for the health of the surrounding communities. The press release outlined the generous pollution control measures the utility would be implementing to ensure the protection of surrounding communities and the city.

Richard thought he could see foam appearing at the corners of the plant manager's mouth as he gurgled inarticulately after reading the press release. The "over my dead body" line had not been received well by the inspectors who let the plant manager know, in no uncertain terms, that they would now be staying through next week and asking for the power plant to run at higher levels. That was the only way to evaluate the size and scope of the pollution controls they were going to require, since the plant was clearly a "major" hazardous emissions source.

The plant manager's cell phone rang, and his face fell as he noticed the caller ID. The number of "Yes sirs" he made while listening said the person on the other end of the line meant it had to be someone higher up in utility management. This time it was the emissions company man who turned with a knowing smile to the camera.

Those gathered in the conference room burst out in expressions of relief, gave a quick thanks to Richard, and then quickly left to get things ready for the press conference. Richard wondered if the smile on his face as headed out was as self-satisfied as the plant manager's expression had been earlier.

Richard had gotten some sleep but was still tired from the night's effort when he arrived back out at the plant site to watch the press conference. Many of the faces who had spoken at the regulatory hearing had returned along with a crowd of others from the various environmental, social justice and faith-based organizations.

He gathered with some of his environmental friends and looked out at the heathy turnout from all the major press and tv networks that were on hand. Their cameras were focused on the impromptu podium placed up on a grassy area atop a retaining wall at one end of the parking lot with the plant in the background.

As the press conference time approached, Richard saw the group that had huddled up in the church van appear out of a building just inside the gate walking out with some of the utility's bigwigs thatRichard recognized including the CEO. They came out of the security gate and walked up the grassy edge of the parking lot to gather behind the podium covered in press microphones.

The press conference was led off by one of the local ministers who had been fighting for the health of the brown and black communities that would be primarily affected by the plant. He was followed by a couple of the regional organization leaders who outlined the differences they had over the years with the utility, but how pleased they were with the breakthrough steps the utility was stepping up to make. Next was the woman from national who said the utility had carefully reviewed the studies that her organization had submitted as part of the regulatory hearing. She said that upon finding the emissions reading taken from the coal fired plant behind her today matched those shown in the submitted studies and realizing the deleterious impacts implied by the emissions sampling done today, she said the utility had responsibly stepped up to take immediate action to cure those potentially harmful effects. She said the coalition of organizations gathered around the podium applauded the actions of the utility, particularly the plant manager, who was quickly on the phone with the top company officers.

She then said, "And now I am pleased to introduce the CEO who will outline the responsible commitments the utility will be taking as a result of today's notable events."

She went off to the side of the podium and started shaking the hands of the utility officers for the cameras as the CEO made his way to the podium. The last hand she shook was the hand of the plant manager whose face was a shade of apoplectic red and was visibly straining to keep his lips sealed as he tried and failed to make his mouth smile for the shot.

The CEO thanked the organizations and groups in attendance and announced the plant would be getting the latest greatest pollution controls that would go above and beyond those on any coal fired plant in the country. He further acknowledged that zero emission generation methods such solar panels, were underrepresented in the utilities' generation mix, and that new efforts to double the use of these renewable methods would be undertaken.

As he finished speaking there was silence for a moment and before the woman from national could be seen starting to applaud.

A healthy round of applause broke out across those attending, clearly surprising the CEO.

The press conference ended and the CEO and several of the organization leaders were asked for interviews. Richard and his friends had been planning to get something to eat after the event and they started walking towards the parking lot. The woman from national caught sight of him and made a motion to the regional organization leader that had gotten Richard involved. The leader came jogging up and asked Richard and his friends to hold up a moment while the woman, in the middle of an interview, asked the reporter to wait and strode through the departing crowd towards him.

She came up to him and took both his hands in hers saying, "Richard, you must realize all the progress we made today came because of your efforts to have that emissions sampling back up and running. I want to let you know that all of us are immensely thankful for you stepping up to make today's outcomes possible. I hope our paths might cross again in the future when there will be more time, but sadly we have a lot to do on our end yet today. By the way - I'm not sure we've been introduced. I'm Ariana."

2

Khadija waited on the concrete apron next to the stack of video equipment cases, scanning the empty sky above. The sunlight here felt comfortably warm on her upturned face, in contrast to the heat that was becoming unbearable at her home base. She had traveled halfway around the world to be here because Ariana had come to her with a special request.

Khadija had been asked to quickly and quietly arrange for travel for a group of NGO coalition leaders and scientists to a retreat at a remote location in the rainforest. Ariana had stressed the importance of covering everyone's travel tracks so no one beyond those involved would be aware of where they were going.

Getting everyone flown into the capital city hotel had been an involved process but with only a few snags everyone had arrived by the last evening. They had all met in a conference room after dinner where Ariana had let the gathered select leaders and scientists know that they would be travelling again in the morning to an eco-lodge in the rainforest. She asked them to wear the comfortable hiking clothes they had been asked to bring and to just bring the essentials for an overnight stay in the rainforest.

Prying the group away from breakfast and herding them into vans the next morning took longer than Khadija had anticipated. The group had been asked to put their phones in airplane mode and Khadija handed out satellite phones that the group was asked to use instead. The driver had made up the lost time on the road out, so they arrived a bit early at the tiny airfield. Ariana had the group sitting on folding chairs in a nearby ramshackle building holding informal meetings they were waiting.

Khadija sat down on one of the equipment cases and thought back to her two homes and the path with the NGO coalition that had led to her being here. She had grown up in a tight knit extended family in a village in Pakistan, but her father, had moved them to London when he had gotten a medical residency there. She had attended schools in London from age 7, but she often returned to her home village with her mother. She had spent large parts of her summer breaks back in the village among her Pakistani uncles, aunts, and cousins.

During her college years, she frequently returned to her home village to be looked after by her extended family there, while her father and mother would provide volunteer medical services to poorer population areas in the region. Khadija would sometimes accompany them on these medical trips and would see the increasingly precarious life many lived in areas affected by extreme weather and drought.

Her father and mother had made arrangements with the NGO coalition to be available for deployment back to her home country to provide medical assistance in the event of an emergency. Due to climate change, their country was now one of the handful of countries most severely affected by extreme weather in the world, and they were increasingly called upon by the coalition.

In college, she had been working part time for one of the western express delivery and logistics companies coordinating shipment deliveries to the more remote towns and villages of her home country. Her familiarity with the multiple languages and dialects of the vast region made her invaluable when it came to getting deliveries through. She was near the end of her third year in college, when the epic floods started to hit her home region.

Her father and mother were deployed almost immediately, and her company was one of many contracted to ship in multiple planeloads of relief supplies every day. She got a call from her dad telling her the flooding was now starting to impact tens of millions asking if she could travel in and go around with the aid teams who were trying to find out what was needed in the towns and villages but didn't speak the language.

She immediately left the university to fly over and was out with the teams the next day trying to get out through the flood-ravaged landscape to see what the local impacts were. The aid organizations soon realized she was incredibly effective at helping them assess the damage and needs in an area and lining up trusted partners on the ground to help distribute the aid and shelters.

On one of the first days that it wasn't pelting rain; Khadija got a call from one of her fellow shipping company workers. She was told that aid flights were getting bottlenecked by the limited capacity of the country's few commercial airports. At this rate, non-governmental organizations were soon going to find it impossible to funnel in the necessary food and aid. Khadija asked for an estimate of the bottlenecked shipments and was dismayed by the reply. It was a vast number, and she realized in an instant there would be no way to do it without pressing military airbases in the country into service.

She had said, "It may be impossible but let me see what I can do to get the military here to allow landings at their air bases. No promises though."

She hung up and called her father to run the idea by him. He said his old friendships with a couple of the air force generals from the village where she grew up might be able to help them out. Khadija then called the central logistics group for the aid organizations and asked to speak with whoever was in charge of the in-country air cargo logistics. The person apologized but Lieutenant Rosen was in flight to check out airstrips in the South of the country and would not be back for a couple of days. "Do you know what strip in the South is next?", asked Khadija and the person let her know.

The strip was not far away, and she had scrambled the Australian driver guy with the jeep to run her down into the valley to the airstrip. They were almost down to the valley when they saw a bush plane fly over and circle the airstrip in the distance.

The plane had just landed and was starting to taxi off the

landing strip onto the gravel to one side when they arrived in the jeep. The plane didn't turn off the engine and turned back towards the runway still rolling. Khadija realized that the pilot probably saw them, didn't know them, and was prepared to make a running takeoff if they got much closer.

She had to do something to head that off, so she leaned out the side of the doorless jeep, took her headscarf off and started waving it wildly as her hair blew back in the wind. Apparently doing something only a crazy western woman would consider did the trick and the plane's engines died as they pulled up.

The rear cargo door opened, and a wiry dark-haired woman climbed out and stood with her arms crossed behind her back sizing Khadija up. Seeing no one else getting out and unable to see past the glare on the windows, Khadija said, "Is Lt. Rosen inside?".

The woman smirked slightly and replied, "Who wants to know?"

Khadija who was becoming less than patient with this standoff in the hot sun said, "The person about to tell him he is wasting his time, if he's hoping to use this poor excuse for an airstrip to stage a major loading operation. Besides, I have a better idea to run by him."

The wiry figure continued to stand there for a moment before breaking out in a chuckle. She let her arms fall to her sides and the gun she had been holding behind her back came into view. She took a small holster out of her flight suit pocket, slipped the gun into it and put it back in her pocket. She stepped forward saying, "Seren Miriam Rosen at your service. Tell me your idea."

Khadija explained how she had grown up in the same village where two of the country's air force officers had lived at the time. They had been friends with her father, and she had played with their daughters as a child. Her father had occasionally seen them on his returns to the country for medical relief trips. After moving to London, the daughters would seek her out of during her summer trips back and were fascinated to find out about life in Europe. When they got older, they would occasionally come to visit her and her family in London and her dad and mom would escort them around to show them the sights.

Their fathers had risen in rank over the years, and they were now generals with decision-making authority over operations at some of the military airfields that were ideally placed for relief supplies to be flown into. She said her dad, who was in the country doing medical relief, was the possible key to getting their permission to use the airfields.

Khadija said, "So, Sar - whatever - Rosen, I think getting my dad to have a talk with the generals has a chance of getting you more than just some potholed dirt airstrips. What do you want to do next?"

"Well, the first thing I want is for you to just call me Miri. Second thing is to tell Kangaroo Jack over there to put down the tire iron he's been hanging onto ever since he saw me with the gun, and the third is to tell me what to call you."

Khadija gave her driver a look, and he sheepishly put the tire iron back and then said, "I'm Khadija but you can call me Khadj for short."

"Well, Khadj, I'm going to get someone on the phone and ask you to her what you told me, then we can work on what will happen next."

Miri got a satellite phone out of the plane, walked under the shadow of the wing, and dialed. Someone answered and after she said the location she was checking out was the worst of the bad ideas that had been sent their way recently, she said that she had been chased down by woman that might have a better idea.

She put the call on speakerphone and a woman's voice asked Khadija to tell her who her father was. She barely got started describing her father and mother before the voice said she knew who they were. The voice then asked to run through her idea of how to approach the generals. After patiently listening the voice said she was putting one of the local leaders on the phone and wanted Khadija to tell them the names of the generals. She passed along the names and heard someone speaking in the local language over another phone in the background.

The woman's voice came back on the phone with confirmation

that the generals were both at the large southern airbase. The woman asked Miri to conference in her dad and Khadija read off his satellite phone number. Her dad's voice came on the call and Khadija let him know in English that they were on a conference call regarding the idea she had run past him earlier. The woman said she had met her father and his wife on a relief effort some years previous and hoped they had been well since. The woman said she liked the idea of having him talk with the generals and got her father's opinion on how best to handle the meeting. The woman asked her dad if he and her mom would be willing to fly out and meet with the generals if they could arrange it. She heard her dad check quickly with her mom and then agreed to do it.

The woman spoke to someone to start making the arrangements, before coming back on to ask where their medical relief team was located. Upon hearing the village name, Miri said there was an airstrip nearby and they could fly over and arrive to pick them up in about an hour.

Her dad said, "Good, then its settled". He then asked, "Would this by chance be Ariana, that I'm speaking with, and will you be able to join us for the meeting?"

The woman's voice replied, "It is indeed and, yes, I plan to join you."

Her dad said he looked forward to meeting her again, but reminded her to bring her husband, and have him voice any comments she wanted to make in the meeting. These are old school military and while they know and will tolerate my daughter, they may be less than receptive to a western woman joining the conversation.

"I understand perfectly…" Ariana said and then paused as someone talked to her. "They tell me the generals look forward to meeting with their old friend in the morning at the southern airbase. Miri, if you would be so kind as to pick up Khadija's parents and bring them back to our logistics camp for the evening, I will have all the airbase info gathered and waiting for you. You may have a long evening ahead to work up our ask of the generals, so I would hurry back. Look forward to seeing everyone in the morning for the flight into the base.", said Ariana wrapping the call up.

Miri told Khadija to send Jumping Jack, back off in the jeep and to get herself up inside and strapped in the copilot's seat while she did a quick walkaround to get ready for takeoff. The twin engines fired up and Miri soon had the plane in the air.

As the autopilot took over, Miri checked the horizon and then pulled out a sectional aeronautical chart showing the country with various landing areas circled. She also pulled out a highlighted map showing the areas of the country that were flood impacted and handed them to Khadija.

"Let's decide which of the dozen or so airbases circled on the map are the best placed for the relief supplies we need to move to the affected regions. We will need a firm list of the airbases and on site asks for your dad to request from the generals by morning", Miri said as they flew.

They had picked up her dad and mom and headed to an airstrip near the relief effort logistics center, where they could spend the night. They had a quick dinner together at the canteen set up for the relief workers and then her parents headed off to their lodging. Khadija and Miri went back to the logistics unit with a long evening of planning in front of them.

Early the next morning they scanned all their work from the evening before and made copies to take with them to the meeting. Khadija had fortunately made all the detail callouts in the local language because they were contacted and asked to email over any materials the generals would be asked to review as part of the meeting.

Ariana and her husband met them at the plane and Miri flew them to the airbase for the meeting. They were met by base airmen and driven to a building with small conference room.

The meeting with her dad and the generals had seemed more a social tea party than an urgent flood relief meeting. Her dad was equipped with a folder that showed the list and locations of airbases they were interested in. Satellite photos of the airbases were marked up with highlighted areas where the oldest hangars and least used areas of the base they wanted to be able to use for their staging and transfer to trucks and other modes of delivery. Khadija was there to translate for Ariana and her husband but for the first twenty-five minutes of their half-hour meeting her dad was just drinking chai and catching up with the generals on their families and things going on in the village and in their respective lives.

Other than an expression of surprise to see "little Khadj" as a "grown woman", the generals largely ignored everyone but her dad for the entire meeting. Eventually they asked what her dad was seeing out in the countryside, and nodded as if already knowing the scope of the flooding disaster he described to them.

Finally, they asked what they could do for her father, who pushed the folder across to them. The generals flipped through the paperwork, asked if there was anything in the folder that had not already been included in the morning email and Ariana's husband was prompted to say "No".

Her dad added something in her local language about maintaining total control over the infidel cargo planes and if they were given any hint of non-compliance to make them sit in the sun for a day and then leave the country in shame with their cargos still aboard. This brought a smile to the generals' faces as they got up to end the meeting, but Khadija refrained from translating it. The generals gave her dad their regards, said it had been good to talk with him, briefly acknowledged Khadija, and then left the room.

Her dad told them not to talk until they were back out at the plane, and Khadija reminded Ariana to keep up both her headscarf and the appropriate appearance of dutiful wife as they were driven back across the base.

Once they were seated inside the plane, her dad let them know he thought it had gone well. He said they would need to really ride herd on the air crews and ground operations folks they brought in to avoid cultural offenses and stay in the good graces of the generals.

When the approval from the generals came through later that day, Miri and Khadija worked hurriedly getting ground crews, loaders and handling equipment, mobilized and ready to fly on the big military cargo planes that Miri had lined up. Ariana asked Khadija and her father and mother if they would travel around with Miri to coordinate with the airbase commanders in the local language while the airbase operations were being stood up. Miri flew them almost nonstop between the base airfields to meet and finalize the detailed operations plans with the local base commanders.

Khadija's mother gathered all the base staff contacts at each airfield and sent out a constant stream of logistics emails as soon as the commanders approved the detailed plans so everyone was clear on the relief flights arriving, the supplies to be unloaded, and the ground delivery distribution that would be running out of each airfield. The flights with loaders, equipment and ground personnel would start arriving the next day, and the flights with supplies as soon as the ground crews were ready.

Within a couple of weeks, the number of flights coming in was staggering and the massive carrying capacity of the larger military cargo planes was starting to catch them up to the scope of the disaster. The food, water purification, and tent deployments to support the millions affected was difficult and imperfect. A couple of thousand died because of the flooding, but many more were saved.

In the wake of the disaster, the NGO coalition was able to obtain permission for ongoing use of some of the airbase facilities including one half of a cold war era military airfield that Khadija now called home when she was not deployed in the field. Khadija, who knew the daughters of the military officers really wanted a western education, suggested that the coalition hire them to work in a girl only section of the new staging and logistics operation at this base. Khadija could not only train them in logistics, but because relief efforts required having a large support staff ready and waiting around for a disaster to happen, there would be large amounts of time for the daughters to take western remote learning courses.

The proposal was included as part of the overall NGO airfield use plan but was dismissed by the generals and base leaders who were reluctant to have woman-lead NGOs running things on half of one of their bases. It was Khadija reaching out to the general's daughters and having them spread the word to the other base military leader's daughters, that created the pressure from their families to close the deal.

The first few months of setting up the base and training the girls in to handle inventory and logistics for disaster relief, kept everyone busy. Soon the staging work was done, and the waiting for the next disaster had begun, giving the girl's free time for their classes and studies.

The sound of a plane snapped Khadija out of her reminiscences, and she looked up to see a twin-engine plane appear low over the trees. The plane banked steeply over the far end of the runway and swooped down to land in smooth motion. The plane seemed to barely slow as it turned off on the first ramp to head directly over to them. Khadija backed away from the stack of cases as the plane pulled up with just enough momentum to come to a stop only feet away from the stack.

As the propellers slowed to a stop, Khadija motioned to the guys to come over and help carry load them into the plane. The wide plane door opened slowly and a familiar wiry woman in flight suit was framed in the opening. She looked at Khadija for a moment, before realization dawned.

She said "Khadj, I almost didn't recognize you without the headscarf and with that styling hair." She jumped down and hugged Khadija, taking in her new haircut, and said, "Why'd they drag your new styling self over to this corner of the world?"

Khadija replied, "Hey Miri, good to see you. For some reason Ariana asked me to gather a bunch of scientists and the coalition leaders out at this strip without raising any non-NGO eyebrows."

Miri added, "Well good to see you too. Ariana drug me over to play taxi driver for this group. Now make yourself useful and chock the wheels, while I get this stuff stowed. That way we can get our guests out to the middle of nowhere for their "special" meeting."

Miri worked with the guys to get the cases stowed as Khadija got the wheels chocked and then headed back to the building to bring out the mix of coalition leaders and scientists going on this flight. She got everyone seated while Miri did her preflight checks. Khadija closed the door and called out to Miri who started the plane's engines. Khadija checked that everyone was buckled in on her way up front, then plopped into the familiar co-pilot's seat and put on the headset to tell Miri that everything was good in the back. Miri gunned the engines, and the plane turned and was quickly headed to the end of the runway. Even fully loaded, Miri had the short takeoff and landing capable bush plane off the ground long before they reached the midpoint of the runway.

On the climb out, Khadija considered how unusual it was to have her step back from worldwide logistics that her team worked on, to secretively take on the travel and equipment arrangements for this small "retreat" meeting. It was likewise unusual for Miri to step back from her coordination role with the worldwide military and air cargo services the NGO coalition utilized, to simply serve as an airborne taxi driver. There was something going on that was limiting the need to know on this "retreat" meeting to only the most essential and trusted members of the coalition.

She looked at the military style flight suit that Miri always wore when flying and considered what she knew about Miri's military background. Miri was a former military cargo pilot, with multi-engine ratings, that now worked for the NGO coalition. She helped the NGOs coordinate with the governmental militaries that were relied upon to deploy disaster airlift deliveries. Miri had a couple of powerful short takeoff and landing bush planes with extended range available to her across the world that she used to airlift in first responders and assessment teams over disaster areas and while she checked the airlift possibilities. She would then work with the air forces and air cargo services to line up flights to get aid and relief deliveries from Khadija's girls out to the affected regions.

As the plane reached cruising altitude, Miri engaged the autopilot, sat back, and they caught up as they flew out over the unbroken rainforest below. They chatted about Khadija's family and how things were going with her logistics and loader women back at the base. Miri talked about her mostly Thailand and Malaysian based relief efforts since they had wound down their flood relief efforts.

Miri said she had also wound down her last relationship had been so scattered in her recent travels she didn't have any men in her life now. She asked Khadija if she had any new prospects since they had last seen each other. Khadija said being effectively cloistered with her women as a condition of being able to use the base was not conducive to meeting men. Miri made a tsking sound and started to say something, but Khadija was spared her usual diatribe on having to find a "good" man, by the autopilot arrival notification and Miri having to focus on getting the plane descending to follow the bends in the river below.

Khadija could see Miri was looking for the landing strip somewhere to their left, but there was nothing but rainforest and the river as far as Khadija could see. A dirty smudge in the unbroken green flashed past on the left, and Miri immediately banked the plane over to head back around towards it. A clearing appeared below with the dirt strip that the encroaching rainforest only reluctantly seemed to allow. Miri lowered the flaps and flew down in a long looping oval around the clearing to see what kind of shape the dirt strip was in.

A figure came out onto the strip to look up and wave welcomingly at the plane. Miri said the wind direction looked like it was blowing in from the river as she lowered the flaps and flew to the opposite end. She banked around steeply and then lowered the flaps even further to what looked like an implausible angle to Khadija. The plane seemed to slow to a crawl with the flaps fully extended, but as they came down to just skim over the treetops, Khadija could see the leaves whipping past just under the wheels.

The trees below them ended abruptly and she saw Miri immediately give a small push of the rudder pedal and a slight turn of the wheel. The plane dropped down smoothly like an elevator into the clearing, and she let the controls come back leveling out the plane right over the start of the dirt. She pulled the nose up to float the plane over the weedy potholes at the end of strip, and then let the plane settle onto the dirt. The plane jounced and bumped until finally slowing at the river end of the runway. Miri made a turn on the ground to face back down the runway, before coming to a stop and killing the engine.

Khadija opened the door and went out to chock the wheels as the welcoming figure that had waved at them appeared around the back end of the plane. He was dressed in worn jeans and a Boston Red Sox T-shirt. His smile, and casual clothes belied the seriousness of the native tattooed pattern on his handsome face.

Miri came out to check the stairway as he said, "Welcome to ...heart ...of ... world." He introduced himself with a long name they could not quite make out.

Seeing their puzzled expressions, he said "Call me Jaha."

A couple of elders of the native tribe came out and joined Jaha in greeting the leaders and scientists as they stepped out of the plane. The elders went off with the group to take them to the canoes they would be travelling in upriver to the retreat site. Jaha stayed to help Miri and Khadija unload the cases. Miri and Khadija slid the cases to the door, while Jaha hefted and carried them towards the river and out on the makeshift pier there to a flat-bottomed boat tied up there.

As they watched him effortlessly lift the biggest case out of the plane and turn to carry it over to the pier, Miri elbowed Khadija in her ribs.

"Sometimes you just have to go native or go home." she said with a mischievous smirk. Khadija shook her head and chuckled but felt herself blushing. She thought the sooner they got this retreat done and she could pack Miri off to meet her next beau, the better off they both would be.

THE "GIFT"

3

It was a warm clear night as Ariana crawled under the sheets of her cabana bed. She had pulled the gauzy curtains across the open front of the cabana but could rely on their open weave to let the cooler night breezes reach into the open living area. The eco-lodge, run by Jaha's tribe, only offered off-the-grid cabanas that coalition leaders and scientists were all housed in for the retreat. The lights of the from the open-air pavilion could still be seen reflecting off the water through the curtains and the sound of music playing could still be faintly heard playing for the few still nursing their drinks and moping about the day's proceedings. Ariana had impressed upon each of the meeting participants the need to quickly gather, far from the watchful eyes of the world, to consider both the dire climate situation they were facing and the new solutions they would be asked to consider.

What she had not yet told the gathering was that her bringing them out to the ecolodge was solely based on a shared dream of a "gift" being given that had come to Jaha and his tribe. Jaha had said that the dream was unusual in clarity, its frequent recurrence among many of his tribe. The dream was specific about the appearance of the gift at the ecolodge on the day of the first full moon after the spring equinox and called for the tribe to enlist trusted partners to join with the tribe on that date who could assist in sharing the "gift" with the world.

Ariana had worked with the tribe for several years to protect the area of rainforest the tribe called home from the oil and timber companies that were doing enormous damage with their extractive practices in the region. The tribal elders had come to an agreement to have Jaha reach out to "the woman from the modern world who wanders the forest" as she was known by the tribe and arrange to bring only the most trusted of her "modern world" associates to help the tribe consider the offer of the "gift".

For all Jaha's earnestness when he had called her to tell her the importance of the dream and the specificity of the "gift's" arrival location and date, he could not say what form the "gift" would take. Ariana had needed to do some arm twisting to get the select group of non-governmental organization heads and science advisors to agree to meet on that date in a place where communication would be largely cut off. Poor Khadija had her hands full to get the group quietly taken from their scattered locations across the world, to this off-the-grid ecolodge location.

The morning had started out with the tribal leaders, opening the retreat with a form of intention or blessing in their native language that Jaha had translated for group. Jaha said the tribal elders spoke about a shared dream of a "gift" that would be offered on this day that could serve as temporary means of salvation for both the tribe and larger world now facing the threat of climate change. It would be the collective formed by the tribe and those that had travelled in from the modern world that would guide the use of the "gift". Jaha finished the tribal leader's blessing with a form of prayer asking that wisdom be given to the gathering to guide them in their steps and actions with the offering to be provided. The blessing, while well received, seemed to be taken in a more metaphorical sense by the gathered leaders and scientists than Jaha had intended.

Being sequestered with a smaller trusted group enabled frank and blunt discussions that Ariana was thankful that the NGO coalition was now having. There had been widespread dismay at the unavoidable impacts of climate change that the presentations by the scientists made clear were coming. The solutions suggested would run up against national and business interest's headwinds and would not achieve the massive scale needed in time. It was as if they were all passengers on a runaway train and the scientists had just shown them how the train was likely to start coming off the tracks much sooner than anyone had previously thought.

As the day had worn on with a flicker of progress starting to be made, Ariana thought the "gift" just might be the act of getting these leaders together, without the pressures or eyes of the outside world to hash out a collective plan for moving forward. As the principal organizer, Ariana found herself arbitrating between competing interests and advocating for breaks when discussions became heated. She had encouraged the participants to take quiet walks out in the village and rainforest during breaks to remind them of what was at stake.

The dinner and planned "celebration" of the "gift" that took place after were subdued affairs despite the music and attempt at celebratory decorations. Only Xanthe, who had presented her findings on the lack of progress on electrification and the new technology fronts, was still halfheartedly arguing some point while most of the group was just standing around to have a drink before they headed off to their beds. Ariana knew that the NGO leaders were having issues with taking doom and gloom prognostications back to their membership and donors after the years of effort their organizations had made. Jaha was the only one who still looked happy as he was leaving the pavilion reception.

As he had passed her, she had said, "Sorry your "gift" didn't come out of today's discussions."

Jaha paused, still smiling, and said, "There is more of today yet. I still wait."

He left and Ariana looked around to see if there was any more damage control needed. Xanthe's argument had drawn to a stalemate, so Ariana had decided she was finished putting out the fires for the day made her way towards the entry to leave.

Ahmed, who had delivered most of today's dour climate news and always refrained from drinking, had artfully entertained himself with a group of white balloons snagged from the entry decorations. With nametag markers from the registration table, he had given each of the balloons oversize mascaraed lashes and smiling red lips. He was now holding them in one hand while he bowed formally inviting them collectively to dance. He had started mock waltzing to the music as Ariana passed him heading out of the pavilion. He had smiled ruefully and gave her a parting wave, before grandly twirling, and mock dipping his balloon dance partners. A balloon with a wry inked smile had taken this opportunity to escape and head for the open-air pavilion ceiling above.

"Your harem is starting to run out on you" Ariana had joked as she paused to watch the balloon bump into the wood beams under the thatched roof.

"No matter" Ahmad had said motioning to the other balloon decorations still intact by door. "There are plenty of others waiting for an opening to cut in. Sleep well."

While walking across the long boardwalks and dry island paths in the dark to her sleeping cabana, she had come across Jaha sitting in front of a fire. She had been surprised to see him dressed in his colorful tribal wear that was usually only worn for ceremonies or notable occasions.

The flicker of the fire danced over the painted patterns on his face as he spoke to her without turning his head "Dreams say "gift" come today. Moon is full. I still wait. I greet it. You should too".

She had said, "Well, there are only a couple of hours left to the day, and you're on watch so, I think the best way for me to prepare for the "gift" after today's circus is to get some sleep."

Jaha looked up with grin and nodded, as she skirted the fire and headed up the path a short way until the deck out back of her cabana had appeared in the bright moonlight.

Now, here in her bed, she hoped all the reactionary trauma, induced by today's reports, would have had run its course by the morning and cooler heads would prevail. She turned over to face away from moonlit deck outside. The rustle of a cooling breeze coming through the loosely woven drapes and the lilt of the distant music soon had her dozing off.

Ariana was roused by the faint percussion of a familiar beat. With her eyes still closed, longing to go back to sleep, she tried to place it. It must be coming from the pavilion, but from what she could see through the gauzy drapes, the pavilion looked dark. Only the slight flicker of Jaha's fire coming from back down the path was visible in the moonlight. She wondered why she could only hear the percussive beat and not the music that went with it. She reluctantly sat up in bed and became aware the percussion was coming from outside her cabana, not the far pavilion.

She got out of bed to find her flashlight, noting the louder beat sounded like someone drumming on the deck boards right outside. She peeked out through an opening in drapes and immediately saw a bobbing form in the moonlight at the far end of the deck. She fumbled to find the flashlight switch,as she poked it out through the drapes. The beam came on, and as she swung it around, a familiar ovoid face came into view. It was one of the harem girl balloons that Ahmed had been mock dancing with. Its marker lashes looked disconcertingly back at her as it bobbed in the air over the deck. Its ribbon was fastened to something dark and small that Ariana couldn't quite make out. It was flipping from side to side on the boards beating out the rhythm of the song in the middle of the deck.

This must be a joke from Ahmed or more likely Xanthe, if she had been up late sipping on the ouzo bottle her brother had brought her from Greece. Since turning on the flashlight, the box had quieted its tapping, but as she just stood there peeking out while trying to work out how the trick was done, it was now again getting much louder and more insistent. Clearly, she would have to go out and play along, or they would never let her get back to sleep.

Wrapping the sheet around herself, she stepped out on the deck, with flashlight in hand, to take a closer look. "Alright guys, you got me" she said as she took a step towards the balloon face. Jaha, who had heard the loud tapping, appeared up the path with a questioning look on his face. Ariana waved him up on the deck to stand beside her, now uncertain that this was a prank. The dark object, in the final beats of the song, tap danced back away from them to the far side of the deck with the balloon face bobbing along in the air above. As the object pounded out the last 4 beats, the song came to her – Tequila! With a whoosh on the final beat something streaked out of the sky to land on the far end of the deck.

It took Ariana a moment to get over the surprise of the object's arrival that had caused her and Jaha to jump back. In the now silent moonlit night, the flashlight beam revealed a dark cube shaped object about the size of the seating cubes she had seen in her niece's kindergarten classroom. The balloon had been blown over to the side by the whoosh of air and now floated back up to hover over the now stationary smaller form next to it on the deck boards. The seating size cube had a slight red glow around the outside that was starting to fade, but the faint smell of wood smoke coming from deck boards under it warned that it was still hot. In the edge of the flashlight beam, they saw the balloon slowly start to rotate until the girlish features were hidden and the blank white side of the balloon was facing towards them.

A couple of rays of golden light projected upward from a pair of tiny boxes attached on one side of the smaller "tap dancing" cube. This golden light uplight created a moving dappled pattern on the white balloon. The dappled pattern sharpened and then resolved into a projection of a smiling child with native tattoo patterns similar to Jaha's across its "face." A small projected hand raised in front of the smiling face and a chubby baby finger pointed at Ariana and Jaha, then at itself and its mouth made silent speaking movements.

"I told you "gift" come today." Jaha said quietly out of the side of his mouth as Ariana stood there gaping.

"Ahmed! - Ahmed!" Ariana shouted as she strode in through his cabana drapes. The flashlight found Ahmed sleeping on his cot and he slowly rolled over to look her way blinking in the bright beam.

"Ahmed – you have to come with me." she said seriously. He

looked dubiously at her standing there in her sheet and started to roll back over mumbling, "It'll surely wait until…", but Ariana cut him off.

"Ahmed, I mean it! You have to come with me right now. One of your harem girls showed up with a child and this cube thing, and Jaha and I need your help sorting this out!" Ahmed's eyes opened wide as he sat up and reflexively said, "I swear by Allah it's not mine."

4

"Miri are you awake?" asked Khadija urgently through the curtains of Miri's cabana. Dawn was just breaking, and a satellite phone call had put Khadija into disaster mobilization mode.

"Maybe" came the sleepy reply from inside the cabana.

"Good, get up! We have a quarantine situation, and I need your help getting control measures in place before the others get up for the day!"

Miri was out of bed in a flash, quickly pulling on shorts and a top that were too colorful for Khadija to look at with her bleary eyes, so she turned to head back down the boardwalk. Miri caught up with her as she was pulling out a couple of glorified kids type wagons that the lodge used for toting luggage and supplies. They each took a wagon and headed around the back of the reception area pier area to the pavilion. They gathered half a dozen folding chairs, some sign making materials, and some of the bright streamer material from last night's decorations in the wagons before heading out the other side of the pavilion towards the far cabanas.

Khadija was monitoring the wind direction with a bit of streamer as they walked and stopped them at a juncture where some of the other cabanas had paths coming out to the boardwalk. She looked down the long run of boardwalk still towards bird watching pier and to where the boardwalk ended on the far shore where the paths to Ariana and Ahmed's cabanas came out of the trees. She could not see anyone on the boardwalk on the bird watching pier jutting out into the water, so it looked like only Ariana, Ahmed, and Jaha remained out that way.

She had Miri place a couple of chairs at each side of the boardwalk and stretch some of the bright streamer material between them while she wrote, "Danger, Quarantine Area, Keep Out!" in fat marker to make a sign. Khadija taped the sign securely to one of the chairs to discourage any other early risers from wandering that way and then they moved on. They blocked off two other access paths to the boardwalk with chairs and signs and then headed back.

At the pavilion, Khadija flipped the lids open on couple of the cases to make sure they contained what they would need, and then they loaded them along with a folding table, into the wagons. They rolled their loaded wagons back down the boardwalk to the quarantine sign and checked the wind direction before heading beyond the barrier. Near the end of the boardwalk, they turn to roll the wagons out onto the bird watching pier.

They set the folding table up under the covered roof area at the end of the pier and placed a video monitor on it at one end. Miri worked to set up the solar panels, battery, and extension cords, while Khadija set up the half dozen cameras, lights, microphones, and long range wi-fi repeater for sending the audio-video feeds. Miri kept a careful eye on the wind direction during this process to make sure the breeze direction would still be blowing any airborne pathogen away from the pier.

Khadija used the satellite phone to check with Ariana and Ahmed on the set up, to say the wind direction was still good, and that her and Miri were clearing out to get things set in pavilion ahead of the morning session and then ended the call. They turned off the lights to save battery life until the sun was fully up and then wheeled their wagons back down the boardwalk towards the main pavilion.

The dawning sun was just lighting the bottoms of a few clouds as the wagon's wheel bumped across the boards. Miri took the moment to ask how Ariana, Ahmed and Jaha had become infected and what kind of pathogen they were being quarantined for. Khadija said that she wasn't sure, but that Ariana said it would be explained in the morning session. She added as long as the wind kept blowing away from the main pavilion, Ahmed thought they should be safe there. Miri's doubtful expression contrasted with her brightly colored clothes starting to glow in the first rays of the sun.

The buzz around breakfast in the main pavilion was heightened as news of the quarantine was announced by Khadija. A group of the tribal elders had arrived by boat from the village and Khadija motioned for them to take their seats at the front. As the morning session time approached, Miri, who had commandeered one of the lodge's bird spotting telescopes, let Khadija know that Ariana, Ahmed, and Jaha could just be seen coming out on the bird watching platform and were setting something up on the table. Khadija and Miri had set up an oversized video monitor on a table at the head of the morning session seating but had turned it off after testing the wi-fi connection. A camera pointed at the seating and a microphone were set up so Ariana, Ahmed, and Jaha on the bird watching pier could see and hear the assembling coalition members starting to take their seats.

Miri saw the lights switch on at the bird watching platform and left the spotting scope to walk over by the still dark oversized monitor at the front of the seating. Khadija, who had set up at a table at the back of the pavilion with a video switcher and monitor array set up, reached down to start the video recorders in the rack case under the table. Ariana's voice came over speakers saying, "If everyone will finish taking their seats, we have something the tribal elders would like to show you."

Miri flipped the power switch on the oversize monitor, and it lit up showing a wide camera shot of the table out on the bird watching pier with Ariana, Jaha, and Ahmed standing behind it. In the center of the table was a dark cube shape, about the height of Khadija's forearm, that could be seen to have an opening running through the center with tapered faces leading inwards to the opening. To one side was a smaller dark cube shape, about the height of a can of soda, that appeared to be a scaled down copy of the larger cube with similar tapered faces leading inwards to a center opening. This smaller cube had two even tinier dark cubes the size of kids alphabet blocks stuck to its sides. The ribbon running down from the balloon was sandwiched between these to hold it in place. The upper faces of these tiny cubes were glowing, and golden tinged rays could be seen shooting upward projecting the image of a smiling child face with the facial pattern similat to Jaha and many of the tribal elders.

The animated facial features of the child on the monitor looked even happier as the child's facial image turned slightly from side to side as if taking in the gathered coalition in front of it. A murmur of perplexity and consternation ran around the room, but Khadija saw the tribal elders smiling and looking for all the world as if this was exactly what they had been waiting for.

5

The sun streaming in through the gauzy drapes onto Xanthe's face woke her and she rolled over to keep from facing it. After a couple of minutes, it occurred to her that the sun should not be as high in the sky as it was, and she reached for her phone to check the time. Only a dark screen reflecting her puffy morning face could be seen despite her repeatedly pushing the power button.

The high sun probably meant she had slept way past her alarm time but, in a way, she was OK with that. She had given all her reports the previous day and the agenda for the morning did not involve her. Besides, she had a bit of headache from last night's drinking, was hoarse from debating her report results, and didn't want to pick up where last night's arguments had left off until she had time for some coffee and aspirin to take effect.

She took her time getting dressed and then walked over to enter from the back of the pavilion where she could get to the coffee and breakfast tables without bumping into anyone. The food and water issues that were scheduled for the morning session were outside her technology monitoring purview, so she figured she would have an hour or so to lounge in a chair in the back until the coffee nursed her back to full debate form.

She came in the back of the pavilion where she would not interrupt the proceedings, plugged her phone into one of the lineup of charging strips alongside the phones and electronic devices of others, and picked up her fully charged tablet. As she headed for the breakfast table, she noticed the meeting format was different than expected today, with Ariana, Ahmed, and the native guy with the long name no one could pronounce, up on a monitor at the front.

Xanthe as was trying to choose between the healthy breakfast options before her when the camera view switched and she got a glimpse of some cube objects and a bizarre looking balloon shown on the monitor. She would find out soon enough what those were all about but she needed coffee and something to settle her stomach first. This eco-minded group was always on about sustainably sourced healthy food options in their menus, so she carefully poked through the food offerings before putting a couple of items on a small plate. She didn't want some hidden bean curd blowing up in her digestive system.

Jaha - the short version of the name the native guy was called – was now on the screen talking about how this "gift" from the puente ruwaqkuna - another long name she would have difficulty remembering -aligned with his tribe's dreams. As she headed for the coffee, Ariana was saying something about how even though the tribe had implicit trust in the ruwaq - good, a shorter name she could remember- they were just one unknown in the array of unknowns that the tribe's "gift" presented. Xanthe got a cup and poured some coffee. She took a long sip to wash down some aspirin from her bag as Ariana was going on about how verifying the intentions of the makers was as important to the coalition group as considering the possibilities of the "gift" offered.

Xanthe topped up the coffee cup and then used her computer tablet like a tray to hold everything, so she had a free hand to pull out a chair behind Khadija. She heard Ariana ask everyone to refer to the "cubes" as the new "clean cooking stove project" while they were being evaluated. Xanthe was glad they were introducing some new type of clean stove, as part of the scheduled food and water session that she could safely ignore.

Xanthe put her feet up on a chair in front of her and lounged back so she could have enough lap for both her breakfast plate and her tablet. She pulled up one the white papers from her To Read folder and settled in to read up on the latest thermal battery developments. Over the top of her tablet, she saw Ahmed turn the large cube over and take out some thin black object from its center. The tech side of her brain heard him mention something about the control unit and large cube had to be biometrically keyed to an owner before the cube would be activated to work. So, she thought, the stove was electric and not just for cleanly burning wood or charcoal in.

The paper was getting to new developments in graphite thermal storage, so she largely ignored the stove presentation as Ahmed put a large pot of water on the bigger cube's top. As she read, she half watched Ahmed make a finger motion on the surface around the perimeter of the pot bottom, and then mime using the control unit to turn on a stove burner. He said the maker thought the large pot of water could be brought to a boil at max heat in under a minute if they wanted. This detail made her look up from her tablet and shake her head. The amount of power needed to boil a pot that big that fast could only come from a hefty electrical outlet.

The coalition's relief efforts were focused on populations that couldn't get batteries for a remote control, much less access to the electricity needed to power some insta-boil stove. This power hog of a stove was a clear non-starter in her mind, so she dug back into her reading while trying to tune out the discussion that seemed to bog down on issues around whether to test the stove or not. Xanthe tuned most of the discussion out as she read on about promising improvements in thermal photovoltaic panels.

As she finished her white paper, Ariana's voice broke into the discussion and suggested they table discussion of the larger cube "stove" issues for the moment and focus on the smaller cubes. That way, she explained the native child's ruwak avatar could make his transition and walk them through the uses of the smaller builder cube and the two tiny communicator cubes. Out of the corner of her eye she saw Khadija switch the feed to a camera showing the smaller soda can height builder cube with, what must be, the two "communicator" cubes stuck to it. She wondered idly as she looked through her reading file for another paper, what tech nerd had come up with "communicator" as the preferred term for those.

The image of the patterned faced native child with a chubby hand waving before fading out on the balloon made her sit up. She had thought the odd face had been printed on the balloon and her mind started working on how what had to be an animated projected image was done. Sitting up she could just see past Khadija to watch Ahmed place his palms on the front of the two tiny cube shapes on the front of the smaller "builder cube" as Ariana seemed to call it. There was a snick sound, and they came off in his hand, releasing the balloon ribbon that had been held between them. The marker drawn female face on the back of the balloon rotated momentarily into view before the balloon floated out of view.

Xanthe got up to get a better view and headed back over to the drink table to drop off her empty plate and refill her coffee. She watched Ahmed set the tiny cubes to either end of the test table and then make a motion with his hands on the top of one of tiny cubes. She thought he must be miming some control movement, but a focused light beam shot upward from the cube.

So, the tiny cubes could serve as flashlights, she thought as she started refilling her cup. She thought about the blowback that anything battery operated would be sure to produce among the group when, wait…. something was going on in the flashlight beam. She paused with her cup half full to turn back and watch. Khadija had switched to a zoomed in view of the tiny flashlight cube and an audible gasp came from the room as dust motes were gathering in to fill the light beam producing a transparent circular orb of dust glowing in the light. The orb density increased until it was softball sized gold-tinged ball that could only be partly seen through. In an instant the orb morphed into the head of the native child ruwa…whatever. A chubby hand resolved in the lit dust next to the now smiling head and waved in a welcoming motion.

A spattering sound broke into the silence in the pavilion. Xanthe paused in her gawking at the screen to become aware of the drops bouncing off her shoes from the tipped cup in her hand. She whirled back to the table to grab some napkins and start mopping up the coffee puddle she was standing in as the discussion exploded to life in the pavilion. With most of the mess mopped up, she started to refill her cup again.

Ariana must have seen her on the camera, because she interrupted the discussion, and said "These cubes are clearly a new technology evaluation issue, so I think we should hear from our technology evaluation lead at the back of the room."

Everyone turned in their chairs to look back at Xanthe who, with a refilled cup, was in mid-slurp. In the silence, they waited for her to respond, as she gulped down the coffee trying to think. Even the native child avatar image seemed to be looking expectantly at her. The native child image animated hologram thingy had caught her by surprise, but it seemed to her this was a case of too many high-tech bells and whistles being added to products that only needed to be a dumb "stove".

She replied, "Well… based on some of the concerns I've been hearing…" Xanthe hesitated, then said "I think you would want to start with testing until you know what you're dealing with, then asking the ruwa….maker to dumb down the product to a level you think you can control, and then turn a red team loose to try an armada of hacks and attacks to be sure it is safe to release for relief use."

The gathered group turned back towards the screen now showing the three out on the pier. Ariana gave a questioning look to Ahmed, and he gave a considered nod back to her.

Xanthe thought Ariana was looking directly at her from the screen as she said, "Xan, I know it is asking a lot and may prove to be dangerous in ways that we cannot anticipate, but would you consider joining our isolated trio at the bird watching pier. We need someone to be the "keyed" person running the "stove" cube through its paces for evaluation, and it seems clear you would be best suited for that role?"

The gathering again turned in their seats to look back at Xanthe. She demurred for a moment, but the earnestness with which

Ariana was looking at her from the screen, made this seem more important than Xanthe thought it warranted.

"I'll be glad to join you down at the pier to check out these cubes…stove… thingies for safety." she said. Ariana gave a smile of relief, and after some other discussion, gave the gathering 20 minutes for the morning break.

Khadija took a call on the satellite phone and then came over to Xanthe and handed her a sheet of paper saying, "Glad to hear you'll be the keyed in as the person to do the testing. Here's the list of test equipment we have immediately available on this side of the ocean. Ahmed said to ask which items you want first, and Miri will have them flown in. If there is anything that is not on the list or that will not run off an extension cord from the solar panels, let me know that as well, because it may take a bit longer to get that shipped in and set up."

Miri glanced down at the list and was taken aback by some of the sophisticated testing and diagnostics equipment included in the container. Why would she need things like a portable Xray and magnetic resonance equipment to evaluate a glorified stove?

Khadija continued, "We'll get your stuff moved to one of the cabanas in the quarantine zone down towards the pier and I'll get a satellite link set up for the four of you so you can keep your home fires burning for the next month or so while you are all kept in isolation."

"Quarantine zone…. in isolation for a month." mumbled Xanthe wondering what she was getting into. She was about to renege on the whole thing when a question that had been nagging at her formed in her mind. She asked, "Wait, you said you only had 120-volt power coming off the panels, but a stove that can boil a big pot of water like that has got to need 240-volt power to pull that off. How are you going to get us that amount of power back here in the middle of a rainforest?"

Khadija looked insulted by the question and said "While the environmentalists in this coalition would hate the thought of it, I could get a diesel generator and tank of diesel to last a month brought upriver by barge in a heartbeat. You don't need it though.

As Ahmed said this morning, the stove power is self-contained and internally powered with no plugs or batteries needed."

"Self-powered? How can that be?", asked Xanthe perplexed.

"Well, Ahmed said the balloon child seemed to indicate it could boil a pot of water the size of a water heater tank for something like a hundred years on the power it generates internally."

As Xanthe stepped back in disbelief, Khadija continued, "The maker of the stove cube appears reluctant to share any details on how they work. I think they want you to use all this fancy pants equipment to tell them how tricks like boiling water for the next century are pulled off. So, you'll let me know on the list…."

Xanthe had turned away to consider the implications of this. She now wished she had been paying closer attention to the morning's session, because there was clearly more to this than she was aware. Ahmed knew she had done her graduate work doing endless tests on various battery materials and chemistries with a lot of the equipment listed.

While she still served in a negotiator role with governments and communities on disaster relief and aid efforts, her job had morphed into consulting for the NGOs on developing technology. Her focus was on leveraging technology that could head off the severity of the climate crisis and improve resilience in the face of projected extreme heat and weather. Her report yesterday had largely centered around needing to more than triple the use of existing clean tech to produce energy, and more than double efforts in energy efficiency and demand reduction.

The projected inability of nations alone to meet these goals in time to prevent massive population dislocations and deaths was the crux of the retreat agenda. Yet, in all her research and time spent following the latest clean energy developments, here was some novel tech she had not even heard a rumor of. She was trying to work out in her head the number of watt hours needed to boil a tank of water for even a year, much less a hundred and wasn't liking the number of zeros in the figure, when she became aware of Khadija waving a hand in front of her face.

"Earth to Xanthe… so you'll let me know on the list, because

Ahmed wants to get testing going right away."

Xanthe glanced down at the forgotten list in her hand and said, "Tell Miri we're going to want all of it starting with the Xray unit. I'm gathering my stuff and heading down to the bird watching pier now!"

6

Richard was just finishing his Monday morning walkthrough of the overseas plant robotics installation when, to his surprise, he spotted a familiar figure. This assistant to the Administrator at his company was usually neat as a pin, so it took Richard a moment to place the rumpled, bleary eyed young man jogging out onto the factory floor looking desperately around for something.

He walked over to head him off saying, "What does the Administrator have you looking for on this side of the world?"

The assistant whirled around with a relieved look on his face and said, "We've been trying to contact you since Friday. Where have you been?"

Richard said that he taken off to go on a weekend climbing trip and added, "I guess the cell phone reception in the mountains around here isn't the best."

The assistant fished an envelope out of his rumpled sportscoat and handed it to Richard. Richard started to put the envelope in his pocket saying "OK, But you look like you've been through the wringer. Let's get you ..." but the assistant cut him off saying, "Open it. Open it now".

Inside was just a note on the Administrator's stationery that said "Richard, This is bit sudden, but need you back, Pronto! My staff will get you set." It was signed with the familiar first name scrawl of the Administrator.

The assistant said "I've got a car waiting out front so, let's get moving. I hope to god you have your passport with you cause your flight leaves in an hour."

They hustled around the back of the pallets of robotic equipment that Richard had used to shelter his workspace from the noise of construction. The assistant asked him to pack quickly and give him his phone, tablet, and passport. As Richard shoved his mobile workstation and essential gear in his travel backpack, he saw the assistant fold and paperclip an unusually large bill in the back of the passport and then remove the SIM cards from his phone and tablet.

"Hey…." started Richard, but the assistant cut him off saying, "You'll get new ones in Austin. Here is some travelling money", he said handing Richard an envelope of bills, "but I will need all your business and personal credit and debit cards."

The assistant sealed Richards credit card the SIM cards from his phone and tablet in an envelope and pocketed them before handing Richard's, phone and tablet back. As soon as Richard had them shoved in his backpack, they were off and running for the car the assistant had waiting out front.

The car shot out of the facility, and the driver seemed to be enjoying himself as he weaved dangerously past traffic and gunned the car to speeds in open stretches of road that had the assistant holding on with a death grip on the handle over the door. Between clenched teeth the assistant asked him for his hotel key and a rundown of what Richard would want shipped back to Austin from the worksite. Other than his tool case, road box and the clothes from the hotel, there wasn't much.

When the car screeched up to the departures curb, the bundle of money the assistant chucked at the driver as he seemed awfully big, but then they were here at the airport in record time. The assistant had the photo of a woman's face on his phone as they hopped out, and a uniformed body belonging to an impatient matching face was there to meet them.

The assistant passed Richard's passport along with a plane ticket inside to the uniformed woman. She flipped the passport open to the back, nodded, checked Richard's face against the photo in the front and then turned to briskly stride away. Richard half jogged behind the woman to keep up as she strode briskly into the departures building, past the regular departure security line full of travelers, and down to a closed set of gate entries at the far end of the terminal. The rollup barriers were all lowered and locked at this end behind a couple of lines set up for security check in.

She flipped on one of the Xray machines and had him place his backpack on the Xray conveyor belt as it started up. She pulled a printed boarding pass out of the inspection station desk and stapled it to his paper ticket while keeping an eye on the Xray monitor as the backpack traveled through. She quickly moved a metal detector wand around him, patted him down and apparently satisfied he was not some sort of smuggler, inserted the stapled paper boarding pass/ticket into his passport and handed it back to him.

A quick look to check that the surroundings were clear, and she raised the barrier just high enough for him to duck under. She pointed urgently saying, "Gate 17 - go fast" in broken english.

He started running and was the last passenger left to board as he made it to the gate. The gate attendant had him hurriedly swipe the end of the boarding pass poking out of his passport, got a positive beep, and waved him onto the jetway saying the plane was already late. She shouted after him to take the first open seat so the plane could leave.

As he buckled in and the plane pushed back, he opened the passport to check and, sure enough, the paper-clipped bill was gone from the back of passport. He was about to put it away in his pocket when he noticed that the assistant's name was on the boarding pass. As the plane took off, he was musing why the Administrator would want him returning home under an alias.

7

Xanthe headed out of her quarantined cabana into the moist morning for the now routine walk to the drop off table. She had lost count of the days since the morning when she had joined the quarantined trio. From the juncture where the path from her cabana met the boardwalk, she looked to see if anyone else was up yet. She could not see anyone on the quarantined end of the boardwalk toward the bird watching platform, but the morning delivery of breakfast to the drop off table could be seen on the boardwalk back towards the main pavilion.

She walked down to the drop off table that had now represented the start of the quarantined end of the eco lodge and saw that the rolling case with the equipment requested for today's tests was already under the table. She looked out across the water towards the main pavilion and could just see a figure or two moving there. She gave a wave, but doubted anyone would see her at this distance. She got the case out from under the table, extended the handle and then poured a cup of coffee from the insulated dispenser that had been brought out with the breakfast tray.

Grabbing the case handle with her free hand she started rolling it slowly over the boards back towards the bird-watching pier as she watched the morning colors change out over the water. The formal retreat had ended with a resolution by the coalition and approval by tribal leaders to start the testing and exploration of the cubes' potential at the eco-lodge. Ahmed had been particularly insistent on keeping the cubes' existence known to just the small circle of those at the retreat and only the minimum of other trusted coalition staff back in what the tribal elders called, the "modern" world. Most of the coalition leaders, who had organizations to run, had already been flown out by Miri. Only a handful of scientists had stayed behind with Khadija to gather in the main pavilion and dream up tests for Xanthe and Jaha to do.

The assortment of equipment for the initial testing had showed up surprisingly quickly so Xanthe suspected that some advance arrangement must have been made to have it ready. With only a few additions, like the specialized equipment that Xanthe was bumping over the boards in the case behind her, all the tests had been managed by the equipment Khadija had already had on her list.

Xanthe had joked with Jaha that, with dreams that paid off like these, that the tribe might try their hand at divining next week's lottery numbers. Jaha, with surprising seriousness, had said the modern world's manic focus on money and consumer goods was at the root of the problems that had come to the tribe's neighborhood. What need did a tribe, intent on living in balance with the natural world around them, have for lottery winnings.

Jaha said the cubes were thought of by the tribal elders as a temporary gift to provide time for the modern world to come around to new ways of thinking that would allow them to "be" in harmony with the natural world. Still, Jaha was so seriously focused on the cubes testing, that she couldn't resist teasing him occasionally.

Xanthe arrived at the birdwatching pier and rolled the case down by the long lineup of solar panels clamped onto the pier railing. She set her cup on the railing, and the case to the side, and walked along pivoting each panel over to the optimum angle for the morning sun. She picked up her cup and headed with the case to the covered end of the bird watching pier.

The challenges with doing the type of sensitive testing they had been doing this past week in a remote rainforest location were many, but the most annoying thing was it Γαμώ το σπίτι σου rained a lot in a Γαμώ το σπίτι σου rainforest. The roofed area of the bird watching deck was only so big and the amount of equipment in active use had grown to fill up the covered area of the deck around the center test table. Because she and Ahmed didn't want any test results being skewed by equipment being rained on, tarps were draped over all the large equipment. She had to elbow her way gingerly with cup in hand through the blue tarp covered test equipment as she walked under the roof.

She maneuvered the case around and through the macrame of wires running to the camera tripods and light stands surrounding the test table to drop it off at the table at the center. The cubes were all in place on the table but the native child avatar hologram on the communicator cube, would not show up until they called it. She went to the far corner of the covered pier where two built-in benches met. She sat and put her feet up on the far bench to look out over the water at the warmly lit clouds in the distance.

As she sipped her coffee, she thought how Ariana insisted to the coalition leaders and trusted scientists that the remote location was necessary for their retreat. Xanthe thought it was odd that the makers of the cubes only fully trusted the tribe and would only deliver the prototypes into their keeping. The tribal elders were charged with seeing that the "gift" of the cubes was implemented in a way consistent with intention of the makers who they referred to as puente ruwaqkuna or "ruwaq" for short. Jaha could not say how the cube technology came to be gifted through his tribe, but only that the technology was a sort of limited time loan to keep the "modern" world from ruining things for everyone else on the planet.

Xanthe took another sip and leaned her head back against the rail. Above her at the peak of the roof was the balloon still valiantly trying to remain inflated. The black marker lashes and red marker lips looked dubiously down at her from the rafters. "I know, I know" she said to the balloon thinking of the commitment to the cube research she had made and the weeks of quarantine still to run.

Her partner back in Athens was used to her taking off at a

moment's notice to mobilize for the disaster du jour. They had planned to get away for a weekend in the sun on the Aegean but with her quarantine commitment, that would have to wait. She was sure Ahmed and Jaha were missing their families and Ariana was missing her husband, so she had their company to console her.

Jaha and the tribal elders had a deep trust in the intentions of the ruwaq and the gift of the cubes that was being offered, yet, with his home just a half hour canoe ride away, Jaha was stoically committed to keeping in quarantine with the three of them.

While there was no measurable evidence of anything harmful about the cubes or the native child dust 3D projection, the interior construction and contents of the cubes remained a mystery. The tarp clad battery of equipment had been used to passively probe the cubes in every manner the scientist team could dream up. With the cube's ability to soak up most electromagnetic and Xray spectrum radiation, there was little they could tell beyond the surface without the cubes' functions being activated.

The tribal elders had indicated their willingness to grant permission to activate the cubes days ago, but the frustrated coalition science team had resisted, hopeful they could still pry secrets from the inanimate cubes. The case she had rolled over held the equipment that was going to be used for the last passive test the science team wanted to perform before they would relent and allow activation of the cubes' functions.

Jaha had been assigned to work with her from the start, so he could explain to the elders what each of the tests the coalition scientists wanted to run would be. The elders would only allow non-destructive testing and would watch the child image's expression for any sign of concern while tests were being run.

There was no manual, or reference information of any sort provided with the cube, just the native child projection that could use its arms and expressions in silent pantomime along with simple animated graphics to help them figure out the possible functions offered by the cubes. Xanthe thought the native child projection was clearly artificial intelligence based. While the "native child" was eager to help answer questions on the cubes' capabilities and operation, it would only smile and ruefully shake its head at any questions about how the cube technology worked, was fabricated, or about the creators of the technology. Xanthe suspected Ariana and the tribal elders might know more, but they were not sharing.

Xanthe knew the cube technology did not exist in the corporate markets or university labs. Her pet theory, based on all the "need to know" secrecy, was that the tech could only have come out of some nation's military development lab. Depending on the nation involved, Xanthe could understand the caution being exhibited. As the week wore on, and test after test proved unable to reveal the interior workings, she was beginning to have her doubts.

Xanthe heard the creak of the pier boards from several pairs of feet coming down the pier, took a final sip from her cup and got up to power up the cameras and monitor for the morning check-in. There was rustle of tarps as Ariana and Ahmed swam their way in and then kept them parted so Jaha could carry the breakfast tray in. As the monitors and audio came on, she could see and hear the scientists milling around back in the pavilion. The tribal leaders were already seated talking amongst themselves and Khadija gave a wave from her seat in the back at the switcher.

Ariana nodded at Xanthe to turn the lights on and then called for the milling scientists to gather. Jaha, as usual, followed with translation for the tribal leaders. Ahmed motioned with his fingers over the small communicator cube and the smiling projection of the native child formed, giving a welcoming wave to everyone with its chubby arm.

Ariana gave a considered look at Ahmed and the native child projection before stepping forward to say, "The equipment for the last passive test of the cubes has arrived, and Xanthe will conduct that test presently. As you are aware, if there are no further issues or concerns raised by this morning's test, then the plan is to do move to active testing of the cubes later today. We have had lengthy discussions on this, and I have received approval from our off-site coalition partners to proceed to active testing if those of you at the pavilion agree. I would like to just poll everyone here to be sure there is agreement to proceed with active testing if nothing of concern turns up in this last passive test."

Ariana nodded at Jaha, who translated for the tribal leaders. Almost as one, the tribal elders indicated their approval. Ariana said "We have the elders' OK to proceed with activation, so it comes down to our science team. How do you vote?" The science team did not immediately respond, and there was some animated last-minute consulting among themselves.

Xanthe knew their dilemma. From all the surface observations that had been made, there was nothing evidently harmful or dangerous, but the cubes' interior workings were entirely concealed. If the native child's assertion that the largest cube, could really contain the power to boil a tank of water for a century, then the math alone raised implications that made the scientists uneasy.

Xanthe's back of the envelope calculations told her that if the cube stove prototype was turned on and somehow all that power was released at once, all that would remain of the bird watching pier would be a steaming crater under a minor mushroom cloud. So, in a way, the scientists were being asked, like the tribal elders, to take it as a matter of faith that the intentions of the cube makers were benign. They could only hope that by activating what was truly a black box, they were not going to unleash a form of Pandora's ills on the world.

Ariana and Ahmed let the consulting discussion back at the pavilion play out, while the native child projection floated with the serene Budda-like neutral expression it adopted when it was not trying to sway any vote outcome. After a bit, there was reluctant agreement, and the scientists voted to allow active testing of the cubes to proceed.

The morning testing had not raised any further concern, so Xanthe and Ahmed, assisted by Jaha began active testing that afternoon starting with the tiny cubes that now produced the native child projection. Based on the motions of the child avatar, and the simplified graphics that it produced in the lit dust, the tiny dark cubes were shown to be "twinned" to one another so that they were capable of transmitting signals and communications between each other.

Xanthe had demonstrated how electrical or optical signals applied to a location on one of the tiny "twinned" cubes, produced the same signal at the same location on its twin. This capability had gotten the tiny black boxes dubbed "communicator cubes" by scientists. The native child indicated the communicator cubes could also be used for supercomputing applications, but Ahmed said they would need an interface designed before those aspects could be tested.

The communicator cubes could do also a neat trick to emulate a video call when set on a desk or table in front of a person. The charged dust particles would form up into a curved plane in front of the eyes of a person where a gold-tinged 3D representation of the other person's or people's faces joining the call could then be seen. The real-time expressions and audible voices of those joining the conference, made it the next best thing to actually being in the room.

Xanthe and Jaha ran another battery of tests to check that there was no harmful radiation coming off the communicator cubes when they were used. It was puzzling to Xanthe and the scientists, that there was not only no harmful radiation, but no transmission signal of any sort being emitted when the twinned cubes were being used in conference calling mode. A couple of wild theories involving entangled particles were floated but again they had no idea how it was being done.

That afternoon Ariana announced that even though the coalition was attempting to keep the existence of their "clean cooking stove project" testing a secret, word of the potential for a need to manufacture hundreds of millions of "stoves" had somehow leaked out. One of the coalition leaders had just reported being reached out to by a company that was very interested in doing production runs of their "stoves" for them.

Fortunately, this corporate actor did not seem to be fully aware of the potential of the cubes, but unfortunately had an unsavory reputation for going to extreme lengths to try to acquire and reverse engineer new technology. The corporate actors knew that a coalition leader had just returned from a conference where a "clean cooking stove" demo model had been shown and had pressed for more details on the conference location.

Ahmed said the leak could possibly be due to the large amount of government monitoring of communications and bad actor eavesdropping going on in parts of the world. He suggested that they cease all use of phones and limit communications to emails and messages sent via direct satellite uplink.

Xanthe joked that the conference call test of the communicator cubes they had just done was probably the most secure method of talking on the planet. Ahmed said that, as they had been actively using the communicator cubes with the native child projection for over a week safely, he suggested that further calls, meetings, or deliberations of the coalition leaders and scientists be done using the communication cube's abilities so that they could not be intercepted or be listened in on.

Ariana asked the native child if the ruwaq could provide enough communicator cubes for all the tribal elders, coalition leaders, and scientists to use in further communications. Khadija suggested they round up the number to an even hundred to include the key coalition staff that would be needed plus a few extra for future partners that might need to be included. The child looked at Jaha with an inquiring expression as Jaha explained to the tribal elders what the request was. As soon as the tribal elders approved the request, the native child nodded approvingly at Ariana. Khadija requested that if the cube delivery was going to drop out of the sky, that it occur out by the drop off table on the boardwalk for safety. The native child had a bemused expression as Khadija mentioned safety but soon smiled and nodded at her in agreement.

Ahmed suggested these communicator cubes have some sort of innocuous looking means to conceal them when not being used. Ariana said they had already planned to give out small wood globe mementos of their retreat to those attending. The mementos were already at the lodge, and she wondered if the bases under the tiny globes could be modified to hold a communicator cube. The globe mementos could then sit innocently out in the open on desks or be packed in travel baggage.

Xanthe mentioned that this would be a good way to test the communicator cube abilities at global distances, while keeping their communications secure. Khadija said she would see if a regional supplier could do a rush order of base add-ons to adhere to the globe mementos.

With the communications resolved, Xanthe and Ahmed, with Jaha's help, spent the rest of the day taking careful electrical and optical transmission measurements of the communicator cubes. Xanthe made up a pair of drilled plastic squares that could be rubber banded onto the communicator cubes for very fine scale tests of the ability of the cubes to "twin" electrical and optically applied light signals applied to a very specific locations on the first cube and capture the output signal in an optical fiber applied to the twinned cube.

Ahmed had made arrangements with his manufacturer friend for an end of the day call with some "hotshot" engineer that was being assigned to them. Xanthe and Ahmed sat down and using a secure satellite uplink, launched a video call. Some unshaven guy in a cowboy hat, looking like he had been dragged in off a dusty cattle trail appeared on the screen. Xanthe, a bit surprised said, "Really Ahmed, aren't we scraping the bottom of the Texas barrel here?" before unmuting the audio so they could get the cowboy's attention.

8

As Richard walked out into the terminal lobby at JFK, he was met by a smartly dressed black woman, who he also recognized from the Administrator's offices. She introduced herself as Sylvia before turning to lead him out of the terminal to a waiting car. The drove them out of the airport and turned to head away from the city skyscrapers on the horizon.

After a drive out onto Long Island, the car pulled into another smaller airport, where a private jet was waiting. As soon as they were in the air, the familiar jet lag tiredness caught up with him, so he reclined his seat and was soon asleep.

The voice of the pilot announcing they were coming into the Austin area woke him and he looked out to see the familiar skyline on the horizon. Instead of heading for the city, the plane banked away to follow the highway South. Richard could see them overfly the exit to his apartment before they descended and then landed at a small airport. Sylvia was on the phone as soon as they touched down saying "We're on the ground".

A black SUV pulled up as the pilots lowered the stairs. Sylvia motioned to him to get into the back as she hopped into the front seat next to the driver. Richard put his cowboy hat on, so his hands were free to push his backpack across the rear bench seat ahead of him as he got in. The driver started off and Richard settled in for the ride to the company office.

As the driver reached the highway and continued past, it was clear they were not headed to the company offices or production buildings.

Richard asked, "So where are we going?"

"Not exactly sure" Sylvia replied. "But it shouldn't be that far."

The driver headed a few miles down country roads past mostly ranchland and a few dilapidated industrial buildings. They pulled off onto a dusty gravel road flanked by scrubby trees and undergrowth. As the road turned to the right inside the tree line, a tall rusty chain-link fence came into view. The driver pulled to a stop in front of a rusty chain-link gate and once the dust cloud settled, Richard could see that it had a new heavy chain with a lock securing it. Sylvia handed Richard a key and asked him to unlock and open the gate for them. Richard heard her tell someone on the phone they were at the gate as he got out of the SUV.

Richard unlocked the chain and pushed to swing the gate open, but it was slightly stuck on the gatepost, so he pushed harder. The gate came loose with shudder, and Richard pitched slightly forward into the cloud of fine white dust that was knocked loose off the gate fencing. The brim of his hat thankfully kept the dust out of his eyes, but the front of his clothes were coated with the dust. He swung the gate wide, and the driver drove in slowly. Sylvia asked him out the window to close the gate but leave it unlocked. Richard swung the gate closed, hung the heavy chain and lock on a post to the side and then attempted to dust himself off before climbing back in the SUV.

Tall material loading conveyors and pipe chutes were just visible in the sky over the ridge of whitish crushed stone along the gravel road was they were following. The backup alarms of heavy equipment could be faintly heard over the ridge and the road looked to have been frequented by heavy equipment that had left deep ruts. Some patches of fresh gravel had been dumped in the old ruts to make the road passable for normal cars, but even so, the SUV jounced quite a bit as they drove.

A metal building came into view ahead and Sylvia told someone on the phone, "We are pulling up outside". There were stacks of small slabs of concrete piled up around the back that all seemed to have been crushed or cracked near the center. A new satellite uplink transceiver was tucked back into some of these concrete slab stacks just outside a large rollup door on the back of the building. The door was already half open and the driver soon pulled right through the door into the interior of the building.

There was another black SUV already parked inside the building that was dominated by a large hydraulic press in the center of the room. Overhead a small beam crane provided a means of lifting and positioning whatever the press was used for. A wall with double doors partitioned off what looked to be offices in the front of the building from the hydraulic press room they were parking in.

As Richard got out, a familiar figure dressed in jeans and hiking boots emerged from the far SUV and started walking towards Richard. He was talking to someone on his headset while walking over but cut the call short with, "I have to go" as he reached Richard and held out his hand with a smile.

Richard smiled back and shook the hand of the Administrator. "Sylvia", the Administrator said to the assistant. "Can you ask the drivers to take a walk outside while we meet. Please ask them to keep to the side of building where you drove in, as we are trying are trying to keep a low profile while we are here.

As she headed off to wrangle the drivers, the Administrator walked Richard over to a folding table near the double doors with a laptop set up on it. They sat and the Administrator asked Richard how things were going on his overseas project as he turned on the laptop and made a connection through the satellite uplink transceiver. Richard gave him a breif update on the project he had just been pulled off of, while the administrator keyed in passwords on the laptop screen to access some site. Richard was still explaining what was remaining to be done at the overseas site as the administrator slid the laptop over in front of him on the table. All Richard could see was a dark screen with a "connection waiting" message reflecting his dusty cowboy hat and jacket. He thought about getting up and taking them off as he finished his update, but the Administrator was already launching into the new project.

"So, Richard… apologies for dragging you back around the

world on short notice, but I have an interesting ask from a friend of mine that requires some interface, robotic remote control, and facility design work to be done on the lowdown."

The Administrator outlined how they were being asked to merge their automated loader platforms with the newest robotic bodies to lift and load small cargo using remote control.

He continued, "These combination robotic torsos on loaders need to constantly work in temperatures up to 200 degrees Celsius and must be remote controlled to enable piece by piece loading by remote operators located up to several thousand miles away. We have teams rebuilding the loaders and robotic torsos with high temperature compliant parts and coming up with a cooled enclosure for the circuit boards and controller electronics.

What we need your help with is everything on the communication interface, remote operator control, and facilities design end. You will be asked for the present to work from this location to maintain secrecy. There will be some remote operator training, and production facility set up travel needed, but for the moment getting the interface going here is the priority. What do you think?".

The administrator paused to give Richard a moment to process everything he had just covered. What Richard really thought was this project must be highly unusual to have the Administrator get personally involved in secretly dragging Richard back across the world to be sitting jet lagged and covered in dust in some disused backwater building.

Richard mused for a minute on the actual project before saying, "Reworking the controller software and expanding it to cover the robotic torso and loader base will take some time but is doable. There is some new VR tech and haptics that could be used to give the remote operators better visibility and touch feedback as they are loading the pieces, so that is solvable. The challenge will be getting a low latency dedicated connection across the all the countries the remote operator communication will need to cross." A voice from the laptop interrupted saying, "We may have some tech that will help with the communication latency, but first introductions." Richard twisted back towards the laptop where a smiling middle eastern looking man and a dark-haired woman with a dubious look had appeared on the screen. The administrator walked over into view of the camera behind Richard and said, "Ahmed, good to see you. I hope all the security hoops we are jumping through on this are to your liking so far. This is Richard, the engineer that I recommended". Ahmed greeted Richard warmly and introduced the woman, who was still looking dubiously at him, as Xanthe.

Ahmed moved two tiny black boxes into view on the table and said that they were "communicator cubes" that they thought could solve the long-distance communication challenge. Richard watched as the woman demonstrated the ability of what she called "twinned" communicator cubes to send electrical and optical signals between one another with no connection terrestrial or satellite networks needed, no interference by metal earth or rock for underground use and zero latency.

Richard was doubting what she was saying about the lack of interference, until she placed the one cube with its electrical and optical test signal generator still connected into a charged isolation cage designed to cut off all possible radio or electromagnetic connection to the receiving cube. And still the signals continued uninterrupted.

This sat Richard back in his seat as considered how this could be possible. Ahmed, seeing the astonished expression on his face, said that Richard didn't have to worry about how the tiny cubes worked or how they were manufactured. They just needed his help with the connection interface, the robotic loader implementation, and the facility designs.

Ahmed said, "This is a long-term project, with a paramount need for secrecy and security that will mean you will need to work in relative seclusion. You will be limited in what you can tell your fellow workers, friends, and family. The project will require some long hours and long stints of travel over the next couple of years. I can however promise that you will find the work intriguing and its altruistic goals aligned closely with those of your activism efforts. So, is this a project you would be willing to commit to?"

Richard thought for a bit, as the woman on the screen crossed her arms and moment by moment was returning to her dubious look. Richard finally said, "Well, if these can relay electrical signals and optical data without interference or latency over long distances, we can definitely engineer an interface and use them for the remote robotic loader control. I'm not sure how you know about my activism efforts, but assuming this project is helping those efforts as well, I'm onboard." "

 Great" said the Administrator and Ahmed smiled on the screen.

The Administrator said, "I'll make the needed arrangements at this end, if you can get Richard several of the communicator cube things to start work with".

Ahmed said, "Indeed, thanks again for lining things up in a hurry and keeping this discreet. We'll be back in touch soon."

Their images faded from the laptop screen until only Richard's dusty reflection remained.

The Administrator said, "Their security guys say this place is about the best location they have found in the area, so let's plan on setting you up here. Sylvia can arrange to have everything you need sent out to set up this front room as testing lab. This back area should be large enough to put the robotic loader prototypes through their run tests with the software you'll be developing. Remember, they have asked that the communicator cubes and all results you find from working with them be kept entirely confidential. You will have security assigned and report only to me and Ahmed on this project."

The Administrator motioned to Sylvia to have the drivers come back in as he packed up the laptop. Richard followed him over to his SUV as he opened the door to get in.

He continued saying, "I would ask that you not come by the company offices or production facilities or let any of your co-workers know that you are back in town. As far as anyone will know, you are still overseas and just getting reassigned to this new "clean cooking stove" project. Sylvia will be your sole contact at the company and can help with getting the equipment and stuff you need sent out. She'll get you dropped off at the nearby house we have for you to stay at and can fill you in on more details."

The Administrator and his driver got into their SUV. As it pulled around the Administrator rolled down his window and said, "Glad to have you onboard for this one!" They headed out the open loading door and disappeared in the dust.

Sylvia was still waiting by the open loading door insistently tapping her foot and the driver was already in the SUV with the engine running when Richard roused himself from his momentary reverie. The rush of excitement from the demonstration was wearing off and jet lag was catching up with him as he collapsed back into the SUV seat for the drive out. They went out back out the gate, locked up, and the driver headed for his temporary house. As they pulled up the front drive Sylvia said, "I have a number of things to go over with you and a stack of paperwork to sign, but I would suggest we wait until tomorrow, cause frankly your dusty butt looks about done in for today."

9

The next day, at the morning meeting, Khadija announced the overnight delivery of the communicator cubes out on the board-walk. She let everyone know the rush order of globe memento base add-ons would come in with Miri on her afternoon flight.

Ariana said, "Good, let's get the communicator cubes keyed to everyone here and make sure those taking extras know who they need to make their handoffs to."

Ariana wrapped up the morning meeting and headed back to her cabana, while Xanthe, Ahmed, and Jaha moved on to test the smaller cola can height cubes they had taken to calling "builder" cubes. The builder cubes looked like 4" high replicas of the larger stove cubes with a similar square opening through the middle and the ends of the cube tapering into the opening with angled faces. The native child's animations indicated that the builder cubes, while useful for a range of excavating, mining, and construction activities, had further structural building potential if specific direction could be provided. Ahmed said they would need their cowboy engineer to get the interface developed before that could happen.

For today, they would rely on the ability to temporarily control the builder cube on the table using a communicator cube. Xanthe followed the projected animated instructions to hold a communicator cube up against a side of the builder cube and make finger motions on the cube sides to have them both glow brightly for a moment. With the communicator cube now able to control the builder cube, Ahmed asked Jaha to let the tribal elders know they were going to begin the tunneling test.

A thick granite stone was resting at one end of the test table and Ahmed now set the builder cube on top of it with the center opening pointed down. He had them put on protective glasses and dust masks, then checked with Xanthe to make sure the test equipment was ready. He got a nod from her and from Khadija to indicate the cameras were recording and then counted down 3-2-1. Xanthe made a motion with her finger on the communicator cube and a plume of dust shot out of the top of the builder cube. In a flash, the builder cube disappeared into the stone as the test table disappeared into the dust cloud. Xanthe hurriedly made a counter motion on the communicator cube to shut off the builder cube, but they had to wait until the dust had settled to see the result.

Ahmed pointed a camera down and wiped off the lens to show that builder cube had made it through the rock, out the bottom of the table, and nearly down through the boards of the pier below. He reluctantly indicated further testing on the builder cubes functions would have to wait until they had the control interface and the software protocal developed to fine tune the control. Xanthe gathered up some of the dust for further testing as they cleaned off the table, swept up the pier, and cleaned all the camera lens.

Once the space was cleared of dust, Jaha set the larger "stove" cube in place on a short equipment case, so the top surface was just above the test table behind. Xanthe positioned all the monitoring equipment and Ahmed refocused all the cameras to Khadija's satisfaction for the tests.

The stove cube had already been included in all the passive testing runs they had done, and like the small cubes, only the surface properties could be ascertained. Like the smaller cubes the stove cube surface was a carbon/silica mixture with an unusual nano-structure construction. Also, like the smaller cubes, the interior soaked up all the Xray, MRI, and other advance imaging equipment energies, so they knew almost nothing about what was going on inside. Only faint particle emissions hinted at some form of power being generated internally.

Ariana had come back out to the pier to be on hand for the initial stove cube tests and watched from the bench by the railing as Xanthe and Ahmed finished setting things up. She reminded Xanthe of the tribal leader's directive that each stove cube be "keyed" to a single "owner" who alone would be able to control and use that specific stove cube for their lifetime. Xanthe knew there was no way to transfer ownership so, once this stove cube was keyed to her, she alone would be able to operate it.

Ariana, knowing the commitment involved, asked Xanthe one last time if she was willing to become the "owner" of this stove cube for the foreseeable future. Xanthe said yes without hesitation and Jaha translated her assent for the tribal elders. Jaha received the approval to proceed from the tribal elders and Xanthe said to the native child avatar that she was ready to have the stove cube keyed to her.

The smiling child's face perked up before being replaced by a series of simplistic animated graphics that outlined the process. When the animation series was done and the child's smiling image reappeared, it motioned for Jaha to pick up the control tablet and hold it in both hands. Ahmed asked Khadija back at the pavilion "Are you getting this?", as everyone could see that the corners of the tablet had started pulsing with a white highlight. The child's hand gestured toward Xanthe as two hand graphics appeared on the face of tablet. The child mimed placing his chubby hands on linework representation of the tablet and then looked over at Xanthe. Xanthe stepped over to Jaha and then placed her hands on the glowing handprint outlines on the control tablet. The edge of the tablet glowed brightly for a second and then faded to a pulsating glow around the edge.

Following the native child's instructions, Xanthe took the tablet from Jaha and walked over to place it on top of the stove cube. Another pair of glowing hand outlines appeared on the top of the cube where Xanthe again placed her hands. The outline around her hands and the tablet edge glowed brightly for a second then faded out and a series of colored lines now appeared on the tablet face. The child beamed and clapped silently with its tiny hands. Xanthe thinking of the long weeks of testing ahead was more circumspect. For better or worse, she was now committed to being the sole person able to operate the stove cube going forward.

The native child presented animation instructions for each individual stove cube function and Xanthe followed along to demonstrate them using the control tablet. The capabilities shown raised a considerable number of questions which the native child would only answer with nods or shakes of its head. As usual, when questioned about the tech allowing the stove cube to do the demonstrated functions, the child image would hold its chubby finger over its lips with a knowing smile and give no more detail.

As the afternoon testing session got underway, Khadija could be seen gluing the globe mementos onto the new wood bases that Miri had returned with. Xanthe had only just started demonstrating the next stove cube function when Ariana hurriedly strode in and interrupted to let the group know that there were further concerning developments that their security team had made her aware of. They were going to need to wrap up testing at the eco lodge by the end of the day and get everyone out to the airstrip.

She asked Miri to fly the scientists out this afternoon, while the arrangements for the quarantined four would be made to leave with Khadija and Miri tomorrow. Xanthe asked Khadija to just keep the camera recording going, so those at the pier would be able to run through the last of the stove cube functions quickly, before packing up. Once Khadija gave them the thumbs up that she was recording, they started again on the stove cube functions.

On the monitor they could see Khadija making the scientists watch her operate the hidden catch on the new wood base addons that allowed the top of the memento with the globe to flip open so the communicator cube could slip inside. The tribal elders "keyed" communicator cubes to each of the scientists along with the extras that some of the scientists would be carrying home to "key" to other coalition leaders. They quickly slid the tiny cubes into the globe mementos and hurried off to pack.

When the time came for the last of the scientists at the pavilion to depart, Ahmed called for an end to the testing. They gave a last wave to the scientists, got an update from Khadija on what the morning transfer to the plane was looking like, and then the monitor went dark as Khadija cut the connection, so she could pack up the media recorder to send with the scientists. The distant sound of the boat leaving the pier taking the scientists back to the village airstrip faded as Xanthe set about packing things up for tomorrow's departure.

10

The next morning, Ariana was walking quickly down to the drop off table on the boardwalk early carrying a small plastic bin containing blood samples from the four of them in quarantine. As her footsteps across the boards made a hurried patter, she considered the latest warning they had just received.

The security team had identified a para-military squad being mobilized that was known to work for the disreputable knock off manufacturer. The security team did not like the mobilization and even less the direction their flight was taking them. Ariana had been advised to have everyone leave the eco lodge with the cubes as quickly as possible.

The blood samples had to be run early today, so Khadija would pick them up, run the testing in the portable lab that she had brought in, and report back to them with the results. The earlier lab results had consistently come back with no sign of any effects of the cubes on the four of them, but Ariana knew that the portable lab equipment they used in the field was only designed to look for known pathogens. Ahmed was worried that any novel pathogen or side effects of working with the cubes could take several weeks to show up, hence, the need to maintain quarantine.

As she reached the drop off table, there was a fabric tote bag on it and a rolling case under the table. She set the small bin down and took alcohol wipes from a container on the end of the table to wipe the bin down entirely. She stripped off the rubber gloves she had used to carry the bin and discarded them in the hazardous waste trash can under the table. She opened the tote bag and saw four transparent plastic packing enclosures, each with a globe memento on its new square wood base. The tiny wood globe was stained in wood tones for land and a blue tint for water. A small, engraved plaque was mounted under the globe celebrating the NGO coalition's new partnership with the tribe. Ariana took out a wood globe and set it on the table. Remembering Khadija instructions, she slid the upper globe backwards on the base. The lid of the wood base released, and she tilted the globe and wood lid over backwards on the hidden hinge until they were resting on the tabletop. A communicator cube was nestled in the wood base and in this open position, could be used for secure calls or leaving secure messages. Once the globe mementos with the communicator cubes were distributed out to the coalition leader and scientists, they should be able to communicate and conference with each other securely.

Ariana hinged the globe upright, slid it until the base was closed, placed it back in its packing, and then put it back in the tote bag. She pulled out the handle on the wheeled case that Khadija had adapted to transport the cubes and rolled it behind her while carrying the tote bag back towards the bird watching pier.

She heard a voice call out in the distance behind her and turned to see Khadija already walking out to pick up the samples. Ariana waved, but the quarantine rules meant they couldn't get any closer. Khadija must be anxious to run the samples first thing and then head back to the airstrip at the village to finish prepping the plane for her, Ahmed, and Xanthe. They hoped to have everything buttoned up at the birdwatching pier to be able to leave before noon.

Jaha would go with them back to the airstrip and then stay in quarantine with his family at a place outside the village. As she headed out on the pier, she passed the lower-level boat dock where two canoes were tied up. Their luggage was already sitting down on the dock and Ariana left the wheeled travel case there and went in under the roofed area.

This morning, they were working quickly to get all the pricey testing equipment fully under the bird watching pier roof, and get the tarps tied over them so they would be protected while they waited out the rest of the quarantine isolation period. As she came around the wall of blue tarped equipment, she could see Xanthe and Jaha maneuvering a large case top over a piece of equipment. She told them that the modified case for the cubes was by the luggage and made her way to the back railing where Ahmed was talking on the secure satellite phone.

She took out the globe mementos out of their plastic sleeves, set them out on the top of an equipment case, and opened them to reveal the communicator cubes inside. Ahmed took a pause in his phone conversation to tell her the morning medical test results looked normal, and Khadija was heading out for the airstrip. As he went back to his phone call, Ariana heard the flatboat's engine start up in the distance. Ariana saw the expanding wake appear as the boat made its way down the tributary carrying Khadija back to the village. She watched as the boat turned and disappeared down the river, before hearing Ahmed wrap up his call and turning back to him.

Ahmed said, "Things are set with the biosafety lab and quarantine house, but the security team is not happy with the progress of our potential visitors. They hope to know more soon, but I would suggest we get these communicator cubes keyed to us, get things buttoned up and be off heading down river as soon as we can.

He had Xanthe and Jaha, who had finished packing the cubes, pause in securing tarps around all the remainder of equipment to come over by the globe mementos on the case. Jaha, who considered the keying of the communicator cubes to be a significant event, had them form a circle around the statuettes. He recited a wish in his native tongue and then asked them to each step up and place a finger alongside his to have a communicator cube keyed to each of them. Each cube glowed brightly as both fingers were applied, and Jaha gave a ceremonial bow to each of them as the light faded.

Ariana and Ahmed pitched in to get the equipment packed and under tarps and they were making good progress when another call on the satellite phone. Ariana could tell by the tone of Ahmed's voice that he was not receiving good news and Ahmed gathered them around the phone as he put it on speaker.

Miri and Khadija's voices were interupted by the voice of the head of security who let them know his team had tracked a jet used by corporation of concern to an airport only a couple of hundred miles north of them. A dozen military looking men with duffel bags had come off the jet and walked over to load onto a single prop bush plane. They were considering them armed and very bad news. That single prop plane was now in the air and its transponder showed it making a bee line towards the village.

Miri interrupted to ask the make of the plane and upon hearing the answer said they might only have about half an hour before the plane arrived in their vicinity. The head of security told them to drop everything and get out of there now. Jaha was already running down to the canoes to get the luggage in as the other three grabbed their laptop cases and the globe mementos.

Jaha suggested Ariana and Ahmed take one of the canoes and get a head start while Xanthe and him stopped by the pavilion to get the eco lodge staff contingency evacuation going. While Ahmed was stronger, she had more experience in canoes and took the rear seat. Jaha shoved them off and then started quickly packing the luggage and cubes into the second canoe.

As they came by the pavilion, they paused for a moment to shout thanks to the eco lodge staff and tell them Jaha was following and would have instructions to clear out. The eco lodge boardwalks passed from sight as they made the turn to the main river and, now that they were paddling with the river current, they were making better time. Ariana asked between paddle strokes, "So how bad would it be if this airborne squad catches up with us?". Ahmed paused for a moment to look back at her and give a simple shake of his head, before again putting his back into paddling hard. Ariana tried to dispel thoughts of some of the black ops military contractors she knew were at work in the world. She decided the sweat breaking out on her brow was not just from the effort of paddling.

As they reached the halfway point, Ariana heard the twin engines of Miri's bush plane rev up from the direction of the village and fervently hoped they would be ready for them. Xanthe and Jaha caught up to them and, as they passed, Jaha handed Ahmed a rope and had him tie it to the front of their canoe. With the tow line in place, and Jaha's powerful strokes they continued at a faster pace until the village pier was just coming into sight around the river bend.

The faint drone of an approaching plane came to them from upriver causing Jaha to dig especially deep with his paddle strokes and both the canoes surged forward for the final sprint to the pier. Ariana had not paddled this hard in years and struggled to compensate for Ahmed's renewed effort in the front to keep the canoe following in a straight line. Jaha headed them into the shadow of the overhanging trees by the bank as the growing drone of the approaching plane came up from behind them.

11

Khadija had just strapped down the last of her equipment cases in the back of the plane when the satellite call from the security head had come in. She listened for a second then stuck her head out the plane door and shouted "Miri, we have incoming and need to scramble!"

She jumped down out of the plane and waved over the tribal elder who spoke some English. During the call with Ariana's quarantine group and the security head, Miri had fired off questions about the exact type of aircraft and number of men and bags loaded into it. The security head was fed quick answers by his team as Miri noted the info down on her clipboard.

Jaha spoke to the tribal elder in his native tongue to get the contingency evacuation of the village underway and then the call ended. The tribal elder called over to the two village guys he had assigned to help Khadija carry items from the boat, and they ran up with the last of her luggage. The tribal elder spoke to them and they ran for the village to spread the alarm. The tribal elder wished them well but said he was needed to help lead the village back in the rainforest to a place they had prepared for this contingency and hurried off.

Miri had a no-nonsense expression as she said, "This incoming squad is really bad news, that none of us really want to be around to meet up with. The quarantine bunch canoeing this way is probably at least 20 minutes out even with the river current at their back, so it's going to be tight to make it out of here before that incoming squad arrives. Get everything inside strapped down for a rough ride, while I see what extra runway, I can scrounge up to make this happen."

Miri ran off toward the river landing and Khadija hefted her luggage into the plane, taking care not to damage the plastic isolation tunnel rolled up by the door. She was finishing strapping the cargo area net into place when Miri jumped up into the plane with a wry expression.

Miri said, "The wind direction will force them to land from the river end of the airstrip and may give us a chance to get away clean if we can hide out under the trees right by the river. Pull the chocks and button up the door and then get up front with me cause I'll need your eyes."

Miri headed for the pilot's seat as Khadija pulled the chocks and then jumped in and closed the cargo door. As soon as the door was secure, she called out to Miri and heard the engines firing up. She made her way up the aisle alongside the plastic sheeting she had installed to isolate one half of the rear area of the plane and plunked down in the copilot's seat.

Miri was furiously doing math of some sort and checking a chart on the back of her pre-flight checklist. She was already wearing her headset and motioned to Khadija to put on the co-pilot's headset as she worked. Satisfied with her calculations, she had Khadija look towards the far side of the wide stone paved ramp down to the river the village used as raft landing for their rainforest river excursions. Miri said, "See those large tree trunks on the far side of the ramp? I'm going to need you to call out distances from the wing tip to the closest of those trunks once I start turning away from the river."

Khadija only got out "OK, but…" before Miri gunned the engines and released the brakes setting the plane into motion. It looked to Khadija, like Miri was trying to take the plane right down into the river as she left the potholed end of the dirt strip and bumped down the stone paver ramp heading into the river. The massive rainforest trees loomed over them as Miri idled the engines. The plane was starting to roll down the gently sloping ramp of its own accord, when Miri braked the left wheel hard and gunned the right engine. The roaring engine pivoted the plane around on the stationary wheel, and the wing on Khadija's side swung out over the river, then around directly towards the alarmingly close tree trunks on the far side of the ramp. Her called-out numbers were getting tight as the wing finally cleared past the closest of the trunks by the river's edge and the plane reached a point of being entirely turned back towards the dirt strip.

Miri shut down the engines and as the props slowed to a stop she said, "Hop out with the chocks and watch as I get better aligned with the runway. When I give a shout chock the wheels only on the downhill side."

Khadija made her way out of the cockpit. Out on the ground, she watched and motioned as Miri let off on one brake and then the other to allow the plane to roll backwards a couple of inches until it was aligned to her satisfaction with the runway. Khadija kicked chocks in against the downhill side of the tires and called "Chocked" in the plane door and stepped back to watch as Miri released the brakes to check that the chocks alone would hold the plane in place on the ramp before locking the brakes.

The plane was now tucked back into the shadows of the over-arching canopy formed by the massive rainforest trees to either side of the ramp. The plane was fairly well concealed from any-one flying over, but Khadija didn't know what good that would do once the bad boy's plane landed and saw them.

Miri called back and asked if she could fill in a couple of the deeper potholes in line with the wheels, while she did some re-vised flight planning in the cockpit. Khadija grabbed a paddle from the rafting collection on the pier and used it to rake some loose gravel and stones into the potholes. She was finishing fill-ing the last of them with the paddle when her satellite phone rang. The security team lead's voice said, "incoming plane is about 10 minutes out still on a heading directly for you". She shouted, "Badboy's ETA 10 minutes!" up at the pilot's window and held up 10 fingers until Miri nodded at her. She ran down to the dock and could see the pair of canoes rounding the bend in the distance. She went back to the plane door and shouted in that the canoes were in sight and unrolled the plastic isolation tunnel out of the plane and down towards the river. The tunnel flapped back and forth in the gusty wind, so she set her paddle on the end to keep it in place. That's when she heard the drone of a far-off plane engine.

The quarantine group in the canoes must have heard it too, because she could now see they were all paddling like mad and sticking to the near bank to keep out of sight. Khadija expected the plane to appear at any moment, but the sound changed and she figured the plane must be circling over the now abandoned eco lodge just up river.

She yelled in the cargo door to let Miri know the plane was over the eco lodge and the canoes were almost there. Down at the river she made exaggerated motions at Xanthe in the front canoe towards the end of the isolation tunnel and then stepped up by the cargo door to give Miri a heads up when the canoes arrived and were clear of the left prop wash.

The wind was blowing briskly past the front of the plane down towards the river, so Khadija didn't worry about any pathogen exposure as Xanthe, Ahmed, and Ariana came running up with their luggage inside the plastic tunnel and started clambering up the steps into the plane. Khadija shouted that the left enging was clear, and Miri immediately started it. Jaha followed inside with the cube case, got a quick round of hugs and was back out fighting his way back down the now billowing tunnel being blown in prop wash from the far engine. Khadija heard the drone of the approaching plane coming their way, as Jaha came out of the tunnel and gave Khadija a grin before disappearing into the forest.

Khadija frantically reeled in the isolation tunnel to keep it from being seen by the approaching plane, jumped inside, and yelled that the plane was overhead as she pulled the cargo door closed. The other engine sprang to life as she squeezed her way along the isolation plastic draped over the three now occupied seats.

Miri called back, "Everybody strap in, this may be a bit of a wild take off," as Khadija hurriedly sat in the copilot seat.

Khadija put her headphones on as Miri ran the engines throttles up further until the plane seemed to be barely held back by the brakes. Khadija wondered why they weren't moving, but she could Miri's lips moving saying, "Wait for it …Wait for it". Miri had her neck craned around looking out the side window when she said, "Here we go everyone." over the intercom.

Miri let the brakes go and the plane leapt forward up the ramp, just as the bad boy plane swooped in over the tree canopy in front of them. They were already gathering speed across the potholes, before bad boy plane even touched down. A cloud of dust was kicked up as the bad boy's plane tires settled on the dirt. Miri went to full throttle and said, "Got you!"

They were a third of the way down the airstrip when the dust cloud kicked up by the landing blew off to the side of the runway. Khadija could now make out the bad boy plane making a turn at the far end of the runway. She could tell the moment the pilots at the far end of the runway saw them, because the plane went from a slow turn to the engine being gunned to whip the plane around and start it coming back down the runway right at them. Miri said, "OK, boys so you want to play chicken…"

The distance between the charging planes was closing rapidly and Khadija thought about saying something but her lips seemed to have lost the ability to form words. Miri was totally focused on her airspeed indicator and seemed oblivious to the head on train wreck about to take place. Khadija saw a grin cross her face as she yanked back on the controls, and they lunged up into the air. Khadija watched the tail of the bad boy plane pass under them with a surprising amount of clearance.

Miri was already banking sharply to the South before they reached the far end of the strip clearing. Khadija could just see men start to jump out of the stopped plane before the rainforest closed in under them and the strip was lost to sight.

Miri now banked sharply back around to the Northeast keeping low in a valley to make them difficult to see. Miri was pushing the plane as fast as it would go as she dodged from one valley to the next keeping them just over the treetops. She asked Khadija to call the security team and keep them on the phone to give them updates on the bad boy plane location.

The security lead on the phone said the bad boy plane transponder showed that it had taken off and was headed South following the direction Miri had the plane pointed when they had first left. Khadija relayed the info to Miri who figured with the haze, they were already near the limits of being visible.

Miri said, "Keeping down on the deck for a bit longer to get us out of range of the bad boy's radar should allow us to get away without being picked up."

After a while of watching Miri weave along the valleys uncomfortably close to some of the treetops, the security lead told Khadija the bad boy plane was still headed South. She relayed the message and Miri started to climb out of the valley while throttling back to cruising speed. She brought up the flight plan on her nav screen and engaged the autopilot which continued to take them in a slow climb towards the mountains. Miri relaxed and then keyed her mic. Khadija heard her voice come over both her headset and the cabin speakers behind.

"Glad you all made it in time to avoid a run in with our party crashers. The security folks are telling us the bad boy's plane is still headed South, while we are now flying away from them to the Northwest. We are now out of their visual and radar range and should be safe. We are being a bit naughty flying without our transponder on, but we can't risk our friends finding us by monitoring the satellite transponder feeds. We have a long way to go, so if you want to get up and stretch, or get something to eat or drink from the bins strapped behind the last row of seats, now would be a good time. Khadija has kindly provided a camp toilet at the back of your hamster run, but I would suggest opening the overhead vents poked through the hamster plastic overhead before availing yourselves of that luxury. We know you had no choice in airlines for your travel today but, still, try to sit back, relax, and enjoy flying coalition air."

12

Richard woke and wondered for a moment where he was. The new smell of the sheets fought with the musty smell of the quilt he was under reminding him he was at the safe house. Richard sat up in the bed and found he was thirsty. In the light coming through the old gingham drapes, he could see the wood bedstead and a worn and scratched up wood dresser that made up the only furnishing in the room. He decided to investigate the bag and cardboard box on the dresser later, as he stepped over the pants and shirt that he had discarded to head out of the bedroom. He padded in his bare feet out through the unfamiliar house to see what there was to drink out in the fridge.

Yesterday the driver had dropped him off at this house tucked back in off a road about a mile from the gate. Sylvia had given him a key and said he would be staying here for the time being. She said there was some food in the cabinets, drinks in the fridge, and that she would be back in the morning with some paperwork they needed to go over before Richard got started. She had told him that he was not to go back to his apartment in town or pick up his car. The security team felt that it was important that Richard appeared to still be working overseas. With drink in hand, he wandered around the dusty ranch style house to find that only the living room, kitchen, and the bedroom, that he had crashed in, had some semblance of furniture. Most of the mismatched and worn pieces looked like they were the leftovers from some rural yard sale. He peeked out past the thick drapes covering the front windows, to see the gravel driveway heading out through the scrub trees. Out the back windows were the remains of an overgrown yard with more scrub trees to the sides.

When he heard a car coming up the gravel drive, he peeked through the front window sheers and saw that it was Sylvia. He unlocked and cracked the front door and then headed back to the bedroom to get some clothes on. From the bedroom, he heard Sylvia come in the front door and he called out to say he would be out in a minute. He just threw his travel clothes back on and came out into the living room where he was greeted by the welcome smell of coffee.

Sylvia was sitting at the rickety kitchen table with a stack of papers and two cups of coffee. She was mixing sugar in one and pushed the other one towards Richard as he sat. He gratefully took a couple of sips, as he looked over the stack of papers she was dealing out on the table.

Sylvia was casually dressed in jeans and a shirt instead of business attire but was still wearing her no-nonsense business attitude. She let him sip on his coffee while she finished her sorting and then asked, "Has the coffee kicked in enough, so you are of sound mind to slog through and sign off on all of this?" Richard nodded over the top of the coffee cup and Sylvia dove in.

Most of it was just updates to the paperwork the HR folks at the company kept on file and a slightly more involved non-disclosure agreement for the robotic loader communication protocol and interface that many of their clients typically required.

There were a couple of items that were unusual though. The first was a grant of permission to use Richard's identity and credit cards to book reservations and make purchases in the interest of concealing Richard's actual whereabouts. Richard was to be reimbursed for what Sylvia called these "red herring" activities. Richard wondered if the assistant, that had bundled him out to the airport, was running around overseas with his credit cards posing as him.

Another was a long list of dos and mostly don'ts that Richard was to follow for what Sylvia called "his continued health and wellbeing". Do stick to the secure safe house and work locations. Do obey instructions of security team member assigned to him. Do exclusively use the work and safe house secure satellite uplinks for only required communications. Don't reach out to local co-workers, friends, relatives, without advance guidance from the assigned security team member. Don't do any of the page of single-spaced bonehead items that would reveal Richard's work details or whereabouts.

The last was a notification that outlined bad actor activity seeking to acquire, by unlawful means, client provided parts, control prototypes or interfaces developed for those parts, and intellectual property related to the parts. It said that attempts had already been made to acquire those with detailed knowledge of the parts, and that strict adherence to the workplace safety guidelines was required to prevent "personnel acquisition" by these bad actors.

Richard looked up from the paper and said, "personnel acquisition?". Sylvia smiled ruefully. "There are some of our less reputable overseas competitors that have learned about the hot potato "parts" you will be working with. They apparently are not above going to extralegal efforts grab these potato "parts" and anyone caught holding them. Looking down at her long immaculate fingernails, she said, "Rumor has it, these guys are not above giving out custom nail jobs to pry trade secrets out of those they "acquire".

The look on Richard's face must have given away his reticence, so she added. "Sorry, just kidding...mostly. Look, just follow the rules, keep your head down, and stick with your security guy if any overeager manicurists come knocking. Are you OK signing off on this notification document?" It was not helpful that she was casually checking her nail polish on one hand as Richard thought about this for a few minutes.

Because he was single, unattached, and willing to travel, he had worked in a lot of places around the world. Some of them had rough sections of town, or rough elements that were not inclined to welcome those from western countries. Richard was used to keeping a low profile when working abroad and had had security escorts in a couple of the locations he had worked at. While it was going to be a novel experience keeping a low profile in his own backyard, was not going to be too much of a burden. Besides, the communicator cubes were nagging at the back of his mind, and not having the chance to find out how they worked was no longer an option.

Once Richard had initialed and signed his way to Sylvia's satisfaction, she had him pull out his laptop and tablet to plug into the satellite uplink cables. He was asked to enter a new password for secure access to video calls and email. She gave him a non-work email address that he could use to securely send her requests for everything from equipment to groceries.

She pulled a satellite phone out of her bag with a corded earpiece. She showed Richard the preset numbers for his assigned security guy, the security team emergency contact number, and her satellite phone number. "You can text or call if you need me or the administrator urgently, but don't wear it out." she said with an expression that implied anything short of a life-threatening occurrence, might become one.

She handed him two keyrings with label machine tags on them. One said, "Qual Test Bldg." and had a pair of commercial door keys. The other said, "T - 9" and had an ignition key and a detachable lock key.

She said, "The first will get in the building at the concrete plant/quarry and the other is for the pimped-out ride waiting for you in the garage. Drive it out, leave the garage open, and then call the security team number when you have it idling ready to go. They have the road under surveillance and can check that the coast is clear before you drive down to the same quarry gate we used yesterday. Use the padlock key on the ring to unlock the gate and relock it once you are inside.

Your clothes and items from overseas will be coming back soon but send me a request for any specific items you want from your apartment in town. Some styling duds to go with your pimped out ride are in the bedroom. Be sure to wear them whenever you are driving in or walking around outside at the quarry.

You will want to work here the rest of the morning, where it's relatively clean. Take the vacuum and cleaning supplies in the garage to the building with you when drive over after lunch."

She asked if he had any further questions as she packed up all the paperwork and started to head to the front door. She paused and adopted a serious tone as she said, "We've gone to a lot of trouble to get your butt back here, without anyone knowing. I need to you to keep it hidden and safe, or I'll personally be handing it back to you in world of hurt." "Later!" she said lightly with only the slightest hint of a smile as she headed out the door.

13

Miri started her descent towards the airport near the biosafety lab and received her clearance to land. It had been a long, but eventless flight, once word had come from security that the bad boys' plane had given up looking for them and returned to the dirt strip.

The tribe was camped out safely deep in the rainforest, so only the abandoned village was left for the foreigners to search. The squad left a mess behind after searching the village and eco lodge but had not done much damage. The squad's unpacking and leaving all the pricey test equipment exposed to the rain was particularly disconcerting to Xanthe, and her rants could still be heard going on back in the cabin. The government forces that were tipped off by the security team had been closing in, so the bad boy squad finally had to give up the search and fly out.

Landing on a regular runway was a piece of cake. Miri let the plane float down the runway for a way before setting the wheels down, so she had enough momentum left to carry her off the last ramp. She pulled the plane around on the concrete parking apron by a white van near a gate in the fence line.

Khadija went out to chock the wheels and pull out the plastic isolation tunnel out of the plane, while Miri went out to meet the official looking vehicle driving up to meet them with all their passports. The officers flipped open and scanned Miri and Khadija's passports, then examined three passports sealed inside double plastic pathogen sample bags with the pages open to the photo page. One of the military police used binoculars to compare Khadija's face to her passport as she finished joining the isolation tunnel ends and called for Ariana, Ahmed, and Xanthe to come off the plane.

One by one they came down the steps, with their suitcases, and made their way through the tunnel, towards the van. The officers asked that they each turn and face them for a moment near the van doors where the plastic was stretched flat so that the man with the binoculars could compare their faces to their passports. With their faces checked and front pages scanned, the passports were handed back to Miri.

Khadija packed the van end of the tunnel inside the back door, while Miri reeled in the plane portion of the tunnel. Khadija got their travel bags placed in the front of the van as Miri secured the plane and then came back over and climbed into the driver's seat. She pulled the van around and gave the officers holding the gate open a wave as they headed out into the city traffic.

On the drive to the biosafety lab, Ariana checked in with Miri to see if she might be willing to continue to help with some of their "clean cooking stove" related efforts. Ariana said, "There are some mining surveys that need to be done, and it would be ideal if you could take those on." Miri said she could certainly do that, if the relatively disaster free period they were in continued.

After a short drive through the outskirts of the city they arrived at the biosafety lab entry. Miri checked in with the guards at the gate and then followed a guard in a patrol car around the parking lot to a rear loading into what appeared to be a new addition onto the building. A couple of pathogen lab workers were already there dressed in isolation suits waiting for the van's arrival. They motioned for Miri to back the van in through the open loading door and had her stop about 20' from the entry to the decontamination chamber. The suited lab workers opened the back doors, pulled out the plastic tunnel, and joined it to a second plastic tunnel end attached to the decontamination chamber.

Ahmed and Xanthe got the cube case and their suitcases out of the back of the van and moved them through the plastic tunnel into the decontamination chamber.

"Goodbye for now my friends" called out Ariana, as the suited workers detached the tunnel and rolled it up into the back of the van. Ahmed and Xanthe gave a final wave to the three of them in the van before the rear doors were closed and Miri drove them back out of the building. Once out of the biosafety lab complex, Miri headed for the house that had been rented for Ariana on the outskirts of the city.

The house, chosen by the security team, was isolated in an area that the city had not yet encroached on. They arrived out in the middle of a section of scrubby desert and turned down a gravel construction road with a new housing development sign. Down the road, they pulled in past a construction office trailer and onto a paved drive. The drive led up to the model house for this new development where one of Ariana's assistants was parked. Miri backed the van up by the open door of the three-car garage, and her and Khadija got out to pull out the tunnel.

The assistant came over to the van and told Ariana that she had clothes and food selected by her husband already in the house and that her computer and videoconferencing satellite uplink was set up at the curved sales desk just inside the front door.

The assistant took Khadija and Miri's suitcases back over to her car as Khadija unrolled the isolation plastic tunnel out into the garage. Miri took the van keys and Ariana's passport into the garage and placed them on a shelf next to the door into the house. They watched as Ariana made her way out of the back of the van with her suitcase and down the isolation tunnel to the end seal. Khadija carefully closed the back doors of the van as far as the plastic tunnel would allow and then taped the doors to keep them closed.

"You both take care and we'll be chatting soon" said Ariana from the end of the tunnel. Miri and Khadija both wished her well as they got into the assistant's car and drove up to the end of the driveway. Ariana's husband would be coming in to join her and they would stay in the house together for the remaining weeks of the agreed upon quarantine. Looking back, they saw

Ariana come out of the end of the tunnel and then hit the garage door button. Miri could see the garage door close as they drove out onto the gravel road and soon the house was lost to view in the dust behind them.

14

It was after lunch by the time Richard had caught up on his emails, put out a couple of fires back at the overseas project he had abruptly left, and had a shower. A couple of pairs of washed jeans were in the bag on the dresser with some new packages of socks and underwear. A new pair of construction style steel toed boots were in the box. There was nothing in the dresser drawers, but some shirts with a concrete company logo were hung in the closet and trucker hats with the same logo were on the closet shelf above. So much for styling duds.

Richard headed out to the garage dressed as Joe concrete worker to find a beat up dusty white pickup truck with the concrete company logo on it. So much for a pimped-out ride. He put the vacuum and cleaning stuff in the back bed, threw his computer satchel in the passenger seat and opened the garage door. He pulled the pickup out of the garage and made a call to the security number to ask for clearance.

After a minute he was given the all-clear and he drove out on the empty road past some fenced ranch lands. The gate leading to the building was only about a mile away. After pulling in and doing the gate unlocking/locking drill, he went up the road and pulled up to park by the loading door. He tried the key that he had been given in the exit door next to the loading door and it opened right up.

Inside the dimly lit hydraulic press area, he flipped on the light switches by the door. In the light he could still see the tire tracks in the dust on where the SUVs had pulled in for his meeting with the administrator. He was glad they had left him a large shop vacuum, as he was going to need it to get the dust off this acre of concrete. As he walked around the press towards the front room, he noticed a set of larger truck sized tire prints in the dust leading close to the front room doors. Just behind where the truck prints ended, a set of heavy caster wheel tracks picked up heading towards the doors. These had definitely not been there yesterday, so he wondered what had been going on since he was last here. The tracks ended on the cleaner tile floor of the front room, and as he looked around, nothing seemed to have changed.

He started off by vacuuming out one of the offices and dusting off a folding table to use as a desk. He set up his laptop on the table and ran a LAN cable in from the satellite modem to get it connected and online. He closed the door to the office and started vacuuming the tile floor of the front room. A fine layer of white dust seemed to be everywhere.

He had just finished vacuuming the front space and had pulled out some taller counters and stools from the front wall to use as a test bench when he heard the loading door out in the hydraulic press space open. Remembering the warning to be cautious, he peeked through the double doors, into the press space. He saw Sylvia by the open loading door waving a black SUV in and then closing the loading door behind it. The SUV drove in around the hydraulic press and pulled to a stop close to the double doors.

Richard went out through the doors to greet Sylvia, but a man in a suit wearing sunglasses popped out of the SUV to head him off with an outstretched arm. The arm had the force of a line-backer behind it and stopped Richard in his tracks. Richard, momentarily stunned, tried to move around the guy, but instant-ly found his arm twisted behind his back and his body forcefully applied across the hood of the SUV. Richard was starting to consider the squashed reflection of his face in the warm black polish as Sylvia called out, "He's with us".

"Sunglasses" released him and looked carefully around the hy-draulic press space before heading through the double doors to check out the front area.

Sylvia came over and greeted him saying, "Apologies, the security guys are a little on edge after some recent developments. Once they check things out, we have a couple of presents for you".

Sunglasses came back out of the front room through the double doors, nodded to the driver, and went around to the back of the SUV. The driver opened a back door, and a casually dressed older man got out of the back seat to greet Sylvia and Richard. He introduced himself as one of the NGO coalition scientists and who had, he said with a wink, been involved with testing on the "clean cooking stove" project.

He had just returned to the country bringing some "stove" parts for Richard. He walked them around to the open back of the SUV where Sunglasses was standing guard and Richard saw the rear floor carpet had been rolled back. A steel plate door covered the area where the spare tire compartment should be. The scientist flipped up a metal cover in the door revealing an inset keypad and keyed in some numbers. There was a click, and the driver leaned in to heft and hold open the thick steel door. The scientist reached in to pull out whatever was so precious it required a safe to be built into the back of the SUV.

Richard wasn't sure what to expect, but the familiar scuffed and dented metal attaché sized case with stickers from his memorable work trips to the far corners of the world was about the last thing on the list. It was Richard's own electronics repair tool case that the scientist handed over to him, along with a cloth tote bag that seemed to have a lot of the tools that should be in the case.

Sylvia led them through the doors into the front room, followed by Sunglasses while the driver stayed with the car. Sunglasses looked out the front entry door windows and then took up station there, while the scientist suggested Richard place his tool case on the counter "test bench".

Sylvia said, "Open it" and Richard dialed the tool case latch dials to the familiar combination. He snapped open the latches and raised the top of the tool case. Instead of his usual neat array of small tools and testers inside, there was a sheaf of papers sitting atop a block of gray foam that was now filling the case. Richard took the papers and flipped through them. They were the documentation on the communicator cube testing he had been promised. The scientist lifted a sheet of gray foam to reveal eight pairs of the tiny communicator cubes set into the gray foam below.

The scientist said, "Now, let's get these keyed to you, so you can get to work with them." The scientist put his finger on one side of the first cube and the cube glowed briefly. He had Richard put his finger on the other side of the cube and the cube glow returned with a pulsating rhythm. The scientist removed his finger, and the cube glowed brightly for a moment and then faded out. They repeated the process to key the remainder of the cubes to Richard, then the scientist suggested pulling over a couple of stools so they could sit while he walked Richard through what he knew of the "stove" part testing.

They had been sitting, talking, and flipping through the documentation papers for about 20 minutes, when the security guy by the door perked up, said something into his radio and pulled out a gun. A large pickup truck pulled into view outside the front doors, being engulfed in the cloud of white dust as it stopped. The driver hustled in from the hydraulic press room with his gun drawn as Sylvia said loudly, "This is one of ours, boys, so please don't damage him."

The pickup truck was a beat-up high ground clearance 4-wheel drive version with oversize tires that was coated in dust and dents. A tall figure got out with his hands casually held up in view as Sunglasses went out the doors to check him out. He allowed Sunglasses to pat him down before he took out some form of ID that appeared to satisfy Sunglasses. He pulled a backpack out the back of the cab that Sunglasses unzipped to check. Richard saw Sunglasses' eyebrows appear in surprise over the rims and new look of respect come over his face as he rezipped and handed the backpack over.

Sunglasses came back in followed by the man who was dressed in dusty jeans, work boots, and work shirt with the concrete plant logo on it.

Sylvia said, "Richard, this is Sam."

Sam took in the entire room, the suits, the scientist and the test bench set up before sauntering over to nod a greeting at Sylvia.

She said, "He'll be looking after your test bench butt while you are working with the "stove parts", that you and Dr. Science are so taken with."

"Good to meet you" Sam said, shaking Richard's hand with a casual yet firm grip. "I see that Sylvia is giving you the same respectful treatment she shows the rest of us," said Sam, grinning at Sylvia.

"Yeah, Yeah" said Sylvia and continued, "Well now that cavalry has clomped in after knocking some concrete worker over the head to take their clothes, let's get the good Doctor back in the car"

As the suited security guys ushered him back to SUV in the hydraulic press room. Sylvia said to Sam, "We just need to make sure the tech cowboy here knows how to put away his toys and I'll be out of your hair."

She asked Richard to pack up the cubes and documentation papers in the tool case and lock it. Sam wandered past the front doors to look out and then over to the double doors to check that the scientist and suits were in the SUV. As Richard closed the tool case and spun the combination dials, he saw Sam heading for the hallway leading to a side building exit door. Sylvia made a motion for Richard to follow with the tool case.

There was nothing in the hallway, but concrete test slabs stacked high along both walls, the bathrooms, and the exit door at the end of the hall. Sam was standing with the Women's bathroom door open looking inside. Richard had peeked into the women's bathroom when he first arrived, but like everywhere else around the building it seemed to be taken up with concrete test slabs, and some heavy measurement device on a piece of plywood on the sink counter next to the toilet. Sam held the door as Sylvia started in, but Richard paused looking uncertainly at the women's restroom sign. Sylvia looked back at him and chuckled saying, "Come on, you think I'm using this dump?".

As Richard came inside, he noticed a new interior steel panel appeared to have been screwed on the inside of the door with 4 hefty sliding bars held by brackets welded to the panel. The concrete test slabs that had been strewn about the place, were now neatly stacked in overlapping rows against the hall side wall. More slabs had been brought in because the interlocking slabs now reached nearly to the ceiling from the door to the far wall. The heavy measurement device was gone from the sink, but the dusty plywood piece was still in place and the detritus that marked the space as disused was still propped up in the corners and next to the toilet.

Richard didn't remember the large flaking plate glass mirror over the sink or the dusty fold down plastic baby changing table on the far cinderblock wall, but the light from the dim overhead bulb didn't really reach back that far. Sylvia was over in front of the flaking mirror and seemed to be pushing on the little clear plastic clips that were screwed in to hold the sheet of glass mirror to the wall.

She finally found the one she was looking for and to Richard's surprise, pushed the clip with the screw head sideways. There was a click, and the entire mirror popped out from the wall, screw clips and all. She swung the mirror on hidden hinges out over the toilet to reveal a large safe set into the cinderblock wall behind. She stepped back in the room and said to Richard "The combination is the same as your tool case plus the four-digit year that the family on your mother's side arrived in this country."

Richard wondered how they had come across that bit of family trivia, as Sylvia and Sam stepped out of the room. He used the buttons on the front of the safe to enter the case combination, and then paused to consider the date he should enter. There was the date that his family had long promoted going back to a revolutionary war general, but his sister, in recent years had determined they were actually descended from an immigrant who arrived during the much later potato famine emigration. He keyed in the potato famine year, and the safe clicked open, so someone had done their research.

He put the case in on one of the shelves in the empty safe and closed it and the mirror. Sam came back into the room and went over to the baby changing station as Richard made sure he knew which mirror clip to slide to open the mirror. Sylvia said from the door entry, "The tool case with the "stove parts" and the documentation you received is to always be stored in the safe, when not in active use. Your laptop, any notes you might take, and any interface prototypes you develop will also want to live in there when not in use.

Richard turned to see that Sam had opened and folded down the baby changing station table. The plastic interior of the unit had been crudely cut away so that two monitors and a remote joystick controller could be fitted inside. Sylvia, looking past Sam at what little remained of inside of the baby changing station said, "While hanging out in dumpy bathrooms with men who abuse baby tables could be called fun, I do have places to be.

You two had better get along, because you will be hanging out together here in bumwad nowhere for quite a while."

Sam chuckled as he casually punched a fist into his open hand and said, "No worries. I'll be fine even if we don't get along."

15

The IT tech, who set up the video monitoring and recording for experiments at the biosafety lab was intrigued. The expansion wing on the biolab complex was still undergoing final fit out when work by all the contractors was suddenly halted last week.

The new biosafety lab expansion wing this temporary client was taking over was just a large open workspace with a center isolation room that only had the glass enclosure built so far. The workspace and isolation room had all the air filtering and basic level 3 three facility protections built in, but none of the actual lab equipment, isolation "fishtanks", or isolation accordion suits was installed yet. The pathogen air filtering system for the general area was hurriedly tested and signed off on by the inspectors, but the rest of the construction would have to wait, at somebody's great expense, until the client was done with the lab.

What was clearly a security team had come out to check out the space, and the rush work order they placed for him to take out the newly installed security cameras in the entire wing piqued his interest. A battery of heavy test equipment was trucked in and brought into the workspace and some office cubical dividers were set up at the two far ends of the room.

The IT guy was surprised to see beds being brought into the cubical spaces and a full kitchen with stove and refrigerator hurriedly set up across the room from the decontamination chamber entry. A specialty camera crew arrived and set up an array of cameras all focused on a table that had been placed in the center of the isolation room. The cameras feeds were run to tables of monitors in the staging space just inside the double doors. A secure satellite uplink was mounted on the roof and tested. Only those working in the biohazard space, watching the monitors outside in the staging space, or with secure access to the satellite link feeds could know what was happening in the room.

The IT tech gave a heads up to some "friends" to let them know something potentially interesting could be taking place. His "friends" were intrigued enough to provide him with an assortment of some miniature spy-tech stuff. As he was removing the existing security cameras called out in the work order, he surreptitiously installed the wireless micro cameras and microphones his "friends" had provided.

Those providing this sophisticated micro tech had an interest in knowing what went on in the facility and paid him well for keeping them informed. The IT tech had his own monitor array setup in the recorder room attached to a hidden switcher that he could switch between his normal experiment camera feeds and the new micro tech feeds he would be recording as well.

He watched the micro tech camera feeds as the hurried set up was completed. The existing "Under Construction" signs and construction barricades were kept in place outside the expansion wing entry doors, while the security team brought in an Xray scanner and some bomb sniffer tech that made anyone entering look like they were going through security at an airport. The client's security team had their own cameras covering the lobby and the parking lot outside the loading door run to monitors on a table just inside the lobby doors.

Everyone cleared out of the biohazard space, as a van was escorted in through the loading door by two figures suited up in isolation suits. The rear doors of the van were opened and the spacesuit looking figures pulled a plastic tunnel out of the back of the van and hooked it up to the decontamination chamber entry. Two figures came through the tunnel rolling cases behind them. Once they had made their way through the decontamination chamber and into the biosafety workspace, the IT guy could see it was a man and a woman. The case was rolled into the isolation room and placed up on one end of the feature table by the man.

He heard them talking for moment about getting some sleep in a real bed, them the man went back and took the computer case off his shoulder to lay on the desk in the office cubicle near the decontamination chamber and grabbed his suitcase to roll back out of the IT guy's sight into the sleeping area behind the cubicle walls. The woman rolled her suitcase over to the cubicle set up at the opposite end of the space, dropped her shoulder bag on the desk and then headed back out of sight behind the cubical walls to the other sleeping area. The guy came back out and set up his laptop and got on the phone. The IT guy saw some sheets being fluffed appearing just over the woman's sleeping area cubicle walls. After bit the woman came out dressed in warm up clothes, grabbed a drink out of the fridge, and brought her laptop over to the couch and TV area that had been set up on her side near the kitchen.

It was quitting time for the IT guy, and it didn't look like anything interesting was going to happen tonight. He sent off photos of the man and woman to his funder friends saying it looked like these two were going to be living in the lab for a while. He checked that all the mini camera recorders were running just in case and headed home for the day.

16

The scientist strolled the long way through the park with fallen leaves crunching underfoot on the warm fall day. He had some time before his next recruitment meeting and decided to take the long path around the lake to enjoy a chance to be outside in the sun. There were still some security concerns for the science team that was familiar with the cube technology, so, the scientist had picked today's meeting location largely at random.

He walked up to the park café and saw the outdoor seating area out back still had a couple of tables and chairs that had not been stored away that would be a good private place to talk. He went around to the front of the café and did not have to wait long before a young black man in a Howard University hoodie with brightly colored shoes walked up. He greeted the young man who said to call him Jamal and after getting a couple of drinks, the scientist led the way around to the deserted café terrace out back.

The front of the cafe had been open to see out to the fall colors of the lower park beyond, but the back terrace was enclosed by the woods behind. The sound of children playing in the distance could be heard as they sat at one of the tables nestled between stacks of stored tables and chairs. The scientist said he was pleased to meet Jamal and that his professor spoke highly of him. He asked about Jamals life since leaving school and the free-lance work projects he was doing.

Jamal related how he had mostly been involved in run-of-the-mill coding and software updating for a couple of companies, while he was saving up to possibly relocate from the east to the west coast. The scientist said their team had an interesting project that would initially involve developing some protocols to access a supercomputing resource for crunching data from a new climate sensor network. The data provided would need to be fed into an upgraded version of their climate modeling software that was in development.

Before he could tell Jamal more though, the non-governmental organization coalition he would be working for, asked that he sign some non-disclosure paperwork. Jamal was intrigued, so he readily agreed, and the scientist pulled a computer tablet out his shoulder bag to bring up the forms to sign. When done with all the forms, the scientist looked around to make sure they were alone and then launched a video call on the tablet in front of him.

After a moment Ahmed's face appeared on the screen. The scientist told Ahmed things looked good to proceed and then pushed the tablet over in front of Jamal. Jamal started in surprise as he saw Ahmed's face. Jamal said, "My old professor said that I might find this project interesting, but he didn't mention you were involved." Ahmed smiled and said, "Yes, your professor and I go way back, and I did impress upon him the need for confidentiality on this project. He seemed to think you were at a point in your life where you would be free to travel outside the country, while being OK working primarily in isolated secure locations for the next couple of years. Does that sound like something you would be interested in?"

Jamal thought for a moment and said, "If it's working with you on interesting stuff, then sure."

Ahmed smiled and said, "You will be working for the NGO coalition and reporting to me. I think I can promise that you will find it interesting. One issue we presently have is the computers we need to borrow time on to run our climate models are limited in their availability and not good enough to process the wealth of satellite and sensor data that is now available in the world. We need to process orders of magnitude greater data in a shorter time to achieve the detailed model projections needed for advance disaster pre-planning. We could use your help with a new approach. Instead of waiting for days of time to become available on the current supercomputers, let's say we would give you full-time access to our own dedicated processing capability. Let's also say that this processing capability can crunch though all the satellite and sensor station data from across the world for real time model projections. There is more we would ask, but that gives you an idea of the potential of the tech you would be working with. Does working with that level of new processing technology interest you?"

Jamal thought for a moment and then asked, "How many sensors with how many data points are we talking about?"

"Let's say just shy of a million sensors with a dozen to a hundred data points being provided in the real time stream by each sensor." replied Ahmed.

Jamal's eyes opened wide, and he paused to think for a moment. Ahmed gave a knowing look as he leaned back to wait. Jamal took a couple of minutes before he finished doing the back of the cranium calculations in his head and exclaimed "I'm not sure that that amount of data could be processed in week, even if we had unimpeded access to the quantum computers I worked with at school - much less in anywhere close to real time!"

Ahmed sat back up and said, "The latest thinking from our, well…, "authority" on the matter is, that if software changes to the climate model could be made, and new protocols to take in the expanded sensor data streams could be developed, crunching the data using our novel tech will be the easy part."

Jamal was lost in thought for another minute before saying, "Well, I guess it would be possible to port the model program over to the new incoming streams and maybe work up some new protocol for getting it sent to the supercomputing hardware, but I have to tell you that your "authority" has some perverse definition of easy, because what you outlined will be anything but."

Ahmed asked the scientist to bring out the "processer unit" and show it to Jamal. The scientist reached into his bag to take out a plastic sleeve enclosure with wood globe memento inside. The scientist took out the globe and set it on the table in front of Jamal. Ahmed was saying something about the matter of coming up with software for the dispatch and guidance of a new global delivery system for aid and relief packages as the scientist released the globe top to flip back. Looking around again to be sure they were not seen; the scientist shook a small dark square out of the bottom and handed it to Jamal.

Ahmed paused in his job scope outline to tell Jamal what he held in his hand was a communicator cube capable of processing way beyond the quantum computers he had worked with at school. He said that the single small communicator cube he held could handle nearly a teraflop of processing. Jamal looked at Ahmed as if questioning his sanity, causing Ahmed to smile.

Ahmed said "These work without the need for cooling and stack into easy to carry 300 teraflop servers. We presently have enough communictor cubes for a hundred servers already being made but would need you to do some initial calculations to tell us if you will need more." Ahmed intentionally paused and the scientist took a sip of his drink as they carefully watched Jamal's reaction.

After a minute of watching the parade of expressions crossing Jamal's face, Ahmed continued, "The great thing is it already comes with ready access to our artificial intelligence "authority" which can learn by having you tell it what you need. Just describe the inputs you will be sending, the functions and processing you would like it to handle, and the output format you want for the results."

Jamal looked doubtful, so Ahmed asked the scientist to introduce Jamal to their "authority" that would be available to guide him. Jamal, expecting someone else to join the videocall, watched dubiously as the scientist reached over, made a couple of quick finger motions on the tiny cube and set it back on the table in front of Jamal. A light beam appeared projecting upward and a gold-tinged fuzzy circular orb started to form, sparkling in the breeze disturbed dust. The orb resolved in a blink into a face and the screeching sound of Jamals chair being propelled backward across the concrete terrace underscored his total surprise.

Ahmed said, "Let me introduce you to our native child friend who can guide you in the programming and the many uses of the cubes".

The smiling patterned face of the native child projection looked down at Ahmed's image on the laptop then raised its head to look at Jamal with a beaming joyful expression. A chubby arm and hand appeared in the dust which was held out in Jamal's direction as if inviting him to shake hands.

17

Khadija, woke and took in the unfamiliar surroundings of the bedroom she was in. Ariana's assistant had driven them back into town to a rental condominium that the biosafety lab frequently used to house scientists. Miri had decided to stay over on the fold out couch and they had stayed up eating popcorn and watching movies last night.

She threw on her robe and walked out into the living room. Miri was already up, dressed and working on her flight plan for the day at the kitchen table. Khadija said good morning and headed to the kitchen to make herself a cup of tea. She did not see any coffee but asked Miri if she wanted a cup of tea as well. Miri said Ariana's assistant had texted to say she was bringing her over a cup of coffee from the next-door condo unit she was staying in.

The assistant would be staying to facilitate things for Ariana and those working in the bio-safety lab during the remainder of their quarantine. Khadija had agreed to stay in town to continue in her role of recording the test proceedings at the biosafety lab and coordinating the secure distribution of results to the various NGO coalition leaders and scientists spread around the world.

A knock came on the door, and Miri jumped up to carefully check who it was before opening the door. Ariana's assistant stood there with two steaming mugs of coffee and Miri invited her in to sit with them. As they all sat around the table, Miri told them about the info Ariana had sent over regarding aerial survey work and the mine area sampling she was being asked to do.

There were thousands of abandoned mine sites across the world and the coalition had selected several of them for her to survey and do sampling tests at. She would be heading back to the airfield later this morning to fly the bush plane out to have it modified for the mine site surveys in the Americas. Eventually she would transfer overseas and pick up the extended range bush plane she used there to fly the Indian subcontinent and sub-Saharan Africa missions that were on the coalition's list.

Khadija said that Ahmed had asked her to consult on the design of the remote operator control centers and manufacturing site loading facilities that would be needed if the coalition and tribal leaders decided the stove cube "gift" was something they wanted to accept.

They finished up their morning coffee klatch and Miri packed the last of her stuff to leave for the airport. The assistant handed Khadija her pass and documents for the bio-safety lab while Miri carried her things out to the car. The assistant asked her if she could give her a ride over to the biosafety lab on their way to the airfield, but Khadija told her with it only being a few blocks away, she would enjoy the freedom of being able to walk outdoors.

Miri gave Khadija a hug and said it had been good to have some time together again. Khadija wished her well in her mine exploration flying. She hoped they would catch up again when Khadija was done with the quarantine crowd and could get back to her home base.

It was a sunny day outside as Miri headed out to hop in the car with the waiting assistant to head off to the airfield. Khadija watched from the front porch of the condo as the car merged into traffic. Well, at least she had a nice day to get outside and stretch her legs a bit before having to head into the biosafety lab.

18

Richard had settled into a daily schedule over the past weeks with Sam out at his concrete plant workspace. His road box of tools had caught up with him, and with the equipment that had been ordered through Sylvia, he had everything he needed to work on his communicator cube interface design and testing. He had gotten far enough on the testing and designs that he was now waiting for the simpler electronic loader interfaces to go into production and the more involved optical interface proto-types to be produced.

Sam electronically "swept" all the equipment and cases that were shipped in for any unwanted "gadgets" that might be included. During his early sweep of Richard's tool road box, he had been surprised to find Richard's climbing harnesses, ropes, and gear in the bottom drawer. Richard, seeing Sam's expression, said he liked to get out on the weekends and do some climbing on the bluffs around Austin. Sam asked if anyone knew him there, and Richard said, "Of course". "Well, then we better just keep our heads down", said Sam with his frequent reply to any extra-curricular activities where Richard might be recognized. Sam also tried to have him avoid phone and videocalls and just do everything via email and texts that were more difficult to trace.

Sam had insisted on taking up Richard's spare time in the early weeks to run over what he called "cont" plans. Richard had let Sam know he had already received the three ways from Sunday secrecy litany Sylvia had subjected him to while signing the stack of paperwork. Sam said that the checking off boxes on paperwork was fine for covering the company asses, but he was here to make sure Richard's actual backside remained intact. He said the security team on this project had called him in because some folks with a bad reputation had been taking a keen interest in things the NGO coalition had been doing, including the "stove part" tech Richard was using. He said the best way to avoid appearing on the bad actor radar was just to maintain a low profile, keep Richard out of sight and make everything look and sound boringly ordinary with the "clean cooking stove project".

Sam suggested less was better when questions regarding where he was and what he was up to came up. Sam recommended always answering truthfully, but minimally and to let assumptions made by others remain uncorrected. Always try and make it seem what you are working on is boring. As a last resort, Richard could say truthfully that the confidentiality agreements that Sylvia had him sign precluded him from saying more.

On the first day Sam had Richard run through the first of his "cont." plans. This plan was simple. Sam would call out "Alpha Go" and Richard would just grab the cubes and any interface hardware that was out on the test bench and head into the women's restroom. Once inside, he was to slide the barricade bars into place, and then open the mirror and safe to store the cubes and interface hardware. He was to pull the radio out of the charger built into the safe, put the earpiece in and turn it on to listen for further updates.

Sam might then pick up the aluminum forms case with its clipboard front, his concrete handling gloves and an empty cup of coffee and make a patrol around the building in a worn concrete plant logo shirt looking and making notes on the concrete sample weathering that the blocks around the building were being tested for. Sam would lock the transmit button on and occasionally hum a tune as he walked. Depending on the tune and lyrics, Richard would have an idea what the situation was outside. If Sam casually hummed Stairway to Heaven, Richard was to stay put and push the concealed panic button, next to the mirror to call in reinforcements. Once Sam had checked that all was clear he would say the word "Sesame" over the radio to let Richard know it was safe to come out.

When Sam had come in from one his patrols after one of their "hole up in the bathroom" practice drills, Richard asked why Sam was doing the clipboard case and coffee cup routine instead of taking one of his submachine guns around with him on patrol. Sam said it was important they maintain their cover as just a couple of workers at the concrete plant. "Besides", Sam said, "the forms case can come in handy if I bump into any unfriendly on the way". He smiled and moved his gloved hand with the coffee cup down by the bulky clipboard, and in a flash a military issue 45 showed up in his bare hand under the clipboard pointing disturbingly near Richard's direction. The glove with coffee cup was still inexplicably in place on the side of the clipboard but no longer attached to Sam's arm. Sam showed him how the trick case and glove allowed him to look innocent, while being able to keep a gun pointed at whoever he might be suspicious of. He could fire the gun right through the front end of the aluminum forms case without even pulling it out if needed.

Sam had made some additional "upgrades" to the building in the early days. Sam had reinforced the doors and toted in some heavy panels of bullet resistant plastic to fasten the inside of the windows on the main entry door and windows in the doors into the hydraulic press space. The panels were tinted to prevent anyone seeing in but allowed Sam to keep a lookout from inside.

He mounted the satellite uplink receiver out of sight on the back side of the roof and installed a host of small cameras and tiny motion sensors underneath the eaves of the building roof. He ran the wire feeds in through the wall and up front into one of the front offices he had taken over. The cameras and motion sensors were run into a desk Sam had set up with a bank of monitors and an AI trained system that supposedly could tell humans and drones from deer and birds.

Sam also ran Richard through his other cont. plans. The simplest was just getting in Sam's truck, that he always parked behind the building, and 4 wheel driving it over the gravel ridge to a car Sam had parked at the ready in the concrete plant parking lot. Another had Richard putting on a long tan coat with a hood and sneaking out the back door by the women's bathroom. The coat would act as camouflage as he would quietly make his way down the dry scrub lined creek bed to duck inside a large culvert opening where the creek bed met the road at the outer fence line of the plant.

So, their days went with Richard doing his work while Sam kept an eye on the monitors, did his daily workout regimen, and made his random patrols. He had put a framed poster up in his office that showed three illustrated duck characters wearing sunglasses lounging in pool side chairs holding drinks. One of the illustrated characters was looking curiously up at a couple of bullet holes in the wall just over his head while the other ducks were lounging oblivious in the sun. Sam said it was a reminder not to get caught being complacent, when there were folks out there willing to put holes in more than just walls.

While Richard waited on interface production, his time was spent sending endless emails and design concepts modification off to a coalition consultant that had been assigned to work with him on the remote operator and manufacturing facilities. The coalition consultant that went by kmasood was frankly a bit of a pain in the ass. No matter how carefully he planned the facilities based on the control chair clearances and maneuvering constraints of the robotic loaders, the constant stream of red marked up revisions and requests for added space he received from this kma... never seemed to end. The expanded support facility requests for remote operators to be able to use to walk around during breaks and between shifts pushed the facility size ever larger. The coalition supported kma...'s revisions but wanted things done in a hurry, so a constant stream of sometimes contentious emails had to be sent back and forth.

When it came to the control chair design, this kma was a particular pain the ass. Some things that were insisted on, like having the operator use their own feet on the ground to simply swivel the entire chair to control the robotic torso turning motion were straightforward. Others, like the ability of the remote operators to pivot the seatback forward to lean the robotic torso forward or be counterbalanced as they stood up and sat down to control the up and down telescoping of the robotic torso posed real engineering challenges. Requests for things like counterbalance lines for the virtual reality headsets, a front monitor so operators could take off their VR headsets while still able to keep an eye on things, and a swing arm steering wheel were easier but still added complications. The expanded footrests added for drive pedals meant the chair spacing had to be expanded and the facility further enlarged. The fold out tray to support a laptop, and holders for books, tea mugs, and water bottles were somewhat easier to accommodate, but in Richard's mind, junked up the elegance of the base design he had originally come up with.

After weeks of work, they finally came to agreement on the 3D model of the control chair showing all the bells and whistles design revisions. Richard sent the designs off to the manufacturer so that two prototype control chairs could be produced for each of them to use in testing.

A week later, Richard modeled a 3D version of the control chair space, and manufacturing facility loading areas that finally achieved consensus between them. Ahmed was relieved when Richard sent the CAD model off to the architects so they could produce construction plans. Now that the flurry of design work was done, Richard was looking forward to a break from the sometimes-hourly emails with constant revisions this kma… person had put him through.

19

The IT tech had been bored by what he had been able to watch going on in the expansion wing workspace the previous day. As he fast forwarded through the recorded video from the micro cameras, he wondered if this project was going to turn out to be a bust for both his "friends" and his bank account.

After all the rush to get the space ready for some super-secret project, the video showed the man and woman seeming to be taking a day off while occasionally playing on their laptops. He slowed the video to watch a young woman come into the staging space through the doors from the lobby. The security team seemed to recognize her right away and her screening in the machines appeared mostly perfunctory. She headed over to the tables of monitors in the staging area and sat in one of chairs there as she fired up the camera system and monitors. She seemed satisfied with what she was seeing and pressed the talk button on the desk microphone.

"Khadija calling Xanthe and Ahmed! Come in, over…"

The IT tech heard the announcement over the miniature microphones he had placed in and around the isolation room. He saw the man on the couch and the woman at her desk perk up and both head into the isolation room. They turned on a monitor where the woman outside's face appeared.

They both greeted her and talked a bit about sleeping better in real beds instead of camping out in the plane aisle for the overnight stop on their trip up. Who sleeps in the aisle of plane wondered the IT tech? There was bit of talk about a couple of other names the IT tech couldn't quite make out, and a bit about catching up on stuff in the outside world, and then they all went back to their corners to play more on their laptops. The only other highlight of the day was when some girl showed up with a bag containing lunch for the outside woman that security felt obliged to run through the Xray scanner.

Today, the IT guy was finding things more interesting as he watched the Zan… woman open the case on the table and lift a large dark boxlike object out to set on the table. The box had an opening through the center and angled in faces on two sides. A smaller black boxlike object with a similar opening and two tiny black squares were also set out on the table nearby. The video feed from the test table in the isolation room was shown on an oversized monitor in the staging area. It was being eagerly viewed by a couple of older scientific types who had run the security gauntlet to join a sort of watch party with the outside woman who seemed to be switching between views and recording the isolation room proceedings.

The IT guy had initially thought that the two being isolated in the lab might ailing from some dreadful disease, the way they had seemed laying around for most of the day before. Instead, today they seemed refreshed and ready to get to work. The Zan… woman wheeled over a large electron microscope and focused it on the larger boxlike object. The IT tech switched micro cams and could see the microscope's image that was being shown on the oversize monitor in the staging area. Other than a pebbled black surface texture, the IT tech could see nothing unusual. The same test was performed on the small box and tiny squares with a similar result. A bunch of other testing on the boxlike objects followed using other oversized equipment spitting everything from alpha particles to x-rays but the interior of the boxlike objects and tiny squares did not show at all. The objects were clearly not that heavy, as the woman had easily lifted them out of the case so, the IT tech wondered what they were expecting to find inside with all this high-end test equipment.

At the end of the testing, all the bulky equipment was rolled out of the isolation room by the man while the woman set up a folding table just outside the isolation room windows. She brought out one of the tiny blocks and he watched as the man seemed to doodle with his finger over its top. The tech saw the gold-tinged rays coming up from the square and the orb of dust gathering. He sat up when he saw the 3D child's face with a pattern across its face form in the dust. The face was animated as it smiled and nodded while looking between the man and woman. The IT tech knew of holography and projections, but this appeared different. The resolution wasn't good enough on the hidden micro cams for him to tell how the effect was done, but at least this was something his "friends" might be interested in.

The Zan… woman picked up what looked like a thin black piece of slate and the IT guy saw some colored lines appear on its surface. The odd child's head had manifested chubby arms that were making motions that seemed to be coaching her. She went into the isolation room and drew a circle with her finger on the top of the large box, and the area glowed faintly. The man carried in a pan of water from the kitchen area and placed it on the glowing area.

They both went outside the isolation room, and while watching through the windows, the woman made a sliding motion with her finger up one of the colored lines on the slate. The glow under the pan turned red, brightened and steam began to come off the pan. She ran her finger further up the colored line until the pan was wildly boiling over. She dialed down the heat and the man walked forward with a heat sensor to measure the heat of the pan, and then lifting the pan off, measured the heat of the still faintly glowing area on the top of the box fading away below.

This heating process was repeated with them going in and out of the isolation room to place different pots and pans on different areas of the top of the box and heat the water in them. The top of the box did not appear to stay hot as the woman could almost immediately draw a new burner shape and heat a different type of pan. At one point a low flat rectangular baking pan with some water was placed on the top of the box, and the woman traced the outline of the pan to create a "burner" of that same size. Both the man and the woman stepped away from the windows before the woman slid her finger quickly up the colored line to the upper limit. The water in the baking pan almost instantly flashed into steam that fogged the windows of the isolation chamber for a couple of minutes. The IT tech was wondering why they needed a Level 3 biosafety lab to test what appeared to be a glorified stove.

There was some discussion among the old guys in the staging area about having already tested the other functions of the "stove" back at the eco lodge and the consensus seemed to be to move to the last line on the slate colored remote control and run the test on it. The woman and man set it up and the IT tech was barely paying attention when it happened.

He jumped up out of his seat to double check that the recorder was running properly. Then he ran the recording back to the moment that had wowed him and there it was. He quickly pulled the recording off, encrypted it and then scheduled it for transmission to his funder "friends." He smiled at the payment they would fall over themselves to make for this intel.

20

As Richard was making his regular morning drive in from the safe house, he considered what was next now that he had the basic robotic loader control interface designed. The interface for sending and receiving the straightforward electrical signals needed for remotely controlling the robotic loaders worked well, and the twinned communicator cubes provided a rock-solid relay connection. The optical interface had been refined and was now in production as well.

The architects were sending drawing sets for him to review for the control chair "arena" and the manufacturing facility loading rooms that the robotic loaders would operate in. There was a hangar somewhere that the coalition wanted to use for robotic loader training. He had come up with a floorplan for a loading and driving layout for the hangar but fortunately, because all the decisions had already been fought over in the facility plans, there was little in the way of comments being emailed from the coalition consultant.

He was considering his next steps on the robotic loader testing, as he did the unlock/lock shuffle and headed in through the gate. He was driving along the ridge of rock screening the gravel road from the concrete plant beyond when something out of place caught his eye. He slowed the pickup truck to a stop, and he worriedly leaned forward to get a better look out past the brim of the trucker hat Sam made him wear.

He could see the front headlight and start of the grill of a large vehicle just visible around the curve of the road. Sam's contingency plans said if anything looked out of the ordinary, he was to immediately get back out on the road and head for the fallback rendezvous point as fast as the truck would take him. He backed the truck slowly down the drive to the turnaround point and was getting ready to turn and head back for the gate when his phone rang. Sam's voice was on the line, and saying, "Weather's clear, come on up". "Weather's clear" was Sam's way of telling him that the coast was clear of any unfriendly visitors.

Richard headed back up toward the building and, as he came around the bend, he could see that a flat deck tow truck was backed up to the open loading door. The heavy tarp Sam was unstrapping was draped over something on the tow deck that was definitely not a car.

Richard pulled up next to the truck and started to turn off the engine to get out, but Sam gave him a look, so he went ahead and pulled around the building and backed exactly into the parking location on the backside of the building Sam had marked with some random looking scrapes on the cinderblock wall. He turned off the truck but left the keys in the ignition per Sam's contingency plan instructions in case hurriedly getting out of Dodge in the truck was needed.

Richard walked back around the building and helped Sam finish unstrapping the tarp. With a yank, Sam pulled the tarp off, and there they were – the prototype versions of the robotic loader and the remote operator control chair.

Sam used the controls to extend the tow ramp backward in through the loading door and tilt it downwards until the ramp was touching the concrete floor inside. Richard walked up the angled ramp on the rubber matting that had been laid down to look at the loader. The robotic torso and arms that were mounted to the upright post at the center back of the loader was bent over entirely forward with its arms and hand clasped around one another encircling the stereo camera "head". The upper robotic torso was resting on the rows of square plywood boxes that filled the entire area of the robotic loader inset base like it was napping on a grade school desk. In front of the "resting" robotic torso, a modern looking swivel chair was strapped down on top of the plywood boxes. An extension of the rubber matting that ran under the loader been rolled up and strapped against its front. Sam was looking quizzically at it, so Richard explained, "The wheels have to be steel to take the heat, but they don't have much traction on a tilted aluminum deck without the rubber mat".

Richard released the roll of matting so that it unspooled off the tilted deck and out onto the concrete floor. Richard stepped up onto the manual operator platform at the back of the loader and powered up the loader drive. He made sure the torso was disabled and double checked that the loader brakes were engaged, before giving Sam a go ahead to remove the rachet chains holding the loader to the deck.

When the chains were clear, Richard manually drove the loader down off the truck, out onto the concrete floor, and across the room to park and power it down near the doors to the front room. The metal joystick with a ceramic ball end he used to maneuver the robotic loader was already feeling cold and a slight bit of condensation was forming on the electronics enclosure indicating the internal cooling system was operating.

Richard stepped off the loader and unlatched the door of the insulated electronics enclosure. The tall stack of electronics inside started with the circuit boards and power supplies at the top, stacks of drive batteries in the middle, with the enclosure cooling unit that taking up the bottom. A central mount in front of circuit boards was provided to receive the communicator cube. Open plug connectors on the circuit boards were ready to plug in the custom interface cables for the cube that had already arrived.

Sam's phone rang and Sam gave a shout that they were expecting visitors shortly. He asked Richard to barricade himself in the bathroom until he could check out the arrivals. Richard was not waiting long before Sam's "Weather's clear" call came.

As Richard came out into the hallway, Sylvia came in through the doors escorted by Sunglasses and followed by Sam. She walked toward Richard carrying a small case saying, "The coalition consultant is also getting a control chair dropped off at their location today. I need one of your stove "parts" to send their way so their chair can also be used for remote testing and evaluation of the loader. If you would take this case, go back in and do your thing behind the mirror, and then bring me out the closed case with a "part" inside, I would be ever so grateful."

The way Sylvia said "grateful" gave Richard the impression that it would just save her the trouble of calling over Sunglasses to work him over until he relented. He gave a glance at Sam who nodded and then popped back in to open the safe and put one of the twinned communicator cubes in the case. He latched the case closed and went back out to give it to Sylvia, but she stepped back and pointed him towards the doors.

Sam followed as Sunglasses led him out to the back of the SUV. The driver was already holding the spare tire area safe open so Richard could lay the case inside. The driver lowered the steel plate down to click it shut and Sylvia went to get into the back of the car with the two.

Sam, watching the proceeding from over by the loader said, "Sylvia, always good to have show up on short notice. If you could give us a bit more warning, we would happily have tea and ladyfingers waiting for your royal arrival. We'd be ever so grateful if your grace would have the sunglasses duo dust off the gate on the way out to keep our outer domain spic and span."

Sylvia gave Sam a wry grin holding up three fingers and saying, "Yeah, well read between these ladyfingers you rascal to see the chance of that happening." before shutting her door and telling the SUV driver to get moving.

21

Xanthe was in the unfinished isolation room, setting up for the test du jour, and having her morning chat with Khadija as she positioned and focused the cameras suitably for the test. They had now been at the biosafety lab for nearly a month and, as the experiments they were doing became more endurance related, sometimes running for hours at a time, they were now spending a lot more time on their laptops and secure phones these days. While the coalition was rapidly moving forward with all the planning for the infrastructure needed, the decision to proceed with manufacturing of the stove cubes and use of builder cubes for facility construction was still awaiting the results of their testing.

When Khadija and the scientists were happy with the camera positions, Khadija said she was turning on the recorder would be over at the table that served as her "desk" working on her training stuff. Xanthe went out of the isolation room to their monitoring table, picked up the dark control tablet for the stove cube and announced the test number into the mic before running her finger up the colored lines to start the multiple functions comprising this morning's test. As she set the control tablet back down on the table, she could see on the monitor that Khadija was already focused on her training work at her "desk" at the back.

As Xanthe headed over to what passed for her own "desk," she thought about what Khadija had told her about the skirmishes she had with the cowboy engineer. The "cowboy" as Khadija had also taken to calling him, typically designed facilities for the lowest cost, most efficient use of space needed for normal shifts of workers. Khadija had said that the climate modeling suggested they were going to need to surge stove cube, and other relief supplies as disasters occurred. Disaster relief efforts frequently had operators working long hours to cover twenty-four-hour operations. It had taken a while to impress on the cowboy the need for the remote operator facilities to be as much a living space as a working space to facilitate these round-the-clock operations.

Also, knowing that those working long hours needed more maneuvering room tolerance, Khadija had asked for changes to the manufacturing facility design. The bigger entrance doors, more maneuvering space in the operational areas, and more gently curved turning radiuses to avoid blind corners, had caused the cowboy to constantly raise the issues of potential cost. As Khadija had been asked to keep cube info on a need-to-know basis, she couldn't tell the cowboy anything about the coalition plans to leverage the cube technology for the facilities. Xanthe heard her frequently come to Ahmed to have him tell the cowboy the extra "costs" that were going to be incurred would be approved.

Khadija had moved on to setting up a pilot training program for some of her remote operator women. To learn the new remote operator ropes, she had been sent a swoopy new control chair and a communicator cube to connect it to a remote loader at an unknown location. Xanthe always thought it looked a bit comical to see Khadija strapped in the chair wearing the VR headset and lifting invisible items with arm and hand armatures. Her motions had picked up speed in recent days and become wilder, so Xanthe had to wonder if she was intentionally trying to break the robotic loader prototype.

As Xanthe sat at her desk, she glanced at the calendar printout that outlined the testing procedures they would perform between now and the highlighted day coming up that marked the end of quarantine. Early on they had run through the gamut of passive testing with the more sophisticated test equipment that had been trucked in but knew little more about the internal workings of the cubes than before. They were now testing the active uses of the larger "stove" cube, refining the control over the smaller builder cube, and soon hoped to have a workable optical interface to unlock the full computing potential of the tiny communicator cubes.

They had a medical lab set up that could do more involved medical testing, but the results continued to indicate that exposure to the cubes had no measurable effect on their health. Xanthe was glad when the coalition scientists and council agreed that the need for quarantine would be done when the current slate of experiments would be completed in a little over a week.

Plans had been made for the cubes to go over to a university lab for the extended duration testing and then lastly the contaminate and element compatibility testing that the scientists were afraid might gum up or otherwise cause the cubes to stop working. Xanthe would still need to be around to start the cube "stove" function being tested with her hands, but she could have 24-hour shifts of graduate students to monitor and note the duration testing results. She had been sent info on some apartments in the university area and was planning to look at them after she dug through her email, when her phone rang.

It was Ariana, who cut her off telling her to pretend to say hi to one of her assistants back in Greece. Once Xanthe did the greeting in Greek, Ariana said that she was also going to get Ahmed and Khadija on the line, she heard Ahmed's secure phone ringtone over in the area he had set up as his impromptu office and soon he and Khadija were also on the call. Ariana said that their security team had received word that their testing in the biosafety lab was being watched and listened to by nation state with ties to the corporate bad actors they had dodged at the eco lodge. There were indications of a plan to grab the cubes and possibly one or more of them as soon as they left the protection of the biosafety lab. The security team was strongly recommending that the cubes and the trio of them be moved to safe locations sooner than the planned end of quarantine.

There had been an analysis of the video that had come from the biolab to determine the hidden camera locations and the plan they were putting into action took advantage the hidden cameras were mostly focused on the isolation room. Ariana said she was texting them over the details for preventive actions they would take on their end in the meantime. They would be doing the morning experiments as usual, but the schedule would be adjusted after lunch for some element compatibility experiments that were being moved up. She asked them to please use their lunch break to prepare for the afternoon experiments and to please continue to act normal even though they now knew they were being watched. Ariana gave instructions for Ahmed to get off the phone first, Khadija to follow soon after and Xanthe to fake staying on a while longer for a couple of minutes longer and then ended the call.

Xanthe pretended to stay on the call, saying occasional responses in Greek, as she wandered around surreptitiously looking for the cameras. She realized that if the security team sweeping the lab had not picked them up, the chances of her seeing them were probably nil. With a pretend sign off to her pretend Greek assistant, she put her phone away. She was heading back over to her office to gather some things, when Ariana's text came in. She raised her eyebrows at the preventive steps the text laid out, but tried to act like it was a normal day as the morning experiments got underway.

Khadija had arranged for stacks of small cardboard boxes filled with test elements to be delivered at lunch and she placed them in the decontamination chamber for Ahmed to carry in and place on the floor to one side of the table for this afternoon's tests. The boxes were marked with labels for the various elements, and some had radiological warning symbols on them. A set of lead lined protective aprons with sleeve and glove arrangements and leaded glass face shields had also been provided by Khadija for handling the radiological elements.

Ahmed set a stack of printouts on the end of the table and, when everyone was seated in the staging area for the afternoon session, Ahmed started unpacking the elements. He held them, one by one, to the various surfaces of the stove while Xanthe ran through the cube functions to test for any interference or effect. They went quickly through one element after another until getting to the elements marked with the radiological signs.

"May as well start with the strong stuff first", Ahmed said flipping his stack of papers to an element test sheet with a radiological symbol. He and Xanthe put on the lead aprons with built in sleeved gloves followed by protective face shields. Ahmed hefted the box with the radiological warning sign on the table next to the papers and undid the thick top off the lined enclosure inside. He carefully lifted the heavy lead top out of the cardboard and laid it on the concrete floor with a heavy metallic clunk that echoed through the room. With 3-foot tongs, he reached into the cardboard box and delicately raised the enclosed glass cylinder containing the element out of the enclosure. He carefully reached out to lower it over the top of the "stove" cube.

The cube flashed brightly with a whooshing noise. The papers and heavy radiation containment box were blown off the end of the table as Ahmed was launched backward flying out onto the stack of element boxes. The falling tongs shattered the glass cylinder and the granules from the glass cylinder were set free to scatter across the top of the stove. Xanthe collapsed to her knees holding the tablet and then fell over sideways onto the electrical isolation mat below her with one arm under her sticking out at an uncomfortable angle. The flashing and whooshing continued with the two bodies lying there until the last of the radioactive granules had rolled off the top of the stove onto the table and floor below and there was stillness in the lab.

Xanthe stirred first after about 5 minutes to the panicked commotion that the scientists in the staging area were generating over the speakers. She slowly managed to sit up. She slowly rolled over and acknowledged the commotion being made by Khadija and the scientists on the video monitor. She said she felt nauseous and weak and needed a minute. Eventually she was able to prop herself up on one elbow to look over at Ahmed. She could just see Ahmed's dark hair just showing above the crushed pile of boxes and packing foam.

She got to her knees and seeing the BBs on the floor, readjusted her protective gear before attempting to stand. She wobbled to her feet, then shakily made her way over to Ahmed. She sat suddenly, crushing more boxes, and lay back on the packing foam while reaching over to check Ahmed on the other side of the pile for a pulse. "He's alive!" she said with a winded gasp leaning her back on the boxes from the effort.

The commotion that once again ensued on the speaker was cut through by Khadija saying, "We have some paramedics on their way. As soon as the biolab staff can get them in isolation suits, they will be coming in through the decontamination chamber to help you."

Xanthe forcibly gathered the effort to turn and make Ahmed more comfortable on the foam packing and boxes he had fallen on. She then laid back on some of the loose packing foam and said, "I'm guessing we'll be here."

Some biosafety lab staff arrived with isolation suits as the ambulance pulled up. Khadija directed it to back into the staging area space until its back doors were near the doors of the decontamination chamber. She opened the back doors of the ambulance and told the paramedics inside the patients were still in quarantine and they would need to get suited up before they could go into the lab area. One of the lab staff climbed in the back of the ambulance with the isolation suits for the medics while the other staff guy put on a radiation vest and then suited up as well.

A few minutes later an isolation suited blonde haired male and female paramedic were helped down out the ambulance by Khadija. They pulled a gurney out of the ambulance, its rolling base expanding down to make a table height bed. Two large medical kits were placed on the gurney while a heavy radiation hazard bin and Geiger counter were added to it by the lab staff. The three isolation suited figures had one last check of their isolation suit seals, before the suited lab staff person picked up a broom and dustpan, walked over to the card reader on the decontamination chamber. He swiped his key card over the sensor to open the entry doors. The suited lab staff member led the way in followed by the paramedics who were bent over as they guided the gurney into the chamber. Once inside with the outer entry sealed, the staff guy swiped his card across the reader to open the inner door to the biosafety lab.

They made their way with the loaded gurney over to the inner isolation room entry where the staff guy made the paramedics wait outside while he hefted the lead lined radiation hazard bin off the gurney and went in with the broom and dustpan. He worked his way carefully in from the door sweeping up the scattered granules and broken glass from radiological cylinder and depositing them in the bin. He worked his way over to the table and set the radiation hazard bin on top of it as he swept the granules and glass off the table to go into the bin. He lastly checked the area where Ahmed and Xanthe were laying, sweeping in that vicinity.

He dumped the few granules from there in the bin on the table and walked back out to grab the Geiger counter. He walked the path from the isolation room entry, past the front of the table, and around Ahmed and Xanthe looking at the readings on the Geiger counter before pronouncing the path safe for the paramedics to enter.

The isolation suited paramedics rolled the gurney over in front of the table and made their way quickly to start checking on Ahmed and Xanthe. One went to check Ahmed, while the other went to Xanthe who was resting with her eyes closed. Opening an eye she said, "Boy am I glad to see you". Ahmed also roused as they started their checks and weakly answered their questions.

Once they were both checked out, the medical kits were taken off and set on the test table while first Ahmed, and then Xanthe werehelped onto the gurney and rolled back to their respective sleeping areas. The female paramedic carried a medical kit back to Xanthe's area, while the male paramedic stayed in Ahmed's sleeping area to treat him.

Both Ahmed and Xanthe were asked to strip off all their clothes which were put in bags labeled radioactive waste that the paramedics held out. The paramedics handed them both hospital gowns to put on while they bent over them to do further examinations and take blood samples. During the examination process both the paramedics and the patients were out of sight of the cameras behind the cubicle walls.

At the end of all the examinations, Ahmed and Xanthe said they were weak but feeling better. The paramedics advised them to stick to their beds with no activity until the tests came back and there was a determination of what was going on.

Once they were both tucked in their beds, the isolation suited paramedics finished packing up their medical kits from the isolation room, placed them on the gurney and headed for the decontamination chamber. Both of the paramedics were hosed down with decontamination fluid, before being allowed back out. The suits and kits were still dripping, when they made it back out to the back of ambulance, packed in the gurney and the doors were shut by Khadija. The ambulance pulled out and the loading door was closed leaving the lab eerily quiet.

The ambulance headed across town to a hospital and the driver pulled into the hospital parking lot at the far end under the roofed ambulance staging area and parked. He made a phone call to say, "We're here." and then he asked the two in the back, to wait until the car pulled around next to them. The driver said he would need to stay around with the ambulance for a while to let any interested parties watching by satellite assume they were being taken into the hospital.

Moments later a black SUV backed in next to the ambulance and the driver, with a ball cap pulled down low over face got out, opened the back and side doors of the SUV, and then walked over to open the doors to the back of the ambulance. He waited until the ambulance area was clear of any onlookers then motioned to the isolation suited figures to come out. As the suited figures walked over, they dropped off a bulky bag in the back of the SUV and then got in. The driver closed the back, checked that the suited figures were settled in their seats, and then drove them out of the hospital.

After a drive across town, and down a gravel road, the SUV arrived at the new gate in front of the driveway leading into the model house. A security team guy came out of the mobile construction office to look in the SUV and then motioned and the gate started opening. The driver pulled down and in through the far open door of the three-car garage. The driver got out, hit a button on the wall to close the garage door, then went to the back of the SUV to get the bulky bag out. He walked over to a table set up in the garage and deposited the bag on it.

Once the garage door had fully come down, the two isolation suited figures got out of the car. A familiar figure entered the garage, gave the driver a hug with a questioning look as the two were just starting to unseal and take off their suit helmets. The driver said the switch went smoothly, and that the two university theater student volunteers were now in place. He said that hopefully it would be while before the corporate bad guys would realize what had happened. The two suited figures now had their heads exposed, revealing awkwardly positioned blonde wigs.

"Well, Xanthe you could pull off being a blonde, but Ahmed, not so much," said Ariana as she and her husband, who had been drafted to serve as the driver, chuckled.

"I think some of your west coast security folks just bought two of the same wigs not thinking whether long haired surfer dude EMTs would pass muster in this part of the country" said Ahmed taking his wig off with a disdainful expression." Ariana chuckled and added, "Well, I'm just glad to have you both here to join our quarantine party without incident."

Ahmed finished stripping off his suit and then went over and opened the bulky bag on the table. He took out the stove cube that had been part of the switch out drama and pulled out and unwrapped the builder cube that had been wedged inside the opening in the larger cube to check them. Satisfied, he pulled the two tiny communicator cubes out of his pockets to set on the table as well.

Xanthe was starting to root through the pile of test equipment stacked inside the door leading into the house, but Ariana interrupted her saying, "Let's get you both some dinner and get you settled into your rooms. Tomorrow will be soon enough to get the garage in shape for testing."

22

Ariana had been working these past weeks in quarantine at the model house to lay the groundwork with the NGO coalition leaders and science team for potential next steps that might be taken with the cube technology. She was seated at the curved sales desk in the front foyer of the house with her laptop. A vetted list from Xanthe of community leaders, and organizers from across the globe the coalition council should consider reaching out to for trials of the stove cubes was up on her laptop screen.

She heard her husband talking with Ahmed and Xanthe in the kitchen before coming back out with two cups. He set one of the steaming cups on the sales desk next to the globe memento and gave her a quick kiss. He said he would be up in the common room area that he was using for his office and started up the stairs.

It had been good to have him in the house with her these last couple of weeks. Ariana had pressed him into work on planning for some of the future climate mitigation projects that the coalition and tribal elders might opt to pursue. She thought Ahmed must really be missing his wife and family by now. Xanthe, who, even though she prided herself on being an independent woman, must be missing her partner as well.

It was coming up on time to get the meeting started, so Ariana slid and hinged open the globe memento to reveal the communicator cube. She called out to Ahmed and Xanthe in the kitchen that she was getting things started and to please wake up the native child to join them. She then made a motion with finger on the top of the communicator cube and watched the rays of light appear.

She was still amazed by the way the dust formed into a semi-circular plane around the front of her face lit by the golden tinged light from the communicator cube. As enough dust gathered, the curved surface showed a ghostly image of the virtual grove of rainforest trees surrounding the circular clearing that they used as a meeting environment.

Ariana thought the meeting environment design by Jamal's team was a little fantastical as she watched ripples spread out from the center of the pool and flow out over the curved rim that some of early arriving members appeared to be sitting behind. Fantastical, but the water effect in the grove of trees was calming.

Calming was a good thing, with some of the contentious discussions they had been having. The tribal elders and Jaha faded into view along the pool to her right while the NGO and scientific leaders were appearing in more random locations around the pool.

Ariana checked in with Jaha and the tribal elders to make sure there had been no further impact on the tribe since they had left the eco lodge and received good news on that front as they waited for the remainder of the council to appear. Ahmed and Xanthe's gold-tinged images appeared followed by the native child as Ariana looked around and nodded greetings to several of the council.

Ariana spoke out, "Glad to see everyone that could join us today. We are especially glad to see Ahmed and Xanthe, who, as you may have heard, got out of the biosafety lab, safely. The security team says there is still potential for a run-in with the corporate ne'er-do-wells they have been monitoring. Many thanks to the university and their look-like theater students who swapped places with them and are still pretending to be ailing in the bio-safety lab. Let's get started with updates from Ahmed, Xanthe and our scientific team…"

After a series of updates on the assigned projects the leaders and scientists were charged with taking on, Ariana opened the group to discussion on the list of potential communities, and trusted influencers they would need to reach out to, should the trial of the stove cubes be determined necessary. Xanthe offered to take on some the outreach to the sub-Saharan countries that she had previously helped with relief efforts in. She knew many of the villages that would be good contenders for stove cube trials there.

They next moved on to Ahmed and Xanthe's facility infrastructure, and staffing proposal that had been distributed to the council. Ahmed said they had now completed facility designs, infrastructure planning, and the prototypes that would enable full coalition control of the stove cube loading, shipping and delivery process. He stressed that acting in advance to build the facilities and equipment needed was the only way to make the manufacture and distribution of the stove cube "gift" possible at scale in the time the climate model projections were indicating they had.

To do this advance work, Xanthe said they would need a coalition council recommendation and tribal elder approval to produce and use the builder cubes and communicator cubes widely. This would enable the proposed advance groundwork outlined in the proposal to proceed. Unlike the stove cubes, these smaller cubes were simpler for the coalition to fully control and required simpler failsafe contingencies that had already been well tested.

She also reminded the council and tribal elders that the builder cubes would also need to be used for autonomous mining of clean transition minerals. The goal was to provide multiple sources of these minerals that would avoid supply bottlenecks and opportunities for existing suppliers to monopolize sources. The sales of these minerals, and the precious metals that would be obtained as a byproduct, would be needed to fund the coalitions distribution efforts, infrastructure, and staffing needs within communities.

While the tribal elders were fully in favor of using what they saw as a gift that could help the modern world transition, there was a wary reticence expressed by the coalition council members and scientists when it came to introducing the stove cubes out into the world. While the builder and communicator cubes had adequate failsafes, the stove cube technology was different. Due to privacy concerns, the stove cubes had only a simple connection back to the control team that only told them the stove was activated, but intentionally could not tell them where or what the stove was being used for. Once stove cubes were widely distributed and keyed to owners around the world for their lifetimes, there was no going back unless the failsafe was triggered to disentegrate the cubes. The scientists wanted more testing and many thought that the release of stove cubes to the wider world should only be an option of last resort. After the discussion had abated, a vote by the council was called. There were enough council votes to proceed with all the groundwork steps proposed and the tribal elders readily approved moving forward.

Ariana brought the meeting to a close and spent a few minutes after the meeting checking in with a few of the newer coalition members. Ariana took the last sips of her tea as she waited for the others that were conversing in the virtual tree glade to finish. The last of their images faded away leaving just the virtual rainforest clearing and rippling pool shimmering in the dust of the projection in front of her.

She made an X motion with her finger on the top of the communicator cube and the projection in front of her faded away. The dust, free from the static constraints of the cube, puffed out into a small cloud in front of her face that made her sneeze. She chuckled at that as she pivoted the globe back upright until the top clicked into place concealing the tiny cube inside.

"What do you two want for lunch?" she called out as she headed back to the kitchen to join Ahmed and Xanthe.

23

The IT Guy had been regularly uploading the proceedings of the testing to his interested parties and, up until the incident, the deposits showing up in his offshore account were the best he had ever seen. The incident with some radioactive element gone wrong had put a total stop to testing. The malingering duo kept to their sleeping areas and only came into view when they needed to walk bent over with the effort to the bathrooms.

Only the regular visits of an isolation suited nurse to check on the bedridden patients and bring food to their bedsides, occurred to break the monotonous hours of recording the IT guy had to review.

In the isolation room all the cubes remained where they had been blown to on the table and the room was still littered with leftover papers and crushed cardboard. Not knowing that the cubicle dividers would be put up to create sleeping and office spaces, the IT guy hadn't thought to put cameras or microphones in the back corners where the malingering patients were now hidden from him.

He could occasionally make out the faint sounds of them watching some entertainment program behind the cubicle walls, or talking on their phones, but the tiny microphones focused on the front isolation room couldn't pick up their conversations. Without anything of note going on, he had nothing worthwhile to forward to his "friends."

Things brightened up a couple of days ahead of scheduled transport of the cubes to the university and the end of the quarantine. The IT tech had been reached out to by some other corporate group that his "friends" must have put in touch with him. They were very interested in learning the exact time when the cubes and ailing patients were going to leave the lab.

He already knew he was scheduled to reinstall the security cameras in the space next week and it only took listening in on the security team in the staging area to hear an armored truck was expected on Friday morning. A quick check of the biosafety lab shipment schedule showed the armored truck company pickup listed for clearance in through the biosafety lab on Friday at 10 AM. It didn't hurt that they deposited a healthy downpayment for the information to the IT tech's account to incentivize him and he readily passed along that information.

On the day the armored truck was expected, the IT tech had come in early. He was watching when a male and female medic came in through the decontamination chamber without isolation suits, to drop off bags with a fresh change of clothing to the hermit-like patients still holed up in their sleeping spaces. The medics stayed with patients to help them get dressed while two of the security team went into the isolation room and carefully packed all the cubes back into their road case for transport.

Just after 10 AM the loading door into the staging area was opened and an armored truck backed into the staging space. A uniformed armored truck company guard got out of the passenger side, came around to open the back doors, and then went back to sit in the cab. The IT guy texted his new corporate friends, to say the armored truck had arrived.

The security team rolled the packed case out through the open decontamination chamber doors, lifted it into the back of the armored truck and strapped it to the front wall. The IT guy texted that cubes were on the truck. One of the medics called out to the security guys from the decontamination chamber and said the patients were weaker than expected and they would need their help. The security guys followed the medic back and soon the IT guy saw the dark-haired woman and man come limping out of their respective living areas, each supported by a security guy and a medic helping to hold them up as they struggled to walk with a hunched over gait. They were so weak, extra security team members had to come over to help get them lifted into the back of the armored truck. The IT guy texted that the two patients had been loaded in with the cubes and to standby for departure. The armored car driver got out, closed the heavy back doors of the truck, got some paperwork from one of the security team, and then got back in and pulled the truck out through the loading door.

The IT guy texted "The truck is pulling out" to his interested party and got a thumbs up emoji in reply. He switched to the outside facility camera feeds provided for the lab security guards. He watched the armored truck pull around through the lab complex and get checked out through the gate. He then switched to a long-lensed camera he had set up specially for his new friends.

This camera on the roof of the lab building was focused on a section of the street that his friends had a particular interest in. The IT guy double checked that it was still transmitting the video out to them in real time and sat back, curious to see what would happen. He watched the regular security cams to see the truck pull out the biosafety lab gates start heading down the only street leading out from the lab to the city. He then turned to watch the added monitor as the armored truck came into view of the long-lensed camera.

The IT tech was nervous about what his newly acquired "friends" might want to use the real time video he was sending them for, but the money that would be coming in as soon as the truck was out of sight, meant he could be done with this lab job. He was just waiting for the armored truck to drive out of view, so he could pull the long-lensed camera off the roof and get on with spending the money that was coming his way.

As the truck reached the section of street the roof camera was focused on, a large panel van pulled out suddenly blocking the road directly in front of the armored truck followed by a smaller van behind blocking in the truck. The IT tech could see something pulled out of the side door of the smaller van, be shoved under the truck, and the rear of the truck suddenly lift up, so it was stranded with its rear tires off the ground. Half a dozen masked men jumped out of the front van with assault rifles, as a team started working with cutting equipment to open the back doors of the armored truck. The IT guy watched, both surprised and fascinated and at the same time. This was one of the possibilities he had planned for and only meant he was going to need to get out of the lab today instead of a month or two in the future.

Then, an armada of police cars appeared at the end of the road, and it all went wrong. There must have been some sort of announcement because the cutting team stopped and everyone with the assault rifles froze in place. A couple of the masked figures by the van started firing up at the surrounding rooftops as they tried to get back in the van, but they were dropped to the ground by what had to be snipers. The rest stopped, laid their guns down on the ground and pushed them away from them before slowly lying face down on the street.

The IT guy in a panic, grabbed his computer bag headed for the door. He would have to get out of the country before they could tie this back to him. As he hurried out into the hall, he ran into four large guys in swat jackets lounging against the walls.

One of them said, "Well this one looks like an aider and abettor. What do you think guys".

The others nodded and the one speaking stepped up and said, "Just lower your bag very slowly on the ground, turn facing the wall, and reach for the ceiling. My guys missed out on the action up the street, so I wouldn't give them any cause to have a more dramatic story to tell about your arrest than necessary."

24

In the week since her and Ahmeds arrival at the model house, Xanthe had become used to coming downstairs at the crack of dawn to check on the duration test that had been left running overnight. She sat behind the curved sales counter facing the front door of the demo house and flipped on the row of monitors hooked to the camera feeds run in from the garage "lab". As the monitors powered up, Xanthe could see the present duration test where a large pot filled with tin was being heated to several hundred degrees on the stove cube.

Xanthe had become tired of constantly filling pots with water only to have them boil over or flash into steam if she was not particularly careful with her finger on the stove line of the slate-like control tablet. Heating tin until it melted, like solder, into a liquid metal state in the pot was a safe way of being able to run the stove at high-power settings for the overnight hours nightly to prove the longevity of the cube's power source.

Seeing the temperature readout shown on one monitor and the mirror sheen of the still molten metal on another, she was satisfied that the cube stove function had run successfully overnight. She picked up the slate like control tablet for the cube and, as the tablet recognized her hands, the colored control lines appeared. She ran her finger down the stove control line to turn the heat off and watched on the monitor to see the glow under the pot fade away. It would take nearly two hours for the potful of tin to cool enough to solidify, so it could be safely taken off the stove for the next test.

Xanthe headed for the kitchen to start a pot of coffee. As the coffee started brewing, she mused over the progress they had made since leaving the eco lodge. The builder cube and communicator cubes now had the control interface needed to unlock their real potential. The ability to know what every one of these smaller cubes was doing and where it was located at every moment made monitoring their use possible. Effective failsafe provisions were also in place for all these smaller cubes as well. The combination of knowing what those cubes were always up to and the ability to literally pull the plug on their partial or entire use at any time, gave the coalition a comfort level with having them widely deployed. The builder and communicator cubes were now being produced in mass quantities and actively put to work on the mining, construction, and computing needs of the coalition.

As Xanthe poured herself a cup and as she sat to consider the day's upcoming tests, was reminded why the larger stove cube was a different story. "Baby Einstein", as Xanthe had started calling the native child projection, had the ruwaq incorporate what were essentially privacy provisions blocking the coalition's ability to tell where and what the stove cubes were up to. Because the stove cubes were meant to be keyed to a specific "owner" for their personal use for their lifetime, there would be no location, usage, or virtual video data provided from them to ensure the "owners" privacy.

The coalition would only be able to know when a stove cube was keyed to owner, when a cube was damaged trigggering disentegraton, or when the owner had died, and the cube ceased to be in use. While the coalition would still have the failsafe ability to pull the plug on individual, groups, or even every stove cube ever produced, it would not have any independent way to determine if the stove cubes were being used in line with the coalition's mitigation mission and goals. The lack of real knowledge about the manufacturing source, combined with the intended lack of ability to real time monitor the stove cube's activities, was at the heart of the science team's reticence to allow the coalition to release them into the world. The one thing they could agree on was that exposure to the cubes presented no detectable health risks, so yesterday the agreed upon quarantine period was ended.

With the news of the capture of another bad boy squad outside the biosafety lab, the security team had given the green light for Ariana and Ahmed to return to their homes. Jaha and his family had also gone home and would be able to interact with the greater tribe. Xanthe was the one exception in the quarantine quartet.

Because the corporate bad actors seemed to know that the original stove cube with all its functions fully enabled was keyed to her so that only she could operate it, the security team still wanted to keep her hidden away safely in the model house. The good news was that the coalition was flying the love of her life in to join her in the house starting this weekend. She was looking forward to having some alone time for the two of them to catch up after the long stretch of isolation. She wistfully poured herself a cup of coffee and headed back up to her room to catch up on her reading, until the others were up.

Later, when she heard movements in the kitchen, she dressed and came down to join Ahmed and Ariana for breakfast. Khadija called in on the satellite phone while they were sitting around the table to run down what the day would look for them. She said Ariana's assistant would be exchanging cars and picking up Ariana and her husband to drive them across the country to their home.

Khadija said she was wrapping up things at the biosafety lab this morning and would be out at the house later to drive herself and Ahmed a couple of hours away to a smaller airport for their afternoon charter flight out. Khadija would transfer to a commercial overseas flight that would take her back to her home base. The security team was making plans to ensure Ariana and Ahmed would be safe at their homes, while Khadija would move out from the city to live within the military base compound for added security when she returned.

Ahmed and Ariana had a morning communicator cube call that they went out into the living room to get on. Xanthe refilled her cup and headed into the garage lab to see if the tin pot was cool enough to move for the morning experiments. The black SUV that had brought her and Ahmed to the house was still parked at the far end, but the rest of the garage had been taken over for stove cube testing. The stove cube had been placed on a ruwaq made base unit about the same height as the cube with a door set into the front of it. It was made of a material that appeared similar to the cube's surface, with a magnetic property that allowed the stove cube to snap into place on top of it. A duct extension of the same material was similarly magnetically snapped onto the rear facing tapered faces coming out from the square opening in the center of the stove cube. The duct was run through an opening in the back wall of the garage so that the air conditioning and filtration capabilities could be tested. Two folding tables were set to either side of the stove cube where experiment monitoring equipment could be placed. Boxes under the tables were filled with jars of contaminated test liquids and solids, yet to be tested on the cube.

Xanthe walked over to the stove cube, moved the temperature sensor out of the way, and checked that the tin in the pot was solid. The pot was still very hot, but it could at least be moved. Xanthe had bolted a beam onto the overhead joists that a beam trolley and small chain lift were rigged on. She grabbed the chain and rolled the beam trolley across over the pot. She pulled the chain to lower the handle hooks a bit, so she had enough slack to carefully hook them into the heavy-duty metal handles of the commercial cooking pot without touching the hot pot surface. She pulled the chain the other way, and the mechanical advantage of the chain lift allowed her to easily lift the metal filled pot off the stove cube. She rolled the overhead trolley and chains holding the pot down to the far end of the table so the still warm pot could hang there and finish cooling out of the way of the morning experiments.

A row of tall double doored metal cabinets had been brought in to flank the entry door from the house. Xanthe went over to open a couple of them that had deep shelves holding an assortment of bench test equipment and measuring devices. She took out the monitoring equipment and sensors needed for today's tests and positioned them on counters to the side of the stove. She checked the array of cameras and sensors that were clamped onto the overhead joists of the garage to sure they all had good lines of sight. She used a stepladder to adjust a couple clip lights to be sure the shadows from the lab equipment and sensors were not falling across the stove cube.

In addition to testing the cube in stove mode to prove that it could consistently put out a large amount of power, other functions of the cube were also constantly tested. Once connected to the ruwaq supplied base and duct, other lines on the slate like control tablet became enabled. One line started a heating and air conditioning process where the cube somehow drew outside air in through the center opening and heated or cooled it to keep the interior at an owner selected temperature. A second line controlled the air filtration properties of the cube. When this line was activated, the air passing through the center of the cube somehow had all the pollutants removed, so that all that made it out into the garage was clean fresh air. The contaminates removed would electrostatically cling to the tapered faces inside the duct and then migrate to agglomerate into a slate colored "shingle" of filtered material on the bottom surface of the opening in the stove cube.

Similarly, any grease or food remains left on the top of the cube when the stove griddle function was turned off, could be cleaned off by enabling what came to be called the "lembas" line. When the line was turned on, any cooking remains left on the top of the cube could be seen to slowly disintegrate into a form of dust. This dust would electrostatically move off the top of the cube, down the exposed tapered faces and into the square opening in the cube's center. The dust would then be incorporated either in the slate-colored "shingle" at the bottom or slowly build up into tan-colored accretions centered on the inner side walls of the cube opening. Additional solids left over from contaminated water, or some of the test solids, like contaminated dirt, that were cooked on the top surface would also break down and migrate growing both the shingles and the tan accretions at a more rapid pace.

These tan formations were what the tribal elders called "unanchasqa mikhuy", but what Xanthe and Jaha had come to jokingly refer to as "lembas." When they reached a certain thickness, Xanthe found the tan "lembas" would snap off into her hand while the accreted slate-colored bottom "shingle" would reach a certain thickness and then break off from the bottom to be shed out into the duct. Xanthe would gather these "lembas" and "shingles" to analyze their makeup.

A large part of the shingles tested turned out to consist of carbon while the "lembas" turned out to have vitamin packed nutritional qualities. Xanthe had seen baby Einstein make eating motions after one of the "lembas" had snapped off unexpectedly into her hand. Curious, she took a nibble and found it tasted like a slightly chewy version of a tea biscuit.

The scientists had stopped her from eating any more, but once they had stash of them, Ariana's husband had secretly tried a test diet eating nothing but "lembas" for a couple of days. He found them tasty but could only eat about half of one at any given mealtime before feeling full.

They found if they put spadefuls of dirt onto the top of the stove cube with the "lembas" line turned on, the tan accretions would grow much quicker. The scientists found out about Ariana's husband's lembas "diet" and put an end to it. They did, however make plans to do studies starting with lab rats using the growing cabinet full of lembas the cube had produced.

While the air was being filtered, a percentage of the water vapor in the air, passing through, appeared to be taken in and stored inside the cube, so that the stove cube gained weight over time. A cup or bowl could be placed inside the opening in the cube up against the upper surface to start clean drinking water flowing. Depending on the front to back placement of the cup or bowl, the water stream would come out either heated or chilled.

The amount of water that could be created by the filtration

process in humid climates was enough to supply the daily water needs of a single person. The amount of water that could be produced in dry climates was limited though, so the native child had showed how they could use the next line on the tablet to make a blue tinted area appear on the top of the cube. Any water brought in and poured slowly onto this blue area, would be filtered down through the surface into the water holding area inside the cube.

Xanthe's testing today involved taking various jars of water containing a range of contaminants and testing the cube's ability to filter out those contaminants to provide clean drinking water. Once she had the monitoring equipment set up how she wanted it, she went back over to one of the tall cabinets near the back corner of the garage. She reached behind the cabinent. She found what she was feeling for, pulled it down and, with a click, the entire tall cabinet was released to pivot into the room. Xanthe easily pivoted the entire cabinent out until it was perpendicular to the adjoining cabinent.

Built into the wall behind was an inset set of shelves normally concealed by the cabinent. On the top shelf there was a tray holding about two dozen of the tiny communicator cubes. Several of the small builder cubes were set on a second shelf below. In the bottom there was also an empty space where the large stove cube could be securely stored when not actively being used for testing. Xanthe took out the tray of communicator cubes, stepped out, and then pivoted the tall cabinent back around until it clicked back into its position up against wall.

Xanthe set the native child's communicator cube on the table close by the large stove cube. She walked over to two folding tables set out in the middle of the garage directly in front of the "stove" cube. Ariana's husband had cribbed together a two-tiered arrangement on the tables for communicator cubes to be set up on. She placed a lineup of the tiny communicator cubes on the table level across the front and along each of the tiered levels towards the back.

She went back into the house to the curved sales desk, checked the camera views on the monitors and then reached under the desk to turn back on the media recorder to capture the test proceedings in the garage. She heard Ariana and Ahmed in the middle of their meeting in the living room and gave a nod to Ariana's husband in the kitchen, who was assembling a pile of luggage from upstairs as she headed back into the garage.

She held a list as she then went one by one along the communicator cubes on the table, making motions with her finger and saying the name of the person that would be joining via that cube. The tops started glowing on all the communicator cubes she touched, but the dust only projected faces above four of the tiny cubes on the table surface in front.

Xanthe saw Jaha's familiar patterned face and asked how he was enjoying his newfound freedom. The gold-tinged 3D representation of Jaha's head grinned and said he had been back to the eco lodge to get it prepped for the next visitors and was looking forward to heading downriver to visit with friends in the town.

The three other faces of the scientists who would be sitting in on the testing today were greeted before Xanthe went over and made the finger motions to have the native child projection appear on the table next to the stove cube. Jaha greeted the native child avatar projection in his native language as Xanthe placed a beaker with a "clean water only" label into the square opening of the cube. She drained all the water the cube had taken in overnight and then moved her finger on the control tablet to have the bluish glowing area for water purification appear on the top of the stove.

Xanthe took the first jar of contaminated murky water from the shelves under the counter, announced the sample number and contaminant contents, and poured it slowly onto the blue glowing area on the top of the "stove" cube. They had found in earlier testing that water and select healthful minerals would wick through into the top of the cube, while the remaining contaminates would be filtered out and left clinging to the top surface.

This dry contaminated dust would then migrate over the front, down the tapered side faces and into the opening to be spread across and incorporated into the next "shingle" the cube would shed. Xanthe waited for a couple of minutes for the contaminated dust to finish its migration before placing a lab sample jar into the opening and draining the test water into the sample jar. Unlike the murky contents of the jar that had been poured onto the top, the water flowing out into the jar below was perfectly clear drinking water.

And so, the morning continued with Xanthe pouring in water samples, with every possible contamination the scientists could dream up, and getting clean water back out to go into the prelabeled lab jars. So far, without fail, the test results had come back as spring water quality potable water.

Xanthe heard a car pull up outside and checked the time. She announced to Jaha and the scientist's gold-tinged ghostly faces that they would need to wrap up the morning testing session. She could hear Ariana's husband greet Ariana's assistant outside and the sounds of luggage being loaded came through the garage door.

The door from the house opened and Khadija came in toting her luggage and a champagne bottle wrapped in a cloth followed by Ariana's assistant with a tray of glass champagne flutes that were both set on the end of the counter. Khadija gave Xanthe a hug and said she hoped that they would have good attendance for the little end of quarantine celebration they had planned.

The faces of other familiar coalition council started to appear above the communicator cubes on the upper tiers of the table, so Khadija and Xanthe turned towards the table to greet them. Ahmed and Ariana came into the garage to join the party. Ahmed took Khadija's luggage along with his own and went over to put it in the back of the black SUV.

Ariana and her husband came in and joined the virtual party in front of the cube table greeting the coalition council members as they appeared. Khadija removed the wire holding the cork on the champagne bottle, and without warning there was a loud pop followed by a thunk as the cork ricocheted off the ceiling and bounced off the hood of the SUV. Xanthe laughed and said that it would be ironic if the only real injury in the all the careful isolation and testing of the cube was inflicted on the last day by a flying champagne cork.

Khadija poured a bit of champagne into four of the flutes and then took the beaker with the clean water label and filled two more. Ariana's assistant came in and took the tray of flutes with champagne around, while Khadija picked up the two flutes filled with cube filtered water and handed one to Ahmed.

"To the end of quarantine, and the beginning of new possibilities for the world", Ariana toasted as they raised their glasses and clinked them together in the lab.

They could see the gold-tinged faces raise a motley assortment of coffee mugs and water bottles while mouthing clinking sounds as they virtually toasted as well. As they celebrated with the virtual gathering, a few of coalition leaders spoke briefly to mark the accomplishments of the coalition and tribal elders since the retreat at the eco lodge. A couple of the scientists, who had been alarmed by the "explosive incident" in the biosafety lab and had not read the memo about Xanthe and Ahmed's acting performance, asked how the switch out at the biosafety lab had been done.

Xanthe confessed that when she and Ahmed were helping each other put on the lead lined apron with attached sleeves and gloves there was a trick involved. She had held Ahmed's heavy apron from the back as he worked his arms down into the sleeves and then she made the ties across the back. Ahmed did the same for her, but as she was making the motions of putting her right arm down into the sleeve and glove, Ahmed was just opening an air cylinder inside the apron and inflating a fake arm in the sleeve and glove while pinching along the arm shield and glove to make it look like he was helping her arm make it down in the sleeve. Her real arm was still under the vest when Ahmed handed her the control tablet for the stove cube. Taking care to hide it from the cameras, she could move her hidden hand to operate the functions of the control tablet with her fingers out through a slit in the front of the vest.

When time came for the acting part, she just started running the lights and filter air flow controls up and down with two fingers as she bent over in fake pain and released the inflated arm and glove to fall back limply at her side. The air filter slider, run up to its max by Xanthe, blew the papers and empty radiological hazard marked cardboard box off the end of the table as Ahmed leaped backwards onto the foam filled boxes. She kept running the sliders on the lights and filter air flow with her hand to keep up the flashing and whooshing until she had finished her collapse to the floor and the last of the fake "radioactive" granules had rolled off the cube and table.

The video gathering laughed and then started to clap when Xanthe had finished recounting the story. Ahmed instantly bent over to take a bow with a grandiose flourish and then looked sideways and made head motions at Xanthe from his bent over position to get her to bow as well. Xanthe did a form of exaggerated curtsy with a make-believe skirt, while Ariana led another ovation of clapping.

After the celebration had wound down, and all the virtual gathering, but Jaha, had faded away, Ariana gathered them around in circle. Jaha expressed the tribal elders wish that they go forward holding a common intention in their minds even though they would be traveling separate paths and wished everyone well. There was a large virtual hug of Jaha's image and individual hugs all around.

Xanthe opened the garage door behind the SUV and Ariana and her husband said goodbye as they followed Ariana's assistant out to the assistant's car. They went out and waved as the assistant drove Ariana and her husband out past the security guy at the open gate. They went back in the garage and Khadija went around to the driver's seat of the SUV while Ahmed settled himself with his phone and laptop in the passenger's seat.

Xanthe rapped on the SUV window, and as Ahmed rolled it down, she said, "Let's all try and avoid getting locked down in a biolab together for at least the next decade."

"If you make it two decades, it's a date," Ahmed said grinning as Khadija chuckled, shook her head and backed the car out of the garage. With a final wave from Xanthe in the garage, they drove out the gate and down the road until only a dust trail remained.

25

Miri banked the plane down towards the town next to the abandoned mine site that she would be sampling this trip. She overflew the town, with its dilapidated shanty houses jammed up in random fashion on one end along the outer fence line of the mine site. She leveled off at the mapping altitude and turned on the downward cameras and topography mapping equipment. She flew back and forth in incremental passes over the abandoned mine site and town to get photos and gather the 3D mapping data of the present site conditions.

The mine site was one extended tailing pile after another and looked like an otherworldly landscape below her. On her far passes she saw the short airstrip inside the fence line she would be using near some collapsed buildings. She finished up her mapping passes and angled around to land. On the ground, she turned the plane around, so that it was pointing back down the airstrip in case a quick departure was needed. She shut down the engines, locked the brakes, and called the security team to let them know she was had landed at the mine site. She told the team she would be deploying a ballooning builder cube shortly to allow them to monitor the area and keep an eye out for her.

She pulled her laptop out of her flight bag and went back past the racks of drones that took up the majority of the cabin, to the tail section where the 3D mapping equipment and camera was mounted onto the floor. She folded down the seat of a comfortable high-backed chair attached to the wall and hinged down an armrest with a tiny tray table that flipped over for her to place her laptop on. While the laptop was booting up, she turned to the mapping equipment and hinged the camera and lidar arrangement up to store it in the curved side of the tail.

A draft of warm air came up through the now exposed square opening in the tail fuselage floor where the mapping camera had been. She unplugged the drive from the mapping camera and carefully stepped around the opening in the floor to plug it into the laptop. She launched the 3D mapping program and started the import and processing of the terrain data and camera images from the drive they had acquired on the flyover.

She then made her way back to the riveted aluminum panel wall at the back of the cargo area. She reached into a space between the wall panels and the outer fuselage and felt for two bolt heads. She found them, squeezed them together, and the bottom panel of the back wall popped loose. She hinged open the panel until it came up against the upper portion of panel and fastened it to keep it open.

On the hinged-up panel section were mounted an array of tiny communicator cubes connected to a small electronic interface box with a long USB cable and a single communicator cube off to one side. Below was an open space leading into the narrower tail section beyond with the open ends of a stack of builder cubes visible just inside. She reached down to pull out a single builder cube stored separately from the others and then ran the USB cable over and plugged it into the laptop on her way to the cargo door.

She opened the cargo door and went out of the plane to look around to check that no one was in sight. She placed the builder cube on the dirt with its opening oriented sideways and checked that the departure flight track for the drones she would be deploying was clear of trees. She came back inside, made a finger motion on the single communicator cube on the panel and went back to the door to watch.

The builder cube lifted a hairsbreadth off the dirt with a puff of dust and the faint sound of air moving through it could be heard. There was slight distortion visible in the air at an open end of the builder cube as the hint of a clear "bubble" shape could just be seen being blown out the side of the cube. The science team had said the builder cube could essentially blow transparent hydrogen bubbles that could be used as a form of balloon to lift the cube. As the bubble grew larger it started to float up from the cube in an elongated tear drop shape. The teardrop inflated sideways until the balloon side of the builder cube started to lift upwards. Soon after the entire builder cube lifted off the ground to start floating upwards. Miri watched as the "cloaking" function of the cube was turned on and the builder cube vanished from view below the barely visible bubble of hydrogen rising into the air. It was soon lost to sight, and Miri closed the cargo door knowing that the security team could now monitor images sent back to them by the builder cube, so they could be on "guard" and keep her posted in case anyone came her way.

She went back to pull out the builder cube array. The array was a square stack of builder cubes magnetically fastened together with a communicator cube attached on one side. She slid the array down into the square floor opening being able to see the dirt of airstrip below through vertically positioned center openings. The plane was already starting to become uncomfortably hot with the cargo door closed, so Miri used her finger on the attached communicator cube to start up the cooling and air filtration functions to air condition the plane interior.

Bending over to look into the tail opening, she could see the welded rails holding plastic sleeves of builder cubes tucked in among the aileron and tail rudder structure angling up towards the tip of the tail. She released and pulled out a couple of the plastic sleeves each containing several builder cubes and carried them back to the drone racks. She pulled out builder cubes from the numbered sleeve and positioned it in her hand with the tapered center opening running vertically. She then reached under the first drone and slid the builder cube up into the center nacelle until she felt the builder cube magnetically snap into place. She repeated this until all the drones had their assigned builder cubes inserted. She then walked back along around the racks of drones unplugging the charging lines and reaching past the tiedowns to flip on the power switches. She went back to sit at the laptop, checking that the mapping data had finished importing, before bringing up the drone flight control program on the screen.

The drone flight control program showed video feed thumbnails from each of the drone's front and downward facing cameras with the distance above the terrain indicated over the image. Miri selected all the drones and then initiated the preflight check out sequence. She heard each of the six propellers of each drone start up, be checked individually and then come on together causing one drone after another to strain against the tie downs.

As the checkout process was proceeding through the drone rack, Miri switched to the drone destination programmer. She imported the terrain map of the mine area, updated with the latest data from their earlier overflight and turned on the drone destination markers. She adjusted the marker locations of a couple drone destinations to avoid fallen trees or rocks that showed up in the detail photos from the overflight and, when satisfied, saved them. She flipped down the other armrest which had a joystick controller mounted at the end and plugged its cable into the laptop.

With the drone checkout done, she went back through the plane removing and stowing all the tiedowns, then opened the cargo door wide and checked things were clear outside. Back in the chair, she activated the drone deployment program. She did a quick check in with security, then clicked on each drone thumbnail, selected the Fly to Destination option then clicked on the flashing "go" button. One by one each drone's propellers fired up to lift it off the rack, move it down the aisle, and then send it flying out the door and over the fence in a blink toward the assigned mine survey locations.

As each drone reached its assigned location, Miri looked at its camera feed to double check the landing area was clear before clicking on the Land option for it. A couple drones were over shrubs or rocks that she had to use the joystick to maneuver the drone to a clear location before landing it.

Once all the drones were on the ground, Miri went to stand in front of the communicator cube array mounted to the hinge up wall panel. She moved her fingers across each tiny communicator cube, initiating the burrowing mode on the associated builder cube out on the mine site. The builder cubes would slide themselves out of the square drone nacelle openings and quickly burrow straight down in flash through the soil to start their boring and sampling process.

The builder cubes would analyze and record the soil and rock elemental makeup as they bored downwards overnight. Depending on the rock density, they might be down over a thousand feet deep by the time they were scheduled to return. They would then reverse to return to the surface, draw themselves back up into the square opening in the drones, and give Miri an indication the next morning when they were ready to fly back to their storage locations in the plane.

Until then, Miri could fold up the empty drone racks to open up the space and pull out the foam cushions that could go over a couple the lower racks to form a couch/bed for her use. With her overnight living space set, she sat back with her computer tablet on the "couch" to catch up on things she had going in the wider world.

26

Ariana sat in front of her opened globe memento at her home looking out at the virtual glade and gathered council around the pool for their weekly meeting. There was so much going on that their meeting agendas were packed. Her role, once the meeting was started, was to just keep things on topic and moving so they could get through everything in a reasonable time.

The meeting had started out with her asking Jamal to talk about his progress with both the smaller builder cubes and the tiny communicator cubes. Jamal described how, with the new interface connectors, the builder cubes could now be fully controlled by communicator cube arrays utilizing his team's new protocols. One feature of the new protocol, developed with the help of the native child, allowed the builder cubes to be formed into coordinated working groupings for a wide range of uses including mining, infrastructure construction, and delivery services.

Jamal said they were ready to start the planned infrastructure construction and expand the mining beyond the pilot facilities that were already in operation. His team was working on building out the current worldwide delivery capacity needed for secure delivery of construction materials, supplies, and eventually the stove cubes, should they be approved.

Xanthe reminded the council that bottlenecks and uncertainty in the supply chain for critical minerals needed for the transition to a zero-carbon world could be relieved by using the builder cubes to mine and refine those minerals on multiple continents. Ariana outlined how existing abandoned mines sites could be easily acquired by the coalition, cleaned up, and put back into service providing these critical minerals. Using builder cubes to do the clean mining and onsite refining processes, the needed minerals could be produced at high purity factors with little environmental impact.

The surrounding populations, usually left high and dry by the abandonment of the mine, could be reemployed for handling, and shipping the minerals. The mining tailings left over from the previous operations could be reprocessed into clean building materials for housing construction efforts for the surrounding population.

Ariana outlined how mineral sales, when combined with the precious metals that were also refined out in the process, were starting to provide funding at the levels needed for the massive scale up of the NGO coalition effort that was planned. Ariana provided the council with a listing of mines and suitable mining sites by mineral that Miri had identified on her flying tours as being suitable. The list had been vetted for ease of acquisition and security of location. The coalition voted to recommend the proposed builder cube/communicator cube production along with builder cube mining at three more locations and the tribal elders approved the actions.

Ahmed reported on how their new climate data processing capability was providing them clearer, more accurate projections of the impacts of climate change projected to occur in the next few years. The warming impacts alone were pointing towards killer heat waves that would make many equatorial areas of the world uninhabitable for several days to weeks a year.

From the rainforest regions of Jaha's tribe to sub-Saharan Africa, to the Indian sub-continent, the model predicted over a billion people to be at risk of extreme heat exposure. Large equatorial populations, living without access to cooling in humid climates were particularly vulnerable to these severe heat waves and the numbers of those projected to succumb to projected severe heat stroke leading to death were massive.

Without options to keep large populations cool enough to survive, the models projected mass migrations would attempt to take place from killer heat wave regions to the safety of cooler latitudes. Nations with livable climates were predicted to be overwhelmed by the migrating seas of humanity and ruthless measures were foreseen to hold back the incoming tsunami of displaced people. Nations in the heat impacted regions, facing the urgent reality of entire populations needing to move and being brutally blocked from doing so, might look to their nuclear stockpiles as a first use means of last resort to pave the way for their uprooted populations. The projected catastrophic scenarios that could be touched off by unbridled use of nuclear weapons were of as much concern to Jaha's tribal elders as the deadly heat they might be facing.

Following Ahmed's report, there had been much consternation and discussion among the council. Jaha said the tribal elders saw the ability of the stove cubes to provide cooling as a solution that would allow populations to shelter in place and survive extreme heat periods. Ahmed said by providing a widespread means for people to survive the heat and shelter in place, the models showed that mass migration could be stemmed, and the associated potential for catastrophic nuclear scenarios be significantly reduced.

While the tribal elders were in favor of widespread equitable distribution of the bridging "gift" of the stove cubes, many of the coalition council and science team remained hesitant. Widely distributing a literal black box technology, with unknown internal workings, from an unknown manufacturer whose altruistic intentions could only be vouched for by the dreams of rainforest dwelling tribe was a steep ask.

Xanthe covered how the stove cube's capabilities had now been rigorously tested and any short-term potential dangers outlined by the red team had been explored and dismissed. Ahmed had said that there was always going to be an element of risk in deploying advanced technology that was not fully understood. Xanthe said that the manufacturer, knowing the sophistication of the technology and potential power contained in the cubes, had clearly taken steps to effectively conceal and deny that knowledge to anyone attempting to pry into the cubes. Ariana pointed out that the manufacturer had also acceded to strict tribal and coalition control over the distribution and use of the cubes to ensure they were used in accordance with the mission guidelines of the NGO coalition.

Ahmed suggested, in addition to the communicator cube and builder cube production, that an initial run of the stove cubes be produced for more extensive duration studies of their cooling/heating and filtration potential. For security and safety, he recommended these be secured in place at a very remote location, before any distribution to populated areas would be considered.

Xanthe said a production run could serve to demonstrate manufacturing capability, production consistency and provide more extensive duration testing results, than just the single stove cube testing she was using could provide. Ariana had Ahmed make a specific motion, and after the discussion had died down, brought his proposal to a vote. While the number of stove cubes that Ahmed's motion called for to be produced had raised some eyebrows, the vote had passed among the council members and was readily approved by the tribal elders.

Due to unscrupulous corporate efforts to steal the cube technology, and the inevitable focus that would occur when the enormous amounts of income started flowing out of mining operations, Ariana said they had spoken to several of their sympathetic millionaire and billionaire doners. They had set up several mining companies along with privately held funds into which the mining profits would be deposited. The coalition could use these funds to direct monies to their efforts on the ground. Should the stove cubes be approved for widespread distribution, these NGO donors would also take credit for their manufacture. Rumors of a dead scientist's breakthrough tech being applied in the cube manufacturing, were to be floated, but the doners were to insist that they were not at liberty to discuss anything about the stove cubes in ways that would build credibility that they were behind the whole stove cube business. Ariana had voiced her hope that the well protected doners could take the heat off of the NGO coalition and tribe so that security measures for the council could be eased over time. Until then many of the leaders and scientists would have to maintain sequestered lives under the watchful eye of the security team.

27

Xanthe woke unusually early, not sure of the reason. She threw on her warmup suit and sneakers and tried to keep quiet on her way downstairs to the kitchen. She now had grad students staying in the model house with her to monitor the extended-duration stove cube tests. The untidy dishes in the sink reminded Xanthe of their full schedule remote classes while dedicating a full semester to live in isolation in the house to help her with testing.

While reheating some of the night shift's coffee she looked out the back window at the barely lightening sky. They were now running a variety of duration tests around the clock to prove the "stove" cube's product life. They had also been using Jamal's new control program for the builder cubes to test their capabilities. Since the approval to start production of more communicator and builder cubes, they had been demonstrating the ability of the builder cubes to work together in swarms at to do excavation and construction.

A red team of scientists who had been assigned to evaluate the cubes, based on the assumption that they were here to kill us all, was still sending Xanthe and the grad students ever more paranoid tests to run on the cubes. Between red team tests, that were usually done while Xanthe was awake, they had moved on to testing all the cube stove functions on a round-the-clock basis. The garage was already drafty, with no heating or cooling, and Ahmed felt it mimicked a large common room in the developing countries the cube might be rolled out to. A variety of samples that, when burned inside the in the garage, produced everything from smokestack stench to cooking fire smoke were used to test the stove cube's air filtration capabilities.

A new shipment of jars with polluted, mildly radioactive, and bug infested soil was also being tested to see if the accreted "lembas" formed on the interior sides of stove cube opening were wholly free of the contaminants. Sensitive air quality monitors would monitor the garage environment's atmosphere, while tables of testing equipment would evaluate the water filtration, contaminated soil to "lembas" formation purity and the carbon/contaminate composition of the shingles that cubes would produce and jettison over time.

Xanthe came back into the main room with her coffee and walked behind the curved sales desk that the monitors for the garage camera feeds were running on. Everything looked quiet in the garage lab, and she was about to take her coffee over to her morning reading nook, when she stopped and looked back. Things were too quiet! There was supposed to be a builder cube test and a second cooking test running that required one of the students to constantly place and cook a variety of food on the "griddle" top of the stove cube.

On the monitor there was only a blackened smoking pile on the red tinged "griddle" area. Where were the grad students? She looked across the other camera views of the room to see what the students on duty were doing and started, as one of the monitors showed her a black masked figure standing behind the bound and gagged students. She lunged for the security alarm button, but an arm came from behind to stop her hand. Xanthe jumped in surprise to see the two large guys wearing masks behind her.

Each with a hand on her shoulder, they escorted her into the garage where the grad students looked a little wild eyed but otherwise appeared to be unharmed. As they marched her over in front of the stove, she looked over to the far side of the garage. What she had not seen on the cameras was all three of the night detail security guys from the construction trailer sitting limply in the seats of SUV.

A voice behind her said "Do not worry…they sleep…night… wake up… small head…ache. Be good - make stove off ."

From the broken English, they were probably a foreign team, but she could not place the accent. One man held up the control tablet in front of her, but she ignored it and continued to look around. She saw the masked broken English guy lounging back in a chair to the far side of the grad students turning over a builder cube in his hand.

"What about the other students?" she demanded.

"They sleep…night…like them." said the lounging guy point-ing with a toe towards the security guards. "Make stove off… now…pleez."

Xanthe was thankful her partner, Eleni, had headed back home a few days before. Clearly the masked men had somehow gotten through the fence perimeter detectors and overcome the security guys. They were probably the reason she had woken up so early and shuddered to think she had probably walked by them on her way downstairs as they were drugging the students in the bedrooms. There was no alarm siren, so probably no alarm signal had been sent out. She didn't see what she could do other than play along and see where this went. Xanthe thought the men were probably unaware of the shelves behind the cabinets where all the other cubes and control interfaces were stored. The voice started again in a more insistent tone, so she reached out, took the tablet, and dialed down all the stove functions.

The circle of heat disappeared and the control tablet was taken from her. Her hands were zip-tied together. The lounging voice got up and walked up next to her to put a hand on her shoul-der, while the other two dismantled the cube stove, and took the base and duct add-ons with them back into through the main house. The voice pushed her along behind them until they were all standing by the front door waiting for something.

The sound of a vehicle coming into the drive could be heard and the voice said, "apologies…must not allow seeing," as a hood was draped over her head.

She was guided out the door and into some large vehicle that required a bit of a step up to get into. A guy sat on either side of her on the back seat and they were soon off driving roughly off across what had to be the construction site. A scraping sound marked the vehicle passing through the cut fence and then were out on smooth roads to where Xanthe could not guess.

28

Jamal was woken by the sound of rap music coming from the communicator cube Ahmed had given and keyed to him. As he hazily sat up, he recalled one of the first items he had coached the native child avatar through was how to sample music for playback as a form of ringtone. This was not a call from one of the scientists on the far side of the globe forgetting the time difference, this was Ahmed's ringtone.

Jamal threw on a sweatshirt and headed out of the room he was camped in, out into the temporary control center area that he was setting up. He sat at the control desk and then reached over to run his finger over a communicator cube on the console in front of him. Ahmed's gold-tinged image formed in the light from the cube with a concerned look.

Ahmed said, "Sorry to wake you so early, but we have a situation that we need your help with." He went on to tell Jamal about the discovery of Xanthe and the cubes being abducted and asked Jamal if he could pull up the tracking and determine the location of the builder cube that was stolen with her.

Jamal switched on the monitor wall and the first rack of optical interface equipment tied into a tall stack of communicator cubes. As the monitors came on and the optical rack stack equipment booted up, a world map dotted with the locations of all the builder cubes appeared. Jamal reached over to another communicator cube on the console and moved his finger over it. It glowed and soon the native child avatar's projection joined Ahmed's on the console.

Jamal addressed the beaming face of the native child saying, "Show me the current location of the builder cube from the garage lab." The native child nodded and the green and blue speckled 3D globe filling the monitor wall rotated until a red circle around a white dot in the middle of the ocean came into view. As the display rotation stopped, Jamal could see that the highlighted dot was moving ever so slightly across the map.

Jamal asked the native child to overlay the transponder locations for all air traffic near the circled moving builder cube and list their airspeed and direction of flight. The child nodded and a tail number appeared at the cube's location with the airspeed and heading next to it. He asked for the flight plan for the tail number and when it appeared, he shook his head knowingly.

Jamal turned back to Ahmed's projection and said, "It looks like the stolen builder cube is about halfway across the ocean on one of the corporate bad ass planes and the flight plan has it heading towards the defunct military base that security team has been keeping an eye on. At the cruising speed they are going, they should arrive in an hour and a half or so."

Ahmed's projection turned to face the native child avatar and asked, "Can you have the builder cube sample the air on the plane and compare the results to the first air filtering test in the garage lab done by Xanthe?" The child nodded and the results appeared as part of Ahmed's projection in front of his face. Jamal saw Ahmed's eyes scanning as he asked the child to scroll until arrived at a line in the data that seemed to satisfy him.

"OK, the builder cube on the plane is sensing Xanthe's distinctive shampoo, so she must also be on the plane," said Ahmed swiping away the information.

"Forward the location tracking info to the security team and I'll need you to start planning a possible rescue plan with them as soon as we finish. That cold war facility has a bunch of buildings and bunkers to take her to once they land. Make sure our "eyes" over the facility are placed, so we can follow where they take her," continued Ahmed.

Jamal said, "I'd like to get a bunch of the mining builder cubes working further South repurposed and sent towards the bad boy base in case we might need them. I'll make sure they balloon down quietly into place overhead so those at the base remain unaware they are there.

Ahmed said, "Good idea. I'll check in with Jaha to get the tribe's permission for their temporary use as rescue resources and be back in touch once we know more." Ahmed's head projection faded, and Jamal looked back up at the monitor wall to see the red circled dot had moved a bit further across the mostly green and blue dotted globe. Jamal rotated the globe view until an area with a cluster of light green dots and a cluster of white dots came into view. He zoomed in until the light green cluster was just visible at the top of the monitors and the white cluster was in view at the bottom.

He pointed to the white cluster at the bottom of the screen and said, "We are going to repurpose builder cubes out of this location to add to the observer builder cubes here at the base".

Jamal zoomed in to look at the handful of light green builder cubes already posted over the facility.

He said to the native child, "Show me new observation solution locations repurposing the cubes already over the site and adding in the incoming builder cubes at detailed observation altitude. We'll want detailed coverage of all the buildings within the base fence line but being sure to leave the runway and approaches clear." Gray reference dots appeared over the base facility grounds clustered closer together around the buildings that could be seen from the air. "Extend the coverage for a mile down all the surrounding roads, widen the runway approach clearances, and lower the density over the hangars." The locations of the gray dots shifted and reformed on the screen.

A text from Ahmed saying they had permission from the tribe to add further surveillance to the facility came in. Jamal said "Those locations will do for now. Please dispatch the builder cubes from the mining location and adjust the positions of the existing onsite monitoring cubes to the new locations. Keep the cubes coming in from the mine over flight level 500 on the way there and have them balloon into detail observation altitude maintaining cloaked mode. Send the security team the locations now and the added builder cube video feeds when they arrive on station."

The native child had him repeat the command with the words "I authorize…" added and flashing lines appeared on the map leading to each of newly assigned locations. Jamal zoomed back out and could see the origin of the flashing lines coming from the white cluster mining location. The start of some of the lines were already beginning to shift to a solid non-flashing line showing where the actual builder cubes were now rocketing out of the top of the remote mine shaft and starting to fly to their newly assigned locations.

One of the aspects of the builder cubes that had been discovered was, like the larger "stove" cubes, they could somehow grab ahold of a cone of air particles some distance in front of the tapered opening, pull the particles in through the center opening, and then accelerate them out the back. The builder cubes could form up into stacks with their center openings aligned to exponentially concentrate and massively accelerate airflow out the back at rates equivalent to a small jet engine. Jamal had to have the native child avatar put limits on the top speed they could travel in their normal stealth mode to keep them to subsonic speeds.

The cubes' surface absorbed all radar, and the surfaces of the builder cubes could light up like a TV screen and produce a cloaking image that made the cubes virtually invisible at any distance. This made them undetectable by air traffic radar and visual systems, another reason the coalition wanted to keep a lid on this tech leaking out. The only potential giveaway was the sound that all that thrust made when they took off.

Jamal was already formulating an idea as he watched the solid lines slow dramatically as they started to approach the base. The cubes would shut off their collective thrust, come apart and individually fall quietly in long arcs towards their assigned locations. The center of the builder cubes would start to slowly blow a hydrogen bubble out into a balloon behind the cube. The increasing air drag on this transparent balloon would slow the cube and the increasing buoyancy of the hydrogen being pumped in would allow it to float silently down to its assigned altitude. Only a bit of sideways propulsion was needed to counteract any wind and maintain the builder cubes' position over the target. Jamal heard from the security team that they were good with the added locations he was stationing the cubes at so, he had some time to wake up and do some planning.

Jamal was dressed and back at the console chugging a power drink so he could coherently think through the crazy idea that had popped in his mind. He had pulled up and was reviewing what was available in the way of plans of the base buildings, when the communicator cube rang with the security head's ring tone. Jamal leaned over to activate the communicator cube, and the head of security appeared.

He let Jamal know that there was no way the coalition could have the local authorities assist with a rescue where the plane was heading. The corporation involved had apparently bought off the police and local government officials who were giving them free rein on their operations out of the base. If Xanthe were to be rescued, it would not be aided by any of that country's law enforcement.

Some time later, Jamal had finished reviewing the plans and was noodling various scenarios on a monitor, when the child gave him a heads up that the plane was approaching the base facility. He asked the child to switch from builder cube to builder cube to keep the jet in view as came into land and taxied. The images on the monitor wall switched to follow the jet from several angles as it landed and taxied over toward the ammo dump end of the base complex and came to a stop. A vehicle drove around to meet the plane as the door opened to create a stairway.

Four darkly clad men got out the plane and marched a hooded female figure with her hands bound towards the person from the vehicle. They were led over to one of what Jamal recognized from the building plans as an ammo bunker with the last of guys carrying a large duffle bag. Two of the guys stayed outside while the rest went into the bunker. Another vehicle pulled up and two military police looking individuals got out and also took up station at the entrance.

After a few minutes, all the darkly clad men came out, with the now empty duffle bag, slung limply over one of their shoulders, and got back on the plane. The man that had first driven up got back in his vehicle and drove off as the plane taxied back out and took off.

Jamal checked that the builder cube from the garage lab was located in the ammo bunker and figured from the empty duffle bag that the "stove" cube probably was probably there as well. He asked the child to track the plane for the security team and alert him to any movements around the ammo bunker. He then texted Ahmed to get permission from the tribe to enable video feed and sensor capability on the builder cube that was in the bunker with Xanthe. Now that they knew which building Xanthe and the cubes were in, Jamal had a better idea about what they could do about it.

29

Ariana called the impromptu council meeting in the virtual tree glade to order. The calming water ripples lapped peacefully in contrast to the air of concern emanating from the gathered council. The abduction of Xanthe had brought them together and many seated around the pool were wondering if they might also be in danger. Jaha and the tribal leaders had stoic expressions and sat silently while many of the gathering were in earnest discussions with worried tones.

Ahmed caught the gathering up on what they knew about the kidnapping. A breach had been made in the back fence leading to the overpowering and drugging of the site security guys and the grad students at the house. All had had woken with headaches but were OK otherwise. The word from the security team was that Xanthe was presently being held at an overseas military base in a former ammunition bunker. A reverse engineering team and interrogators were expected to arrive on site tomorrow and that's when the security team felt things could become really dangerous for Xanthe.

Ahmed asked the native child avatar to bring up the video images of Xanthe provided by builder cube from the inside of the bunker. A view of Xanthe appeared over the center of the reflecting pool, and the gathering could see her walking around an oddly shaped old concrete walled room with a water bottle in hand looking at the surveillance cameras mounted in the corners. Ahmed said these corporate actors had a reputation for ruthlessness and many who were abducted by them were not seen from again. Ahmed asked Jamal to tell the gathering about his idea.

Jamal said that had come up with a plan, that the security team considered risky, but that might be the only option they had. He asked the native child to bring up the animation showing what he was proposing. A rotating see through view of the bunker construction appeared along with representations of the furniture and placeholder figures representing Xanthe and the guards outside. Jamal asked the child to run the animation of his proposed plan and the chatter in the meeting glade quieted as the animation played out in the floating 3D model over the pool.

There was a momentary silence after the animation finished and then the gathering erupted back into conversation. Ariana was having trouble getting the attention of the council, until the conversations were cut through by chanting coming from Jaha. When quiet was again restored, Jaha said the tribal leaders would agree to the plan if it met with the approval of the council. Jamal and Ahmed fielded questions until finally Ariana called for vote. With no other option available, and Xanthe in real danger once the interrogators arrived, the vote easily passed.

Jamal suggested the plan be put in place after nightfall at the base and said he would work on a way to let Xanthe know her essential part in the plan. Ariana thanked Jamal who said he needed to leave the gathering to start the plan implementation. The gathering echoed thanks as he faded from view.

Ariana said the implications of this rescue attempt would hint at the further capabilities of the cubes, making the cube technology even more desirable for this bad actor to acquire. They might go to unpleasant lengths to get information from the science team members and potentially the other council members as well. She said that increased security for the council, scientists and their staff was going to be a fact of life for all of them after this.

Ahmed outlined how a remote village in a rift valley co-located with the main cube manufacturing facility was the planned safe relocation place for any of the coalition leaders and scientists that came under threat. He said the security team was already recommending that a couple of the scientists and their key staff that were potentially under threat relocated with their families to the rift village as soon as possible. He said coalition leaders and council members would have added security and individual backup escape plans put in place in case the threat level expanded.

Ahmed said one way to remove the incentives for bad actors and lessen security concerns would be to simply move up the timeline for their plans. By publicly announcing donor plans to have the coalition widely distribute "their" stove cubes in impacted regions and providing example stove cubes to any government or corporate actor that wished to evaluate them, they could lessen the threat and buy some time. Once the stoves had undergone field trials and widespread distribution had started, the threat to all but some key scientists should be greatly lessened.

Ahmed reported that the tests of the massive installation of stove cubes that were being fixed in place had been going well and had proved the production capability of the manufacturing facility by the rift valley village. The extensive testing of the stove cube done for the red teams at the model house had determined the stove cubes were as safe and dependable as any new technology could be.

The council had already come to agreement that only the cooking, water purification, air conditioning and filtration, refrigeration and lighting functions would be enabled when the stove cubes were deployed. He pointed out that the council now had as much information as they were likely to ever have to decide on whether to release the stove cubes to the world.

Ariana said, based on the increasing threat, that coming to a decision on deploying stove cubes would be better if done sooner than later. She asked if any of the council was willing to make a motion to recommend that stove cubes be distributed to governmental/corporate actors and to the remote villages that had been selected for field testing. After a motion being made and subdued discussion by the council was conducted, the council finally voted to recommend this limited stove cube distribution. The tribal elders' approval to proceed was quickly obtained and voiced by Jaha.

Ariana thanked everyone for gathering in such a hurry and for making the commitment to proceed. She said the gathering glade would be open for those who wanted to return to watch Jamal's evening action as it took place. As the gold-tinged images of the council and elders faded from the glade, she heard Jaha next to her say, "Funny - at end - council come to "believe" in "gift" just like tribe." She glanced to the side in time to see his virtual Cheshire cat grin fade from view.

30

As the hood was removed from her head, and the zip ties holding her hands to her belt were cut, it took Xanthe a moment to be able to see. As her eyes adjusted, she could see she was seated at the front of a small private jet. The pilots were hidden behind a cabin door at the front, and as she looked around was disturbed by the fact the three men no longer wearing masks. The man with the voice, seated directly across the aisle from her, asked her to keep her seatbelt buckled and to not touch the lowered window shades during the trip.

All of the accent and broken phrasing he had used in the garage was gone, and the voice sounded a little too polished and calm for the situation. His serious expression let her know he would not tolerate any monkey business now that her hands were free. One of the other men said they had drinks in the back and asked the voice if he wanted anything. The polished voice said, "We should start with our guest" as he looked over at her. Xanthe asked for some ginger ale and anything they might have to eat.

Xanthe was concerned as she munched on snacks with her drink. Letting her see their faces could only mean they didn't expect her to have a chance to give descriptions to the police. Aside from being built like soldiers, their white Anglo faces were fairly non-descript with no identifying scars or features. The polished voice said "I know you have a bunch of questions, but you've probably worked out that I can't tell you anything. We'll fly for a while and land, and then, unfortunately, we'll need you to put the hood back on while we're changing planes for another flight."

The hood went back on for the plane changeover in an echoey space that had to be a hangar, followed by a long flight in another jet where she was fed and asked some preliminary questions about her background and employment roles with the NGO coalition.

As they prepared to land, she was again hooded, and her hands zip tied. She was ushered off the plane at the destination into a building a short walk away that smelled of damp and mildew. She was taken down a short hall and into an echoey room in which the stale air was at least dry. She was guided to sit on a cold metal chair; her wrist ties were cut and footsteps headed back across the room followed by a heavy door clanging shut.

With her hands free she undid the drawstring around her neck and pulled the hood off. The dingy old concrete "bunker" where she found herself, was only lit by a single dim bulb in the center of the ceiling above. The high ceiling was only flat for a section down the center running over to the door wall. The three other ceiling faces angled down to meet the room height walls on the sides and back.

The concrete looked to be cold war era construction cast using forms made from individual planks so the plank edges and even a bit of wood grain showed in the concrete walls. The door was a heavy sheet of rusty steel with riveted reinforcing bars that were rolled at the ends into hinges. The layers of paint had almost entirely flaked off the door leaving just a rust and primer color.

The beat-up green paint of the steel office chair she was sitting on had resisted the rust better than the door and matched a metal office table in similar beat-up condition to one side of the room. The table had the cube stove, the stove's control tablet, and the builder cube set on it. A couple of bottles of water had been left out at the end of the table.

She walked over to the table, picked up one of the bottles and opened it to drink, as she paced around. The stove base and duct were on the floor to one side of the table. An old, splayed horn type public address speaker was on the wall over the door. There were no windows, and the only outside light Xanthe could see was a sliver coming under the door from the hall beyond. The heavily stained concrete floor showed signs that heavy steel racks of some sort had once been bolted to the floor.

On the side of the room opposite the table, a worse for wear mattress was on the floor. A folded pile of threadbare bedding and clothing was tossed on top of it. The clothing was just some an old style warm up hoodie top with a matching draw string bottom. The only new things were the cameras mounted up in the corners. The construction reminded Xanthe of the bomb proof munitions storehouses that had been in use during the cold war. Stiff from being cramped in airplane seats, she stretched out on the mattress trying to work out her escape options with only the stove cube and a builder cube she did not have the means to control.

An hour later, with no good ideas coming to mind the steel door was unlocked. A tray of food was shoved in through the partially opened door, and she walked over to pick up the tray, she checked the door again for any way to get through it. Like a lot of cold war era construction, it was overbuilt from a solid steel plate. From what she could see of the heavy hinge and hasp construction through the crack in the door, it looked like it would take a tank to knock it down.

She carried the tray to the table, placed it to one side of the stove cube, and pulled over the chair. The tray and heavy plates the food was piled on were an institutional type common in eastern Europe, but the plastic fork and napkin packet had salt and pepper labeled in English. Even lukewarm the first forkful made her realize she was hungry. As she was finishing eating, having decided any plan to escape based on using a plastic fork would be futile, a subtle change in surface of the stove cube next to her caught her eye.

On the front face of the of the stove cube portions of the matte black face appeared to be turning a slightly lighter charcoal tone. She had to move her head to just the right angle to make out the slight shift in tone that spelled out, "Act casual, tap fork 3 times."

It was a message! And being sent in a way that she could barely see and those watching the camera feeds from the room would surely be unaware of. The coalition must be able see her using the builder cube capabilities. If they could see her, then builder cube location transmitting ability must be telling the coalition where she was. She turned slightly sideways looking away from the cube while she ate a forkful of food and tapped the fork idly three times on the table in view of the builder cube.

Out of the corner of her eye, she saw the subtle writing change to read, "We have rescue plan. 3 for Yes". She took another forkful of the food and then tapped her finger three times on the table while she chewed.

"Tap 1 for forward, 2 for back". As she played with her food, to act casually, she tapped her finger once, and a graphic sequence appeared in the charcoal tone outlining what she should do. After she played it through, she was done eating, so she leaned back in the chair and idly double tapped her finger on the side of chair in view of the builder cube rewinding and then running through it a second time.

"Tap 3 if understand." She tapped the three times, and the instruction came, "Take builder cube to 4 corners?"

She got up and walked over to the end of the table picking up another water bottle and opening it, before casually picking up the builder cube to turn it over idly in her hands. She wandered with it as she took sips from the bottle of water. She carried it over under one of the corner cameras and as she said, "Anybody home out there?" She casually placed the builder cube into the corner as she leaned in as if listening for a response.

She walked around to a couple of other corners and repeated the question in different languages to those cameras as she leaned the builder cube into the corners of the room. At the last corner, she stood on the toilet so she could get up and put her face directly in front of the camera. She waved the builder cube back and forth between her face and the camera before leaning it into the corner so her face could get up close to the lens. She said loudly in her regional form of Greek, "Hey, fuckers of one another's mothers. Can you get your fingers out of each other butts for a moment and answer me?"

Getting no response, she hopped down and paced back over to the table. The words on the stove cube changed and she saw "Good we have location". As she plunked the builder cube on the table as the words changed to "4 hours to extract time." She tapped 3 times with the water bottle and a faint countdown clock appeared on the front of the cube.

She set her bottle of water on the table and carried the food tray over and set it on the floor by the door. The room was a bit cold, so she put on one of the hoody sweatshirts. She checked the bedding for any clues to its origin and finding none went ahead and made her bed. She kicked off her sneakers and put on the baggy warmup bottoms on over her running leggings. She sat on the mattress and discovered from a certain position on the bed she could just make out the countdown clock time.

She lounged there, trying to gauge what part of the world she was in. The second jet had flown long enough that could have crossed an ocean and she could be almost anywhere on two continents by the time they landed. It was a more humid and chillier climate but that did not narrow the possibilities down much. She figured her new captors were under instruction not to communicate with her until whoever would be conducting her interrogation could be brought in. Good, she thought. To-night's rescue operation would not be likely to be interrupted by the start of an interrogation.

With about fifteen minutes to go on the countdown clock, she sat up, put her shoes back on and went over to the table. She took a sip of water and set the bottle down next to the stove cube. She picked up the tablet and builder cube and then pulled the chair around so she could sit with her feet propped up on the table. "Ready in 10?" the cube spelled out and she idly tapped three times on the tablet with one hand, while turning over the builder cube in a playful way with her other hand. She brushed the front of the stove cube with her fingers to make sure it was in reach as she blindly groped for the water bottle while playing with the builder cube.

At a minute to go she put her feet down on the floor pulled the sweatshirt hood up over her head. Instructions reminding her to keep her arms and legs inside the plane of the sides of the chair scrolled up the front of the stove cube at the countdown reached 10 seconds. She had stopped playing with the builder cube and was holding it up agaist the metal chair frame, while she reached over to set the water bottle on the table by the cube stove.

Dust was starting to stream down from ceiling onto the food tray by the door as the countdown reached 5 seconds. The builder cube she was holding against the side of the chair with the opening facing up magnetically attached itself to the metal frame of the chair with surprising force. This was Xanthe's cue to stretch sideways and snatch the "stove" cube off the table. The words "Tuck and Duck" were flashing in lighter charcoal tones as she yanked it off the table into her lap. She extended her arms straight over the top of the stove cube and intertwined her fingers as she brought her feet together centered at the front.

Before she could fully duck her hooded head down onto her arms, she saw small square openings appear around a six-foot area of the ceiling showering shards of concrete down in front of the door. A stream of builder cubes came flying in through the square openings and down towards her chair. In machine gun succession, the builder cubes snapped together into vertical columns onto the sides of the chair forming two protective side walls.

There was yelling and a commotion starting in the hallway outside. As the builder cubes reached the height of the stove cube in her lap, she could feel it become locked into place, and she put her head fully down on her arms. Air being accelerated down the open center of the growing columns of stacked builder cubes finally generated enough thrust that the chair start to lift off the ground. In that same instant a 3-foot-thick slab of the concrete ceiling crashed down, obliterating the food tray dishes by the door.

With her head down, she could barely peek out as the builder cube flanked chair started sailing up over the fallen slab towards the newly made ceiling opening. She pushed her head back down onto her arms as the chair entered the concrete dust cloud over the slab and then shot up through the gaping ceiling opening into the night sky. She just got a glimpse of the panicked guards opening the door to find it blocked by the concrete slab as she sailed into the night.

Her hood was flapping like storm flag in a hurricane from the increasing speed, until more builder cubes joined up in mid-air to form the other sides of a box-like enclosure. Once she was totally enclosed and protected, there was enough room for her to sit upright and stretch her legs. The acceleration and increasing whine of the wind outside the cube enclosure indicated she was probably flying at airplane speeds. She had to admit, this was a novel way to skip out on a "party" thrown especially for her by some pretty unsavory characters.

31

On the night of Xanthe's rescue, Miri had been waiting for her at a remote airstrip just over the border. She could only hear the whistle of thrust and feel the whoosh of air as the builder cubes had set Xanthe down only a short distance away. It was not until the builder cubes turned off their cloaking and disassembled to fly off that Xanthe's sitting form had been revealed facing away from her. Xanthe had jumped up and pranced around with the stove cube over one arm and holding the builder cube aloft like winning prize fighter saying, "Chew on that you scummy ..." followed by a long train of invective in Greek that Miri was glad she did not understand.

At some point in her jumping around, Xanthe had noticed the plane, pulled back the hood and to make out Miri standing there in the dark .

Miri had said, "Don't let me stop your victory dance and cussing jag. It was just starting to get interesting."

She had flown Xanthe out to safety and, since then, the security team felt Xanthe would be safer as a moving target doing remote community visits.

Miri had spent the past couple months ferrying Xanthe, her pair of community organizers, and the stove cube around to remote towns and villages bordering the north African deserts. Ahmed's climate models projected these towns and villages would be some of the hardest hit by early extreme heat occurrences. Due to their remote location and small tight knit communities that already knew Xanthe, they would be among the first to do the field trials of the stove cubes.

Today, Miri maneuvered the bush plane around one of the towering cumulus clouds as she started her descent. Xanthe looked at the cloud and said, "Well, at least there is a chance of rain to help the crops around the villages we are visiting this week. The increasing droughts have been really hard on those trying to get by in these villages."

Xanthe and her team would be dropped off to travel by land rover to meet with trusted leaders and members of the village communities. Xanthe would outline the projected extreme heat impacts projected for their villages and would then demonstrate the stove cube as practical solution to help their communities survive these heat events. Lastly, they would get buy in from the local leaders to have community members do field tests of the stove cubes to prove their value.

Miri did a flyover of the mining site to see how the mine building construction with its large internal mineral holding areas and the site tailing amelioration was going. She was pleased to see the building looking nearly finished, the hills of poisonous tailings gone and the formerly otherworldly site covered with soil and sprouting grass. Done with the mine site flyover, Xanthe asked if they could circle over the adjacent town, so she get a feel for the current living conditions of those left behind by the mine closure.

After a loop around the town they headed for an actual paved airstrip, unlike the dirt strips or roads they frequently had to land on. As they came in to land, Miri could see the dusty four-wheel drive vehicles that they had requested, already waiting at a paved area near the far end of the strip. Miri floated the plane just over the end of the strip but let it run for a bit before smoothly touching down. The groundspeed carried the plane to the end ramp exit and across the taxiway towards the apron area with the vehicles. Miri pulled up near the vehicles, cut the twin engines and checked in with the security team to be sure they already had eyes in the air above the site to keep them safe.

Miri said, "My first mine site inspection visit is just a short drive from the airstrip we are landing at, so will I stay in the neighborhood this time until the three of you are wrapped up with your first set of meetings. Remember to keep your satellite phone close so you can scoot back to the airstrip if security sees anything untoward happening."

Xanthe opened the cargo door, set the steps in place and chocked the plane wheels, while Miri worked with the organizers to get all their stuff, including the stove cube pulled out. Xanthe backed the land rover up until it was just a few paces from the plane steps, took a careful look around before giving Miri a nod that it was clear to pull out the case that housed the stove cube. The organizers packed all their overnight camping and presentation stuff in the back of the rover around the stove cube case to keep it hidden from view.

Xanthe called out the window to say she would check in once they had their initial meetings and could confirm the departure window. Miri reminded her that, even though security had flown in builder cubes to watch over their camping location by the village, the mine site, and the airfield, to always to have her team keep an eye out.

Miri watched as they drove out of the gate exit then headed back up to the front of the plane to grab her laptop bag from behind the pilot's seat. She had a mining site to file a review on before she could kick back in the plane and enjoy the evening.

32

Richard was at the test bench running some extra-curricular tests on the communicator cubes, when Sam came out and announced something had triggered one of his motion detectors, so he was going out for one of his patrol walks. Something was always triggering the motion detectors, so Richard nodded and didn't think much of it. Sam keyed the mic on his radio to check that Richard's radio on the test bench was turned on before heading out the front door and making Richard lock it behind him.

Sam had been increasing his random patrols with the aluminum inspection form case/clipboard he used as his concrete worker cover. Sam had been particularly alert, since word came of a kidnapping of a coalition member that had been involved with the cubes. When that had happened a couple of weeks back, he had abruptly stopped Richard from sending emails or communicating with anyone on the outside. The backlog of work Richard needed to get sent out on the training and designs for the facilities was now building up to an uncomfortable degree.

Sam seemed pleased that Richard was uncomfortable. Complacency was one of Sam's biggest bugaboos, and he was constantly varying their arrival/departure schedule and taking measures to keep them in constant readiness in case one of his cont. plans was needed. Even the increased cont. plan drills and the work were becoming increasingly routine for Richard now that the electronic and optical interfaces were done and in production. After a couple of weeks of tweaking and refining the control protocols, the remote control of the robotic loaders was running smoothly.

There had been long days of sitting in the prototype control chair testing and refining the control protocols while putting the robotic loaders through their paces with the haptic controls. The kmasood consultant also had a control chair and a second robotic loader to run around for testing in the hydraulic press room. Richard had sometimes looked out and seen that second loader making wild quick movements that had already broken a couple of parts that had to be reengineered.

He had to admit the consultant was very quick to pick up the control chair interface with the loader. One day when they were both in the chairs practicing loading the plywood boxes, they got into an informal race. The consultant had soon put Richard to shame loading nearly double the number of boxes in the same amount of time.

As with everything else on this project, it only took a couple of days for the consultant testing the control chair to ask for substantially more that he had ever planned for. It came in the usual "red ink" email that asked for changes to what Richard had already designed or proposed. This email asked if he couldn't use all the 3D modeling of the manufacturing facility spaces, that he had already done for the architects to produce virtual training simulations. By providing an accurate virtual environment that those training in the control chairs could navigate and interact with, the consultant thought the learning curve could be substantially shortened. The "laundry" list of interactive training simulations being requested was extensive and .

Ahmed who was copied on their "red ink" emails, chimed in saying it sounded like a good idea that their software team could help with. Richard had modified a 3D model for the simulations and sent off the scenario, animation, and interactive rundown based on the consultant's "laundry" list, for Ahmed to pass along to the software team. With the high resolution needed, and massive model he was sending, Richard figured it would take them a couple of months to get those simulations ready to review.

The chair and robotic loader testing had concluded, and the prototype control chairs, and robotic loaders had been taken away to be stripped down to look for wear. For the last week of duration testing, Richard had the robotic loaders moving jerkily while their arms spelled out Y...M...C...A, and danced back and forth around the hydraulic press room. He wanted to be sure there was nothing more that could possibly break on the production models that the consultant could give him future greif about.

Now that the final versions of the control chairs and robotic loaders were in production, Richard and the consultant were supposed to be drafting a remote loader operator training manual. The communications blackout imposed left him unable to communicate with the consultant on the those, but Sam could still get hand delivered simulation updates from the software team for his review. Now that he had free time, while waiting for the software team to make revisions to the simulations, he had bigger fish to fry.

The biggest fish he had been trying to fry was getting to the bottom of how the communicator cubes did what they did. Richard had gone through all documentation the scientist had provided him with summarizing their testing results. To verify the science teams findings, and to satisfy his own disbelief, he had placed the twinned communicator cubes in everything from separate boxes of lead, to signal proof Faraday cages to try and interrupt the signal, but the control communications still came through cleanly.

There was basically no way he could detect the connection and data transfer between the twinned builder-cubes, and yet they had worked consistently and collectively without fail for now over a thousand hours of trial testing. Today, he was reviewing the latest results at the test bench in a bit of a funk. After throwing everything he could think of at them he had to face the fact that some other engineer had managed to produce a bulletproof communication technology that was simply beyond his ability to measure or understand.

That morning Sam arrived late but brightened Richard's day by presenting him with a memory stick with the final version of the virtual training simulations from the software team. Sam went out for his morning patrol and Richard had put the memory stick in his pocket impressed by the speed the software team, while he cleared and repacked the equipment from his latest failed communicator test. He was just stacking the equipment cases by the door and getting ready for a morning session in the control chair to review the simulations when the radio on the test bench crackled to life.

Sam was on the radio saying conversationally, "Go to cont. Alpha plus - Go Alpha plus, this is not a drill."

Reflexively, Richard popped the communicator cubes in the tool case, picked the case up and said into the radio, "Alpha plus going". He ran over to his office to grab his laptop and the satchel with his hat hanging off, before heading to the women's restroom. Inside, he slid the bars in place to lock the restroom door, placed the tool case with the cubes and his laptop inside the safe, closed it and swung the mirror back in place to hide it. He pulled a radio earpiece from the pocket of one of the oversize tan overcoats Sam had stashed in the bathroom, plugged it into the radio and slid it over his ear.

He keyed the mic saying, "At Alpha, awaiting plus". Sam keyed his mic, but only his casual humming of a tune let Richard know, Sam was aware he was locked in the bathroom with the cubes stored in the safe waiting for Sam to join him.

A few tense minutes passed before Sam's transmission came over his earpiece saying, "Entering front, stand by for plus". He heard the front door open, and heard Sam come into the front room. He was whistling the tune over the radio to sign that it was OK for Richard to open the door.

Richard relaxed, unbarred the door, and looked out. Sam motioned for Richard to stay put as he placed heavy steel bars across the front door and then did the same across the doors leading in from the hydraulic press area. Sam had told him the bars were just to "slow down curiosity seekers" to give enough to give time for the calvary to arrive.

Sam grabbed his backpack and laptop, then came down the hallway towards the bathrooms. He double checked that the heavy bolt locks were still in place on the end of hall exit door and then joined Richard in the bathroom, motioning for him to slide the bars on the bathroom door into place..

Sam put the phone on speaker so that Richard could now hear the ongoing update being given by the security team. Sam went over the changing table unit on the wall, folded it down, and powered up the monitor and joystick controller. Sam flipped through the outer camera views on the monitor until one showed a drone moving back over near the ridge between the building and the quarry at the top of the drive in from the gate. Richard could hear someone on the satellite phone say, "Drones look like they have finished perimeter fly over and appear to be to now be taking up station to watch gate and plant road exit paths."

"Do we have a twenty on the drone operators?" asked Sam to the phone."

"Drone operators appear to be in car parked in pull off on plant main entrance road. No other spotters that we can see, wait - we have two cars pulling up at an unused back gate. One person has gotten out and appears to be cutting the lock on the gate." said the voice on the phone.

Sam said, "Look for cars coming to the new gate entry we use. They are going to want to box us in."

Sam flipped through the camera feeds to check that the drones were still in position towards the other side of the building and then flipped a couple of switches on the joystick controller. Richard heard the engine on Sam's truck start up outside. The engine revved as Sam moved a control to the side of the joystick.

"Get the coats ready – we may be going to Bravo", Sam said as he opened his backpack and pulled out a vest harness with multiple clips of ammo and two guns in holsters that he strapped on. He quickly checked the ammo clips in each gun and then put them back in the holsters. Sam pulled a small submachine gun out of the backpack, shoved a clip of ammo into it and was slinging its strap over his head as the phone voice started speaking quickly, "The old gate is open - man cutting lock is armed - cars starting to move up drive – Police have been notified of break in by armed individuals – cars have pulled up and are waiting at bend just before access road from plant."

Sam said, "Stand by for plan Delta, repeat plan Delta. Expect Bravo if enough leave the scene."

Sam slung the submachine gun to his side, took one of the tan-colored oversized coats to put on, and glanced over at Richard to make sure he had his coat on over his satchel and was ready to go. He switched the monitor view to a wireless camera mounted inside the windshield on his truck running outside which vibrated as he revved the truck. He then switched back and forth between the cameras focused on the road approaches to watch for their incoming visitors.

The phone voice continued, "Two cars at new gate… man getting out to approach new gate." Sam told Richard that they may have an opportunity for a Bravo exit, so to be ready to move calmly and quietly if Sam called for it just like they had done in drills…

The phone voice interrupted, "New gate open – cars now approaching from both directions- prepare for incursion".

Sam said to the phone, "Plan Delta is Go, repeat plan Delta is Go! Advise on any intruders or drones with line of sight to side door exit to allow for Bravo."

The phone voice said, "Copy Delta, monitoring for Bravo – cars will be to you soon."

Sam was switching intently between the camera views now showing the pair of cars coming from each direction kicking up a cloud of dust behind them as they sped. Sam switched to the camera view pointed out the front of the truck and his put hands on the joystick controls counting to himself. He flipped a switch and then gunned the engine using the joystick controls.

The camera view lurched, and Richard could hear the spinning truck tires throwing up gravel against the building as it peeled out. Using the joystick, Sam drove the truck around onto the side drive between the building and the rock berm as if to get away from the cars coming in from the front of the building. Another pair of cars could now be seen angling from the back of the building to cut them off.

"Watch this" Sam said as he yanked the joystick over. The truck, with its oversize tires, veered to head diagonally up the side of the large rocks forming the berm. Some gunfire broke out as the angle of the sky shown on the monitor seemed to tip over impossibly steeply. A bullet hole with radiating cracks appeared in the windshield as the truck cleared the top of the berm and started down the other side.

"Road is clear to the left." said the voice on the satellite phone as Sam bounced the truck down the berm to reach the bottom on the other side. The pursuing cars were unable to follow, so he turned the truck to the left and sped off on the rim road following the giant hole in the ground that was the quarry.

The voice on the phone let Sam know that one of the drones was attempting to follow the truck overhead while one was still on station by the back of the building. Three of the cars had turned and sped back out down the gate roads, but one car was still outside. The three cars were having to drive the long way around the plant to head the truck off on the far side of the plant complex.

Sam had the truck flying around the quarry rim road but slowed a bit to make his way through the cement plant to the main entry. The truck breezed right by the surprised gatehouse guy and skidded out onto the main road. Sam opened up the throttle on the truck, so that it flew past the drone operator car a short way down the road.

Sam nearly missed the turn onto the road he was looking for and had to jam on the brakes to make it. The truck was now running down an overgrown dirt track pitted with potholes leading back throught the overgrown trees whose branches slapped against the windshield. The voice on the phone told Sam that the drone car had started pursuit and that the other three cars were closing in from two directions.

An abandoned ranch house and barn appeared in the truck camera view, and Sam angled the truck towards the barn. Sam gunned the truck straight toward the remains of the doors on the barn and crashed through them. The truck rammed into some rusty equipment in the barn and flipped on its side. He cut the truck engine and started to switch feeds on the monitor to the outside building cameras, when he paused, "Oops, gotta deflate our doubles in the truck in case the drone can get in to take a peek.", he said as he flipped another switch on the joystick with a grin.

The voice on the phone said the remaining car had pulled up out front and that three men were sneaking up to the sides of the front doors while a fourth was getting some sort of battering ram out of the car. Sam asked if there were any intruders or drones that had the side door in view and got a "Negative" reply.

Sam flipped through the camera feeds to satisfy himself the other drone was still in place behind the building where the truck had dissapeared over the berm. He checked that all the intruders were by the front door, before cutting the power to the monitor, picking up the satellite phone, and closing up the baby changing table.

"Plan Bravo is go, repeat Bravo is go" said Sam to the phone. "Copy Bravo is go" said the phone as Sam plugged his earpiece into the phone cutting off the voice. Sam unbarred the bathroom door and led Richard out of the bathroom and over to the exit door at the end of the hall. They pulled the tan hoods of the coats up over their heads as Sam silently unbarred the side door, pulled out the submachine gun, and waited.

There was a huge pounding sound on the front doors and Sam immediately popped the side door open. They ducked out keeping low behind Richard's truck as they scooted over to the fence. Sam kept the muzzle of the machine gun pointed towards the front of the building as he waited. The click of the side door automatically closing sounded overly loud in the silence.

A second heavy thud hit the front doors, and Sam hit the fence where the escape opening was located. A slit tore open in the fence that Richard stepped through, followed immediately by Sam. Richard knew from the drills not to wait for Sam and quietly made his way down through the scrub trees. Sam used a couple of zip ties from his coat pocket to close up and hide the slit in the fencing behind them.

The goal during the drills was to make sure to follow the winding path keeping to the cover of the trees until reaching the dry creek. Richard was not to wait for Sam, but to follow the eroded arroyo keeping bent over so as not to show himself. He was working his way quickly, but as quietly as possible down the arroyo's dry bed, when he heard footsteps behind him crunching on the gravely sand. Richard turned to look, but it took him a moment before he could make out Sam's tan-colored coat in the shadows of the scrub. Sam paused to listen to the commotion still going on at the building and then motioned for Richard to move faster as the arroyo widened out approaching the road. They skirted along a fence line marking the outer boundary of the cement plant /quarry and came to a large culvert run under the road bridge spanning the arroyo. Sam stowed his gun, and they half-crawled under the bridge.

Sam paused in the shade on the other side to get an update from the phone and scan the sky for drones before they again bent over covered by the hooded coats to continue. They kept moved hunched over to keep out of sight in the arroyo until it reached the scrub tree line. Richard was holding his hood up enough to see the tattered plastic bag caught on the branch of a small tree that marked the turnoff. He started up the bank into the scrub trees as Sam kept an eye out behind them.

Once in the scrub trees, Sam took the lead until they were near a secondary service road a couple of miles away from the cement plant. Sam had been getting updates from the security team over his earpiece and stopped them in the woods short of the turnaround at the end of the service road by some electrical lines.

The sound of a vehicle could be heard coming up the road and an extended cab pickup truck pulled into the turnaround.

Sam stowed the submachine gun out of sight and buttoned his coat before walking out of the woods to check in with the driver. Satisfied, Sam waved to Richard, and they were inside the truck and driving off in a moment.

Sam handed a ball cap and sunglasses back to Richard who he asked to lay across the back seat until they were further away from the plant. After a bit of driving and an update on the phone that told Sam the imminent arrival of the police on the scene had sent their visitors racing away, they took off their coats. to get comfortable for the trip. The driver swerved a bit when he caught sight of the submachine gun and Sam's wearable armory that had been hidden by the coat.

Sam saw the driver was eyeing the vest and guns and said, "Things went so well with the bug out, I haven't had to fire a single shot…".

"Yet" he added with a grin and then had to make a hand motion to get the driver to again pay attention to the road.

33

Ariana was chatting with the projections of Jaha and the tribal leaders as the images of other coalition council members started to appear around the rippling pool. Today was going to be the key meeting to decide whether or not to proceed with the full roll out of the stove cube program.

She had asked the tribal elders and Jaha to join her early, so she could be sure they were all fully resolved on the issue. The tribal elders had individually let her know through Jaha that each was fully in favor of proceeding with what they considered the full giving of the "gift" to the "modern world".

Jaha started off the meeting with the tribal elder's reminder that momentous decisions are frequently best decided after taking time to ground oneself in the natural world. He asked the council to take a moment to breathe deeply and reflect silently on their part in the natural world represented by the virtual glade surrounding them. After a minute, one of the elders quietly voiced a blessing for wisdom to be given to council in his native tongue. Jaha translated saying that the "gift" the coalition would be passing on to the "modern world" should be given in the beneficial spirit in which it was offered to the tribe. Jaha thanked the council on behalf of the tribal elders for their thoughtful consideration and turned the meeting back to Ariana.

Ariana said the field trials in the villages had gone well, but that the governments and corporate actors that had been given stove cubes appeared to now trying to get inside them causing disentegrations. There had been increasing requests not only for more stove cubes to experiment with, but for their doners to reveal how they worked and how the manufacturing was done. Fortunately word of the builder and communicator cube capabilities appeared limited to the one corporate actor who was not sharing it. Without an understanding of the technology behind the stove cubes, they would remain a curiosity on the back burner for most of the government and corporate entities. Ahmed recommended they continue to provide stove cubes but slowly so that this back burner testing could only occur at a slow pace. As knowledge of the inner working of stove cubes continued to elude these entities and the implications of the coalitions wider use of the other cube technologies for delivery and infrastructure became evident, the attention given to the coalition would go from back burner to a spot light focus. The national security and corporate bottom line concerns the cube technology presented, once more fully understood, would set off a race to acquire it.

Ahmed said that the security team was doing well with their expanded personal protection and contingency relocation plans that were now in place. The scientists, key staff and their families had finalized arrangements to move into the housing in the remote village near the manufacturing facility. Ahmed said the entirety of the coalition council membership and their key staff should plan should follow security team guidelines to minimize their public exposure for at least the six-month period between the public introduction of the cubes and their widespread deployment. He said Xanthe would be kept safe by her constant movements and Richard, their interface engineer that had recently been under threat, was being relocated overseas to a safe location.

Jamal reviewed the failsafe controls that that would ensure the coalition could literally pull the plug at any time on any or all of the cubes that would be deployed. Jamal also stressed the coalition's strict control over all loading and transport that would ensure only stove cubes with failsafe contingencies incorporated could get out into the world. He said the logistics centers and delivery systems were well underway and that construction on the remote loader control centers had started.

Ariana said, "Now we come to the moment of decision. Should we make widespread use of the "gift" of the stove cubes to counter the near certain impacts of extreme heat and climate crisis disasters that Ahmed's models now predict - or do we sit by due to the uncertainty of not fully knowing what we are releasing into the world." Ariana asked for a motion to start the voting process on the stove cube production and deployment. After some last-minute discussion to clarify the severity of the projected forced migrations and some final hand wringing by a few of the scientific advisors, the council voted unanimously to recommend moving forward with the widespread introduction of the stove cubes to the world. The smiles of the tribal elders and Jaha who translated their approval to proceed, stood in contrast to those of Jamal and the council members who were more soberly facing the massive amount of work they had just voted to undertake.

With the breif time frame to get production and deliveries to scale before the first of the extreme heat events were projected to occur, Ariana also felt the starting gun pressure and the enormity of the challenge before them.

34

Khadija gratefully cycled in the cooler shadows of the old concrete perimeter wall on her way to the remote operator building where the women she trained worked. The aged pavement of perimeter road she was riding on ran between the inner concrete wall and the outer razor wire topped fence that encircled the military airfield.

The road had been used by guard patrols in the facility's military past. Now security cameras had replaced the guards to monitor the perimeter area, so the road was little used. This doubled combination of perimeter security was only broken by the handful of security staffed entries and railroad access gates.

Khadija, due to security concerns, had moved out of the city and into the former on-base barracks where the other working women on the base lived. The military airfield was a couple of miles across, and the distance between the barracks and the training hangar, where she was headed today, was too far away to walk. The irregular schedule and misogynistic attitudes of the shuttle drivers made using her bicycle preferable, if she could keep to the shade of the perimeter wall on the way.

Women using bicycles were traditionally frowned upon here in her home country, but spending much of her teenage years growing up in England had accustomed her to using a bicycle to get around. The sight of independent western women bicycling the perimeter road, even with the obligatory headscarves, inspired frequent resentment and outbursts among the men commuting on the roads just outside the fence.

She was reminded of this as some angry guy on a motorbike started to hold up traffic as he slowed to follow Khadija on the road just outside the fence. He started to make leering faces as he spouted invective and sexual inuendo at her through the fence to humiliate her as she rode. He grew increasingly angry as she continued to ignore him, not even glancing his way as she cycled at a brisk pace.

Fortunately, she was not far from the entry gate with the opening in the perimeter wall. As soon as she could make it through the inner wall entry, she would be rid of the angry tirade being shouted at her by the weaving motorbike guy.

Entering workers were formed up into a line at the entry gate. Some were purchasing tea and food from the vendor carts that always set up by the gate. Traffic slowed to pick its way around the carts and past the line of workers filling the near side of the street.

The guy on the motorbike was slowed by the snarl of traffic near the entry gate and she was starting to get ahead of him, when the guy recklessly gunned his motorbike into a narrow open space right next to the fence catching up to her to continue his tirade. She waited until he would have to stop for the tea cart parked by the fence, before turning to face him squarely.

She said in her native language, "Hey momma's boy, save what you're shouting for your sisters once your momma makes you come home."

The motorbike guy was dumbstruck staring at her and only managing gurgling sounds as bits of foam appeared at the corners of his mouth. The sound of the motorcycle hitting the first tea cart sounded like a clap of thunder, and the rain of hot tea falling back down through the clouds of steam produced satisfying yelps from his sliding body now careening over onto the adjoining food cart. Food from the top of the cart mixed with the onrushing tea to form a minor breakfast tsunami in front of the sliding body.

A western man wearing a cowboy hat only saw the hot tea and food tsunami coming at the last second. He spun around and tilted his head back just in time, so the brunt of the steaming wave broke over his hat and back. From the top of his blue work shirt down to where his jeans met his boots his entire back was a wet mess with pieces of food streaming off. He tipped his head back down, turned, and the eyes under the brim of the food caked hat were fixed on her. She looked back at him as he seemed to be sizing her up with those eyes, but the moment was broken by a guard grabbing the western man and a struggle on the food cart. The motorbike guy extricated himself from the cart and jumped angrily back on his feet. She saw him start shouting and wildly looking around so, she quickly turned in through the perimeter wall entry to disappear from sight.

35

It had been a bit of a whirlwind for Richard, since he and Sam had made their escape from the concrete plant. They had met up with Sylvia at an airfield where a small plane waiting for him. She had walked him briskly over to the door of the plane, taking his phone and handing him an envelope saying it was the best they could do on short notice. She had chided him with a slight grin, "to keep his patoot out of trouble."

Richard had shaken Sam's hand to thank him for all he had done to keep him safe. Sam had said, "Well, it's not every assignment that you get to put cont. plans into action and walk away without any unwanted holes in your duds."

As the plane left the ground, he had watched Sam give him a casual wave while Sylvia stood by impatiently with her arms crossed. Inside the envelope was an authorization document in both English and a flowing foreign script, some foreign money, and a note from Sylvia telling him where to show up and counting the ways not to be "stupid" until he got there.

Somewhere along the northern coast of Maine, he had transferred to a private jet that flew him across the ocean and down to airfield just over the arid mountainous border into his destination country. A small beat-up car had met him and driven him all afternoon along the coastal mountains and into the city, dropping him off at a guest house close to the military airbase at the address he was to go to in the morning.

The room he was led to was ramshackle and hot, but with jet lag already catching up, he was soon asleep on top of the covers, before the glow of the sunset had faded.

He awoke well before dawn and pulled out his tablet to see what it had of the training materials he had been developing. The training manual itself was back on his laptop, still locked in the safe at the concrete plant. The tablet had his early notes for the training manual, so he cribbed together an outline to work from for the first day and then shut down the tablet which was running low on power.

He had left the charger for both his tablet back in the cement plant building office and would have to figure out where to get replacements that would plug into the local power outlets. Sylvia's "don't be stupid" instructions included not making calls, connecting to any wi-fi or in any way getting back online. Without being able to call or in any way to send a message, Richard had no way of letting anyone know he would be arriving.

Richard washed up in the sink and put back on his jeans, cowboy boots, and the blue work shirt with cement company logo. He gave a goodbye wave to the matron of the house as he headed out to walk the mile to the military airfield. Even the early morning sun was brutal, so he put on his hat, while keeping an eye out for an electronics shop that might sell compatible chargers. The mix of residential area and basic food shops did not have the chargers he was looking for but a restaurant with outdoor seating looked inviting.

He ordered coffee and pointed at something that looked like it could pass for breakfast from the display case inside. He enjoyed traveling and exploring new places, but he usually had the benefit of the translator on his phone when he was in off the beaten path locations where no english was spoken. Without being able to use his phone, the smile, point, and guess method had to be used for today's breakfast selection.

His cowboy hat had elicited an excited reaction from the man behind the display case but seemed to receive mixed reviews from those on the street walking past him. The coffee was dark and strong, but he could feel it perking him up. The pastry wrapped item, that he had picked out from the case, tasted good but was very spicy. From the table, he could see down the street to the military base gate at the address he had been given. The gate was not yet open, but vendor carts were starting to set up to either side and workers were already starting to gather outside.

Richard wanted to get in early, to leave time to check in with the base authorities and find his way to the training location, so he headed down to join the crowd forming at the gates. He was glad he made it down to get in line when he did, because the crowd was starting to spill out into the street by the time the military guards opened the gate. The line surged forward as the guards at the gate started checking ID passes, and Richard was pressed forward by those in line behind him. He pulled out the entry authorization document Sylvia had given to him as he reached the gate entry and was next in line for entry.

The roar of a wildly revving motorbike was suddenly heard over the slowed traffic near the gate. Richard could see the motorbike rider speeding along the fence line toward the vendor carts he was next to. The motorbike guy seemed preoccupied with yelling at a woman on bicycle as he fast approached the carts. The cycling woman on the other side of the fence said something that stunned the motorcycle guy who seemed to forget about the vendor carts ahead of him until it was too late.

The motorbike crashed into the tea cart catapulting the guy into the tea urns. The falling tea urns were flung by his flying body and crashed into the stacks of food on the second cart. A wave of tea soaked steaming wet food was kicked up and Richard barely had time to spin and tip his head back, before the scalding slurry broke over his back and hat.

The flying slurry carried right through the open chain-link fence to also half cover the man in front of Richard and the military guard who had just finished checking his badge. The guard and the man in line ahead of him howled in pain from the scalding wave and Richard could feel for them as his back also burning from his slurry covered shirt.

The military guard shouted as he jumped forward, shoving the man in front of him out of the way and Richard backpedaled a couple of steps to let the guard pass. The sight of his cowboy hat, no badge, and attempt to move aside in the crowd, made the guard reflexively grab Richard's arm. Richard saw the woman on the bicycle pause,until the motorbike guy, covered from head to toe in food slurry, jumped down off the food cart with an angry wail. She looked straight at Richard for a moment before giving glance at the motorbike guy and disappearing through the opening in the concrete wall.

Reinforcement guards came running out of the gate, and one of them yanked Richards arms behind him to snap handcuffs on him. The entry authorization document, that Richard had been holding, fell out of his hand and he watched the slurry covered document land in a crumpled pile at the base of the fence.

The reinforcement guard clearly did not understand Richard's english as he looked through his satchel and then led him in through the gate. The more Richard tried to direct his attention back to the crumpled authorization document, the rougher the guard handled him. Richard was shoved into the back of a military vehicle that had a metal cage divider between the front and back. The guard got in and ignoring Richard's pleas drove the vehicle in through the opening in the concrete wall and turned to drive off around the airfield.

It was a surprisingly long way around to what Richard guessed was the opposite side of the base where the guard drove towards a metal building with flowing script squiggles on the sign over the doors. The flowing script contrasted with the sternness of prison bars over some of the windows on the side of the building as the guard pulled around the corner the building. The vehicle stopped next to a hose on the building wall and the guard motioned for Richard to get out, with a look of disgust at the mess on Richard's back.

He gingerly took the wallet out of Richard's back pocket and proceeded to hose the food mess off of Richard. Richard tipped his head back so spray from the hose would clean off his hat as well. Thankfully, his satchel was fairly waterproof so his tablet and phone inside were protected, but everywhere else on his body was getting thoroughly soaked.

The guard gave up trying to get any more of the dug in food out of Richard's shirt, hung up the hose, and marched Richard's dripping body around to the front entry of the building and in through the door. Inside in the entry area, the guard said something to the military police looking individuals behind the counter, and Richard chimed in with "speak english?". The military police guys seemed to, at least, recognize the language he was speaking but one could only say "no english" as he was led around to a door leading out of the entry area.

The military police guy stepped out into the entry and his guard escort kept a hold of Richard by the handcuffs from behind, while handing him Richard's wallet. After looking through Richard's wallet and checking his driver's license, he then took Richard satchel and put with his wallet on the entry counter. He patted Richard down from head to toe, checked under Richard's hat, then held the door open for the guard to march him inside.

They escorted him down a cinderblock gray hall that seemed to suck up the feeble light the overhead fluorescent tubes were trying to put out. They passed various office doors on the way and then turned the corner at the end of the hall where a series of barred doors lined the back corridor. The MP guy opened one of the barred doors with a key from his ring and Richard was marched inside by the guard.

The military police guy removed Richard's belt, and then Richard was placed facing the wall while the guard removed the handcuffs from Richard's hands. As they went out locking the barred door behind them, Richard asked, "What happens now?" "No english", was the only reply as their footsteps disappeared back down the hall.

36

Khadija cycled up outside the training hangar, grateful to be back on her home turf. She pulled up and placed her bike in the long bike rack under a roofed shade structure by the side of the hangar. She took a moment in the welcome shade to cool off and to reacquaint herself with the familiar vista of the air base.

On the near side of the military base were the old structures used by the NGO coalition, whose shade she had availed herself of on the ride over from the gate. Many of these were older hangars not in use by the military that Khadija and Miri had included in their request to the generals. As a condition of the continued use of the military airfield after the flood disaster had been dealt with, the generals insisted sufficient supplies be stocked within the country for the future projected disasters that would again require relief efforts. Many of the old hangars were used as staging warehouses for these supplies which could be readily deployed for coalition relief efforts in other countries in the region as long as the stocks were replenished.

Khadija had helped coordinate the installation of the tall palette racks that now filled these old hangars with this stock of supplies. The old buildings and hangar warehouses gave way to a concrete apron of shipping containers on truck trailers and beyond were stacks of shipping containers 4 high covering a football field of area next to a rail siding. Most of these were empty, left over from the influx by rail of disaster aid following the epic flooding that had taken place last year in the region. The lower containers were pre-staged with more tents and heat-resistant food supplies. These containers could ship out on truck trailers or be loaded onto the shipping container carrying train cars. The upper containers were presently empty and would be pulled down and sent out on trains when the warehouse needed a major restocking after a significant disaster or relief supply effort. These could be pulled down by the large container handlers parked near the shipping containers.

Out toward the airfield were new white temporary storage structures that had been erected for pre-staging the most critical relief supplies. This allowed them to be quickly pulled and loaded on emergency relief cargo planes. Beyond those were the white arcs of the temporary airplane hangars which cargo planes could taxi under to park out of the direct sun for loading.

Between the stacks of shipping containers and the white hangar shade structures, were several shipping style containers built into mobile offices with silvery one-way windows on three sides at one end. These were used as supervisor locations when a disaster called for rapidly loading cargo flights. They had insulation, air conditioning, and satellite-based communication connections and could also be deployed in the field as mobile logistic offices. Khadija had her logistics post set up in the farthest mobile unit so she could easily keep an eye out the window on the planes being loaded.

Just beyond her mobile unit started a row of electric bus sized vehicles with their large roof mounted solar arrays unfolded to create an almost continuous shade structure spanning between them. These were mobile medical units but, between deployments, were used as air-conditioned flight crew ready rooms and places for pilots to get some sleep while waiting for their planes to be loaded. Beyond the white arcs of the hangar shade structures, she could see the lattice of taxi ways broken by the three broad runways. In the hazy distance beyond, Khadija could see the newer buildings, hangars and living quarters actively used by the military. The hectic jumble of the city visible beyond the far fence line quickly faded into the rising smoke of cooking fires that could already be seen hanging in the air.

The palpable heat radiating off the corrugated metal roof above the bike racks reminded her how the rusty metal roofs and walls of the hangars absorbed the sun and turned the metal clad hangars and warehouse buildings into ovens for most of the day. This had presented a challenge for those needing to run forklifts and loaders to stock and deploy supplies out in the full sun and in the furnacelike hangars and building warehouse spaces.

Khadija had remote controlled forklifts and loaders brought in that could be run continuously in the heat to load both the shipping containers and planes during the long hours and tight turnaround schedules of relief operations. Being familiar with running loaders and forklifts from her commercial logistics days, she had learned, largely on her own, how to operate the new remotely controlled forklifts and loaders. During the flood disaster, most available men had been deployed out into the field, so she had been drafted to train the local women to run the remote-controlled forklift and loaders at the base.

Since the newer hangar shade structures had been put up, the huge old hangar she was walking along was now little used. When the move to the new remotely controlled forklifts and loaders had been decided, Khadija had requested the use of the air-conditioned hangar and offices for both the training and work operations of the women remote operators that were being recruited. Promises had been made to the base commanders to keep the training and remote-control work areas as women only areas. Khadija, because she had gone to school with some of the base commander's daughters, she was considered an acceptable chaperone by both the base commanders. Their daughters jumped at the chance to sign up and work for an international coalition run by western women.

As she walked from the bike rack around to the front side of the hangar, she saw two of the remote-controlled loaders near the front doors These remotely operated loaders were normally inside being used for training, but the girls liked to park a couple outside as lookouts for any approaching male visitors. There were several construction trucks and service vans parked outside the loading door at the far end of the hangar. A couple of contractors were hanging out by the loading door there, which is probably why the girls had the lookout loaders out front. She could just see a sliver of the male guard shack inside the loading door where all the male contractors needed to check in.

Khadija saw the green power lights on the loaders' camera arrays and waved as she walked by knowing her women would be watching inside. She went in the women's only front entry and the coolness of the office lobby air conditioning felt chilly after the heat outside. Looking over the counter she could just see the entries to briefing and ready rooms that had once been used for military operations. They now held the control station tables and break areas for the remote operator women working there.

She could glimpse through the far doors into the old engine repair bays. There had originally been additional control stations in the former engine repair bays, but Khadija had relocated that group of women into the control tower building to make way for the conveyor system for the upcoming new training.

She chatted with the familiar security "scarves" women who just nodded at her badge, took a cursory look through her large handbag and then had her place her palms on a new surface that had been added into the counter. Satisfied they had a good scan, she was waved through the electronic screening enclosure and escorted over to the stairwell doors. She was told to place her palm on the pad by the stairwell doors and there was an audible click as the doors unlocked.

They went in and Khadija saw that new lights had been installed in the stairwell and a fresh coat of paint had been applied on the walls that now brightened up what had been a dingy decades old utilitarian stair. She started towards the stairs, but the security woman led her around the back side of the stairway over by the emergency exit doors. She was surprised to see a set of new set of elevator doors in the wall where for years nothing had been but a blank wall. The construction team must have been busy while she had been on the far side of the world.

The security woman had her place her hand on the dark pad

next to the doors and they opened to reveal a brand-new, well-lit service elevator.

The security "scarf" said, "Just place your palm on the pad and swipe up to go upstairs or halfway down to come back down".

She let the doors go and as they closed, Khadija looked at the new elevator. There were sets of doors at both ends, so the rear doors must lead out to the aircraft hangar interior. There were no buttons or floor level indicators inside the elevator, just a dark palm pad at each end of the elevator next to the doors. Remembering the security woman's instruction, she placed her palm on the pad and swiped it upwards. The elevator smoothly started upwards and soon the doors opened onto the second level landing of the stairwell.

She went through the second level doors into the darkened former aircraft repair manager's area, where she conducted all her training. She turned on the lights in the darkened space and saw that the regular training control stations had been moved back near the rear of the space and the couches and comfortable break area chairs had been rearranged. Seven of the sleek modern swivel control chairs were now lined up along the window wall looking down into the hangar. The half height wall with upper windows on the hangar side had been replaced with a new floor to ceiling glass wall, so that anyone sitting in the control chairs could see down across the full width of the hangar without having to stand.

These were the latest version of the control chairs with swoopy supports arcing up from behind the head rest to hold the video monitor out over the front of the chair and a cleaner cable arrangement coming down to the VR headset, The footrest with pedals had cleaner lines and the incorporation of the futuristic looking gloves to the styling rod armatures coming out of the seat back at shoulder height gave these control chairs a sleeker look.

She walked back to one of the old control stations and slung her handbag strap over the back of the chair. She took off her head scarf, pulled out her tablet and checked her email. Still radio silence from the "cowboy" engineer on the outline for today's training, the training manual, or confirmation that he would be joining in on the videoconference she had set up for them today. Khadija had picked up Xanthe's disparaging way of refering to the engineer as "that cowboy" and it had stuck.

The training area was a head scarf optional area except when a local military commander or other men were entering the women's only portion building. Her remote operators and the security scarves kept a sharp eye out for men of any sort coming their way that might compromise the fragile independence they maintained at the base.

She took her lunch out of her handbag, put it in the refrigerator, then went over to the wash station counter she used as place to set up tea and coffee. She filled the hot water pot and turned it on to heat. The tea and coffee supplies were running low, so she got some more out of one of the lockers while she waited for the water to boil. She made herself a cup of tea and walked over to the new glass wall to look down in the dimly lit hangar as she sipped.

The cargo plane she had used for training had been pulled out of the hanger. Instead of trailers holding shipping containers for forklift practice there were only the two rusty shipping containers, that she had requested the backs be cut out of, placed up against the engine repair bay loading doors below her. Directly below her, a single conveyor belt emerged from the conveyor filled engine repair bay. It angled down to a large circular rotating catch turntable. Square wood boxes were spaced out on the conveyor belt and several boxes had come off the end of the conveyor and slid down the angled face of the catch carousel. When the conveyor system was in operation, the catch carousel would start rotating like a baggage carousel at an airport baggage claim.

The maneuvering area around the conveyor and catch carousel was defined by orange plastic traffic barriers that marked the location of the walls in the manufacturing facility. A truck width gap in the barriers led to another orange barrier defined room with yellow parking stripes taped down. A further gap led out of the second barriered "room" to the open hangar.

Yellow parking stripes were taped down on the concrete floor to one side outside the room barriers and seven of the new production loaders with their robotic looking upper bodies were parked in the spaces there. On the posts at the back of each parking spaces were charging dock connectors, that the charging connections on the new loaders were "parked" into. Yellow road markings were taped down forming a two-lane road around the outer perimeter of the hanger circling back around to a yellow tape defined loading area in front of the two shipping containers.

Off around the end of the offices, Khadija could just see a couple more of the new robotic loaders as well as the remote forklifts and loaders she had used to do her regular training with. Looking at the other end of the hangar, there was some temporary construction fencing with fabric screening. This separated the training area from the construction staging area that had been set up on that end for construction of the elevator. Construction equipment could just be seen over the top of the fencing stretching between the new elevator and the loading door where the contruction crews entered at the far end of the hangar.

The oversize TV, camera, and microphone she had requested was set up on a rolling cart near where the full height glass wall ended. It was intended for the remote videoconference connection to the missing cowboy who was supposed to be joining them online for the training. The Director of NGO coalition operations at the base had asked to join the video conference to talk to the women for a few minutes at the start of today's training. Khadija got her small laptop computer out of her handbag, connected it to the oversized TV and the camera/mic and went ahead and launched the videoconference.

She was hoping the cowboy engineer, who had been missing in action for a couple of weeks, might join the call early, so they could talk through the day's training before it started. She checked that the videoconference was live, but it was still early and there was no sign of the cowboy on the call.

She thought about the hundreds of women that she and her

lead women had trained since she had first set up operations here. Things were cool enough in the hangar during the mornings so the women could just walk out and watch up close as Khadija and her lead women, demonstrated some of the trickier loading and unloading maneuvers from one of the monitor control stations upstairs. The women could then come up and practice in the air-conditioned comfort of the second floor running the forklifts and loaders around in the hanger below. As the women completed their upstairs training, they would move downstairs to the ready rooms to do their work shifts there.

While a certain amount of work was done daily for general warehouse and shipping container stocking, there were long stretches of free time available to the women until relief supply requests came through. Because the coalition insisted on a controller staffing level that could continue around the clock loading operations in the event of a disaster, there were easily three times the number of fully trained women available than could ever be utilized for the typical half day of warehouse work and shipping container stocking. Usually those who had been recently trained and needed the experience were assigned this half day of work, while veteran women would be in the room to keep an eye on their work and help them out as needed.

Because deliveries and shipments came in waves, there were frequently extended periods, even in full mobilization times, when the women had to wait on planes, trains, and trucks to be ready for loading or unloading. While control stations lined the walls, the entire center of the rooms was filled with couches and comfortable seating for women to use when not actively running remote equipment. With extensive paid time with little to do, laptop computers were given to all the women, and they were encouraged, to enroll in online secondary education and college courses that the coalition would pay for. This was an attractive benefit for young women raised in the repressive patriarchal culture of the region. The first ones breaking down the doors to apply for training positions in the program were the daughters of the commanders and generals who ran the base.

While these military decisionmakers were not happy with setting up a virtual women's learning center within the confines of their base, they also knew many of the political and military leaders, blamed for the lack of governmental response during the flooding disaster, had been booted from their jobs. Those generals and leaders left in power, due in no small measure to the NGO coalition's efforts, saw the value of maintaining the coalition's logistics operation and major storehouse of relief supplies at the base. With the NGO coalition presence benefiting both their country and their continued careers, they endured the learning center aspect as long as the women kept it quiet.

When there were urgent requests, emergency flights, or a full-scale aid mobilization all the women might be working long days to manage the workload. As compensation for the occasional long hours, the coalition would also pay for women, who had worked a year or more as a remote operator, to attend real brick and mortar universities, in or out of country. The condition was the woman would need to work a couple of days every 6 months to keep current on operating the forklifts and loader.

Theses women would also serve as reservists and be available in the event of concurrent major disasters to return as a remote operator for the days or weeks they were needed to load and dispatch the doubly massive aid supplies that would be running through the facility.

Khadija sipped her tea and waited for her women to arrive. This training had many of her most experienced women, and she had no doubt that they would figure this out together, cowboy or no cowboy.

37

The morning had passed sitting around in soaked clothes, before a light blue military uniform appeared at the door with two MPs carrying Richard's satchel and belt. From the number of chevron stripes on the uniform he looked to be a military officer of some sort. He had the MPs open the door and hand Richard back his belt. They waited while Richard got his drying boots from where he had them propped against the wall and then walked him down the hall.

They unlocked a gray metal door, and ushered Richard into a utilitarian conference room with metal chairs and a gray linoleum topped metal table that matched the drab cinderblock décor. The officer motioned for Richard to take a seat and then sat on the opposite side, while the MPs stood to either side just behind Richard.

Because trying to speak to the other guards had provoked a negative reaction, Richard waited silently as the officer opened a file. The officer looked over what was written on a report of some sort inside and then took the satchel from the MPs and pulled Richard's passport and wallet out of the front pocket. The officer took his driver's license out of the wallet and compared the photos from the passport and driver's license with Richard's face. He then flipped through the passport looking at the stamps from Richard's fairly extensive travels.

The officer set the passport and wallet aside and then took everything out of Richard's satchel. In addition to his phone and tablet, were the concrete plant baseball cap, a couple of papers from work, the taxi instructions in the local language and the receipt from checking out of the hotel. He looked through all of those, while keeping an eye on Richard to gauge any reaction he might have.

He handed the phone to Richard and said, "Turn it on and unlock it." Richard immediately perked up and said, "You speak English!" The officer nodded and sternly looked at the phone. Richard unlocked the phone and handed it back to the officer, who went to the call history and noted down recent call numbers as he scrolled down. He then handed Richard the tablet and gave him a look that Richard took the meaning of and turned on and unlocked the tablet. The officer took it back and looked through the programs on the tablet. He launched Richard's email program and handed the tablet back over so that Richard could enter his password. The officer opened a few of the emails and used his phone camera to take pictures of them. He asked a couple of questions about Richard's most recent emails to the coalition consultant and seemed to react oddly to his answers.

The officer sat back for a moment as he considered Richard sitting in front of him, with only the sound of Richard's still damp shirt and jeans dripping onto the floor. The officer finally sat up and said "Alright, my guards seem to think they have caught a spy trying to use a diversion at the gate, to infiltrate our base for espionage purposes. The penalties for spying are severe in our country, so I need you to tell me why you are here."

Richard explained that he was being sent to help with remote operator training at the base for the new robotic loaders his company had developed. He said that the entry authorization document he had been provided had been knocked to the ground by the gate.

He was saved from having to give a fuller explanation, by the officer having the entry guards hunt down, rinse off, and text him a photo of the entry authorization document Richard had dropped outside the fence. A return call from one of the coalition Director's assistants who had turned up a cryptic note from Ahmed that told the director to expect a loader technician to arrive today did the trick.

The officer had Richard pack up his all his stuff from the table while he made some marks in the file. He gave the MPs some instructions and then told Richard the MPs would take him over to old hanger and turn him over to the coalition security, so they could have Ka… somebody sort him out. The officer implied this Ka… person was a troublemaker and was glad to get Richard out of his hair so he could become this Ka… person's problem. The serious expression on the officer's face was broken by the hint of a satisfied grin at this prospect. He gave a dismissive wave, and the MPs ushered Richard out the door.

38

The ding of the elevator doors opening out in the stairwell brought Khadija back to the current days training. A group of head scarved women came in through the doors, many of whom Khadija recognized. She greeted them and pointed them towards the morning tea and coffee. Khadija saw the work lights out in the hangar come on and a couple of her lead women appear that she had drafted to help with the setup of the training area in the hangar.

The hangar training plan and conveyor assembly instructions for the engine bays was the last information that she had received from the cowboy engineer. She had sent a few suggestions for modifications to the plan to provide more clearance, but this was a couple of weeks back before the replies to her emails had suddenly stopped.

While her current group of veteran controllers in the training would not miss the curve, she knew that this would be the point where a misjudgment by future trainees could easily run a loader into the hangar beams. Without word from the cowboy, and needing the road defined for the training, the lead women were out taping down the curve at a location that would provide greater clearance.

Women for the training were both arriving via the elevator and by coming up the old stairs. With the amount of sitting involved with their jobs, Khadija knew some of the arriving women would opt to take the stairs for the exercise anyway. Many of the women, upon arriving for their regular shift on the first floor and finding their schedule open, would take morning walks for exercise out in the hangar while it was still cool. A path around the outer perimeter of the hangar had been kept clear as a sidewalk for use for these morning walks. Fixing the curve clearance also kept this perimeter path clear for use by the regular shift women controllers.

As the time approached for the start of the training, Khadija saw the Director join in on videocall with her camera off. Khadija walked over to the microphone by the oversize TV to let the Director know that she had not yet heard from the engineer and didn't know if he would be joining them. The Director suggested they give the engineer 10 minutes and then they would get started.

Khadija announced to the group they might be starting a little late and with any luck they would have an engineer from the robotic loader company joining them on the TV. She let them know he was a man, but jokingly said he was an infidel from Texas so, they needn't bother with putting their head scarves back on while he was on the call. She asked them to go ahead and roll chairs over from the control tables to gather in front of the oversize TV while they waited.

Khadija checked out the window and the lead women had finished taping the road curve. She could see several women from the regular downstairs shift were now out walking the perimeter with their headscarves down on their shoulders enjoying the relative cool in the hangar.

The face of the Director appeared on the oversize TV to ask the women to take a seat in the chairs. The Director welcomed the gathering and stressed the importance of the remote operator work they would be doing. She said that the "clean cooking stove" units they would be helping distribute was part of the coalition's climate crisis mitigation efforts. The coalition mission was to enable those living in affected areas projected to be impacted by extreme heat and weather events to be able to shelter and continue living in their homes.

The Director stressed the need to keep what they were working on confidential and simply refer to what they were loading as "clean cooking stoves." The Director talked about the ability to continue their educational pursuits in their new remote operator roles during training and once the transition to their new daily work had begun. She ended by saying she had every confidence in the women she saw before her and, smiling ruefully, had every confidence that Khadija would be able to make the morning productive even though the engineer from the Texas robotic loader company looked like he would not be joining them.

Fortunately, the cowboy had shared an animation of how the remotely operated robotic loader and its control chair would work so, Khadija found her copy of the animation in the laptop files and brought it on the oversize TV. The animation started by showing an orbiting view of the control chair with an unclothed generic male figure sitting and strapping into the chair that raised a few titters from the gathered women. The figure placing its arms and hands into the haptic controller armatures and then pulled down the virtual reality headset and slipping the chin strap on.

The video cut to an orbiting view of the new loader with the robotic upper torso. The animation went to split screen with the control chair on one side and the robotic loader on the other. The animation showed how the movements of the person in the controller chair were mimicked by the upper body of the robotic upper body mounted on the back of the loader. As the animation progressed, Khadija explained that the virtual reality or VR headset was counterbalanced by the cable coming down from above. It had to be gently pulled downwards, and how a chinstrap was used to keep the headset in position on the operator's head. The VR headset would show the operator a stereo view from the cameras on the top of the new loaders. The animation showed the operator figure turning its head while wearing the VR headset to either side and up and down, and the cameras on top of the robotic upper bodies of the new loaders following the figure's head motions.

The animation zoomed in on the "arm" armatures extending

from shoulder height mounts attached to the padded chair back section. The armatures led to a padded "elbow" joint and then to the end of the pair of forearm rods where the touch sensitive gloves were. Again, as the animated figure moved his arm and made motions with his fingers, while on the split screen, the arm and fingers of the robotic torso moved in synchronization. The animation moved on to focus on the chair back, that the animated figure was strapped into, to show how it moved as he leaned forward with the robotic torso on the other split screen bending over forward at the same time.

The animated figure demonstrated how the base of the chair could be swiveled around by his feet on the floor, and the split screen image of the loader showed the twist occurring of the robotic upper torso on the new loader. The animation then zoomed in on the footrest with the pedals and the foot operated buttons. It showed how the two pedals controlled the ability of the loader to be driven forward, backward and pivot around on a dime as needed. The pedals could be operated with two feet to maneuver around or one foot like an accelerator pedal for straight driving when the small steering wheel was pivoted into place.

The animation was just starting into the loader deck controls when an urgent sounding announcement came over the PA in the local language. "Forecast calls for rain, forecast calls for rain. Please have all rain covers in place to prevent leakage". The experienced women in front of her pulled up their headscarves and immediately went back over to their old control stations to put away their laptops and take out bits of sewing and tatting to occupy themselves with. Khadija put her headscarf on and looked out the window to be sure the women down in the hangar walking were doing the same as they came back inside. Khadija headed out into the stairwell and flew down the stairs.

As she came out on the first floor she ducked in behind the counter where one of the security women pointed to a monitor showing a military vehicle with three men headed their way. Khadija said thanks and headed into the first of the control station rooms. In the first room all but one of the girls had their headscarves on, all the laptops were already put away and signs of sewing were appearing out of bags.

"Headscarf please" said Khadija as she passed the woman on her way to the control desks monitoring the view from the front remote loaders on sentry duty.

She asked the woman at the control station to zoom in on the vehicle and saw that it had military police markings. She reminded the woman at the station to switch off the monitor once their visitors arrived and was off to check the next room. The next controller station room was a picture of domestic bliss with everyone wearing their headscarves and, in addition to sewing, a couple of women had broken out bags of vegetables ready to start slicing them whenever the men triggering the alert would appear. All laptops and educational materials were put away and it looked like the women were behaving as obedient wives and daughters demurely doing domestic chores in their spare time. She went out and into the engine bay with all the newly installed conveyors where a couple of her lead women were coming in from their taping work.

Khadija said, "Looks like MPs coming. Head back to the control rooms and keep an eye on the new girl's domesticity performance until we find out what is going on."

Khadija went back out into the entry lobby and played with some forms at the far end of counter until the doors opened. Two serious military police officers entered escorting a bedraggled man in jeans with a seriously soiled blue denim shirt. Khadija wondered for a moment who he could be and why they were bringing him here, until she saw the food-stained shirt.

In a flash she realized he was the guy at the gate who had taken the brunt of the tea and food cart tsunami. She looked down and pretended to be working at the logistics counter half hoping he wouldn't recognize her. As a squabble between the security women and the MPs started up, a text came in from the Director. It said the engineer from Texas who they had been expecting to join in on the videocall had somehow turned up here at the base. The text went on to say the director was having some difficulty finding out where the problematic captain had put him.

Khadija texted back to say that their least favorite captain just had the MPs bring their guy in through the women's entry and were dumping him on the security scarves. The Director texted, "Sounds every bit like what the captain would pull to embarrass us. Get our engineer sorted out, and the hangar operations back to normal, while we work on the proper paperwork for him to be on base."

Khadija acknowledged the text and then wrote on one of the warehouse stocking forms, "Tell them he is a loader technician we have been expecting. Have them escort him outside to the loading door construction entry and put him in the loader parts lock up. I'll deal with him from there."

Keeping her head averted to avoid the gazes of the police or the engineer, Khadija casually walked over to the security end of the counter and placed the form there, taking care to catch the eye of the security woman nearest to her. She went back down to the end of the counter and watched as the security women nonchalantly yawned and stretched so her fingers just touched the form allowing her to slide it across under the overhang of the upper counter section to keep it out of sight of the military police. The security woman's eyes widened ever so slightly, and she took the form down and slid it in front of the other security woman searching but not finding any records on the monitor.

The second security woman looked down momentarily at the form and then up the first security woman who made a barely perceptible nod in Khadija's direction. She made an exasperated motion as she pretended to find the guy's records saying it looked like he was some full of himself loader repair guy coming from the land of the great Satan whose records had been buried so that he would be given deserving grief when he arrived. She instructed the MPs to take him around to the loading door being used by the construction workers so they could lock him up until the hangar was clear of women for him to begin his repairs.

The military police headed back out the door and Khadija

checked in with the security "scarves" before they went out to lock the guy away. She poked her head in the control station rooms and told the women there was not going to be an inspection, then went back upstairs to the training space. She told the women that the military police had shown up with their engineer in person downstairs. Just to be safe, she said they would wait for the sunny forecast to come over the PA, and once things got back to normal and she could decide what they would do with him.

She called the Director's office and got her chief of staff on the phone. "Our erstwhile engineer just showed up in person at our door with two MPs. There was an incident with me and a fundamentalist on a motorbike out by the entry gate this morning that resulted in him being covered with projectile food and being hauled off by the military. Looks like they gave him some grief on the military side of the base before they dragged him back over to dump him on the security scarves. We have him in the loader parts lockup for the time being until I can work up a way to sequester him for the training. In addition to a badge and the paperwork to make him legit, I'll also need some guidance from the Director on the ground rules for working with a fox in our proverbial henhouse.

Don't think I don't hear you chuckling. I do not want to hear any rumors about me getting a western guy in trouble, drug across the base by the military, and then locked up until I am ready for him."

39

Ahmed's wife roused him from sleep. He had left his phone out in the living room when he headed to bed and but even across their condo, he could hear the shrill alarm ringing on it. His wife jumped out of bed and was heading out the door saying, "I'm getting the kids," before he was fully aware he needed to get moving.

Hopping out bed, he headed for the living room, slipping on some shoes on the way. He picked up the phone, pushed the button to stop the alarm and asked, "OK, what are we looking at?" A voice on the phone suggested Plan C saying that a man had entered, overcome the condo tower night door attendant, and was now sitting at the desk keeping an eye on all the entry and exit cameras at the desk. "Confirm C, we're moving now," said Ahmed as he shoved his laptop and tablet in his travel bag, grabbed his wallet and a lanyard with card and a key and joined his wife with her travel bag and the kids at the front door.

He connected an earpiece to his phone and heard the voice say that a squad of men were entering the building. The voice suggested they would be at the bottom of all the stairways covering the emergency exits so Plans A and B were not viable. The voice said to expect visitors to come up in the elevator shortly, but Plan C was still viable if they could make it to HVAC room. Ahmed opened the door slowly and glanced down the hall towards the elevator before moving quickly out into the hall. "Plan C" he said to his following family as they passed by the elevators and turned down the far hallway.

They were at the end of the hall, when they heard the ding of an elevator arriving at the floor back around the corner. Ahmed held the card on the lanyard to the sensor on a door marked "Service Personnel Only. It opened and he ushered them inside a dimly lit room filled mostly with large motors running large air handlers for the open common spaces on the floors below. An oversized set of doors on the outside wall were barred with a wood beam. It had safety rope clipped across it with an orange fabric flag that warned of danger of falling when the doors were open. A heavy steel I-beam mounted to the ceiling had a second extendable I-beam just below with a rolling lift point. This I-beam lift arrangement ran the width of the room right up to the center of the outside doors. It was normally used when they needed to haul up replacement motors or heavy equipment parts for the AC air movers from the alley behind the condo tower.

Ahmed turned on the light on his phone and then unscrewed the single light bulb by the door that was dimly lighting the room. Handing the lighted phone to his wife, he removed the bar from the doors and then cracked one of the doors to peek out.

It was a sheer drop right outside the door to the alleyway below, but the alleyway looked clear of any of the incoming squad. He saw a darkly dressed man come out onto the second-floor bridge between the condo tower and the parking garage across the alley. The man held the bridge access door open with his leg as he stretched out to look around. The man stepped back in out of sight, but Ahmed did not hear the door to the bridge close, so the man must be leaning against the open door as he kept watch on the exit.

Ahmed held his finger to his lips as he looked over to his wife and motioned to indicate the squad member below. He opened both of the equipment loading doors quietly until they were both pointing out away perpendicular to the building. The drop to the alley below looked farther than he remembered from the drills, and he reminded himself to have the kids sit down in the basket, so they couldn't see.

He walked back across the room to a large metal enclosure on the opposite wall. He used a key off the lanyard to unlock the padlock and then opened the doors. He let the lift cables running out of the top of the cabinet hang freely from the lifting eye on the beam roller right overhead. One end of the lifting cable was attached to a collapsible work basket and the other end to a large, motorized drum that the lift cable was spooled onto inside the cabinent. He pulled the collapsible work basket off its hooks and let it fall on the floor. He uncoiled a length of cord attached to a lever on the drum out across the floor and left the last of the cord on the floor by the door.

He pushed the industrial looking button on the crane controls by the doors and the lower I-beam started extending out through the door opening. As the I beam travelled out over the alley, the moving lifting eye trolley dragged the work basket towards the doors. It started to rise off the floor as the slack in the lift cable was taken up by the moving trolley on the lower beam. His wife guided it so that it would come to rest against the safety rope. Ahmed paused the I-beam extension, so his wife and kids could clamber into the work basket. He reminded the kids to sit down and then he fully extended the I-beam out over the alley taking up all the lift line slack in the process. The workbasket was now raised a small amount off the floor, and only the straining safety rope held the workbasket back from swinging out over the alley. Ahmed picked the thin cord off the floor and handed the end to his wife to hold tight to as he clambered over the top rail into the suspended basket.

He pulled a utility knife out of a pocket in the basket and reminded everyone to be quiet for the ride as he cut the safety rope. The freed basket suddenly swung out of the doors into the open air above the alley, with an unsettling movement. Looking down in the basket, the kids seemed to be enjoying themselves, but his wife with the cord held in her white knuckled grasp on the top of the basket was definitely not having fun. Once the basket swinging settled down, he nodded at her and while she kept a firm hold on the rail with one hand, she pulled the cord with the other. The cord pulled the release lever on the lift line cable drum, so the drum started to unspool causing the basket with them to descend. The clutch on the drum kicked in to limit the how fast they would descend and the trip down into the dark alley below was silent and surprisingly smooth until they landed softly.

Ahmed had been watching the squad guy on the second level bridge since they had swung out into his view, but he was standing in the bright light inside the door looking away from them towards the street in front of the condos. Putting a finger to his lips as he pulled down on the lift line to lower the collapsible work basket to the ground, he helped the children up, and they all padded quietly across the alley to the grass strip running along the parking garage.

The parking garage was a series of concrete ramps that continuously angled up around a wide central opening running up through the entire structure. They made way their way to the far end where they squeezed through a gap in the shrubbery planted up next to the open sided concrete structure. In this back corner, Ahmed led them to a fenced off storage area at the back of the lowest level.

Going up to a side gate, he again used the key on his lanyard to open the padlock. Gently pushing aside a heavy looking stack of snowplow blades, a space behind was opened up that his family filed inside. The minivan hidden inside was nondescript and more than a little the worse for wear. His wife opened the sliding side door and asked the kids to get in and buckle up while Ahmed made his way around behind the vehicle. Easily sliding a heavy stack of scaffolding bucks aside, and yanking down the paint spotted drop cloth on the back wall of the garage, a large steel plate with a black pad next to it was revealed.

Placing both his palms flat on the plate, the edge of the plate glowed briefly, and the steel plate started to slide open. Ahmed rushed to the front of the minivan to unlatch the gates and push on the tall piles of ice melting pellet bags that hid the minivan. The hidden casters under the bags allowed the bag stacks to pivot around smoothly with the gates clearing a path for the minivan. Taking a quick look to make sure the garage was still clear, Ahmed turned to head for the driver's seat. He could just glimpse the stream of builder cubes forming up under the van as he climbed in and closed the driver's door.

He took out the globe memento from his bag, set it in a cup-holder and opened it to reveal the communicator cube inside. He made a motion with his fingers on the cube and then checked with the security team on the phone as he waited for the native child avatar to fully appear. The security voice gave him the go ahead to proceed with Plan C evacuation as the slight rocking of the minivan settled down after the last of the builder cubes had fastened themselves in position.

"Everyone get ready?" he said, and his wife and kids adopted the ducked down position they had been taught in the drills. The native child image had fully formed so Ahmed said, "Plan C evacuation, execute". The child nodded and smiled as a whooshing noise arose and the minivan lifted slightly upwards and then floated forward across the garage. Ahmed was fastening his own seat belt as the minivan floated towards the curb bounding the grass in the center clearing of the parking garage. Looking up, Ahmed could see a face appear over the railing. It was the squad guy from the second level bridge who had heard the builder cubes' thrust. Ahmed could hear him radioing to others in front of the garage exit to cut off their escape.

The minivan lifted easily over the curb and headed out over the central grass area under the star filled sky framed by the parking garage. With an even louder whoosh, the minivan started flying straight up the central opening in parking garage. Ahmed could see the surprised look on the face of the squad guy as they rocketed up past him and shot out into the night sky above.

A nearby helicopter must have caught sight of them, because it turned and tried to use its light to illuminate the minivan as they started to gather speed over the city. Ahmed told the child projection to keep climbing to avoid that light, and head out west for the time being. As the darkened minivan was lost to sight in the night sky, the searching light from the helicopter probed in vain behind them.

Once the minivan was out of the city, Ahmed asked the child to take them down right over the treetops to and start heading for the rendezvous site. Ahmed learned from the security voice that they were also pulling the other science and modeling teams that were at risk out. Ahmed and his family would join them at the rendezvous site to leave town with them on the electric drive bus they used for secure travel.

Ahmed checked in with the scientist driving the bus who said he and the others were already at the rendezvous site. Ahmed said they were only minutes out and to keep a lookout for a helicopter that was working with the kidnapping squads. Ahmed looked back at his kids who took the idea of a flying minivan in stride and were eagerly looking out the windows. His wife gave him a forced grin, not liking that the minivan was entirely supported by a bunch of builder cubes controlled by the smiling native child image floating between them.

The minivan cleared the tree line and started angling down into the rendezvous site coming up ahead. He asked the native child to land the minivan near the excavated depression that was to be the center reflecting pond so that the headlights could illuminate position 4 and the "pond" area just in front.

The site was supposed to be a new business development, but the construction had been halted so that not much beyond the basic grading and excavation work had been done to the site. The coalition had leased the site as a location to build one of Jamal's logistics control centers, but the increasing threat had forced the planned control centers to be relocated to more remote places. As the minivan touched down, Ahmed turned on the minivan headlights. In the headlights, he could see the bus was aligned on the number 4 painted on the concrete edge of the drop off into the reflecting pool area under construction. The dry reflecting pool area had been dug out and a foot high concrete perimeter wall had been poured, but the bottom of the area was still just gravel.

A searchlight in the sky turned towards the site and Ahmed, seeing the approaching helicopter, told his family to quickly get on the bus and buckle in. He told the voice on the phone that an unfriendly helicopter was headed their way and they were evacuating on the bus ASAP. Ahmed cut the headlights, and blurted to the native child, "Plan C3 express departure is now in effect. Initiate transport platform assembly and don't wait to finish the sides before departing." He grabbed his travel bag and picked up the open globe memento with the flickering native child projection and ran towards the bus.

The faint sound of the approaching helicopter was now drowned out by a continuous series of whooshing sounds starting in front of the bus. A long black platform the width of the bus was assembling itself builder cube by builder cube at lighting speed in the reflecting pool just in front of the bus.

Ahmed jumped up the steps and set the globe with the native child on the level dash area by the scientist driving saying, "Take the bus out on the platform until the child motions for you to stop and then kill all the lights. Hurry, we have company."

As the scientist pulled the bus out onto the platform, walls of builder cubes were already assembling along the sides of the bus at a rapid rate. The native child kept waving its little hand in a forward motion, but as soon as the rear tires of bus were on the platform, Ahmed felt the platform lift and saw it start moving out over the reflecting pool area. The child held up an open palm telling the scientist to finally stop the still rolling bus a moment later and the scientist set the bus parking brake and turned off the headlights.

The side walls of builder cubes were now fully formed, and they were fast sealing in the front, back, and forming a roof of cubes over the bus when the bus started to lift. Ahmed asked the native child to put the cubes in cloaking mode with interior visibility and the solid black of the cube walls around the bus abruptly turned transparent.

The outside darkness was suddenly pierced by the searchlight beam of the approaching helicopter. The light beam swung erratically across the building site, momentarily flashing over the moving bus, before fixing on the minivan. The bus, hidden from its view by the builder cube cloaking, banked up over the far end of the construction site gaining altitude as the helicopter arrived and started circling over the site. Ahmed could see a large van with the squad arrive and the men pile out to check the minivan and cars. He could see the squad fan out to search the construction site before it dwindled in the distance behind the now fast-moving bus. The scientist driving was breathing hard as looked back at Ahmed and the stunned faces behind him.

Ahmed said, "We should be safely on our way to the remote manufacturing facility and village. It will take several hours to get there so make yourselves comfortable. We should be flying level enough now for you to get up and find drinks and snacks in the kitchen area. By the way," said Ahmed turning toward the scientist in the driver's seat, "I think you can turn off the engine now."

This produced a relieved outburst of laughter on the bus as they flew across the night sky.

40

Richard tried and failed to sit comfortably in the fenced parts storage area that the scarf wearing security woman had locked him into. He was inside a large aircraft hangar that the MP's had driven him back across the military airfield to get to. The MP's had seemed to find it amusing to drag him in the front door and cause the female security women some agitation.

One of the scarved guards had found something on the computer that had made the MPs take him back out and around to a loading door entry into the hangar where they again met up with the pair of security women. As they walked past construction equipment in a fenced off area of the large hangar, Richard noticed one of security women had her hand on the taser holstered on her belt. From her looks, it looked like she was more focused on the MPs who were enjoying all the kerfuffle they had caused, than on him.

They arrived at a small fenced off parts lockup under the windows at the front of the hangar where forklift pieces were set on shelves and larger parts were strewn across the floor. One of the security women opened the locked fence gates while Miss Quickdraw McTaser stood by itching for an excuse to light up one of the chuckling MPs. Richard was shoved by the MPs into the storage area who then turned and headed back towards the loading door exit. As lock clicked into place on the closed gates, Miss Quickdraw pulled her taser out to point up to a camera, and then threateningly in his direction. He got the impression if he tried to climb the fence or get out, she would be happy to track him down and vent her bottled up frustrations with the MPs on him.

The security women left through a door, just beyond what looked to be a newly installed elevator in the old, stained wall of the hangar offices and Richard looked out to see where he was. The arch of the hangar swooped up and over to disappear behind the office wall and the tops of giant sliding doors that could be seen on the opposite airfield side of the hangar. Everything lower down was blocked by the screening mesh attached to the construction fencing run that divided off this back section of the hangar. Richard was wondering where he was, but a glimpse of the robotic loaders through a gap in the mesh, told him he must be in the hangar set up for the remote operator training. At least he was in the right place, so hopefully all he had to do was wait for someone to dig him out of this lock up.

As the morning wore on, the hangar started heating up to an uncomfortable degree and the steepening sun rays coming through the hangar windows behind him were fast eating away at what little shade he had remaining. Being in the direct sun was unbearable, so he had to build up a pile of parts to create a small area of shade he could huddle within. Huddled up, wearing his hat and using his satchel to try and fend off the sunlight from the side, he wondered how long it would be before heat exhaustion set in. The only upside of all the heat was his shirt with the concrete plant logo and his jeans were finally drying. The stiffness left by the residue of food was starting to itch making him doubly uncomfortable.

There was little other activity the rest of the morning, and Richard was starting to worry about being baked alive, by the time the two security women came out to unlock the entry. He kept his head tipped forward so his hat would keep his face out of the brutal sun streaming in, slung his satchel over his shoulder and was motioned into the elevator by the security women. Miss McTaser was looking nervously at his hat as he walked by her into the elevator, while the other scarf wearing guard placed a hand on a dark pad to close the doors and start the elevator.

As the elevator doors opened to the upper level the cool inrush of air was a welcome relief after the heat of the hangar. They escorted him down to some doors, held one door open as far as the pulled-out cubicle divider panel on the other side would allow and pointed him into a small cordoned off area. The area was sandwiched between cubicle dividers on one side and floor to ceiling windows looking down into the hangar below on the other. He heard the security women slide the loose cubicle wall into place behind him, sealing him in this impromptu holding area. The high cubicle panels opposite the windows ended in a half cubicle height panel running across to block the end with a counter height surface on top of it. Beyond the counter was another run of high cubical panels that formed a narrow corridor that blocked his view out into the second-floor space.

A table with three monitors was placed in front of the counter height portion of the wall. The monitors were on and showed three views of an area with a line up of the new control chairs. He leaned on the back of the worn office chair and bent over the table for a closer look. On the monitors he could see women having lunch at some tables with monitor arrangements like the one in front of him. More women were gathered on couches and comfortable chairs eating and talking. A few were kneeling on prayer rugs on the far end of the space in prayer. There was something odd about the scene before him, but he couldn't put his finger on what it was.

He swung his satchel up on the table, and was about to take off his hat, when he saw a figure on the monitor striding over to the entry the end of the cubicle cordon. He stood there a moment unsure what to do, when dark eyes framed by styled hair walked into view on the other side of the counter to look sternly at Richard, sizing him up. After a moment Richard started to ask, "Do you speak English…" but she cut him off saying, "So you're the cowboy they had to get rid of on the next flight out and dump unannounced in our neck of the proverbial woods."

There was the flash of a mischievous grin for a second before the façade of sternness closed back in. Richard had the odd feeling he had seen her before, but there was no way he could have missed that hairstyle in a land of headscarves. But, if you covered the stylish hair style in front of him then… "Holy bullpucky it's you from the bike by the gate this morning," Richard blurted out.

The stern look turned to a wry grin as she said, "Yes, I'm Khadija Masood and yes, my run in with the motorbike guy caused you some grief at the gate this morning. But, in all fairness, we didn't know your cowboy derriere was going to be dumped on our doorstep. That rascal of an air force captain, instead of just contacting the coalition Director's office when you showed up, thought he would use you to cause a kerfluffle instead. Having his MPs show up unannounced and drag you in through the women's entry, put all my women through a domestic servitude scramble."

Richard said, "Sorry about the lack of notice but security made me get out of Dodge quick – wait - what's a domestic servitude scramble?"

Khadija replied, "Something that will quickly make you even more unpopular around here if you are ever the cause of it again. This entire hangar is a woman only facility only permitted to exist by the grace of Allah and the pressure the daughters of the generals in command can apply. There are those around the base, including the captain, who would like nothing better than to shut us down and send all these women back home to be subservient wives and daughters. We have worked hard to get things to a point where these women can have some freedom within the confines of this hangar. I will not allow anything, much less the three-ring rodeo of your getting dropped on us out of the blue, to compromise that."

She let that sink in before continuing, "So, this is the deal. You can only be in the building as contractor if you are kept separated from contact with the women working here. You are to remain in this cordoned off area during training where you will be permitted to observe the training remotely on the monitors per the original teleconference rules that had been agreed to. You are to provide feedback and comments only to me and are not to talk to or interact in any way with the women in this training. If you so much as look in the general direction of any of these women in an unprofessional way, I will have the security scarves tase your ass and leave you in the parts lockup until you are roasted beyond recognition. So, no talking, no interaction, and only businesslike facial expressions if we ever bring your image up on the monitor in front of the women. Am I clear?"

Richard nodded and then said "Wait, I'm locked in here?" A disconcertingly satisfied look flashed over her face before she said, "It's better than having a security scarf constantly guarding you with a nervous taser finger."

Richard reluctantly nodded and said, "By the way, I saw that motorbike guy pestering you this morning. I don't know what you said to him, but I was not sorry to see him get his due, even if I was on the receiving end of the blowback."

Khadija smiled before saying, "OK, so now that we have you here, we have some training to do. I haven't heard a peep out of you for weeks, so I hope you've got something in the way of simulations or a training manual to show for all the emails I've sent.

"Emails?" Richard said questioningly then the realization hit him. "So you're the k.masood consultant that's been sending me all the changes. I ran off without my laptop that had the manual on it, but…", Richard paused as he fished in his pocket and found the memory stick, "…I do have the latest simulations that could be loaded into the control chairs."
Richard reached over to set the memory stick on the countertop and said, "Glad to finally meet the coalition consultant I have corresponding with."

As Khadija reached for the memory stick, Richard reflexively lifted his arm back up to shake her hand. Khadija stepped back with an annoyed expression.

"Remember, Absolutely no physical contact! Don't make me put bars across this opening and have to ask what you want brought in for meals."

41

For as bumpy as the day had started off, Khadija thought the training settled down nicely in the afternoon after prayer time. "Cowboy," as Khadija had taken to calling him, actually had a nifty 3D training simulation that her women could use to practice.

Khadija had explained to the women that they would be taking turns in the new control chairs training in a simulation mode for the first couple of days, until they got the hang of operating the virtual robotic loaders. Next week they hoped to get the chairs communicating with the real robotic loaders down in the hangar and start the women practicing with the conveyor and the plywood boxes.

She sat the first seven of the women trainees in the control chairs and got them comfortably strapped in, with the VR headset on and then launched the 3D step by step training. Khadija watching on the monitors behind the chairs could see the women mimic the step-by-step motions of the small guide 3D animation movement by moving their arms and hands inside the haptic gloves and watching through the VR headset the realistically rendered robotic 3D arms and hands match their movements in the simulation. The haptic gloves allowed them to feel when they touched objects in the 3D training simulations, pick them up, and load them onto the simulated loader bed. The other women walked behind the control chairs watching the monitors suspended out over the front of the chairs to get feel for what the simulation training involved, until it was their turn to take over a chair. And so, the afternoon went with each of the women getting a couple of turns at the control chair and completing the first two training scenarios.

At the end of the day, one of the security scarves came into the space and handed Khadija a large envelope with the cowboy's name on it. Khadija took the envelope and peeked inside, as the second security scarf appeared, got a nod from her, and started to unlock the cubicle panel by the exit door.

Khadija went around to the counter opening and said, "Hey cowboy, the chief of staff's car is out front waiting for you, and he has sent your paperwork up."

She reached over and dropped the envelope onto the table in front of him saying, "Inside is a temporary badge and authorization paperwork to make you a legit contractor here. Put the lanyard with the badge on and make sure you carry the papers around with you while on the base."

She saw the security scarves pivot the end cubicle panel open so the cowboy could be herded back into the stairwell and said, "Well, as it's said, all's well that end's better, so you better get your derriere moving and not keep the chief waiting."

As he was ushered out the door, she turned back to her women and the training. Looking at the sophisticated animations and 3D virtual environments up on the monitors as she walked along behind the control chairs, and saw that the women were learning quickly. She was impressed that the cowboy could produce this level of work and, for a moment, considered that she might have to revise her opinion of him. She shook that thought out of her head, as the last of the women finished their second simulation tutorial. She gathered the women to get their feedback on the tutorials so far and set a staggered arrival schedule for the next day. She made sure all the women knew how to how to power up the chairs and boot up tutorial scenarios three and four before letting them go for the day.

When the last of the women had left, she strapped herself into the first controller chair, launched the first tutorial scenario and strapped on the VR headset. She wanted to check through these latest versions of the simulations, to be sure all the changes she had requested were incorporated, before heading back to the barrack dorms where she was living. The simulations turned out to have all the changes and other improvements that she had asked for neatly incorporated.

She still felt an echo of the resentment that had built up for the cowboy for not responding to her recent emails, not sending the info on the tutorials in advance that he had promised and being dumped on her doorstep in the most disruptive manner possible. He had better have good reasons for all this. If not, well, she had him as a literal captive for the coming days and could dole out the appropriate grief as needed.

42

The satellite tech was comparing methane readouts from the previous day when the monitor to his left with a live feed from the satellite momentarily flashed a deep green. Puzzled, he rolled his chair down to that section of the table and pulled up the latest readings from the satellite sensors. All the sensors appeared to be operating nominally, and as the satellite was now travelling back out over the open ocean, he sent a request for a full sensor check up to the satellite to have it do a once over on its own systems. A deep green flash in that location had to mean something was glitching in their new analysis program.

Any glitch like this could undermine the broader credibility of the satellite's data, so the tech wanted the glitch tracked down and fixed as quickly as possible. The satellite had the latest in spectrographic sensors, designed to finely analyze the air quality and gaseous mixture content of the atmosphere the satellite was looking down through at each moment of its orbital travel.

The satellite had been launched so it orbited north to south, and the slight east to west offset of each orbit allowed for a slight overlap in sensor coverage at the widest equatorial point of flight. The satellite could pick out everything from methane leaks and industrial smokestack carbon emissions to monitoring melting permafrost outgassing.

The communication of all this gaseous data to the ground now took advantage of the constellation of communication satellites it now orbited among. Instead of having to sort and save the relevant data on the satellite to only download the data when in range of a normal ground receiving station, using communication between satellites made it so cheap that the full deluge of data was just sent back to the ground in an ongoing basis.

The ground computers had areas of interest geofenced so that only the data from those areas was saved out of this uninterrupted data download. The software designers had added bright colors to represent the various gases of concern overlaid on the ever-scrolling view passing beneath the satellite to make identification easier for the analysts. The neon coloration of carbon, methane, and other harmful emissions contrasted with the green tint that had recently been added to finely monitor oxygen content.

Massive tree plantings were being funded, and new direct air capture facilities were being piloted to pull and sequester carbon out of the air. The governments and entities paying for them wanted detailed independent feedback that the carbon they were paying to have removed with these and other methods, was meeting the levels advertised.

The satellite could show the difference between the level of carbon removal by mature forests and newly planted saplings on logged terrain. It could also compare the amount of carbon in the air being drawn into the front of a direct air capture plant and compare it with the oxygen rich air flowing out the back once the carbon was removed. Even with the biggest of the direct air capture facilities, the amount of change in oxygen level only showed up in the displays as a tiny tinge of green. The oxygen rich air created by mature forests absorbing carbon in peak growth months would barely achieve medium green plumes on the displays.

The tech searched the buffer data and found the abrupt shift in color to dark green along a ridge line in a place that just didn't fit. The tech looked up at the monitor as the beep indicated the satellite sensor check was completed. The report indicated everything in the satellite hardware was operating normally.

He saved the data from that dark green section of the overflight and passed it on to the software folks in a bug report. In case the bug might show up again in future orbits, the tech geofenced a wide perimeter around the remote area, so its data would be saved. That way he could monitor the area for the recurring error until the software geeks could get this latest bug worked out.

43

Richard had slept on one of the hospital beds that were in the back of the bus vehicle that the chief of staff had dropped him off at last night. He got up, put on his jeans and T-shirt, but left the concrete plant logo shirt that had caught most of the food tsunami on the floor.

Recreational vehicle type slide outs made the bed area at the back wide enough for two beds with an aisle left between them. The bus was clearly set up for medical aid with hospital like monitors on the walls above the beds, hooks for IV bags and oxygen type ports between the beds. Richard walked out in the main area where additional slide outs made room for the desks and examination tables along the outer walls.

On the drive over the chief of staff had said they needed to keep Richard within the confines of the coalition base for his security so the medical support vehicle would serve as his living quarters while he was with them. He had been handed a bag with drinks and snacks that was sitting out on one of the examination tables.

Richard went over to look in the bag, yawning as he opened it. He was considering whether a warm cola or just a bottle of warm water was the least offensive way to start the morning, when he noticed a piece of cardboard pinned to the windshield under the wiper. He walked up front so he could read the message through the glass in bold marker that said, "Coffee in logistics container" with an arrow pointing back towards the warehouse. Richard yawned again and thought that sounded better than a warm cola, so he put his boots on, grabbed his hat and satchel and headed out.

The muggy heat outside was already oppressive as he walked along the shady side of the handful of bus vehicles parked near his. He was used to heat from living in Austin, but it never came with this amount of humidity. He soon left the shade of the bus solar panel arrays and saw the words "Mobile Logistics" on the first of the shipping container-like work units he came to.

The modified shipping container also had an overhanging roof of solar panels that kept the corrugated metal sides of the container shaded. There was mirror tinting on the windows at the one end so he could only see his rumpled reflection as he walked around the far side to where the entry door was located. A fabric tote bag with what looked like plastic food containers was sitting by the entry door.

Before he could try the handle, the door was popped open by someone hanging back in the interior shadows. Richard stood there a few moments squinting into the dark interior before a familiar voice snapped, "Well grab that bag and get in here before anyone sees you or me without my headscarf! I need to get back on my call."

Richard picked up the tote bag and stepped quickly into the cool interior. He could see the sunlit view out of the windowed end of the mobile logistics unit that allowed a view from the warehouse on one side, all the way out to the shade structure hangars by the taxiway out the other side. It took a moment for his eyes to adjust from the brightness outside to see the Ka…. woman, sitting in a chair in the darkened back half of the unit.

She pointed towards a single serving coffee brewer in the kitchenette area and went back to her laptop that had some video conference in process. Richard set the bag on the kitchenette counter and found the makings to start a cup of coffee brewing. As he waited for the coffee, he looked at the interior of the logistics unit.

The front of the unit had a couple of desks with multiple monitor set ups positioned by the large windows that wrapped around that end. The back of the modified shipping container was totally enclosed without windows. Beyond the kitchenette, the rear floor transitioned to carpet with a couch and two comfortable chairs filling the space. The back of the unit did not have any windows, but two oversized monitors mounted on the walls above the couch on one side and the chairs on the opposite side were turned on and showed camera views from outside, so it was like having windows there.

The monitor on the door side looked towards the warehouse while the monitor on the opposite side looked out towards the hangar shade structures and runways. A couple of divider drapes were gathered up against the side walls suspended from a ceiling track. They looked like they could be pulled across to separate off the kitchenette and rear lounge area from the front work area.

The smell of coffee seemed heavenly as it streamed down into the cup. On the end of the couch next to the kitchenette was a large handbag. It had a travel tag with names written in both the flowing script of the local language and english. He could see the name K h a d i j a spelled out on the tag, so he at least he now knew what the Ka... woman's first name was. The coffee finished brewing, so Richard carefully took the full cup and sat in the other chair.

The video conference on her laptop sounded like it was being conducted in english, so it was probably coalition related. He couldn't make out what was being said in the video conference, so he sipped his coffee and looked at the view shown on oversized monitor opposite him above the couch. he view, shown in this direction, looked out past the bus vehicles he was calling home, and the white shade structure hangars on the coalition side of the airfield to the runways of the airfield. On the far side of the runways and taxiways, the only visible activity was a fuel truck that appeared to be refueling a military plane in front of more modern buildings and hangars. He watched as a tiny figure in the distance unhooked and stowed the fuel hose.

The fuel truck was starting to drive off beyond the view of the monitor as the video conference ended. The Ka… woman - K h a d i j a - finished typing in notes, before looking over at him. She sized him up for a moment before saying, "There's breakfast in the delivery bag you brought in, so go ahead and dig in. I still need to make a few calls, but then we need to go through all the balls that you dropped while they were kicking you out of the country."

Richard was about to object, but again saw the flicker of a mischievous grin, so decided silence and breakfast was the better course. He was starving but steeled himself to eat whatever spicy food might be considered breakfast around here as he headed over to the counter. As Richard opened the food containers, he was pleasantly surprised to find familiar breakfast fare inside. He looked back towards Khadija to ask if she wanted any food, but she was looking down at her laptop while talking in the local language to someone on the earpiece connected to her phone. He served food for himself, brewed another cup of coffee, and sat back down in the comfortable chair to dig in.

She finished her calls and took her cup over to the kitchenette to make a plate for herself and get another cup of tea. Richard finished eating quietly, not sure what to say, as she was sitting back in her chair. The silence stretched to an uncomfortable length as she sat watching him while silently eating her breakfast. Her stern look was momentarily broken by the mischievous grin as she said, "Alright, I guess I want to hear what bad things you did to get booted overseas only to have your karmic comeuppance catch up with you out at the gate."

Richard smiled and related his escape from the concrete plant and travels leading to yesterday's run in with the base guards and air force captain. She slowly sipped her tea as he told the tale of his and Sam's escape. She sat, lost in thought for a moment after he finished.

She then said, "OK, I guess I need to cut you some slack, if you were actually dodging guys with guns. I'm going to have you monitor today's training from here in the logistics unit. With the women just doing tutorial simulations in the control chairs, there won't be a need for you to be at the hangar. We'll get you put back in your prison cell there when we have the women take your robo-loaders out on your little go kart training course.

Training aside, there is a lineup of folks who need decisions on everything from facility set up to loading and shipping planning for the "clean cooking stove" project. So, lets put away the breakfast dishes and you warm up your coffee while I get things set up so we can monitor the training from here and then let's start working through the backlog."

Khadija asked Richard to bring his tablet and went down to the one of control tables at the front of the unit. She brought up the same three views on the monitors that Richard had watched the previous day and then asked him to sit at the desk. It was still early, so the monitors showing the training space only showed one woman. Khadija made a call, and Richard could see the woman shown on the monitor answer her phone. They talked for a moment in the local language and then Khadija hung up.

"Just needed to check in with my lead woman for the morning. She will see that those arriving in staggered shifts this morning are set to run the virtual tutorials. I also asked her to remind the others that they will be on camera being observed by you during the day for those who want to keep their headscarves on. OK, let's get you back in touch with the outside world" she said bringing her handbag down and sitting at the other control desk across from him.

She pulled a satellite phone out of her bag, turned it on and showed him the numbers for her, the director, and her chief of staff. For security reasons, he was not to call or text any work associates but could use it for talking with personal friends or family as long as he did not discuss his location. She then guided him on how to connect his tablet to the satellite uplink Wi-Fi in the mobile unit.

She said, "You are only to communicate back to your office and friends via email or video conferences with your camera turned off. Whenever communicating do not give any indication that you are here at this base. We want to keep your trigger-happy fans from getting wind of you being here."

She then shifted subjects saying, "I stayed and ran through the first four simulations last night, and have some questions and suggestions ..." Sitting across from him with her laptop, she dove into her notes and quizzed Richard about the overall training picture. As she questioned Richard, Khadija watched the first shift of training women get their tea and then strap in to run their simulations.

After Richard had run through what he could piece together from the notes for the training manual off his tablet, he apologized that the radio silence restrictions had prevented him from sending the draft training manual ahead of time. He promised that her further training questions would be answered whenever he could get his laptop out of the safe in Texas and sent to him. She had already given him a bunch of changes that would need to be made, so he wasn't sure how helpful the manual would be going forward except as a starting point to edit and refine.

By mid-morning, they had moved back to the comfortable chairs in the back so that Khadija could replace the view of the runways on the oversized monitor with his design plans for the control chair arenas. She had him talk through the functioning of the facility and said she had a few suggestions but suggested they get in a lunch order before they got into that.

She bought up a menu from the coalition commissary, had him choose some items, and digitally placed their order. She asked Richard to set the bag of empty reusable containers from breakfast together to put outside the door while she found her marked-up version of the facility plan. Khadija had him wait a moment before going out the door while she checked the monitor to be sure that there were no military or contractors in view on the warehouse side of the mobile unit to see him.

Khadija explained that, while the coalition didn't really care, it was important to maintain at least the appearance of separation of the sexes in her case with the military patriarchy that ran the base. She did not want to give those running the base, like the captain that had dumped Richard on them, any reason to further resent her or her influence with the generals. But there was work to be done so norms had to be bent so she could have his undivided attention until their collective projects were back on track.

"Speaking of work", she said bringing up a version of the control chair facility plan covered in red markings, let's talk about fitting out this space.

They had only gotten through discussing a few of the markups when the sound of a vehicle pulling up outside could be heard. Khadija looked at the monitor behind her to see the coalition commissary delivery van outside and the guy getting out to drop a tote bag with their lunch by the door. He carried the tote bag of empty containers back to the van, got in, and her phone beeped with text saying the food had been delivered. The van was off soon out of sight on its way around the front of the warehouse, so Richard stepped out to snag the bag.

As they sat down with the warm food, Richard said, "OK, your turn. Tell me how you came to be working here and involved with remotely operated lifts and loaders."

Khadija told about getting involved with the coalition during the flooding disaster in the country. She outlined her and Miri's efforts to get permission to use the military bases and to get the disaster relief supplies distributed to places impacted by the flooding. She talked about the decision that allowed the coalition to continue to use the base and how, with all the men mobilized to rebuild the country, she had developed the remote operator program using local women to continue the ongoing relief logistics efforts and warehouse stocking.

Due to security concerns, she too was being asked to live within the protective confines of the base. She described living in a former barracks that served as dormitories for the women who lived on base during the week and traveled back to their homes on the weekends. She said the dorms were noisy and crowded, so she took advantage of her access to the logistics mobile unit, in the mornings and evenings, and only returned to the dorm to sleep.

They spent the afternoon through her notes on the facility design until she announced it was time for her to head back over to the hangar to brief her lead women on the program for the next day. She said she had an evening meeting, so he was on his own for dinner, but he could use the mobile unit.

She gave him the passcode for the door, then packed up her laptop and put on her headscarf. She then walked over to the front windows to look out and make sure the coast was clear before slinging the strap of her large handbag over her head. She said she would check in with him over the phone if anything came up and headed out the door.

He took a drink and his tablet and headed back to the couch to get online. As he sat, Khadija was still in view on the oversized monitor cycling off towards the hangar. He couldn't quite bring himself to start anything right away as he sat distracted, watching her disappear in the distance.

44

Xanthe and her organizers were bounced around as the van negotiated its way along the rutted road to their next village stop. The road was too rough for Xanthe to get any reading done, so she could only look out over the dry scrub terrain passing by and think of the weeks of effort that had brought her here.

The community stove cube trials had been completed with positive feedback and those communities were now signing up residents for future deliveries of stove cubes to their communities. Xanthe was now working long weeks to expand the community organizer outreach teams needed to obtain the community buy in needed for widespread distribution of the stove cubes. They needed to exponentially grow the numbers of teams, so Xanthe was constantly working with new organizer recruits to train them.

The van reached the village where three local leaders, who had the trust of the community, and two additional trusted community members were waiting to be picked up. The community members were toting a couple of metal pans and jugs of water with them that they stowed in the back of the van. The community leader directed the van driver up a road past the local community center and out to a secluded spot surrounded by scrub trees where they would set up.

When they arrived, Xanthe asked the community leaders to select a location in the secluded grove to place the relief tent while her organizers worked with the community members to pull the tent out from the back of the van. Xanthe watched as the organizers had the community members bring the tent over to the selected location, pull it out of its storage bag. Because the stove cube tech was so unexplainable, Xanthe had found it best to have everything in the set up examined like a magic trick to counter any doubt. The community leaders were asked to examine the tent carefully as it was rolled out and the community members followed the step by step illustrated instructions on the storage bag flap to get the tent set up. Soon the white relief structure was standing in place with the community leaders certain that it was just a tent.

The leaders and the community members were then asked to take the stove cube along with its base box and duct section and examine them closely outside before carrying them into the tent. A set of camp chairs, a camp table, and a case of glassware were also pulled out and examined, before everything was carried through the screened in front canopy area and into the tent interior.

The relief tent structure had a domed center family gathering area flanked by two side area sections that each could sleep up to three. Following the organizers direction, the community members positioned the dark base unit near the rear wall of the tent and placed the stove cube with the opening facing into the tent on the base unit. There was an expression of mild surprise as the magnetic force snapped the stove cube into place on the base unit. The duct was magnetically snapped into place around the rear stove cube opening and a square flap the size of the duct in the wall of the tent was unzipped to leave a square opening to the outside. The entire stove cube assembly was then scooted across so the duct slid out the tight-fitting flap opening to protrude just outside the tent.

Xanthe explained that the stove cubes could be installed in homes, by running the duct out a window and filling in the side gaps with expandable insulated fillers much like a window air conditioner. The camp chairs were set up and then the community members were asked to get their pans and jugs of water.

Two of the pans were set on the "stove" top, and the community members filled them with water from the jugs. One of the organizers brought in the thermometer from the tree branch and hung in the tent which still had all its windows zipped up and was getting uncomfortably hot in the midday sun. Xanthe pointed to the rising thermometer needle to show how the tent in full sun was getting hotter by the moment.

They watched as Xanthe took out a slate looking tablet with one hand and then, using her finger, drew around the bottom of the pans to define glowing areas with her other. She showed the leaders as she ran her finger up on the two red lines that appeared on the tablet, and the areas under the pans started to glow red. Before long, the water in the pans began to boil, and Xanthe pointed again to the thermometer which was reaching an even higher temperature with the steam coming off the boiling water, making the tent interior unbearably hot.

The leaders and community members were then asked to watch as Xanthe moved her finger up the other colored control lines on the dark tablet turning on the air filtration, room cooling, and refrigeration functions of the "stove" cube. The leader and community members were asked to feel the fresh cool air now flowing out of the tapered front opening of the cube from the outside duct and note the reading on the thermometer as the tent started to cool to a more livable temperature.

The leaders and community members were asked to open the base unit door to feel the cold underside of the cube cooling the area inside the base unit down to refrigeration temperatures and to place a second thermometer inside. Xanthe had a community member lift one of the pans off the stove and she immediately placed her hand on the surface where the red glow was fading. She pointed out the cube heated the pan itself and that the cube surface under the pan was only left warm to the touch.

The organizers unpacked a tray with glasses, two large clear pitchers, a couple of teacups, and a clear funnel with a clear plastic hose run off it and set them on the camp table. A community member was told to take out the packet of brightly colored spice powder they had been asked to bring, walk outside, and throw it as hard as they could into the duct opening.

Xanthe had the community leaders and members lean forward in their chairs to look through the front tapered opening through which the sunlit tree trunks outside could be seen. The body of the community member could be momentarily glimpsed followed by an arm movement and suddenly the entire duct opening was filled with the brightly colored spice powder. Even though the air conditioning function was drawing outside air in through the duct, the spice powder was somehow prevented from being drawn in through the center opening of the stove cube. The powder soon settled revealing the surprised face of the community member looking in through the duct. Despite hurling the powder forcefully, only a dusting of the brightly colored powder had made it inside the cube opening. It had been immediately drawn down to deposit onto the bottom face of the short internal tunnel that ran through the stove cube. None of the colored powder had made it into the tent.

Xanthe explained that the air filtration function could not only prevent blowing dirt, sand, and insects from entering but could filter out wildfire smoke and other air pollutants of concern. Xanthe knew that, once the air filtration was activated, it would also constantly remove carbon dioxide and other greenhouse gases as well, but improving interior air quality was the feature that would most benefit the villagers.

She asked the leaders to continue to look from their bent over positions as she moved her finger over another line on the tablet. On the upper face of the short tunnel the leaders watched a glowing oval with a color gradient that ran from blue at the near end to red at the far end. A community member was given a teacup, that Xanthe added a tea bag to and was asked to reach down inside the square tunnel to place the cup up to the glowing red end of the oval. As the cup was raised to touch the far underside face, a stream of water could be heard running into the cup. When the sound of the stream cut off, the community member pulled out a steaming cup and showed the leaders the teabag starting to steep in the hot water.

The other community member was given one of the clear glasses to hold under the blue end of the glowing oval in the opening. The leaders watched as it filled only about a quarter of the way up, before the glowing oval started flashing along with the blue line on the control tablet. Xanthe explained that the water they saw in the teacup and glass had been extracted by the stove cube from the humidity in the outside air since they had been running the air filtration. They had only been running the water condensing functions for under an hour, so the "stove" cube had only condensed and stored a small amount of water in that time. She asked the community members to take a sip of their hot tea and chilled water, and got their nod that things tasted fine, before asking them to set their cup and glass back on the tray.

Xanthe asked one of the community members to bring the jug they had brought full of muddy brown liquid and fill one of the clear glass pitchers with it. The water they poured in the pitcher was an unhealthy-looking brown color taken from the most polluted water source in the local area. Xanthe asked them to take out the other pollutant and poisonous samples they were asked to bring and add them into the brown water in the pitcher. The community members poured in a variety of additives from motor oil to colored antifreeze, to a yellowish-colored liquid that Xanthe did not ask about. When the pitcher, now with a floating oily foam on top, was full, Xanthe asked one of the community members to scoot a chair up next to the opening in the cube and sit. He was handed an empty glass pitcher and the funnel with the clear hose.

Xanthe asked that the end of the hose be placed into the pitcher and the pitcher set on the tent floor in front of the re-frigerated base. She asked that the funnel be held up against the flashing blue end of the oval as she went over to the cube. The first pan was still boiling away, as the leaders watched Xanthe move her finger on a blue line on the control slate. She then moved her finger across the cube's top surface in an irregular shape skirting the boiling pan creating a glowing blue outline.

As her finger came back around to touch the starting point, the drawn outline filled in with glowing blue. She asked for the other community member to take the pollution filled pitcher and pour it into the center of the glowing blue shape. The curdled oily foam plopped down onto the blue surface before the polluted water started pouring out of the pitcher. The brown liquid spread quickly out to fill the blue glowing shape but was held in place from running beyond by some invisible force at the outer edge. The community member, fascinated by this boundary effect, started pouring faster until the water pool held back at the boundary edge was nearly a finger thickness high.

A flow of water began to come out into the funnel and down the clear tube to start filling the empty pitcher on the tent floor. While the water being poured out of the pitcher above was an opaque oily brown, the water flowing down into the pitcher below was perfectly clear. With all the contaminated water finally poured out above, it took a minute before the stream of water flowing out into the pitcher below stopped. The blue area on the top surface was left nearly obscured by the dry powdery pollutants that had been filtered out in the process. Xanthe moved her finger on the control slate to end the water purification process and had the community member take the funnel and pitcher of clear water back over to the tray.

Xanthe pointed to the powdery substance on the top surface of the stove cube which was slowly working its way over the front edge, moving down the side tapered faces, and heading into the bottom of the center opening. The leaders watched as it migrated to form a brown coating that covered over the dusting of brightly colored powder across the bottom.

Xanthe opened the base refrigerator door and took out the thermometer which was now showing a temperature suitable for most food refrigeration. She also pointed to the thermometer hung from the tent to show how the cool air flowing from outside had now reduced the temperature inside the tent to a comfortable level.

The organizers brought in two easels, to set up to either side of the stove cube. They placed set a of printed maps of the locality on one, and a graphic chart showing the projected increase in heat for the locality over the coming years on the other. Even with the light coming through the white tent fabric, the charts were a little difficult to see in the dimness of the interior.

Xanthe said "Oh, and one more function that comes in handy." They watched her run her finger up the white line on the tablet causing the sides of the "stove" cube to glow a bright white. The light filled the interior of the tent making the map and chart on the easel clearly readable.

The organizer that spoke the local language gave some background on the NGO coalition and the communities' experience collaborating with them during drought induced famine periods when food aid had been a primary concern. The organizer pointed to the easel with the chart showing the increasing temperature projections for the region in coming years. The second organizer then flipped through the map cards starting with the current year map colored mostly comfortable green to future date maps where the yellow, oranges and finally patches of deadly red heat in the locality were becoming the norm. The organizer explained the red indicated periods of days to a week or more where the combination of temperature and humidity could make their region unlivable without some means of cooling to prevent death from overheating.

Xanthe said the coalition was asking community leaders and community members who were widely trusted, to try out the "stove" cubes in their homes for a couple of months first. She said, if they gave their approval, then the coalition would be willing to "gift" a stove cube to everyone in their village that would allow them to shelter in place through the coming heat and extreme weather.

Xanthe and her organizers stepped out of the tent to let the leaders discuss this offer that the NGO coalition was making to all the villages and towns in this affected region. Xanthe gave the organizers feedback on their presentation, and they discussed plans for the organizers to be issued stove cubes so they could take the presentation and coalition offer to other villages and towns in the region.

Xanthe would move on to training additional organizers fluent in the languages to rapidly expand the outreach. She knew they only had a few months to obtain buy in from thousands of community leaders representing millions to allow for time for stove cubes to be put in their hands ahead of the projected heat waves and extreme weather that would be coming. Xanthe also knew there were other features to the stove cubes that the coalition wanted to keep concealed for the moment, but in time the need for revealing those would likely come.

After a half hour of discussion, the community leaders invited them back into the cool of the tent. They said they would gladly accept the coalition offer to try the stove cubes and looked forward to collaborating with her community organizers on further outreach to their communities once they approved the stove cube's use.

Xanthe asked the community members to pour some water into each of the glasses from the filtered water pitcher and hand them around to everyone. She concluded the meeting by raising a glass to toast to the future wellbeing of the village in the challenging years to come and let them drink the water from their "gift" to come.

45

Khadija walked behind the control chairs in the hangar training space watching the women negotiating the simulated route they would take with their loaders on the screens above each chair. Most of the women now had the hang of stacking and driving the virtual robotic loaders, so Khadija had less coaching to do these days.

These days… She thought back to mornings and evenings the past week in the mobile logistics unit spent with the "cowboy" reviewing the manufacturing facility plans and set up logistics. The Director had urged her to push Richard a bit to get decisions made so that all the facility support items could be ordered and fabricated. Thankfully, the women Khadija had selected for in this training contingent were some of the most experienced remote loaders and forklift operators on the base, leaving Khadija time to work through the backlog of facility set up and logistics decisions needed with the cowboy.

It was proving fast to train this group, who were already careful in their movements and safe in their driving. They already knew the consequences of running a forklift into a towering rack of palettes or the damage even the slightest bump of loader into the aluminum fuselage of a cargo plane could do. They had run all the 3D training simulations and picked up the operation of the robotic loader quickly, with little supervision needed early on.

The new control chairs were a significant improvement over the basic joystick controls the women used for remote operations at the base. The gloves and arm rods would provide resistive and touch feedback whenever the simulated robotic hands met the box shapes that they were now loading. The ability to reach out with your own hands, feel the touch feedback from the haptic gloves and rod arms made it a very natural process to use. The women were already comfortable enough with the control chair functions, and bored enough with the simpleness of the tasks, that they had fallen into the kind of ongoing conversation that they would have when they were working their old-style loader shifts.

They had completed all the tutorials and were now doing virtual loading and shipping runs in the simulator program. Khadija was spending today at the hangar doing last minute coaching to get all the women up to a proficiency level to operate the real loaders. She was determined to get the last of the women's check out runs completed before the midafternoon end of shift, so they would be ready to start operating the real loaders on Monday.

It was Friday, and today's training shifts would end early in the afternoon for the religious observance. Many of the women staying in the dormitory during the week, used the early ending workday to travel home to their families for the weekend. Khadija would wander behind the line of control chairs and watch each woman's progress on the control chair monitors. She would coach and occasionally chime in to playfully counter the teasing she was getting from having what they were calling her "mail order cowboy" delivered.

Her "cowboy" was proving to be much more interesting than she had expected and the ease and familiarity their planning sessions had taken on had started to produce a warm fuzzy feeling that ... She shook off the thought as she saw one the women lined up askew for her virtual container approach and stepped up to suggest rerunning the approach with a wider turn radius.

As the last of the women successfully completed their virtual loader runs, Khadija wished them a good weekend as they put on their headscarves and departed.

Khadija received a text from the Director that that the communicator cubes needed to connect the robotic loaders to the control chairs would be delivered before training started on Monday. The text included a brief mention about some of the cowboy's stuff from back home also catching up with him soon. She called Richard to tell him about the text and to say that they had wrapped up the training at the hangar for the day. Khadija resisted the urge to tell him she would be coming right back over to the logistics unit. Instead told him she was going to stay and run through a few of the updated simulations to make sure all the changes she had asked for were workable.

She found herself babbling on with cowboy about having them having run out of commissary menu items to try for dinner as an excuse to stay on the phone. Cowboy wasn't sure what he wanted so she said, "OK, snooty boots, just pick out something and call me back after 5:00 so I can get the order in," and ended the call.

If the simple opportunity to talk with a western educated man turned her from a professional trainer and logistics expert into a babbling fool, there was something wrong. She admonished herself for being so silly as she strapped into a control chair and launched the updated conveyor room simulation.

The simulation started with four robotic loaders in position in the conveyor room by the conveyor belt, a fifth loader by the catch carousel, one loader fully stacked out in the cooling room, and one empty loader in the "on-deck" parking space in the cooling room. Her virtual robotic loader started in the on-deck parking space.

When a loader came out through the virtual raised door, she would drive into the conveyor room to the catch carousel position. She would pick up stove cubes that the loaders by the conveyor missed and had slid down onto the carousel. When one of the loaders next to the conveyor was full, it would drive out of the room, and she would maneuver around to park in its vacated spot alongside the conveyor. She picked cubes up as they passed by on the conveyor and stacked them in layers on the loader bed. She could feel the magnetic snap as she stacked the cubes together with openings vertically oriented to fill up the loader.

Once the simulated loader was stacked full, she would drive the it out of the conveyor room back through the raised door into the cooling room to an empty parking space. Accelerated clock icon hands ran quickly around the dial to represent the time needed to cool before the temperature readout reached an acceptable degree of coolness.

Once the load showed as cooled, she could then drive the loader out onto the main four lane road and take a long drive around to the shipping area where shipping containers were docked. It was a straightforward maneuver to turn and drive the loader into the back of the shipping container. Proximity readouts told her when the front of the loaded stack came up against either the back wall of the shipping container, or a previously loaded stack.

An automated program could then be engaged that lowered the loader bed tray to the floor. It then simultaneously pushed the entire load of stove cubes off the front of the loader while backing the loader out of the shipping container leaving the entire load of cubes in position on the floor in the shipping container.

After a long drive back to the parking area just off the four-lane road she was ready for a second run. She had only made it inside the virtual cooling room to the on-deck parking spot when her phone rang, so she paused the simulation.

Somewhat annoyed that cowboy was interrupting her before she was done, she just hit the speakerphone button and said in a mock western drawl "Why howdy there snooty boots. There must be rustlers attacking the ranch for you to be calling this early."

An unexpected but familiar female voice said, "OK, who is this with the bad accent and what have you done with my friend Khadija?"

Khadija sat up and said, "Miri, I'm surprised to hear from you. How are things in deepest driest Africa?"

Khadija, wondered why her phone had not rung with Miri's distinctive ringtone.

Miri said, "Hey Khadj – It is you. I thought for a moment

the ghost of Dale Evans had possessed you. I've left the dunes behind, and I am out of Africa for a couple of days on a special mission. They made me keep radio silence on the way, so I've just now arrived where I can give you a call."

Khadija struggled against the straps as she pivoted to take the phone off her belt to talk directly into it asking, "So, where are you now?"

Miri replied, "Somewhere where I can see you've taken up a bondage fetish in Mr. Gadget's swoopy chair."

"What?" said Khadija, looking towards the cameras sending pictures back to the logistics unit.

Miri continued, "At least your new hairstyle looks nice. It sets off your disbelieving squinty eyes, and your far too wide-open mouth nicely."

"You're here???" said Khadija.

"Yep, keeping your ever-loving snooty boots company until you are done with whatever bondage voyeurism you two are into." said Miri. She added, "What do you know, snooty boots cute cheeks look even nicer when they're blushing. You better hurry back here. You know I can't be trusted when left alone with a handsome man who's into hardware."

The cowboy seemed to be trying to protest in the background but was having difficulty producing words so Khadija jumped in, "Don't say another word and keep your hands to yourself, I am on my way."

"Good" said Miri with self-satisfied expression and added, "On the way, could you bring along a loader. Cute cheeks comes with a lot of baggage and your mom sent a couple of stacked coolers that I need to get out of my plane."

Khadija left the hangar and cycled back over to the warehouse where the electrically driven remote loaders were lined up outside the warehouse. She unplugged a loader, put her bike on the platform, and then stepped up to the manual controls. She soon had the loader running at its top speed and was hoping that Miri was behaving herself with the cowboy, as she pulled the loader up in front of the logistics unit. She pulled her bike off and set it up against the metal container wall of the unit before keying the code to open the door.

Inside she found Miri lounging on the couch while the cowboy was still working on his tablet in one of the chairs. Miri hopped up off the couch to give her a hug and then pulled down her headscarf to check out her new hairstyle. Khadija said there was a hair salon in one of the international airports on the way back, that she had stopped in at during a layover. Miri suggested they get the stuff out of the plane so she could lock it up and then they could relax and kick back for the evening. Miri and the cowboy walked out to the plane, while Khadija drove the loader over and pulled it up by the cargo door.

There were a bunch of suitcases with the cowboy's stuff, Miri's travel bags and two large coolers that cowboy helped Miri lift onto the loader. Miri handed the cowboy a bag with his laptop and chargers, then opened the coolers revealing stacks of food storage containers with neatly written labels. Cowboy, who had been watching the opening of the coolers looked puzzled.

Khadija explained, "My mother, who seeks to save me from the unhealthy food she thinks they are serving at the cafeteria here, goes a bit overboard whenever she learns Miri is headed my way.

Miri added, "Kahdj's mom is a fantastic cook, and she knows that if she can get her food in Khadj's hands, she will always wind up preferring it to the commissary food offered on the base."

Miri was pawing through the containers clearly recognizing some of the dishes and marveling at the amount saying, "In fact, there is so much here, I think eating in and having one of our movie night's is obligatory."

Miri looked at cowboy and said, "Considering the assortment of heathen food the commissary has probably been foisting on you, you would be spiritually offending Khadj's mom unless you joined us for dinner and stayed for movie night."

Khadija thought her mom would have a different take on her hanging out with a strange man watching movies after feeding him her cooking but, strangely couldn't really bring herself to object. Cowboy looked hesitant at first but when Khadija didn't object, he said "Sounds like a plan."

Miri, carefully watching the reactions between her and cowboy, jumped in before Khadija could back out saying, "Its decided then. Let's drop off stuff at the buses and plan to meet at the logistics unit at 6 for dinner."

Cowboy started off walking towards his bus with his laptop bag and Khadija waited until he was out of earshot before looking at Miri and saying, "What do you think you are doing?"

"Just helping things along." said Miri and added, "I can tell you are as taken with him as he is with you. Just don't let me get caught between the two of you when all that repressed energy decides to let go. All right, drop my travel bag at my bus and let's get "snooty boots" his suitcases, so he has something clean to wear."

46

Richard came out of the tiny closet of a shower in his bus to look through the pile of suitcases that Khadija had delivered to him. It looked like someone had just pulled all the clothes out of the safehouse and added a mix of other items from back at his apartment to fully stuff the suitcases. He pulled out some clean jeans, a western shirt that showed the least wrinkles, and another pair of cowboy boots that were near the top. He would have time to dig through and unpack the suitcases over the weekend.

Showered and dressed, he wandered back over the logistics container and found Miri and Khadija already pulling food containers out of the microwave to set out an impromptu buffet. Miri had changed out of her flight suit into a very colorful top and brightly colored loose-fitting pants. She pulled out plates and utensils and then announced she was digging in. Richard noticed one of the comfortable chairs had been pulled over by the couch, the divider curtains were pulled across separating the kitchenette and back lounge area from the front work area, and the start of a movie was paused on the large screen across from the couch.

Miri finished spooning a variety of food out onto her plate, grabbed her drink, and headed to the chair in the other room. Khadija looked hesitant for moment, but Richard had said "After you," so she proceeded with her plate and then went in to sit near Miri on the couch. Richard got something to drink out of the refrigerator and then spooned out samples of a couple of the dishes onto his plate to try. Everything tasted good, if a touch spicy, so he made a plate with several of the dishes.

Miri was talking about her recent trips to evaluate abandoned mines with impacted or distressed communities around them as he carried his plate back to set down on the side table by the last place on the couch. Miri talked about the three mining sites that had been acquired by the coalition and were already in operation. A community benefits trust had been set up so that half the profits of the mine would go to benefit the surrounding communities.

Miri insisted there be no talk of work the rest of the evening, so they shared stories about places they had visited and interesting things they had seen while eating. Richard gathered the dishes and took them back into the kitchenette as Khadija started the movie and asked Richard to turn off the lights in the kitchenette.

The movie was good, and they found themselves laughing at the situations that the actors found themselves in. About three quarters of the way through the movie, Miri got up saying something about personal needs the tiny bathroom in the logistics unit would not be adequate to contain. She made them keep watching the movie as she let herself out hurriedly.

The movie finished a while later, so they sat around talking about the world depicted in the movie for a while until it was clear Miri was not returning. They cleaned up and put away everything in the kitchenette and then Khadija packed up her laptop to go.

The large wall monitors were back to their exterior views out towards the warehouse, so she looked at the monitors in both directions. Seeing no movement, put on her headscarf and slung her handbag over her back. She then turned off the monitors and had Richard turn off the kitchenette light, leaving them both in darkness.

She opened the divider drapes and walked out into the windowed work area lit by the outside lighting from the airfield and warehouse in the distance. After reflexively looking out the windows, she headed for the door. "See you in the morning for breakfast?" she asked. "Sure…" was all Richard could say before she was off on her bicycle into the night.

47

Ahmed was woken by the security team with the coalition climate sensor supervisor on the line. The supervisor said, "Tsunami alert, Southern coast of Chile, ETA 55 minutes!" Ahmed was instantly awake as a text dinged in and he pulled up the highlighted map of the coast showing the projected wave height and impacted areas.

Ahmed said, "I show Commander Gonzales of the Chilean Navy as our key contact. I'm going to see if I can get him on his personal phone to give him a heads up and see if he can get the word out this is not a drill. Get with Jamal's group to see if this is one of the areas where they have the capability to trigger the tsunami sirens and phone alerts in and have them stand by. I'm switching lines to call the commander but will be back on the line shortly."

Ahmed texted the impact map to the commander's phone and then called the number. Ahmed greeted him in Spanish when he answered and introduced himself saying they had met some years before during coordination meetings regarding new sensor buoys in their national waters. He gave him the now 53-minute ETA on the tsunami arrival at the southern coast, those sensors would soon be reporting. He asked him to look at the text he had just sent with the projected impacts. The commander looked at it and agreed it looked catastrophic.

He asked Ahmed to hold while he called the alert monitoring folks to see if they could start the evacuation sirens and text alerts. He came back on the phone saying they saw the tremor, but didn't have enough evidence to be certain it would cause a significant tsunami, so their head of emergency services refused to sound the alerts.

He asked Ahmed if he was certain his data was solid. Ahmed said with the new sensors that could detect the actual pressure wave in the water, and the dramatically improved model processing, the prediction was very solid. Ahmed said only the casualty count was in question depending on how fast they could get people evacuated.

The commander expressed the wish that he could personally trigger the alarms, but that power rested with the head of emergency services. He said that he doubted that person, a political appointee that was woefully unqualified, would consider triggering an alert before the incoming wave hit the beach he was standing on.

Ahmed asked "If you could order the alerts to be set off, would you? The commander instantly replied "Yes, I would." Ahmed asked the commander to hold on the line for a moment and switched over to the call with security and the sensor supervisor. "Do we have Jamal's team on the call, and can you trigger the sirens and text alerts for the red and orange highlighted areas of the map?" he asked. "Yes, and yes," said a voice Ahmed recognized as one of Jamal's team leaders. "Then I hereby authorize you to set off the tsunami sirens and text alerts for the red and orange highlighted areas of the Chilean coast." said Ahmed. "Acknowledge permission to set off sirens and text alerts," Ahmed heard the supervisor say loudly so those in the control room where he was stationed could hear the command. "Sirens and alerts are now activated" continued the voice to him. "Thanks" Ahmed said and switched back to the call with the commander.

He could hear a siren in the background and a text alert ping in on the commander's phone, as the commander exclaimed "What the devil!" Ahmed apologized for keeping the commander waiting but said his people were detecting that sirens and alerts were fortunately being set off in the red and orange highlighted areas of the map as they spoke. "Perhaps your gun-shy service head finally saw the approaching danger and acted?" Ahmed said innocently. The commander snorted derisively and said, "I don't want to hear another word from you about this and I'll probably deny we ever talked if it comes up.

Many thanks though for looking out for us. I've got to get off and get the relief mobilized for all those likely to be homeless but alive in the morning." The commander rung off, and Ahmed switched back to thank the sensor supervisor, Jamal's team leader and the security team for the quick response.

In a follow up meeting later that morning Ahmed learned that large swathes of the southeast coast had been hard hit by the tsunami, but everyone who heeded the sirens and alarms, made it to high ground ahead of the disastrous rush of water and survived. The coalition saw to it that relief supplies and tents were mobilized to the region in record time to house much of the southeast coast population whose homes had been destroyed.

When later in the day he received a call back from the commander to thank him for the extra advance warning, Ahmed asked that his team not be credited with the discovery as he needed to keep his team's capabilities under wraps for a while yet. He was amused when he later read in the online reports that, for lack of other information, the head of emergency service's wife's psychic was being credited for the timely alerts being triggered.

48

The next morning was a Saturday, with no scheduled training so Richard rooted through the suitcases and pulled out his running shorts, tee shirt and a thin warm-up suit. With his running shoes on, he grabbed his satchel headed out the door to get some coffee at the logistics unit.

It was early but the humid air still held the made it feel uncomfortably warm outside. It made him thankful for the air conditioning in the bus and logistics unit as he looked out across the runways with the air above them already shimmering in the heat of the morning sun. Khadija's bike was not outside, so he went in and had logistics unit to himself.

He brewed a cup of coffee, sat down in one of the chairs, and took his tablet out to catch up on some reading. The now familiar sound of the commissary van pulling up outside to drop off breakfast could be heard and after the van left, Richard brought in the tote bag to set on the counter.

He was halfway through his second cup of coffee, when he heard a noise outside, followed by the door opening. Khadija came in, saw Richard, and said, "Good morning there Dash!" as she set her handbag on her desk and took off her headscarf.

"Dash?" said Richard puzzledly.

"Yeah, you look like you're ready to run some sort of sprint. Did I miss a cowboy dress code memo somewhere?" said Khadija.

"Oh, The cowboy union says we can hang up our hats and join the casual crowd on weekends," joked Richard.

"Well, OK Mr. Casual Cowboy, why don't you dig out breakfast while I get a cup of tea. Maybe then we can run through the long-lost training manual on the laptop you abandoned back at the OK Corral," said Khadija.

Richard grinned and started taking out the food containers. Khadija had him put aside a couple of containers that were for Miri, but they were soon eating and having their usual morning conversation. After they had eaten, Khadija hooked up Richard's laptop to the large monitor over the couch and they sat in the chairs. Richard scrolled through the manual pages shown on the large monitor and Khadija made notes for changes as they went.

Miri appeared in the door, again clad in colors that were too bright to look at when lit directly by the morning sun. She came in, saw the food waiting for her and said, "Thanks Khadj!"

She brewed a cup of coffee, kicked off her shoes, and then propped herself up on the couch to enthusiastically dig in.

"How did you two do after I left?" she said.

Neither of them were sure how to respond immediately and there was a mischievous glint in Miri's eyes as the silence lengthened. She waved it off by asking what they were planning to do for fun over the weekend.

Khadija said, "I hoped to get in some practice with new loaders, but we're dead in the water until the communicator cubes arrive."

"Oh yeah, umm, about that…" Miri said chewing.

Richard perked up and said, "About what?"

"Well, I was given specific instructions to turn over a metal briefcase to either the Director or her chief of staff. The Director is travelling, so I left word for the chief of staff to call Khadj when he was ready to meet and receive it. I wonder if it might contain the communicator cubes you're looking for?"

"Is the metal case kind of beat up with a lot of travel stickers on it?" asked Richard.

"Yes, it is, though it does have combination locks on it, so hopefully the chief of staff will know how to open it," said Miri.

"I know how to open it!" said Richard continuing, "Great, we can head by the plane, get the case of cubes, and have a couple of loaders up and running in the hangar this morning."

Miri said "No, not until the chief of staff gets in touch and arranges to meet me to accept the case. My orders are specific so, sorry, that's what's has to happen."

Khadija checked the time to make sure it was late enough in the morning and then pulled out her phone and texted the chief of staff. Moments later, she received a text back.

"The chief says he can be back on base to meet us about 1 PM".

Miri said, "Good, I need to arrange for refueling and do some planning of my own for next week, while you two chat amongst yourselves about this idiot's guide to robo-loaders snooty boots has come up with."

"Manual" Richard offered.

"Whatever - see you back here for lunch," said Miri with a grin as she headed out the door.

Richard sat through Khadija's dissection of the manual, and they were onto updating supply lists for the facilities, by the time Miri returned.

They again dug into Khadija's mom's containers to fix plates of food and sat on the couch and chairs. Over lunch Khadija and Miri were telling him disaster relief stories when Khadija's phone rang.

It was the Director's assistant, saying the chief of staff was just getting back to the base and could meet them in half an hour at the logistics unit. Miri said she needed to get ready to meet the fuel truck after their hand off of the case and headed back to her bus to get her flight suit on. Richard and Khadija cleaned up after lunch and Miri returned just before the chief of staff's car pulled up.

The chief of staff greeted Miri like an old friend in the baking heat of the day outside the logistics unit. He shook Richard's hand saying he was glad he could join them at the base, then ushered them into the coolness of the car. He drove them out to under the hangar shade structure where Miri had the plane parked.

Miri unlocked the plane and went inside while they stayed in the car. She reappeared and handed Richard's tool case through the window to the chief of staff.

"I've got a fuel truck to meet so I'll stick with the plane and meet you later for dinner in the logistics unit."

The chief of staff wished her well before rolling up the window and driving off. On the drive over to the hangar, Khadija updated the chief of staff on how the training was proceeding. She said she was planning to check out the robotic loaders as soon as cowboy could get the communicator cubes installed and them running.

The chief raised an eyebrow at her calling him "cowboy," but they were pulling up in front of the hangar entry next to another car with coalition markings, so he let it go. He asked Khadija to go in the women's entry and let the taser twins know that they would be in the hanger environs for a while. He said he and "the cowboy" would pull down to the loading door end and meet her at the elevator inside.

Khadija headed inside the building and the chief of staff drove them down to the far end of the hangar and unlocked the door for them to go inside. Only the emergency lights were on in the hangar, so they walked along in the dim light back over to the elevator. Richard noticed all the construction equipment was now cleared out and only the divider fence remained.

Khadija came out the door from the stairwell and joined them by the elevator. The chief of staff put a hand on the dark featureless elevator call pad followed by a finger motion that caused a glow to appear around the edges of the pad. He asked Richard to put his palms on the pad, one after the other, and once done, the chief stepped back up and put his other hand on the pad. The glow around the pad brightened then faded out. The chief of staff repeated the process with Khadija and after the glow faded asked her to now place one of her palms on the pad to call the elevator.

The elevator doors opened, and they all walked into the large service elevator. The chief of staff suggested Khadija now try placing her hand on the taller dark pad by the doors and try swiping down halfway and then sliding her hand sideways off the pad. Khadija did so and the elevator headed downward. The doors at the back of the elevator opened to a dimly lit space and the smell of fresh paint and new construction reached them as they stepped out. The lights sensed their motion and came on to reveal a small lobby of sorts.

Opposite the elevator was a floor to ceiling curved section of steel with the high polish of a bank vault. The lobby was well lit with only a touch of construction dust left over from the contractors that had been working here.

The chief of staff went over to another dark hand pad next to the curved bright steel and they repeated the keying process for both he and Khadija. When done the chief of staff suggested Richard place his hand on the pad. Richard did so and the curved steel section in front of them started to rotate.

An opening appeared leading into a circular room about the diameter of the elevator length. As they reached the center the wall rotated back closing off the lobby and simultaneously opening an entry into a short tunnel of roughly hewn rock.

A layer of grit and dust extended a distance out from the roughhewn tunnel onto the smooth floor of a well-lit large room ahead of them. Khadija looked puzzled, but the chief of staff smiled but said nothing as he walked across to the smooth floor where his shoes started leaving footprints in the dust. Richard noticed another single set of footprints was already showing in the dust leading into the room.

The room was about the size of a basketball court with a high ceiling lost in the darkness above. Only square white lights around the walls lit the floor and the branching corridors running off of it. Doorways leading to a series of rooms could be glimpsed down these corridors that the white squares seemed to do a better job of lighting.

A wiry well-dressed woman appeared at the end of one of the far corridors that Khadija recognized as she made her way across "court" area towards them. Khadija let him know she was the Director of the coalition's base operations.

The Director came up to Khadija saying, "Khadj, great to see you. With everything going on, it has been a while since we've had a chance to talk. And Richard, good to have you here after your hurried trip over to join us."

The Director shook his hand while looking intently at him and then back at Khadija with a pleased look. The Director explained the "court" space was going to be one of the regional control rooms overseeing logistics for their new "clean cooking stove" deployment as well as for aid and relief supply deliveries for the region.

The Director said, "Let's see if we can get some more light in here," as she reached over by the entry to swipe on a dark pad. Richard was still wondering why stoves needed a subterranean control room to run their deployment when additional rings of white square lights around the upper walls turned on.

Richard was struck by the distinctive look of the arched roof and wall construction. It looked like the room was carved out of the solid rock with a symmetrical flowing white structural ribbing reinforcement that looked more like interwoven Art Nouveau decoration than any structure Richard had ever seen before.

The Director, seeing Richard's expression, said, "The builder cubes do this construction and created this space over a month ago. Once the shell was done, we flew in "busloads" of outside finishing crews to put in everything from doors to electric outlets to finish out this facility. They finished all their work last week and caught their "bus" flights back home yesterday. The local construction crews working from the other side at the same time put in the elevator lobby and the turning wall security entry. They also wrapped up cleared their stuff out of the hangar at the end of the week. This space and the lower facility has been kept entirely isolated from the surface until last night when the builder cubes excavated the connector tunnel from this space over to the turning wall security entry leading to the elevator. Let's take a look around starting over here."

Richard with a puzzled look mouthed the words, "bus flight

and builder cube?" to Khadija as they followed the Director, but she gave him a look that said she would catch him up later.

The Director was describing the function of the facility as she led them on a quick tour of the complex of rooms. There was a surprisingly large number of finished and furnished spaces ranging from larger community rooms and kitchen areas to the smaller personal bedrooms and offices they walked past. The Director said the logistics control staff tended to be younger and single so they would both live and work in the spaces once they were brought in on their bus flights for the two weeks to month long stints at a time.

They came through large heavy automated doors into a large space that felt a bit like a parking garage. Its vertical walls, with the white patterned structural tracery, funneled into a large rectangular shaft that a blue whale could have been comfortably lowered down. The elegant flowing lines of white continued up to the top of the shaft far above where they ended in what looked to be a rough gray concrete ceiling. The Director said this was the arrivals area is where they would ferry in personnel and supplies for their "islanded" logistics and other operations in the adjoining facility. The garage area was full of shipping containers with several forklifts parked and plugged in at one end of the space.

The Director said, "Jamal has his techs and specialty contractors coming in later next week to start installing the logistics control and "clean cooking stove" monitoring equipment to get this space operational. Some of the techs and contractors will also be assigned to you two for the setting up of the lower facility. For security purposes, none of the equipment installation techs or contractors know where the bus is bringing them or where these facilities are located. You and a select few of Jamal's team will know the actual location, but we ask you to keep it secret from the contractors and technicians that will be assigned to you."

She led them out into a high-ceilinged wide corridor that led down to a large set of heavy loading doors with a dark palm pad on the side wall. The chief repeated the keying process for the palm pad with both him and Khadija before opening the automated doors. The doors opened into a wider room already full of palettes of control chairs with another set of heavy loading doors at the far end. As they reached the second set of doors, the chief asked Richard to try his hand on the palm pad. The automated doors opened but the corridor beyond only ramped down a short distance before ending into a roughhewn rock wall.

The Director said, "This will be a secure loading transfer area to get large deliveries between this area's arrival area and the ramped access to the lower facility." She led them over to one side of the transfer space where a familiar looking curved section of the high sheen bank vault steel was set in an alcove. The chief placed his hand on the pad next to the wall and the opening into the circular room appeared. They had to go into the room and use a second palm pad to get the walls to rotate and open into the elevator.

They all went back on the elevator and the chief suggested Khadija place her hand on the tall pad and swipe fully down. The elevator started down again and soon the doors opened on the opposite end into a much larger lobby with a larger floor to ceiling curved bright steel section in the center of the opposite wall.

The chief of staff went over, and they repeated the keying process on the dark pad by the curved steel, and when done, Richard placed his hand on the pad. As Richard did so, the curved steel section in front of them started to rotate. An opening appeared leading into another large circular room, and they walked in. Again, as they reached the center the wall then started to rotate back closing off the lobby and simultaneously opening an entry into another roughhewn tunnel in front of them with grit and dust extending out onto the finished floor beyond.

The space beyond was immense but dimly lit. The Director walked out of the end of the tunnel, found the lighting controls, and turned on more lighting. Looking out past the rough opening Richard could now see a brightly lit expansive circular space easily as large as the hangar above.

The tracery pattern of the structural support flows blended into the domed white ceiling that gave an airy daylit feel to the room. As they walked out of the elevator, Richard recognized the space immediately as the shell of the remote operator facility that had only been lines on a plan only a couple of months before. He could see where the concentric circles of controller chairs would mount, radiating out from a raised center area that would hold a massive videowall display tower. Monitor desks that the shift leads could coordinate loader efforts from would encircle the raised center platform.

Outside the chair mount locations, was a zone that plans had specified should contain everything from, comfortable couches and seating, to areas set up like fitness centers to prayer areas to computer and call cubicles that would be interspersed between. An outer walkway had circular openings in the floor for small local trees to be planted. Inside the walkway the floor was a sand color running under the chairs up to the center monitor banks. The outer curved wall, which reached up to the dome, had a sweeping mural of the desert and mountains of the region that gave the entire room an outdoor like feel. He kept being drawn back to find himself staring, in disbelief at the scale of the interwoven structure decorated dome span.

The Director said, "We've been trying to move timelines up, so the shell construction and excavation began on this started as soon as you both approved the facility footprint. There are some worrying trends in the latest climate model projections that may cause extreme heat outbreaks sooner than originally anticipated. I've been asked to enlist the both of you to help to get this facility set up as quickly as we can."

As they walked out into the control chair area and the chief of staff mentioned that the containers in the arrivals area were all full of supplies for the arena and pointed out where the bottom of the ramped loading corridor came out into the arena space. The Director asked Khadija to have the women learning the new loaders, when they were not in training or in class, to go back to the manual forklifts to unload the containers and deliver the palettes of chairs in the transfer room down into the remote operator arena.

The Director said Ahmed would like Richard to get the equipment racks and control desks installed and then work with the incoming techs to install the center monitor wall. She asked Khadija to assign a couple of the women for running all the power and optical feeds harnesses in the cable troughs up into the center monitor area lower rack room.

She also asked Khadija to come up with a plan that could use the women in training to get the furniture, trees, shrubs, food, and prayer areas set up to their liking. The director said once training for this group of women was done, the control chairs on the upper level would be brought down into the domed arena to make up the full 150 control chairs capacity of the arena.

Further training would take place in this arena. The plan was to train a full two hundred woman contingent for the new robotic loader workforce at this location. The director thought they would draw many from the already experienced remote forklift and loader contingent and work to train new replacements for those roles but would leave it to Khadija to work out the details.

The chief of staff pointed out that the arriving techs from Richard's company would not be aware that they had left the US, or that the time zone difference between their home and this base was nine hours. They would stay on their US time, start work in evening, and finish in the early morning to maintain separation from the Khadija's women who would be working during the day.

There was a wing of bedrooms designed for visiting contractors and extended shift workers to be able to nap or stay overnight in as needed. The Director said worrying developments were causing the coalition to take further security measures to keep those involved with the cubes safe. As soon as the room furnishings and beds could be brought in, they would plan for Richard to officially leave the base and be brought back into the airfield surreptitiously to move down to one of the rooms here for the rest of his stay at the base.

As soon as the area was set up and the training was far enough along, Khadija should plan to also relocate underground. Once the control chair arena was set up, Ariana had asked that they both travel to the manufacturing facility to get things set up and running on that end.

The Director led them to an office area built off the side of the arena and to a door with a dark pad next to it. The chief of staff did his hand keying process with the two of them and then had Richard use his palm to open the door. An inset area was formed in the wall of the storage room inside. The chief of staff set Richard's tool case up on the counter height shelf.

The Director suggested the communicator cubes be stored here when not in use so they would be secure during the training. She asked Richard to open the case and verify all the cubes were present. Richard dialed in the combination to open the latches and raised the top foam layer to see that all eight pairs of the communicator cubes were in it.

The Director said during the training process, the communicator cubes should be taken out of both the chairs and the loaders at the end of each day and kept down here. Richard relatched the case and left it on the counter slab as the Director led them back out.

The Director said she and the chief of staff had to leave but suggested the two of them stay behind to spend some time working out how best to accomplish what they were being asked to take on. They walked over to the turning wall entry and the Director and Chief stepped inside once the wall had rotated open.

The Director turned to say, "Oh, by the way, the last of the builder cube construction will going on tonight between midnight and five in the morning to clean up the entries and open the loading access to the transfer room. I would suggest not being down here while that is occurring. Also, Khadj, please catch Richard up on all the cubes capabilities. I understand for security reasons his need to know has been limited to just the basics of the communicator cubes up until now. It is now time to give him the full rundown on the builder and stove cubes and introduce him to the native child. Thanks again to both of you for all we are asking you to take on."

The curved metal wall rotated closed on the Directors thankful expression and Richard and Khadija turned back to look out over the expanse of the domed space. It was taking a moment for the realization of the scope they had just been given to settle in.

"And here I was looking forward to putting the girls on cruise control for the rest of the training and kicking back to catch up on my reading," Khadija said.

Khadija led him up the steps and out onto the center monitor platform where an irregular car sized stack of what looked like black boxes was resting. Khadija went over and took one off the top of the stack and handed it to him saying, "This is a builder cube."

The builder cube in his hands was about twice the size of the communicator cubes he was familiar with and had tapered faces on two sides leading to a square opening through the middle. Khadija outlined the basic builder cube capabilities but said Miri and "native baby einstein" could provide better answers when they met for dinner.

She then talked about the stove cube, a big brother version similar in look to the builder cube that the robotic loaders would be handling and shipping millions of.

After she ran down the list of functions the stove cubes could do, she said, "I don't know how all the cubes do what they do, but I do know we need to keep it totally secret. Word on the various cubes' abilities has leaked out and your gun toting fans want to get their hands on them in the worst way. This has the coalition literally taking operations underground for our own safety."

Richard pulled up the plans for the controller chair "arena" as they had taken to calling the space on his laptop. He and Khadija spent the afternoon walking through the space and planning out an approach that would allow things to happen working outwards from the center monitor display and controller chairs to the outer seating, plantings, and food/drink support facilities. They wrapped up late in the afternoon and took their separate routes out of the hangar with the agreement to meet with Miri back at the logistics unit for dinner.

After being in the air-conditioned arena all afternoon, the outside heat hit Richard hard. He missed the shade of his cowboy hat on the sweltering walk back and the high humidity made him a sweaty mess by the time he walked up to the bus. As he went inside to the cool interior of the bus, he found himself looking forward to relocating his living quarters to down to the control chair arena.

Later, after a shower and a change of clothes, he walked over to the logistics unit. Miri's voice from inside shouted "Come on in" before he had come up to the door. Richard entered and saw Khadija was already pulling out food onto the kitchenette counter while Miri was pulling a chair around to face the oversize monitor showing the view looking towards the warehouse.

Richard started to ask a question about builder cubes, but Miri cut him off saying, "I am not going to have my last evening in town ruined by a ruwaq tech discussion, so stuff it and save it for after breakfast tomorrow. Besides have we ever got a guy movie for you lined up for tonight."

Khadija shook her head at Miri as if being reluctantly dragged into a movie choice she might regret, saying, "Not at all a guy movie, but it should be fun anyway. Food's ready so dig in."

49

The satellite tech crossed the center of the center of the tech campus at a brisk pace. He had just been called by the office assistant who let him know the head of operations had a last-minute cancellation on his schedule and the tech could get in to talk with him in the opening before his next meeting.

The software geeks had compared the data coming in from the new area he had geofenced and had proudly announced there was no problem in their software or display graphics. The hardware on the satellite was sending off the chart carbon and other greenhouse gas reduction readings from the location that consistently showed up as a deep green plume of just the oxygen rich air billowing out downwind.

When the satellite was originally being tested, several companies had been contracted to provide measured releases of various gases at a time when the satellite was orbiting overhead. By comparing the measured release with the data captured by the satellite, the accuracy of all the hardware and software could be verified. The tech had discovered there was still an open contract with a supplier whose web site listed oxygen on its list of available gas products.

The tech had calculated when the next overfly of the gas storage yard would take place and had asked the supplier to vent an amount of oxygen equivalent to the concentration in the remote plume.

On the day of the supplier gas yard overflight, the tech was recording and actively watching the monitor displays. The gas yard had just come into view when a light green plume appeared at its location. The plume quickly shifted to medium green, then finally dark green as the oxygen released reached levels to match the calculated concentration of the remote location plume. After about a minute the source at the gas yard shut off and the display started to clear of the green.

The satellite tech entered the lobby and was ushered up to the conference room near the head of operation's office. He plugged his notebook into the display inputs in the conference table then turned on the large display to bring up his screen.

The head of operations strode into the conference room with his no nonsense manner, greeted the tech and got right to it, "So what have you got that has all our hardware and software teams up in arms and firing off accusing memos at one another about?"

The tech brought up the colored displays starting with discovery of the abrupt shift in color along the ridgeline. He highlighted its persistence and expansion over time even further along the ridge. He showed the head of operations the pale green tint blowing out of the most powerful of the direct air capture pilot plants that were set up to strip out carbon. He then showed the recent test release of oxygen that achieved close to the same dark green level of concentration as the remote plume. The head of operations mused this for a moment then said, "So what you're telling me is that one of these direct air carbon removal schemes that has barely been able to filter out their own farts, has suddenly hit the mother lode with a process that rains out carbon black?"

"Not quite" replied the tech. "The satellite imagery doesn't show any sign of a normal facility along any of the ridges affected. Just a thousand-foot-tall rock outcrops that regular air hits the face of and only air cleaned of carbon and greenhouse gases comes off the back. The only thing the air is missing from the front face to the back face appears to be mainly carbon." the tech added.

"So, they've built it underground", said the head of operations. "Well, If I had a kick ass process that would put the other air capture pansies to shame, I might well want to hide it until I had it ready for prime time. How much carbon are they getting out" he asked.

The tech said "Roughly the equivalent of five hundred train cars filled with carbon black every day. It's orders of magnitude beyond any known direct air carbon capture tech being piloted at the moment."

The administrator sat up, considered this a moment, then said, "Are you saying some pencil pusher tech wiz has come up with a way to strip 500 train cars of pencil lead from the air between the front and back of some mountain ridge every day?"

The tech hesitated a moment at the ludicrous proportions of what he was outlining, but the satellite data was clear, so he replied, "Yes sir."

"We should find a ground team nearby to send out along the ridge line downwind to verify how much carbon they are removing and to see if we can identify who's behind it." said the head of operations.

The tech replied "I think that will be difficult sir. The ridge line is like really inaccessible and really long."

"How inaccessible and how long?" the head of operations asked.

The tech zoomed out from the washed-out imagery of the rock face until the fuller extent of the region became evident and overlaid a dimension measurement of the width of the dark green plume.

"It's that inaccessible and that many miles long" said the tech as the administrator's eyebrows raised.

The administrator pulled out his phone and dialed a number.

"Get me General Morris." he said pausing while they found the general.

"Jim, good to hear your voice." He continued. "Listen I've run across a situation that I need to get to the bottom of and I need some of your southern flyboys to help me look into it."

50

Richard took his morning walk from the bus to the logistics unit, for breakfast. Inside Khadija and Miri were sitting on the couch looking at a plan of the controller chair arena on the oversize wall monitor. Miri was back in her flight suit this morning, while Khadija was in a more stylish version of the baggy pants and loosely fitting top she always seemed to wear.

Richard made a cup of coffee and pulled a chair around so he could see the screen while Khadija finished describing the facility. Miri said, "It looks like an oasis that will be great for your girls."

As Khadija got up to take her and Miri's breakfast plates back to the kitchenette, Richard asked "So, now can we talk about bus flights and builder cube-built structures?"

Miri looked at Khadija, who nodded and said, "He's been cleared by the Director to be let in on all the functions of all of the cubes."

Miri took a deep breath, steeled herself and then said, "I can only tell you what they can do. Don't ask me how they do it. For lifting and flying deliveries, the builder cubes have the ability to form up into vertical stacks and generate downward jet-like thrust to fly things as big as shipping containers around.

For bus flights where the coalition does not want the contractors to know where they are being taken, autonomously driven buses are used with all the windows blacked out. The builder cubes form up to fly them but can mimic road vibration, turning forces, and roadway surround noises amazingly well while in flight. Those seated inside feel like they are just being transported by an autonomously driven bus down the highway to a secret location a few hours from where they boarded. In fact, they may be in the process of flying across entire oceans to underground facilities like we have here.

For builder cube structures we need a bit of show and tell. Khadj, can you grab your globe so that we can have miming native baby Einstein run one of his goldilocks animations."

As Khadija went over to her handbag to pull out her globe memento, Miri described how the builder cubes could tunnel through rock like a hot knife through butter and could extrude a structural material along their tunneled path. She said that Jamal, who ran their software team, had developed a protocol so that the native child projection avatar they called "baby Einstein" could translate 3D models from the architects into actual built spaces.

Khadija closed the drapes in front of the kitchenette to cut off the view into the back, slid one of the side tables over in front of Richard and took her wooden globe out to set on the small table. Richard watched as she slid and hinged it back to reveal the communicator cube inside the wood base. She moved her fingers over the communicator cube and a lit orb of dust began to form in the beam of golden light coming up from the tiny cube.

Richard leaned forward fascinated to see how the dust was being controlled. When the orb resolved with a snap into the beaming projected face of the native child, Richard jumped back in surprise. After a moment his curiosity made him again lean back in to see how it was done. The head and eyes of the gold-tinged child followed him as he leaned over to look at the projection from each side.

He gave Khadija an asking glance as reached his fingers out toward the rays coming up from the inset cube. She nodded and Richard ran his fingers through the projection beam making portions of the child's face dim with his movements. He then moved his hand through the lit dust of the child's face which scattered aside, before reforming and resolving back into the child's image, now with a bemused look now on its face.

Khadija asked the child projection to show the arena structural construction animation in virtual mode. The child avatar nodded at Khadija and his avatar face dispersed into a gold-tinged cloud. He heard Miri in a resigned tone say to Khadija, "Get set for a "how's that possible" day." as the cloud resolved into a gold-tinged image area showing a view looking down from a point over the training hangar.

Richard watched as the hangar and airfield apron faded to a ghost of transparency allowing a 3D line drawing of the control chair arena and the control "basketball" court sized area to appear below the ground with the elevator sketched in in between. The animation showed the elevator, lobbies and circular security rooms appearing in solid form first.

The animation then showed the rapidly crossing paths of the multitude of builder cube extruded "rebar" like runs forming the wall and roof structure in the solid rock for the arena and control court and tying in well below the floor to foundation piers. As the "rebar" animation section completed the roof structures, it resembled the dense woven steel belt of a radial tire. The rebar roof faded to show the added main support columns and patterned support structure extruded out below the roof. When that structure was done, the entire arena dome and arched control court roof and walls were complete but still totally encased in solid rock.

The excavation of the rock under the dome and arched control court roof could now be seen with the builder cubes zig zagging back and forth to chew up the rock and pump the excavated material out of the picture to one side. The lowering level of rock revealed the center monitor platform and steps and the excavation and reinforcement of the outer rooms around the control court.

The tall whale sized shaft going up out of the parking area ran right up to under the concrete of a section of airfield apron surrounded by a perimeter of double stacked containers. The concrete was shown to lift and slide to one side in the animation to let a representation of a bus like Richard was living in, fly up and out of the shaft. The animation made one last fly around as all the furnishing and fixtures were added in before again letting the surface hangar fade back in and concluding.

Richard collapsed back on the couch thinking a mile a minute, as Khadija put the globe memento back in her bag. In the intervening silence he barely heard Miri saying "Wait for it…. wait for it…." in the background before he sat bolt upright exclaiming "How in the world is that possible!"

"There it is.", said Miri putting the last of her flight materials in her case.

"Well, it's been fun hanging out with you two, but I've got to get airborne. Khadj, you take care and look after wonder boy here."

She hugged Khadija warmly and then came over, pulled Richard up while still in a daze and gave him a quick hug as well. She thumped Richard on the chest and looked over at Khadija with a mischievous look saying, "Might be some promise in there."

With a wave, Miri was out the door and heading out to her plane. Khadija came over to Richard, still standing in a daze, and pushed him towards the kitchenette.

"You've got one more cup of coffee to snap out of it before we are going over to the hangar and set me up to run a real loader around your mini Grand Prix training track."

51

Jamal was on the final leg of his long series of flights to take him over to Greece. He looked eagerly out the window as the plane came down through the clouds and the Mediterranean landscape was revealed below. The security team had put him through some dodgy moves just to get him here and make sure he was not followed. A bunch of flights with tight connections had brought him here. He had been too excited by his first trip overseas to really sleep on the plane over and he could feel the tiredness start to catch up with him as he sat looking out the jet's window at the sea far below.

He was glad to finally be out of the shipping container support-ed structure with the living quarters and computer lab perched across the top that he had been living and working securely out of with many of his lead programmers. The work on the climate model, production scanning, supercomputing hardware, and lo-gistics/delivery systems had been all encompassing since he had started.

With the help of the native child avatar, the programming for the sensor network and computer climate model inputting had been ridiculously easy. The child was some sort of advanced artificial intelligence that he could literally talk with to create the code used for the climate model program. The sensor data off ever the ever-growing network of satellites and ocean drones was converted by the translation protocol into a form of quan-tum processable data code that the climate model program could understand. The climate model could then be run on the communicator cube processing arrays using the optical interface the engineer had come up with. The hundred or so "supercomputing array stacks of communicator cubes they were using had the ungodly umph to process the data and update the climate model projections in real time. With that kind of computing capability, no wonder he and his team were sworn to secrecy three ways from Sunday and guarded like they had been given the keys to the kingdom.

His team had pioneered the hardware that allowed for scanning of stove cubes inside loaded containers to ensure quality control and adherence to coalition failsafe specs. Most recently they had specialty shipping containers delivered to them that his tech had outfitted with scanning hardware before they were taken off for use in the manufacturing facility. The last of those had been sent off, along with his team, to the manufacturing facility. Now that the logistics and monitoring software had been handed off to the red teams, he was now relocating to the other side of the world along with the lab/living quarters.

The security team no longer wanted all those arrays of computing eggs to all be in the one lab basket, and was sending Jamal to lose them in various remote locations so they could never fall into the wrong hands. He was supposed to meet up with an explosives expert who would fly around with him to the remotest of locations for placing failsafe explosive charges inside the communicator cube supercomputer cases as they were buried.

But that was tomorrow. Today all he had to do was enjoy the novelty of an overseas flight and the prospect of novel places to visit. The view of the city made him again look intently out the window as they banked back out over the sea before coming into land.

As he came out of the gates with the multitude of tourists that had been on his flight, he was met by an attractive girl, with short, cropped hair, and an array of tattoos peeking out beyond the sleeves of her top. She was holding a small canvas, on which some previous art attempt had been primed and painted over with bold brushstrokes in purple spelling out "HEY M.I.T.

COME WITH ME." She seemed to recognize him and pointed the canvas at him with a questioning look, until he acknowledged he was the object of her search.

She strode briskly through the airport throng leading him, with his carryon bag in tow, out to where a small car was parked. He no sooner had his bag and self in the car before she was off for the exits like the thought of having to deal with the airport tourists for one more minute was going to be unbearable.

Out on the road, she settled down and he managed to learn that she was Eleni, that Xanthe was her partner, and that she did not want to hear any shop talk about any "stove" or his work while he was visiting with them.

When she learned this was his first trip abroad, she took expanding his travel horizons on as something of a challenge. She took him on a route from the airport that would drive them past some of the sights of Athens. They went by a number of ruins and notable sights, but she said they could see Athen's primary attraction better from the apartment.

After a speedy tour of the city, she drove them up toward the top of a hill in a neighborhood that was bit worse for wear. The area had interesting murals painted on the walls, artsy cafes, and interesting restaurants with outdoor dining lining the street. She pulled them off in a narrow side alley and he followed her with his bag and backpack up the stairs, and into a second-floor apartment.

As he entered, a tsunami of color threatened to overwhelm his color senses. A panoply of expressively painted canvases clashed with op art intensity against one another within the limited wall space throughout the small apartment. She said the paintings were her work and as he walked around looking at the paintings, she seemed to be gauging his reactions almost as if the paintings were some Rorschach test set before him.

The apartment itself was small with just two bedrooms, a combined living room and kitchen, and a sofa that Eleni said they could make up for added guests that came to spend the night. As they passed the guest bedroom, she suggested he leave his bag and stuff in there for the time being.

She pushed him out the back door onto balcony to look at the attraction she had mentioned before, saying he must be starving and would get some lunch together for them.

The balcony was a large teak floored deck extending the width of the apartment with wrought iron railings and uprights supporting the stretched green canvas canopy overhead. A table and chairs was on the kitchen side and a couple of lounger chairs were over by the French doors leading out from the far bedroom.

Unlike the busy street and city out front, the view from the back balcony looked away from the city to the hills beyond. A telescope was over by the railing and Jamal was looking through it at some of the homes built up in the distant hills when Eleni came out with a tray. She set the plates and dishes of food out, then filled the wine glasses with a vintage that Jamal "just had to try." She made a toast to "broadening his horizons," and then they dug into the food.

Jamal commented on the how nice the view was, and Eleni said the only drawback was the dozens of tour buses always mobbing the hill over to the right. Jamal hadn't really looked that way and asked why that many people were up visiting a few ruins on a barren hilltop. He was given a "you've got to get a life" look from Eleni before she said in her accented English, "The ruin at the top of hill is the Parthenon – t h e Parthenon! Half the tourists on your plane probably flew here to just to see that."

Jamal got up, turned the telescope towards the hill, and the iconic colonnades and triangular pediment came into sharp focus. "Wow, I didn't know," he said moving the telescope in small increments to see the other buildings that a crowd was surrounding.

As he looked, she made him tell her about his family, girlfriends, and everything he did for fun that was not work related. She snorted when he said he hadn't had a girlfriend since college, dismissed any mention of playing videogames as "fun," and said threatened to sic Mir… somebody on him to see that his other "horizons" were suitably broadened in their upcoming travels.

Eleni saw the combined effects of the wine, warm breeze, and jet lag start to make Jamal nod off. She said she would be picking up Xanthe when she flew in later and wanted him rested to join in celebrating Xanthe wrapping up her Africa community organizing tour at dinner. She ushered him back into the bedroom where his bag was, and said to go ahead and climb into the bed so he could rest well. After she left, Jamal changed into shorts and a tee shirt, hung his travel clothes on the hangers on an empty rack in the corner that looked like it had been taken out of sixty's clothing store, crawled under the covers for a short nap, and was instantly asleep.

He awoke to the sound of voices talking on the balcony and looked out the front window to see the sun was nearly down. As he padded out in his bare feet, he passed by another suitcase in the room and saw some brightly colored clothing items that had been added on the rack alongside his clothes in the corner.

He went through the house and peeked out onto the balcony to see what was happening. He was instantly spotted by Eleni and dragged, bare feet and all, onto the balcony. She introduced him to the love of her life Xanthe, and that pesky Miri who had been spiriting her Xanthe away to the far reaches of Africa. Xanthe was wearing a loose-fitting linen outfit, while Miri was in running shorts and a brightly colored Hawaiian shirt.

Eleni sat him down on one of the lounge chairs and put a glass of wine in his hand, and they picked up their conversation about the next regions they would find themselves in to explore. They had dinner with more of Eleni's wine and looked at the evening stars over the hills as the evening deepened. As the evening wound down Eleni pointed out this was Jamal's first trip out of the states, and appointed Miri to educate him on other places to go and experiences to be had out in the wider world.

After dinner and a final round of toasts, Xanthe and Eleni went into the kitchen to put away things but insisted Jamal and Miri stay out and continue their wider world conversation. They sat out chatting until Xanthe's head poked out through the French doors on the bedroom side to say that they had left bedding out on the couch and that her and Eleni were heading to bed. She reminded Jamal that they would be off early in the morning and wished them a good night.

Jamal told Miri he too was winding down and would get his stuff out of the bedroom. They both walked back into the bedroom while Miri talked about Eleni's wish that he get out of his programming rut and have a more well-rounded travel experience. She said sleeping on the couch was not the best and seeing as they were going to be travelling together, and he had already rumpled the sheets on one side of the bed, he should just join her for the evening in the bedroom.

Jamal started to protest but Miri stopped him, suggested he take a moment to think about it while she stepped into the bathroom to pee. She could find out how he really felt when she came back out.

She talked out the open door of the bathroom, while listening to Jamal's continuing halfhearted protests. Jamal was pulling his carry-on bag around to repack it, as the toilet flushed and Miri said, "I think there has been enough discussion so let's put it to a vote." Miri emerged from the bathroom with all her clothing held in one hand which she laid over her suitcase. Standing in front of him like one of the classical nude sculptures he had seen on Eleni's tour, she said, "All in favor of sleeping in the bed with Miri raise a body part."

Even the simple motion of her raising an arm to vote in favor struck Jamal as incredibly sexy, and he felt a flush come over himself as he just stood there unable speak. Miri glanced down towards his midriff and smile crossed her lips as she said, "In the opinion of the court, the ayes have it."

She came over, closed the door, and led Jamal toward the bed.

52

Ariana was woken by the emergency alarm tone of her phone. She jumped up out of bed and hit the silence button on the phone. Her husband was stirring and looking her way as she said, "Evac alarm – get ready to go while I find out what's happening."

Saying "Emergency Update" into the phone and putting it on speakerphone, she threw on a bathrobe and put on her slippers.

A voice on the phone speaker told them an attempted kidnapping looked to be in progress. Two vans had pulled up at the end of her cul de sac street and two teams of men had gotten out. One team was now working their way through the woods to come up behind her house while the other team was coming down the street in front of her house. The vans were positioned so they could pull across the road and block off the end of the street if a driving escape was attempted. The voice said they could only count on a couple of minutes before the teams were in place to make their entry into the house. The voice advised evacuation plan B.

Ariana acknowledged evacuation plan B and kept the voice on the line as she was following her husband out of the bedroom without turning on any lights. They quickly made their way down the steps in the dark into their home offices, scooped up their laptops and tablets into the bug out bags they kept at the ready and headed out through the kitchen. They ducked under the window over the sink, to keep out of sight, and opened the door into the garage.

Her husband took her bag and jogged over to a paint-speckled tarp covering a car-shaped form. He pulled off the tarp revealing a small black car with heavy armored plating bolted on around the outside.

As Ariana half ran to the utility shelf behind the car, he opened the drivers side door, then went around to the passenger side to get in. The utility shelf was piled with paint cans, gardening supplies and large terra cotta planting pots on the back wall of the garage. Ariana pushed on a bag of potting soil and the shelf smoothly slid to the side revealing a large metal plate set into concrete in the back wall. She placed both of her hands onto the black tablet on the front of the steel and it slid open allowing builder cubes to quickly stream out.

Ariana hopped into the driver's seat, quickly closing the door, and took the opened globe memento her husband was holding for her. She motioned quickly to start the native child projection and as the face started to coalesce, she said, "Evac B go – repeat Evac B go." She heard the whoosh of jetted air and felt the car lift as she looked out through the heavy bulletproof glass panels crudely fastened inside the windows.

She had no sooner strapped in herself, when the garage door flipped open, and the builder cubes shot the car forward. They were down her driveway, and out onto the street in the blink of an eye. She could see delay in reaction of the dark figures they sped past, unsure of what they were seeing . A couple of shots rang out behind them alerting the two vans, who she saw pull across the end of the street to block their way.

Darkly clad figures were jumping out of the vans and scrabbling for their guns when their armored mini-car lifted off the road and shot into the sky over their heads. There was a look of surprise on their upturned faces as the black car was lit briefly in the streetlights sailing over them. As shots started to be fired, the native child triggered a bright flash and the car zigged suddenly to the side in the dark sky. Out the side window, she could see the blinded kidnapping squad give up shooting at the location where the dark car had zigged to disappear into the night sky.

"Well, that should make their report back to whoever had ordered the kidnapping interesting," thought Ariana as she and her husband settled in for the long flight.

53

Jamal woke while it was still dark to the unfamiliar yet comforting presence of Miri's body in the bed next to him. He eased out of bed, put his shorts and T shirt back on, and then got a glass of water from the kitchen to take out to the balcony. He watched the dawn breaking and took a long look through the telescope at the Parthenon appearing in rosy tones on the top of the hill.

Some activity started in the kitchen, but he didn't want to deal with anyone just yet, so he stayed outside enjoying the Mediterranean morning. Miri emerged in a colorful wrap with a cup in hand to announce there was coffee ready in the kitchen. Jamal got a cup and came out to sit next to her and they both silently watched the pink-tinged hills turn to a glowing warm orange.

Jamal started to say that the evening had been special, and while he enjoyed her company, he wasn't sure how they could keep in touch once he had to head off to the airport... when Miri gently cut him off saying, "You do realize you are flying with me today, don't you?"

She could see by Jamal's face that he didn't, so she said, "Well, you can save your goodbyes, cause you're going be stuck flying around with me so I can rig explosives to your super powerful computer junk."

Jamal's relieved emotions were countered by a realization causing him to say, "So you're the explosives expert I'm meeting?"

Miri laughed and said, "Wow, the security team didn't tell you anything before they sent you out of the country. I not just blowing up your junk, but I'm..." Her reply was interrupted by the clattering appearance of Xanthe and Eleni with a breakfast tray to set on the table.

Eleni said, "Well, Miri they certainly didn't warn him about your jaded reputation. Blowing up Jamal's junk sounds interesting, but no talking shop during breakfast."

It was clear to Jamal that Eleni had seen the untouched bedding on the couch. She couldn't suppress a knowing smile when looking at him and Miri. Xanthe seemed to take his evening with Miri in stride and started talking about getaways from the city that her and Eleni had been checking out. Eleni led the chatter about new exhibitions and things that were going on in the city that they should do when he and Miri could return to Athens.

Xanthe said to forget about the city, and suggested that they should join them out in the countryside to relax the next time he and Miri found themselves with a weekend free.

Inevitably after breakfast, Xanthe couldn't resist talking to Jamal about work stuff, so Eleni with a shrug of her head relented and said she was going to head inside. She reminded them they needed to be in the car heading out in about an hour. Miri said she needed to do some filing, so she followed Eleni inside.

Xanthe, pleased to meet the man behind her successful rescue, had Jamal tell her about how he had come up with the idea to use the builder cubes and pulled it off cleanly. He talked her through the rescue operation, and she, in turn, described how it had gone from her end.

They moved on to talking about the progress Xanthe's organizers were making in lining up populations to receive all the stove cubes his team was gearing up to be able to deliver. Xanthe related her experience with presenting the "clean cooking stove" cube to trusted community leaders. With all the community organizers she now had trained and the buy in they had gotten from towns and villages across the projected heat affected regions, they would be ready for the target date for widespread stove cube distribution.

She said that they had also made progress with government

approvals to distribute "stove" cubes directly by "drone" delivery at night, to avoid container nabbing by corrupt local officials or militias looking to hold the shipments for ransom. She said that her organizer teams were getting the stove bases, ducts, and control tablets to the millions who had already signed up, and that process would only accelerate in the coming year.

She said it could only be hoped that the massive drone delivery program for the stove cubes, that had inexplicably been put in the hands of some tyro hacker, had a chance of keeping up. Xanthe grinned knowingly at Jamal who grinned back and said that he had it on good authority the tyro hacker's team would have things ready by the roll out date and would soon after be waiting on her organizers to keep up.

Jamal said the biggest challenge the tyro team needed to solve was the need for the NGO coalition to retain failsafe control over all of the stove cubes, communicator cubes, and ruwaq related tech they would be introducing out into the world. He said they just had to get through the red team trials of the software failsafe controls and they would be ready launch the widespread distribution effort. He said the hardware like the communicator cube suitcase sized computer servers were going to have a cruder explosives-based failsafe that apparently Miri was going to provide.

Miri poked her head out to say she was done with her filing, so they needed to get moving. She asked Xanthe if she could use the shower in their room, so Jamal could use the one in the second bedroom and Xanthe said of course.

Jamal followed Miri back to the bedroom where the just the sight of her bending over her suitcase in the oriental wrap to get her toiletries produced a reaction that both made Miri smile and shake her head.

"Instead of us showering separately, I think you need to come with me."

Jamal found a surprising intimacy in washing each other in the shower, which hadn't been present in the previous night's lovemaking. After a bit of energetic effort at the end, they were clean in a manner that left Jamal needing a bit of recovery time on the bed afterwards.

His eyes were drawn to Miri as took off her towel to put on a sports bra and shorts style panties. She took her colorful tops off the rack to pack, leaving just a long khaki outfit. She was just zipping up the front of her flight suit when Jamal saw the sewn-on insignia and abruptly sat up.

"Wait, you're not just going on the same flight to do explosives… are you the pilot too?"

"Yes, I am…," said Miri in an all-business tone, as she rolled her travel bag to the door, "…and this pilot needs your butt dressed and down in the car pronto!"

54

Miri looked out the plane window across the sparkling reflections off the Mediterranean Sea and told Jamal that they should be seeing the coastline of Africa soon. She had been telling Jamal how this plane, with a front propeller in the nose and a second propeller directly behind the passenger/cargo cabin provided the safety and performance of a two-engine plane but its short takeoff and landing (STOL) ability allowed her to get into the more remote villages Xanthe had visited on her tour.

To get around the rear prop, twin tail sections with smaller tail rudders extended back from the wings and a tail/aileron spanned between the twin tail sections to box out the back of the plane. Miri told Jamal how they had run across the STOL plane at a military airfield in Africa sitting disused with one engine not running. Miri had said it was shame they couldn't have one like it to get to the villages that could only be accessed by landing on roads or very short dirt strips. Xanthe had said that if she wanted it, she had a couple of ideas how arrange it for her .

Xanthe had the science team work with an aircraft engineer do some calculations using the twin missile mounts under each wing as added thrust locations before she had persuaded the country's military to donate it to the NGO coalition. She had Miri fly the plane on one engine to an electric engine retrofit shop where the old gas-powered engines and avionics were removed, and new high performance electric motors, batteries, and avionics were installed.

Xanthe told her about the coalition scientists having worked with native baby Einstein to use the induction properties of the stove cubes to produce electricity. The ruwaq manufacturer had produced a form of transformer/inverter "plugging strip" that could be magnetically fastened onto the side of a stove cube stove with outlets for a range of common AC and DC voltages. Xanthe got a stove cube keyed to Miri and gave her one of the oversized "plugging strips." Xanthe had thought using the stove cube electricity to charge and power Miri's electric plane would be a good way to test the "plugging strip" prototype.

The result was a plane with powerful electric engines providing great short take-off performance and virtually unlimited range. If the oversized "plugging strip" ever failed, the full batteries would still easily fly the plane a couple of hours to a safe landing spot. The plane, being able to get them into places that might have only been accessible by roads, had saved Xanthe weeks of driving time. She said Xanthe had also worked with baby Einstein on a second nifty system for the plane, but said Jamal would see it in action later.

The coast came into view and Miri flew an approach towards the coastal airport that was their waypoint. Miri flew high over the airport and flipped off the transponder on the plane as they passed over the far end of the runway. She headed back out to sea far enough to be just out of sight of the land before turning to follow along the coast.

She explained to Jamal that the new paint finish that the builder cubes had coated the plane with minimized its radar signature, so without the transponder they were off the radar at this point. Miri set the autopilot on a vector to follow the coast and settled in for the last leg of their trip. As they approached the latitude and longitude coordinates that Jamal had given to her for their base camp, she banked to head back in towards the coast and throttled back to slow the plane.

She reached down to the communicator cube mounted in secure enclosure with a second set of Left and Right throttle levers along its sides. With her finger she made a motion on the cube and the native child avatar's face appeared over the throttles beaming up at her and Jamal. Miri said, "OK Kid, standby for VTOL In Flight Deploy." And the child nodded its head in acknowledgement. Miri allowed the plane to slow a bit further, told Jamal to watch out the windows, then said "VTOL In Flight Deploy ...GO!"

Out of a small opening under the rear engine enclosure dropped a stream of builder cubes that fell for just a few feet before flying up alongside the plane. Jamal watched as, one by one, they attached to the modified missile mounts under the wings to form long single square tube with the openings aligned so that air could pass through from front to back. Additional rows of builder cubes flew up to form similar long tubes to the right and left of the first tube. Looking out the opposite window past Miri he could see the builder cubes on her side finish assembling their formations in perfect synchronization with the ones on his side. Jamal could barely see the individual builder cubes swoop up and attach to the outside face of the tail fins.

The child avatar which had been moving its little hands in a circular motion stopped and gave two chubby thumbs up when the builder cubes were all in position. Miri lowered the landing gear to further slow the plane and said, "Kid, Standby for VTOL Transition To Vertical Flight and potential Abort." The child again nodded its projected head in acknowledgement and waited as she throttled back the propellers allowing the plane to slow to near stall speed at the high altitude. Miri watched the airspeed indicator for a minute before saying, "Kid, VTOL Transition To Vertical Flight GO!".

Jamal looked out the side window to see the outer portions of the builder cube tubes in front of and behind the wings split in half with the front and rear portions each slowly pivoting on the center builder cube stack towards vertical. Jamal could feel the drag of these cube stacks slow the plane further as they reached a vertical position. A band of condensation formed around the top opening "intakes" of the vertical builder cube stacks as air jetted downwards to lift the plane. Miri was watching the altimeter closely as the airspeed dropped below the stall speed of the plane. She was ready to call out the abort command that would scatter the cubes off the plane leaving it again free to fly unencumbered if there was any problem.

The plane maintained the same altitude as the airspeed continued dropping far below the stall speed at which the airflow over the wings would no longer support the plane. She pulled slightly backwards on the two throttles attached to the communicator cube to further slow the plane. When the airspeed read zero, Miri pushed the throttles back to the center and the plane hung motionless in the air supported solely by the columns of vertical jetting air from the builder cubes. Jamal could see the now vertically oriented builder cubes "jets" on the tailfins also working to keep the plane level.

Miri turned the plane control yoke slightly to the left and the plane started pivoting slowly around towards the left. Another turn of the yoke to the right and the plane pivoted back around to the right. She pulled back gently on the control wheel, the vertical thrust increased, and plane rose straight upwards until she let the wheel return to its neutral position and the ascent stopped. She pushed wheel forward and the builder cube vertical thrust decreased to lower the plane slowly straight down. Jamal could imagine the staggering amount of artificial intelligence processing going on in the communicator cube behind the blissful face of the native child avatar to provide the millisecond-by-millisecond fine adjustments to the vertical thrust needed to keep the plane perfectly under control.

Miri leveled off and for the first time since the start of the process she seemed to sit back and relax. She said it looked like everything was working fine with the builder cube Vertical Take Off and Landing set up. She glanced down at the child avatar to be sure it was still giving her two thumbs up with its pudgy projected hands, before moving the throttle levers forward to start the plane moving forward again. She checked her heading and pushed the control wheel slightly forward so the plane slowly lost altitude as it headed in towards the coast.

Jamal could see they were headed towards a small bay formed

by an indentation in the rocky faces of the cliffs in the coastline. Jamal asked Miri if she saw any sign of bystanders at the site, but as they floated downon their approach the location was evidently clear of any human presence.

Jamal called his team on the satellite phone and asked them to decloak and open the lower parking area of the of the container house. A large wall of black winked into view in front of the cliff and a portion of the front started breaking down into builder cubes that scattered then flew into storage openings at the sides. A space large enough to use as a hangar for the plane was revealed.

Miri slowed the plane to a walking pace as they floated in over the wave tops of the beach area enclosed by the cliffs. Miri adjusted the centering of the plane in the building opening by slight turns of the yoke, before lowering the plane until the wheels touched down. Moving the builder cube throttle forward the plane very slowly, the plane advanced into the "hangar" space until the front propeller cone was just a short distance from the the back of the hangar. Miri idled the builder cube throttles and engaged the brake before saying "Kid, confirming VTOL On The Ground, please Zero All Thrust."

As the whoosh of downward air ended, Miri shut down the regular props and avionics. As they opened the plane doors to climb out into the hangar space, the perfectly level sand floor they stepped down onto felt hard and did not give a bit under the wheels of the plane. As Miri looked back out toward the beach area they had landed on, the plane had not left any wheel marks from the point they had touched down on the "hard sand" to where they finished taxiing into the hanger. She realized this "landing pad" had been treated by the builder cubes in the same manner as the hangar floor to create a solid landing surface. As Miri set the wheel chocks and did her post flight checklist, Jamal looked at the familiar structure around them.

The sides of the hangar were each formed by two 40' shipping containers stacked one on the other resting on the melded sand floor/foundation. Overhead the living and computer lab space's dark supports spanned across with long thin transparent floor sections that allowed daylight to come through from the living space above. The back of the hangar was presently open to the rocky cliff face only a dozen feet beyond.

Miri said the last thing they needed to do was get the landing lights deployed so they would be ready for their evening flight. Jamal went through the double doors into the shipping container and reemerged with a rolling case and a thin shovel. Miri pulled the radio control box with the pre-wired harness and landing lights out of the case and uncoiled them in the hangar, while Jamal went out and started dragging the shovel around the outer perimeter of the melded sand landing pad to make a furrow for the landing light harnesses to lay in.

Jamal showed her where the radio control box could plug in and attach to the side container. Miri laid the harness of lights in the furrow and Jamal followed along filling in the furrow with sand to bury the harness. With Miri carefully positioning each light, and Jamal filling in the harness trench with sand, they had lights in place in short order. Jamal brought out some floodlights to hang on the container sides that would focus out on the landing pad and plugged in their control boxes to the harness connectors.

Jamal checked that the control boxes were powered up and then had Miri get in the plane, set the plane's radio to the control frequency. She keyed the mic on the frequency to turn on the landing lights and then floodlights in increasing increments of brightness with each mic click. Miri, satisfied everything was working, shut down the plane systems.

Jamal said he had some rocks to find and walked toward the cliff, as Miri was kicking some last bits of sand to hide the transition from the outer edge of the hard melded sand to the soft surrounding beach. Jamal as walked back around from behind the building with two chunks of fallen rock in his hands. He placed a chunk at each outside corner where the black builder cubes met.

Miri looked at him questioningly, but he said, "Why don't we take a walk down the beach to get clear and then we can close up the hangar.

They walked down along the football field width strip of beach ending in the cliffs at each end with their feet leaving footprints in the damp sand just above the level that the incoming surf was reaching. The shallow water was paler green than the deeper blue of the sea further out and looked inviting. Miri said she was going to head for the water right after they got things set up in the living quarters.

At the far end of the beach by the cliff face, they stopped, and Jamal called his team to ask them to seal up the hanger, cloak the enclosure, and put the ceiling in the living space into shade structure mode. Miri saw the builder cubes swarm out of the upper side containers to start stacking themselves up to fill both the back and front openings into the hangar. It only took a minute for them to finish stacking into unbroken walls of black that shimmered momentarily before the whole structure disappeared.

The "cloaking" effect was amazingly good, and the structure remained effectively hidden even as they got closer to where the building must be. Only the small green tops of the landing lights and the 4 chunks of rock Jamal had placed at the corners were visible. Miri walked toward the corner rock with her arm extended to feel for the builder cube wall.

Jamal said, "It's good to keep an eye out for the corner rocks, because walking blindly into a corner will definitely leave a mark."

Miri felt the corner and walked with her hand feeling along the builder cube side wall to the back corner marked by the rock chunk just a short distance in from the cliff. As she felt her way around the corner a door eerily appeared set into a small visible surround of shipping container. Jamal joined her in front of the door and placed his palm on a dark plate on the visible shipping container wall next to the door. He left it there for a couple of seconds until a pulsating glow appeared around the edge. He then had Miri put her palm on the dark plate and hold it there until the pulsating glow flashed brightly and went out. He then had her reapply her palm to the pad and the click of the door unlocking could be heard.

Jamal started to go in past Miri when, with a modest hip motion, she body checked him up against the back wall with some force. Speaking in a mock Southern belle accent she said, "Ladies first", grinned and headed in. Jamal collected himself with a rueful shake of his head and followed her inside.

They came into a 40' steel shipping container with corrugated heavy steel walls and worn wood plank floor. The space was well lit by white squares arrayed along the ceiling and a variety of cases, boxes and equipment were strapped off to the walls. Just inside between the door and the outer wall was a floor to ceiling glass enclosure with a large glass door leading into it. Her eyes followed the black stacks of builder cubes running upwards in the corners of enclosure through the square openings in the container floors above. Sunlight was streaming down through the opening from above.

A single door had been set into the hangar side wall immediately inside and a set of double doors occurred in the same wall towards the other end.

Jamal opened and held the single door to the hanger saying in a gentlemanly tone, "After you". They came out into the hangar and Miri was surprised to see the builder cube walls that had formed up to close in the front and back of the hangar looking like tinted glass sheets that she could see out through out to the beach and out to cliff. She looked questioningly at Jamal who said the builder cubes flat surfaces could duplicate the photons hitting the outside surface with identical photons emitted off the inside surface they were looking at. He said the outside cloaking works in a similar way, except the brightness is not dialed down.

Jamal started to talk about the level of difficulty to compute the raytracing calculations used in the cloaking, but Miri stopped him and said, "Why don't we grab our luggage and get moved in. We can continue the raying whatever discussion at another time when I am not being distracted by the waves outside."

Jamal grinned, said something getting a dolly unstrapped, and headed for the shipping container on the other side. Miri got out her carry-on suitcase, her shoulder bag, and two worn backpacks of other clothing she had brought for the weeks they would be operating out of here. Jamal rolled up with a dolly that had two of his suitcases already on it and a box with fresh bedding linens and towels. He grabbed his backpack out of the plane and added it with Miri's stuff on the dolly. Jamal rolled the laden dolly through the door back into the shipping container and asked Miri to open the glass door in the corner. They both went inside with a couple of suitcases and the glass door closed behind them. Jamal said they should avoid touching the walls and keep as close to the center as they could. She squeezed in next to him and he reached over to a dark pad on the wall and made two upwards swipes with his palm.

The dark floor section they were standing on started lifting like an elevator. As they passed through the second level shipping container, Miri saw boxes of food and supplies near the elevator, and a divider wall about a third of the way down the container. She thought that beyond this divider wall must be the space where all the builder cubes were stored when the hangar was opened up.

As they came up into the sunlit third level, the elevator opened out into a surprisingly modern looking open plan space. The coolness of the air-conditioning reached her as she opened the glass door, and they came out into the space. To the right of the elevator was a modern kitchen area dominated by two enormous commercial refrigerators. A counter with stool seating partially separated the kitchen from the main living and working areas.

Like the hanger below, the entire front and back of the living area was floor to ceiling transparent builder cubes. The structural uprights and roof supports of the frames spanning across over the hangar below were visible but finished with what looked like a light wood veneer. The builder cubes forming the ceiling displayed a wooden shade structure that appeared to be built over the top of the space with an expansive view of the sky above.

Jamal saw Miri looking up perplexed and said, "It's the builder cubes doing their view of the outside again. Only the architects recommended some ceiling or shade structure elements be added by the native child, so the place would feel cozier. The floor was again a light wood look with transparent runs of builder cubes set into the floor and bridging the gaps between the sectional spans. Miri could see the plane in the hanger below through these transparent floor sections.

Jamal pointed out the three small bedrooms on the far side and the two larger bedrooms in each front corner. Workstations with large expanses of monitors were arrayed along the back window wall and comfortable furniture was arranged in the living room area looking out over the beach. Jamal explained the workstations had been staffed by his regional builder cube and "stove" cube logistics teams while the underground control centers were being constructed. That team had now moved on to live in and outfit those control centers. They walked through the living room area and Jamal said it was a comfortable space to sit and read or watch entertainment programs on their tablets or on the large display in front of the builder cube wall at the front.

Miri said for now, she would take the larger front bedroom by the kitchen and Jamal could have the larger front bedroom on the far side. She smiled and said the sleeping arrangements might be negotiable, but she wanted them each to have their own space while they got more familiar with one another.

Jamal dropped her stuff in off in the room and then headed back down on the "elevator" to send up the rest of the luggage. Miri got out of her flight suit and into her shorts and one of her colorful tops then pulled the elevator loads of luggage off the arriving elevator. Miri made her bed and organized her bedroom while Jamal sat on the couch with his laptop, checking in on things with his team. When Miri emerged from her bedroom in her wrap with a towel over her arm, she said she was off duty until their evening flight was scheduled, was going to go take a swim, and invited him to join her. Jamal said he just needed to finish check-ins with his team and then he would then dig out his swimsuit and join her. She gave him a bemused look before taking the elevator down.

When finished with his check-ins, he closed his laptop and looked out to see Miri already swimming with strong strokes out across the bay. He put his suit on, grabbed a towel and headed out for the beach. He spread his towel on the sand next to hers, took off his shirt, and headed into the warm water to start to wade out. He was knee deep in the water when Miri saw him and adjusted her swimming direction to head his way.

She swam into the gentle surf line and then stood in the waist high water to greet him as he waded out. Jamal immediately saw he was overdressed for the occasion, but Miri didn't seem to mind, and they headed out to the deeper water to float and talk. Miri said the trappings of civilization become optional when you have your own secluded beach miles from civilization.

"Besides," she said, "Eleni's urging aside, I led you right off into the deep end last night. We need to find our footing to be able to work together, so that when the time comes for me to put on my flight suit, you are over the novelty and focused on the mission."

"Aye, aye sir" he said playing at standing at attention and saluting, as she started to float past him on her back.

From her reclined position she casually punched him in the kidney just hard enough to hurt and said "I mean it. We can have some fun during the day but come mission time I need you to be all business."

She stood up and walked up onto the beach, her body glistening in the sun. As he watched her towel off and put on her wrap, he was thinking this may be more difficult than she knew.

55

Miri spent the afternoon lounging on the couch reading and watching things on her tablet. Around five, she said she was getting hungry, put her book aside and stood to stretch.

She saw Jamal's body express instant interest and said, "Well you have clearly made progress this afternoon, so I think you deserve a treat before dinner." She came over and pulled his interested self out of the chair and led him back to her bedroom. Jamal figured Miri must have been hungry, because with her energetic efforts it was barely fifteen minutes later that Jamal was laying in the bed spent, while Miri was walking around in the kitchen pulling out things to eat. They ate and chatted and then Miri said they both should get some sleep in their separate beds ahead of the evening mission.

Jamal had rarely slept so soundly, and it was getting dark out when the alarm he set went off. He came out of the bedroom and saw that Miri was already dressed in her flight suit with a cup of coffee in hand sitting on the couch. She had a map displayed on the large monitor in the living room and she said there was coffee made in the kitchen. As he joined her on the couch with a cup she asked, "So, how is this game of bury the cube stack supposed to work?"

Jamal said they had just over a hundred of the communicator cube server stacks to bury and rig the ground loop antennas for the explosives signal. The idea was to spread them out in desolate places across the remote desert where they could be buried and never located again. There were circles identified on the map where Jamal wanted to fly to the approx. center of. They would turn off the Nav and GPS, pick a direction and a distance at random, and fly to that random point.

They would bury three of the communicator cube server stacks, fly back on the opposite heading about the same distance and then turn on the Nav to get them to their center of their next circle.

Jamal said, "By doing this totally offline, with random locations at night, in desert areas, the security team's hope is they will never be able to be found."

Miri said, "Based on your locations, we will probably only be able to do about three locations per night and be back by sunup. I've got your three starting locations for tonight entered as waypoints, so let's get the plane loaded and ready to go."

Miri went down to start her preflight check while Jamal pulled out nine stainless steel cube server enclosures plus one spare that were about the size of a medium suitcase. He was careful not to disturb the coiled wire shrink wrapped to the top as he loaded them in the plane. He then got an arrangement of builder cubes, and a case with a communicator cube inside loaded in. Lastly, he handed ten of the cardboard boxes marked Danger Explosives to Miri in the plane.

Miri arranged and strapped off the cube servers and explosive boxes securely in the back, then went up to the pilot's seat. She took four communicator cubes out of her bag and slid them in holders by the two front windows and two side windows and ran through her preflight checklist. She made a motion with her finger over the communicator cube down by the throttle levers and the native child avatar's beaming face appeared.

Miri said, "Kid, standby to Initiate Night Vision… and Initiate Night Vision Go!"

Each of the cubes in the windows projected a transparent gold-tinged view of what was outside across the windows.

Miri said, "Kid, take Night Vision Brightness down to 3 and standby for VTOL On Ground Deploy."

With everything loaded, Miri keyed the mic to turn on the

green landing light and the landing pad flood lights. Jamal turned off the interior hangar lights then got in as Miri finished her checklist. She told Jamal they were ready to head out and Jamal phoned his team. The builder cube walls at the front and back of the hangar scattered and soon both ends were open to the night outside.

She said to Jamal, "Alright, here we go," as she let off the brakes and pulled the communicator cube "missile" throttles slowly backward as the native child watched attentively. The plane started rolling backwards out of the hanger. out onto the landing pad. She pivoted the plane around until it was facing out to sea. With the brakes locked, Miri said, "Kid, standby for VTOL Ground Hover".

The builder cube tubes still pointing toward the ground started to make a whistling noise as low-level airflow started passing through them. Miri ran up the electric motors to check the propeller thrust and then set the props throttles to idle. She checked that the yoke was in its neutral position and said, "Kid, VTOL Ground Hover Go!"

The vertical thrust increased until the plane was just hovering a few inches off the ground. She did her maneuvering checks to the right and left to make sure everything on the builder cube vertical takeoff and landing arrangement was operating properly and checked that the dim gold-tinged night vision cube projections laid over the windows were aligned with the outside world. She then slowly pulled back on the wheel to increase vertical thrust and advanced the builder cube "missile" throttles to increase forward thrust.

The plane started to gain altitude and move out over the sea. Once the plane had enough altitude, she turned to fly them back towards the lit hangar and the lit landing pad with its green dots of light marking the perimeter and increased the forward speed so they were flying above stall speed. She gave the "Kid" the commands to transition to horizontal flight and soon the builder cube thrusters were again pivoted up to their horizontal positions. The airspeed increased as builder cubes came up into this position, and satisfied the plane was flying fine on just the builder cubes, Miri retracted the landing gear.

The lit hangar and landing pad was the only sign of civilization in the surrounding blackness with just the gold-tinged image of the cliffs and shoreline faintly visible in the night vision projections. Miri keyed the radio mic to turn off the hangar and landing pad lights and the darkness was complete below them.

Miri had the "Kid" increase the brightness of the night vision projections to 7 and the world outside brightened into a gold-tinged twilight that Miri and Jamal could clearly see the landscape below passing by. Miri pushed both the electric prop and the builder cube throttles forward and started the climb out to their cruising altitude for the first leg of their evening trip.

Miri told Jamal the collective builder cube thrusters in horizontal flight configuration could put out an amount of power comparable to private jet engines. She said while the max allowable speed for the plane could never begin to use all that power in level flight, it was possible to open them up a bit when climbing to cruising altitude like they were doing now. She pointed to the climb rate and said it put the normal climb rate of the plane with its regular props to shame.

Miri said it got particularly silly when she had tested short take offs and landings with all the builder cubes left in the horizontal flight configuration. She said for her first short takeoff trial with the plane loaded to weight capacity, she had not quite calibrated the throttles on the builder cubes sufficiently with the native child. She was on an isolated grass strip when she ran the electric propellers up to full power with the brakes on and then throttled up the builder cube "engines". The tires started sliding through the grass like the plane was on skis, so she released the brakes, and the plane leapt forward and upwards like it was being launched off an aircraft carrier. She had the plane flying nearly straight upwards on the builder cube thrust before she leveled off and throttled back.

As they reached their cruising altitude for the evening Miri eased both the prop and builder cube throttles back and set the autopilot for the first waypoint. Jamal had her turn off her phone and he took out a couple of specialty gaming dice that had so many faces they nearly appeared round. He said they were going to use the dice as a means to randomly determine the direction and distance they would head from each of center points they were flying to tonight. He rolled the larger one which came up with a 31 on the top.

"310 degrees is our vector from the upcoming waypoint." Jamal announced.

He rolled the smaller of the two dice and it came up with 22.

"22 minutes out from the center point once we reach those coordinates."

Miri looked over dubiously at his method, but when they got to the center point coordinates, she turned off the GPS, banked the plane around to the new vector, and started her timer.

Before long they were approaching the time and she pulled back on the throttles to start their descent. She had the native child put the night vision to 10, and standby to go to vertical lift. At 10 the outside view was approaching daylight brightness, and she adjusted their glide path to head towards a flat area at the base of some dunes. As she leveled out and the airspeed dropped, she had the child trigger the transition to vertical flight. They dropped down to just over the dune tops before Miri slowed them to a cautious pace for landing.

On the ground she shut things down, leaving the builder cubes where they were on the wing and leaving the landing lights on to light the sand out in front of the plane. Miri turned on the interior cabin light and made her way into the back of the plane. She unstrapped three of the communicator cube servers, three of the boxes containing the explosive charges, and the builder cube arrangement that Jamal had worked up. Jamal lifted everything out onto the ground in front of the plane and then pulled out a shovel and a couple of metal tube tools.

Miri put the spandex straps of a headlamp over her head and turned on the light. She carried the builder cube arrangement that had been made from her mine exploration builder cubes, the communicator cube case and one of the metal tube tools some distance out from the plane.

The builder cube arrangement was a dozen builder cubes magnetically fastened in a 3 wide by 4 long assembly with all the openings facing up. She set it on a level area of the dunes and then stepped back to the upwind side. She opened the case top and made a motion on the communicator cube inside. Immediately a thick plume of sand shot into the air as Miri counted to three and then stopped the process.

She took the metal tube tool over and stuck it down to measure the depth of the hole. She needed just a bit more depth, so she stood back and again made a motion with her finger to have the builder cubes dig for just half a second more. She checked the depth again with the metal tube tool and was satisfied. She stood back again and slid her finger quickly upwards and immediately back down on another line on the tablet and the builder cube arrangement popped out of the hole to land in an ungainly way on the dune's surface next to it.

Miri shut down the communicator cube controller and told Jamal the hole was ready. Jamal carried the communicator cube server over and set it on the ground by the hole. He removed the wrapping off the antenna wire on top and laid the tan colored wire on the ground to one side. He unfastened the top and set it to one side. Inside the enclosure was a stack of communicator cubes that filled the interior. Four vertical openings in each corner were provided for the explosive charges.

He drew with his finger across one of the corner communicator cubes and a pulsating glow started on it. He made a swiping motion with three fingers and pulsating glow spread to the entire communicator cube stack. He placed both his palms onto the top of the stack and the entire stack glowed brightly for a moment and then dropped to a very dim constant glow showing the server was now running. The green LED indications told him the server was interacting with the control room properly. Jamal's team would now see the added processing come online back at the control room.

Miri had brought over one of the "Danger Explosives" labeled boxes to set on the ground by the server enclosure. Jamal uncoiled the antenna wire and he and Miri started laying it out across the dune in a long oblong loop that was nearly the wingspan of the plane. Using the shovel, Jamal buried the wire in the sand.

Miri had opened one end of the "Danger Explosives" box and set it upright for Jamal to hold. She pulled out a tall piece of right-angled steel with explosive charges spaced along it. It had a wire lead off one end that provided voltage to the detonators. She carefully slid the steel angle down into one of the vertical openings left in a corner of the enclosure, so the explosive charges faced inward. She repeated the process with the other three charges, sliding them carefully down.

She confirmed with Jamal that he had good signal from the antenna and then tested the trigger voltage herself with a small light up meter plugged into each of the four connectors on the electronics box. She then plugged in each of the four wires leading to the corner explosive charges to make them live, before Jamal fastened the top of the enclosure back in place. Miri handed Jamal one of the metal tubes, and they used the hooks at the ends to lower the enclosure down in the hole. Jamal arranged the slack on the antenna wire and then used the shovel to push the buildup of sand, back in the hole to bury the enclosure.

After all three server enclosures had been buried and the sand leveled to conceal the fact anything had been done to the dune, they packed up, fired up the plane's vertical thrusters and took off to backtrack on the opposite heading for about the same number of minutes, before turning on the GPS and heading to the next center point on their route. Jamal told her this process ensured that the enclosure would be unable to be found, even by themselves, after they left the area. Only the fail-safe shortwave signal could ever reach the enclosure antenna and trigger the explosives in the event the server needed to be destroyed.

Jamal asked Miri if she thought the just the small blocks of explosive in the corners were enough. Miri said the explosive was powerful enough that only one or two of the explosive verti-cal arrangements would be more than enough to break down the cubes. Having four of the explosive vertical pieces was intended to not just vaporize the cubes but blow the lid off and spread the ashes out to make it difficult to tell what had been there. In her testing all that was left of the cubes after triggering the explo-sives was just a crater in the sand you could drive a car into.

Miri said, "This is why we will be double checking everything and doing every enclosure burial by the book. It would be best, for both of us, if only the cube servers get buried in this process."

56

Khadija had gotten in the habit of riding over early in the morning to the hangar to meet Richard down in the control chair arena for breakfast. He had moved out of the bus and was living in the furnished bedrooms in the wing off the back of the arena. He was working overnight shifts with the technicians that had arrived earlier in the week. Their shift wrapped up around the time Khadija arrived, so they could have breakfast and do some planning before the training day began with women in the hangar above.

The women in the training had moved from the simulations to remotely operating the robotic loaders in the hangar. They had fired up the conveyor room assembly that fed the plywood boxes onto the belt and were practicing the loading with the boxes coming at ever increasing speed as the women became more comfortable with the loading process. From today on, they were going to be operating continuously for the entire day with the conveyor running at full speed.

Richard would go up and be locked in his cubicle corral to watch the start of the training. The women operating the loaders were surprisingly good and there was little for him to comment on, so he was getting to head back down to bed earlier each day.

Khadija would order dinner after training wrapped up and bring it down for the both of them to eat. They would watch some entertainment in the common room until the time came for her to head off to her dorm ahead of the techs arriving for their overnight shift.

Khadija checked in with the security scarves to let them know she would be down the control chair arena and then headed for the elevator. Richard was up on the center platform tinkering with one of the control desks when she came out into the arena. She could see, with the techs' help, they had already made considerable progress on the install of the control desks, and the massive video wall arrays.

He looked up and she waved the food bag as she walked over to the eating area. She set the food on the table, got herself something to drink from glass front coolers that had been recently installed and sat down to chat with him. Khadija made him follow Miri's rule of not talking about work while they were eating. They had fallen into the habit of chatting about things in the world or in their lives growing up during meals. Only after they had finished would they segue into the work and training plan for the day.

As they were eating, they heard the circular wall entry turning and saw the Director walk out and look up at the center tower of video wall being assembled before heading their way. She greeted them both, pulled up a chair at the table and took a globe memento out of her purse. She opened it to start up the native child projection and asked to be connected to Ariana and Ahmed. Before long, their images appeared as if sitting directly across the table from them. Ariana greeted her and Richard, gave a nod to the Director, and asked how they were getting along. She spent a bit of time checking in on what they had been up to since Richard's arrival and seemed pleased with their responses.

Ariana nodded at Ahmed who said, "Word is both the training and control chair arena is on track to be largely completed by Friday. Is this so?"

Richard and Khadija nodded, and he continued, "Then, we would like to ask you both to depart Sunday evening for the remote village where the manufacturing facility is located. We would like to have the first robotic loaders set up, and ready to start loading as soon as possible and we think sending the two of you there to make it happen is the best plan at this point.

Ariana asked, "Does this sound like something you both are up for?"

Richard and Khadija looked at one another to check then back at Ariana and Ahmed to say they were good with it.

Ahmed asked, "Khadj, can you have your lead women step up and oversee the transition of the trained women down to the control chair space? You can check in with them from the manufacturing facility end to get them up and running. Richard, if you can get your techs set up to finish the last of the check out, before you leave, that would be great. We would like to have you set up the maintenance bays when you first arrive at the manufacturing faciliity. A case with the twinned communicator cubes is waiting for you in the transfer room there. If you can get one of the pair installed in the chairs before you leave and take the twinned cubes along with you to the manufacturing facility, you can get them plugged in to the robotic loaders, so they are ready.

Ariana said, "Glad you can join us at the manufacturing facility and thanks again for all you have accomplished in this short time."

Ariana and Ahmed's images faded as the Director ended the call. The Director said there would be a bus flight waiting for them in the upper control facility "parking" area Sunday night. They should have all their clothes and items they wanted to take with them for an extended stay loaded on the bus before midnight. She suggested the two of them finish up their work as early as possible and get out for the weekend. She said it sounded like it might be a while before they got another chance.

They sat there in silence watching the Director walk into the distance and disappear behind the turning wall entry. Khadija said, "Well, Cowboy Richard, it sounds like our trails are going to run together for a while, so we better get along. Speaking of getting along, it's time for me to get upstairs to the training. I would suggest you skip the training session and use the time down here to get the control chairs cubes installed. Be sure to use the list of the chair locations the women have picked out when installing them and hang their avatar face graphics on the front and back of their chairs. That way the women will know which chair is theirs when they transfer down here next week. I can tell by your yawns that my scintillating banter is wearing thin. Get some sleep and we'll figure out how to get this all done over dinner tonight."

Richard yawned again while trying to agree, so Khadija shoved him towards his bed and headed off to the elevator to meet her morning shift of women.

Khadija's phone rang midway through the morning training session with Xanthe's ringtone. Khadija answered it saying, "Aristotle's Falafel – if it can be gummed up in grape leaves, we've got it."

Xanthe's voice on the phone said "Hey Khadj, speaking of grapevines, I heard that you might have a weekend free coming up. We have a large vineyard house booked in the countryside and Miri is already coming to visit and is bringing Jamal. Miri says you and the cowpoke engineer have some chemistry you've been trying to paper over and thinks we need pry the two of you out of that high tech playground to join us. Don't even think of saying no and tell cowboy there he's coming, or I'll have Miri hog tie him and strap him in the cargo hold. It'll be fun, so be ready for Miri to you kidnap you both, one way or the other, Friday afternoon. Gotta run!"

The call abruptly ended, and Khadija knew Xanthe had intentionally hung up before she could protest or turn down the invite.

She told Richard the plan over dinner down in the arena and said that she suspected Ariana had a hand in arranging this. Ariana and Ahmed knew that the coalition had other control chair arenas to set up, and over 1500 remote operators to get trained. Ariana knew the coalition would be relying on both of them to take on a large part of that work. Khadija thought Ariana wanted any personality issues resolved between the two of them before they were sent off on Sunday. Richard looked dubious when she mentioned the threat of Miri hog tying him, but Khadija's expression said the matter was not in any doubt.

They spent the evening watching a program in the common room until the start of his techs' shift was coming up. As she left him in the arena and headed up in the elevator for her evening ride back to the dorm, she realized that she had shifted away from her disparaging habit of calling him cowboy and had started calling him by his actual name. She found herself having a warm fuzzy feeling about spending the weekend with him. It occurred to her that maybe Miri knew more about what was going on with the two of them than she was willing to face up to herself.

57

The captain was standing in front of the topographical map pinned on the wall running over a marked route when the door opened and the last addition to his investigative ground team finally arrived. The captain looked disdainfully at the last addition and motioned for him to grab a seat at the back of the uniformed group gathered.

He said, "Alright boys, this is our air sniffer. We need to get him up on the side of the mount near the end of this ridge here to sniff around."

The last addition looked at where the captain was pointing on the map quizzically and piped up with "Climatologist".

"Clima-what" said the captain.

"Climatologist" repeated the latest addition.

The captain, somewhat miffed, continued pointing at the map "Well, Mr. Sniffer, the rest of us are apparently being yanked off our stations to get your Clima-whatever backside out across no-mans-land to sniff the air off the back of this ridge. We don't know who's putting out the stink you'll be sniffing, so the guys here are along to make sure we all get back if they prove to be unfriendly. With luck you may get your sniffing done without anyone losing extremities in the process."

Moving aside so the team could view a second map, the entire marked route could now be seen.

The captain continued, "We'll be flown in here and will be heading out past the mount here on this route to the ridge."

Unless the climatologist was missing something, the dashed

rectangle they were being flown into looked to be the middle of the sea miles away from the mount.

The captain looked at his watch and then over at the climatologist with an expression of disapproval before saying, "Alright boys that's it. Get your anoraks packed, cause we're heading out for a nunatak in the middle of nowhere".

In the bustle that followed, the climatologist could be heard asking, "What's a nunatak."

58

Khadija woke with the rays of the morning sun shining all too brightly through an unfamiliar window and making her squint. Unfamiliar window? She sat up suddenly to find herself fully dressed in a strange bed in an unfamiliar room with a bit of a headache that made it difficult to think. It took her a moment to remember it was the weekend before she relaxed and lay back down to drowsily piece things together.

It was all the fault of Eleni and her quest to find the best vintage from the ample stocks of the vineyard house. From the moment they had arrived, Eleni was constantly putting glasses with just a "taste" of yet another novel vintage in everyone's hands. They had been sitting out under the portico in back of the large house enjoying the mild warmth of the Aegean late afternoon, sipping wine, and chatting. They had been celebrating something about Jamal and Miri having finished successfully losing all the communicator cube servers in the Sahara.

For dinner last night, Xanthe had brought out a variety of steaming dishes from the house while the ever-hospitable Eleni topped up their glasses. Khadija had been cheerfully feeling the influence of Eleni's new vintage samples to go with dinner, but the celebration had also been a little bittersweet. Miri would be losing Jamal who had to head back to the western world after the weekend and her and Richard would be heading for the wilds of the remote village by the manufacturing facility.

Khadija, who never drank in her home country and rarely drank when deployed, had found herself needing to get away from Eleni's continuing parade of after dinner cognacs to take a walk and clear her head. She had wandered through the twilit rows of vines and had somehow come to rest on a bench over-looking the sea.

She had watched the orange edges of the clouds reflected in the sea fade to indigo as the shades of night started to move in. She had thought she should be getting back but seemed to lack the ability to stand. As she had made a wobbly second attempt at getting up, a familiar figure came into the clearing. He had caught her just as she was starting to list severely to starboard, and she had grabbed around his neck to keep from falling.

She found herself looking directly in his face as he eased her back down on the bench and had seemed unable to control her arms to release her him. She had inexplicably leaned in to kiss him and he had patiently waited for her to finish the kiss and pull back in surprise to the limits of her arms that were unwilling to let go. As he suggested helping her back to the house, she had cut him off with a more passionate kiss and this time he responded in kind.

After some time with her hugging him on the bench, he had somehow used her firm grasp around his neck to get her to a standing position. She vaguely remembered him supporting her as they started hobbling together back down the rows of vines towards the house. Her last memory of the evening was of being carried, like her father had when she was a little girl, back into the house.

Now in the morning light, the memory of the evening and the aftereffects of the wine left her uncertain, but she forced herself to get out of bed and face the day. The sea breeze coming in the window held the promise of another warm day, so she showered to shake off the cobwebs. She selected shorts and a top from her overnight bag, thankful for a break from the head-to-toe cover-age of her home country clothes.

She walked down the hall to the kitchen where Miri was sitting in the nook with a cup of coffee.

Miri said, "Well good morning, apparently there is life after a run in with the vineyard's best after all!"

Khadija replied, "I'm not so sure you can call it life, but at least I survived. I must have been embarrassingly out of it after dinner last night. I know I took a walk and was on a bench at some overlook, but it's kind of fuzzy after that. Richard must have come up to check on me and I had my arms around his neck trying not to fall – and I kissed him and – then I kissed him again and he kissed me back and I don't really remember anything after that. Oh Miri, what have I done?".

Miri said, "What you've done is make some progress with your cowboy, that's what you've done. It was touching to see him carry you into the house and tuck you in. We were giving him a bit of grief for only taking your shoes off, but he started acting all Lone Ranger honorable and you seemed comfy enough, so we let you be. I'd put off worrying about it this morning until you've had a cup of tea and you're thinking clearly."

Khadija wasn't sure how she was going to face Richard this morning, but tea sounded like a good idea. She put the kettle on and asked if anyone else had been up yet.

"The girls usually stay up late when they first get together, so I wouldn't expect to see them anytime soon. Your cowboy was up when I came in and has already headed out on the vineyard range with Jamal."

"Good, I need a bit of time before I can face him this morning", said Khadija.

She took her tea out to the portico and looked out over the morning lit rows of vines. It was peaceful there, so she had sat to enjoy a morning to herself and her thoughts – which annoyingly were mostly thoughts about Richard.

A while later the girls were up preparing breakfast, when Richard and Jamal returned from their morning outing. He must have seen something of her inner embarrassment because he walked over by her and said in low voice, "No worries about last night. Let's just start over by being ourselves at breakfast and see what the day brings."

Xanthe and Eleni brought out breakfast and they had a leisurely morning at the table laughing and telling stories. She was feeling more herself after some food and found herself inserting herself into the verbal sparring that was Miri and the Greek girls' way of conducting a conversation. The two men held up well in the fray with four headstrong and opinionated women and seemed to be having a fun time despite being on the sharp end of some of the verbal jabs.

They had spent the afternoon poking around some lesser-known local architectural ruins, had lunch at a restaurant Eleni liked in town, and then found themselves again with wineglasses in hand on the portico as evening set in.

That evening Eleni was under strict instructions not to ply her with multiple vintages, so she was only slightly tipsy after their early dinner. The girls were heading back into town for an art gallery tour that Eleni participated in every month, and while they were all welcome to attend, the car would only hold four. Miri immediately chimed to say that the art tour was something Jamal should see as part of his horizon expanding and suggested, with a mischievous smile, that she and Richard could use some quiet time to take on the dishes while they were out having fun.

After the car pulled out and they were alone together, they fell into what had become their usual banter while dispatching the dishes and walking back out to the point to sit on the bench and watch the sunset. It was with her wits fully about her that found herself again kissing Richard and snuggling against him as the breeze cooled with the appearance of the stars. They walked back to the house hand in hand, and she didn't seem to mind him removing her clothing as they kissed in her bedroom in the dark.

And so it was, they found themselves comfortably spooned together in her bed as morning dawned. They sat up and fell into their normal morning chatting routine in bed as they looked out the open window. Being in a climate where you could open the windows during summer without expiring from the heat was a pleasant change. It was only the awkward moment of getting up to retrieve their fallen clothes that reminded her of the turn their relationship had taken last night.

When they finally made a late appearance for breakfast, there were supportive smiles and expectant looks all around but a silence broad enough to run a cargo plane through.

Khadija finally had to say, "Alright already, yes we slept together and yes we are still talking to one another, so let's get back to our regularly scheduled programming here."

They all laughed and broke out into their usual banter over a casual breakfast. They spent the day relaxing around the house and vineyard, until the time to leave approached. Khadija felt a pang as she changed out of her shorts and back into her all-encompassing home country clothing for the return trip. She was looking forward to the remote village, where she would no longer be bound by the cultural limitations and dress of her home country.

With their overnight bags in the car and Xanthe getting in to drive, they said their goodbyes to Jamal and Eleni. Richard seemed surprised by the bro hug he was given by Jamal and even more by the enthusiastic hugs Eleni was giving each of them. She and Richard were sitting in the backseat of the car for a while before Miri's lips could gently disengage from Jamal's and her flight suited form leave his embrace. Eleni escorted Miri away from Jamal who looked like he could go lip to lip for a second round.

With Miri in the car, Eleni leaned over to the window and whispered, "I said expand his horizons, not become them. You better treat him well and not just fly off and break his heart."

By the wistful look on Miri's face looking back at Jamal as they pulled out, it was clear there was little chance of that.

Xanthe drove them back out to the plane at the small airport nearby. Xanthe hugged her and Richard, saying, "Richard, it's been great to meet you. I am so glad to see Khadj in such good hands. You look after her while you two are off toting cubes somewhere on the far side of the world." Richard nodded and Xanthe turned to give Miri a quick hug saying, "I am not going to miss being crammed in your tiny cockpit, but I will miss you. Fly safe until I see you all again."

They strapped into seats in the small plane and gave a final wave to Xanthe on the ground as they flew off.

59

Miri flew them back to the airbase, and after another round of goodbyes, took off into the setting sun. As her plane disappeared into the distance, Richard wondered when they would see everyone again. As they started walking rolling their bags behind them, Khadija checked in with the Director's assistant to say they were on the ground and to give them half an hour and then pick them up at the logistics unit.

Unlike the temperate climate they had come from, they were already sweating and hot after only the short walk across the baking concrete to the logistics unit and gratefully went inside where it was cool. Khadija packed up some last-minute stuff from her control station as he pulled out the last of her mom's cooking from the refrigerator to put in bag to take with them.

The assistant pulled up and came inside. The assistant asked them for their satellite phones and badges, before getting them loaded into the car. The assistant dropped them off by the hangar loading door and held the exit door open for them to wheel their travel bags and stuff in. He said they should use the transfer room back entry into the control center "parking" area where the bus would be. That would minimize their interaction with the control center team and contractors that were now working there. He said the Director and Chief wished them well on their journey and thanked them again for all their work to get the facilities here ready.

They headed down into the control chair arena to see what they could crib together for dinner from the containers in the bag he had toted along. They sat in the common room eating and have a regular evening watching entertainment on the large monitor until late. Khadija was leaning with her head on Richard's shoulder fighting off sleep when the time came for them to depart.

All of Richard's and her suitcases, plus the boxes of things Khadija had cleared out of her dorm room before they had left for the weekend were waiting on a large shipping dolly. Richard added the travel bags and Khadija's last items on the dolly and was starting to push it across the arena towards the ramp to the transfer room when the beep of forklift came up from behind him and Khadija's voice saying, "Hop aboard."

Once he was securely seated next to her, she effortlessly positioned the forks under the dolly, lifted it and they were off heading around the floor full of control chairs. They passed some of the training women's avatar face graphics hung of the top of the chairs.

Khadija said, "Oddly I'll miss the women and this place but don't worry, we'll see enough of those faces on the loaders where we are going."

The arena was lost from sight as they entered the ramped tunnel leading up to the transfer room. Richard opened doors and Khadija drove them through the transfer room and out into the arrivals "parking" area where the bus was parked. The control center work shift was over, and the arrivals area was deserted for their departure. Richard pulled all their luggage and boxes off the dolly and started loading them in under the bus as Khadija drove the forklift and dolly back through to the other side of the transfer room.

He saw her looking up at the large rectangular shaft extending far above them as she walked back across the "parking "area towards the bus and said, "I hope that section of concrete is moved out of the way before the builder cubes shoot us up out of here."

Richard closed up the storage compartments, and latched the bus entry door behind them as they sat in the front bus seats and fastened their seat belts. Khadija pulled out her globe memento, opened it and made finger motions on it to start the native child projection, before wedging it in the dashboard. When the smiling patterned face appeared, she asked the child to notify the control center team that they were ready for departure. The child nodded and turned to the side as though talking to someone else.

Seatbelt warning dings rang out inside the bus and red warning beacons started to flash around the walls of the arrivals parking area with the sound of sirens. Khadija said the bus flight would be handled by Jamal's control team and they shouldn't have to do anything but make sure they were buckled back in once they heard the seatbelt warning dings ahead of their arrival. Rectangular wall outcrops above all the doors leading out of the arrivals area started to lower covering over all the door openings like blast doors. Richard looked around the space to see if there was anything left out that the force of the builder cubes jetting them out would disturb, but everything looked to be put away. Khadija reached down to the dash to flip on a couple of lights inside the bus as sirens and flashing beacons stopped and the lighting in the space started to dim.

Builder cubes came whizzing in to quickly form up to enclose the bus. The lights in the garage went out so only the flashing of the red lights lit the space. The view out the front window was soon obscured by the builder cubes forming up in front and back of the bus until nothing could be seen but their own reflections in the window. There was a brief time where nothing happened, and then with an audible whoosh, the bus rocketed upwards pressing them down in their seats.

Unlike the faux road motions and sounds used to bring workers in unawares, the builder cubes did not bother to conceal the sense of being shot upwards several thousand feet in the air and being accelerating forward at a rate that pushed them back in their seats. There was a bit of buffeting that felt like the bus might be going up through a cloud layer that abated after a few minutes as Khadija guessed they reached, for lack of a better term, their cruising altitude. Soon the seatbelt dings were heard to let them know they could move about.

They must have been high in the air because their ears popped, and Khadija flipped on the bus heater to try and fend off the cold now seeping in. They sat on the sofa in the back, but the bus heater was having difficulty keeping up with the cold of the altitude they were at. Richard pulled out travel pillows and thin blankets while Khadija found the fold out sofa in the lounge area at the back. She suggested they cuddle together on folded out sofa and double up the blankets to stay warm. He took off his boots and laid down, and she kicked off her shoes to join him. The warmth of laying together under the blankets made them fall off to sleep soon after their heads hit the pillows.

60

The ding of the seat belt warning woke Richard and found himself still comfortably spooned up against Khadj's warm back on the fold out couch. She had heard the ding as well and was starting to stir saying, "Looks like we are arriving."

They got up off the warm fold out couch and made their way, with blankets wrapped around them through the cold bus to the front seats and buckled in. The bus was buffeted again as it descended but settled as it banked around on its approach. There was a floating feeling with very little movement for a minute, followed by a settling motion and bit of a thud as they settled back on the ground.

They sat there for a couple of minutes as the builder cubes disassembled and flew off. Corrugated metal building walls to the sides of the bus were barely visible through the fogged windows. Some source of air seemed to be warming the outside of the bus, so the condensation soon dissipated. After a few minutes, the bus windows were entirely clear, and a large steel door was revealed in front of the bus. The steel door rose vertically into the air and the bus lurched forward.

They emerged into an expansive dock area enclosed within a giant building with untold numbers of truck size doors along the wall they were entering through, extending off in both directions. A wide maneuvering area and parking area with a couple of long rows of neatly parked shipping containers on trailers filled the center of the space.

As the bus maneuvered around the outside of the parked

containers, he could see neatly a dock height level running across the entire opposite side where more shipping containers on trailers were docked. Odd looking trailer tugs were attached to all of these trailers, and he saw a couple of the tugs towing trailers around without anyone running them, so he figured they must be autonomous. The dock level side of the building appeared to be built up against a rock cliff with a couple of large well-lit tunnels openings running out each end. A variety of openings with automated doors rising we spaced along this rock wall.

A host of manned forklifts were busy loading skids coming out of the openings into the lineup of containers along the dock. A long run of windows was set into the rock on an upper level overlooking the dock, where it looked like some people were seated while eating. The bus reached the end of the line of parked container trailers and pulled up alongside the far wall where a truck width ramp came down from the dock level.

Khadija opened the door, and a pleasantly warm breeze greeted them as they stepped out of the bus. The space was abuzz with the movement of forklifts up on the dock level and the autonomous trailer tugs pulling the full shipping container trailers back over into the truck bays. He opened the storage areas under the bus and was wondering what they should do with their stuff when a 4-seat golf cart towing a small trailer pulled up. An older man hopped out and Richard saw it was the scientist that had brought the communicator cubes to him at the concrete plant.

Khadija also recognized and greeted the scientist who said, "We're stretched a bit thin around here this time of day, so Ahmed asked me to swing down to meet you and get you settled in." Khadija was looking across at the logistics operation and as they watched, they could see one of the heavy 6" thick truck sized doors raise to allow an autonomous tug to tow a shipping container into the garage-like bay. On the far side of the bay, they could see another second heavy loading door that was closed.

Richard raised an eyebrow at the scientist, who just shrugged and said "All the shipping containers are scanned and checked in the outer bays, before being allowed to enter or leave. Security is kinda tight around here. Jamal's team is still working out some bugs, so let's get your stuff off the bus before the control algorithm decides enough milliseconds have elapsed and decides to drive it away for its next trip."

He helped them pile all their suitcases and possessions into the trailer and then drove them up the ramp to the dock level. Looking back down the long dock there was a swarm of what looked like a hundred bright yellow forklifts, picking up container height stacks of dark pieces as they slid out of openings in the rock wall. There was a constant crossing of the two marked lanes on the concrete expanse by forklifts running the stacks down and into the waiting trailered shipping containers docked there. The scientist said, "In addition to the advance shipping of the flat packed "stove" bases and ducts, this is where incoming containers with supplies for the village and items for the ongoing facility construction come in."

They watched a couple of drones zip overhead and the scientist said they tested their drones out in the shipping building before they were deployed to do the ongoing boundary spraying for insects that kept the village safe from disease.

The scientist turned the cart away from the busy dock and in through the large tunnel entry where the road expanded into four-lanes with a wide yellow striped median. This loading wing tunnel had the same telltale reinforcing structure pattern as the control chair arena and was coated with a white reflective surface that allowed for bright lighting. The wing had dozens of exterior loading docks with more of the heavy raising doors. Several of the loading doors were raised and Richard could see the interiors of empty shipping containers docked against the foam pads and dock bumper designed to keep outside weather at bay during loading. The scientist said these "exterior" docks were where the stacks of "clean stove project" cubes carried by the robotic loaders would eventually be loaded once the control team rolled out their drone delivery system. He said there was another wing of exterior docks like this one on the other side of the open shipping area they had come from, but for the time being all their loading would be done in the central area.

The scientist said, "They are running two shifts of forklifts loading the "stove" bases and ducts, so we have your robotic loader activity scheduled to occur when those shifts are over starting at midnight local time. You crossed nine time zones to get here, so it should be an easy transition for you to work the midnight shift.

Khadija said, "With the nine-hour time difference that means midnight here is nine in the morning back at the base when my women will be ready to load, so that should work". The scientist said, "Speaking of starting at midnight, we have a bunch of containers with your robotic loaders that will be docking after midnight. I would suggest getting to bed early this afternoon so you will be rested and ready to ferry loaders when midnight rolls around."

Even driving at the scientist's fast lane pace, it took several minutes to reach the far end of this exterior dock wing where the four-lane road curved around into a tunnel cut through the rock. The arched tunnel had the same telltale reinforcing structure pattern with a white reflective surface. Bright rows of lighting pointing up at the arced rock ceiling along the sides made the tunnel feel fairly airy as they followed the curve around out of sight of the exterior docks.

They were only in the tunnel for a minute before a patch of rosy lit clouds appeared through a widening opening in the tunnel ceiling ahead. The arched ceiling divided, leaving an opening in the center showing morning lit clouds above. The four-lane road widened and started to be divided with planted medians between the lanes located under the now continuous opening in the arched ceiling above the road.

"They call this the beltway" said the scientist as he drove down past various alcove entries and parking areas with carts saying some of the labs and control rooms were inside those areas.

He exited off onto a ramp curving up from the beltway below. The ramp took them up and out into a park area where the sky dotted with rosy clouds could be seen past the manicured park trees. The "drop off" as the scientist called the continous opening running above the beltway median, was screened from view at the park level by groupings of artfully placed rocks and manicured shrubs. On the far side of the "drop off" to the roadway below, things went from manicured, to entirely wild and overgrown. There was a high cliff wall rising up from a tangle of trees and prickly undergrowth at its base trying vainly to clamber up the rock face.

The cliff wall appeared to stretch around in an undulating manner that seemed to entirely wrap around the village that it encircled. The scientist said that the remoteness of this "rift" valley, with the village, and underground manufacturing plant made it the ideal location to keep the coalition "clean cooking stove" project hidden away.

They passed several people and families using the park as they turned from the outer road, in towards the village and saw a couple of people in kayaks out on the small lake. Everything seemed perfectly normal, but something about the way the recently planted ornamental trees were lit by the morning sunlight nagged at Richard. The thought was pushed to the back of his mind as they came into the village.

The village had small streets, a surprising variety of restaurants and pubs at street level, with an eclectic mix of housing on the floors above. Everything was jumbled in tight to the streets in a manner reminiscent of an old European village but with a South American flair. The scientist skirted up around the hill at the center of the village to finally pull up in front of a modern looking two-story apartment building on the outskirts.

The building looked brand new and the landscaping out front was still a work in progress. A rack for recharging electric bikes and scooters was located to one side of the entry sidewalk with a number of brightly colored scooters ready for use. They got out and each grabbed some luggage to take in.

The scientist led them into an atrium in the center of the apartment where a garden and some casual outdoor furniture was placed. A casually dressed girl and guy were sitting at one of the furniture groupings with cups in their hands and their notebooks open on their laps, earnestly comparing some sort of graphs just visible on their screens. The scientist said hi to the two, who barely looked up from their screens just giving a wave of their cups. He shook his head saying something about the science staff being oblivious to their surroundings and led them up the stairs.

As they arrived in front of Khadija's door, Richard could look over the railing and still see the two in conversation in the atrium below. Khadija looked at the scientist as if expecting him to open up, but he just motioned her towards a dark pad set next to the door. As she laid her palm on the pad a click could be heard as the door unlocked and they went in.

The apartment was spare and bit on the small side for his Austin size liking with a bit of a Scandinavian vibe. Glass and punched metal dividers set off the bedroom and bathroom without using doors while an overall light toned wood surround made up large areas of the walls and floor. A modern couch, desk, and office style chair were in the main area with a kitchenette along the far wall. A pair of glass doors opened onto a balcony with a couple of pieces of the outdoor style furniture like they had seen in the atrium.

The scientist suggested Khadija drop her stuff and start getting settled in while he went next door with Richard. Richard followed him back out and down to the next door where Richard placed his palm on the pad to open the door. They went in to find an identical apartment set up to Khadija's. He just dropped his luggage off inside the door and placed his satchel on the desk next to a binder.

He and the scientist made a couple of more trips down to the trailer to get everything carried up finishing with a load of Khadija's boxes they dropped off in her kitchen. They left the heavier case with the communicator cubes in the trailer and the scientist said he would drop it off to them later in the East maintenance bay Richard would be working out of.

The scientist asked them to bring their phones and tablets out on the balcony and headed out through the sliding glass doors. Richard went back to his apartment and pulled out his tablet from the satchel. He saw a binder laying there on the desk and flipped quickly through it to see that it seemed to have a bunch of information on living in the village. He took it along with his tablet and phone out through the sliding glass doors onto the balcony.

The balcony was a single deep continuous run of concrete running the length of the building with a deep roof overhang that provided shade along its back half. A stack of shoulder high planters were way down at the far end of the open balcony while stacks of chairs and tables were at the other end.

The scientist had pulled over a table and a couple of chairs and seated himself outside Khadijas apartment. He saw Richard looking at the planter walls as he sat and said that they were probably meant as dividers to eventually be installed between apartment balconies. He said a lot of the finishing stuff had to be put off with the moved-up arrival of folks like themselves.

Khadija came out of her sliding glass doors onto the balcony with her handbag and handed over her phone and tablet. The scientist put new SIM cards in his and Khadija's devices as they looked out across the park and at the panorama of cliff wall encircling the village.

The scientist made a satisfied sound and said, "There, you should be on the correct time and have a secure connection to the outside world now."

He pointed to the binder in Richard's hand and said, "Your guidebook will have all your background info and guidelines for getting around and living in the village. All the info on all the restaurants and amenities is also in the book. The guidelines basically come down to not being reckless on the electric scooters, not getting involved with any of the snakes or nasties they say hang out over by the cliffs, and whenever talking to friends, family, and co-workers in the outside world just stick to your cover story, and you'll do fine. I'm locked up in the lab areas most of the time, so I probably won't see a lot of you, but I'll text you my number if you need to call me. Not everyone here knows where this village is located or about the tech we are dealing with, so keep what you know to yourself unless Ariana or Ahmed clear you to tell them. Again, stick to your cover story to keep us all safe here, and otherwise try and squeeze in a little fun while trying to meet the crazed schedule we all are working under. Good to have you here, but I need to get back to the lab and my team."

The scientist got up and started walking down the balcony towards the stairs at the far end.

"So where are we exactly?" Khadija called after him.

He paused at the top of the stair with a grin to say, "In the rift village of course – just stick to your cover story," and headed down to the cart.

61

Richard said, "Rift village - stick to your cover story - whatever did that mean?"

Khadija said "Well, whatever it is, it will have to wait until after we get settled in and have something to eat."

They ordered breakfast, then agreed to meet back out at the table on the balcony after showers and a change of clothes. Richard got a text that their food was delivered to their order coordinates as he was dressing, and when he went out the plates with insulated covers were already set out on table. Khadija came out and sat and ate while paging through their guide binders calling out interesting items they ran across.

Richard, flipping through the guidebook binder starting from the back, thought looked a lot like the kind of books you would find in a hotel. The back of the binder largely talked about all the places to eat and things to do in the village. The middle told how to "do" all the things to live, get around, order groceries, make calls, and even operate the TV. One of the services they had just used was the ability to order food from any of the restaurants. Food along with groceries, clothing, or other needs from the on-line commissary could be delivered to your living space or office.

The only "don'ts" appeared to be don't play on rocks or in shrubs by the drop off to the lower level, don't maim yourself riding bikes or scooters recklessly down the ramps down to the lower level or into the docking bays, and don't try any parkour tricks to leap over the drop off to the outer ring by the cliffs.

The guide was particularly insistent about not messing around with the wild outer ring by the cliffs. It insinuated that there were nasties waiting in the outer perimeter, and much worse beyond the cliffs. A couple of photos of venomous snakes hiding in trees and info on the malaria-ridden mosquitos and pests that could come over the cliff underscored the point. The constant autonomous drone patrols and spraying done in this cliffside perimeter to keep the village disease free and to monitor for outside nasties implied this was a place you should never want to even think about going.

He reached the front pages where personalized information appeared. On the front page was his name, his work title and the description of his job, and a brief bio, probably taken from his company's website. Below in the area titled "Cover Story" he learned that he was supposedly flown to Quito, loaded on a blacked out bus to drive somewhere to a coast, the bus driven onto a ferry for a long ride at sea, landed at a location where a long bus ride was needed to get him to the village an undetermined number of miles outside of Esmeraldas Ecuador.

The cover story said the NGO had taken over an abandoned "village" and had built it out as a home for all of the employees it needed at the manufacturing facility site. It noted that his cellular calls would be routed out through the cell towers in Esmeraldas. It recommended that videoconference calls be limited to the living room desk or lower-level office areas with a blank wall behind. Video calls from the park or other areas where a larger overview of the village could be seen were to be avoided.

Khadija said her cover story was similar only it had her location outside Tumbes Peru. They finished up breakfast and decided some exploring was in order.

Khadija and Richard pulled a couple of scooters out of the rack in front of the apartment and headed back out across the park towards the drop-off. They carefully negotiated the ramp down to the beltway access road. To either side of the grassy median below the drop off was a fast lane for golf carts or speedier vehicles, a slow lane for loaders/equipment and an outer bike/scooter lane. As they made their way along in the scooter lane, they passed alcove entries where carts and bicycles were parked outside the entry doors to the lower-level rooms.

The guide binder said that only your phone compass app could tell you which direction was which in the valley. Real compasses were apparently unreliable down in the rift valley due to some characteristic of the surroundings. They checked the direction and then scooted off to follow the gradual curve of the belt-way towards the Northern shipping docks. A large parking area opened on the inside of the road where service elevators and regular elevators from the village level above opened into. They saw a man lift being driven out of one of the service elevators and passed other construction equipment driving in the slow lane of the beltway. The guide binder said stairs were located next to the elevators for those wanting the exercise.

A pleasant voice said, "On your left" directly behind them. They had been scooting side by side in the fast lane around some slower forklifts carrying landscaping shrubs in the slow lane, so Khadija sped up and Richard pulled in behind her to make way for those behind. A two wheeled gyroscopically stabilized waiter robot, or "waitbot," as they were called at Richard's company, whizzed past them carrying covered food trays and drink racks someone had ordered for delivery. The pleasant robotic voice thanking for moving aside trailed off as it sped into the distance.

They passed a number of storage bays with specialty lifts and large telescoping work platforms and a maintenance area where all the forklifts, loaders, carts, and other equipment could be serviced. The drop off opening to the sky above and the grassy median below ended as they headed into the connector tunnel. The road widened back out with a paint striped loading area marked off in front the long line of Northeast exterior dock doors they were passing .

When Jamal had his delivery system ready, Khadija's women could quickly fill the exterior containers docked here so the container loads could immediately depart for their destinations without having to wait in the outside "trucking yard" that the guide said that the central building truck bays led to. Corridors carved into the inside rock wall near the end of the wing could be seen leading to dock level offices, service elevators, and cold storage areas for palettes of food.

The docking wing opened into the main shipping area building where the forklifts and trailer tugs were keeping the several hundred trailered shipping containers in the building in a continual motion. Several workers, running around on self-balancing personal transports, were weaving in and out among the shipping container trailers to close and seal the doors on loaded trailers that had pulled out away from the dock. They saw them also open the back doors of the parked lines of empty containers waiting for a space along the dock to open up.

The electrically driven autonomous tugs that picked up and took the trailered shipping containers into the entry bays for scanning and then outside into the trucking yard were controlled by one of Jamal's coding teams programs the scientist has said. They looked like smaller robotic versions of the kind of low-profile tugs commonly used at airports to push airplanes back from the boarding gates.

Numbers stenciled on the floor and printed on signs hung in from the ceiling above defined the docking locations along the unbroken football field length of dock platform. As they drove along the dock between the shipping containers, they had to keep an eye out to avoid the forklifts constantly crossing over with loads to go into the docked shipping containers.

Richard looked over at the dozens of openings in the rock where the parade of flat pack "stove" base and duct pieces slid out on forkable skids from what guide called a high heat environment behind where the pieces were manufactured. Khadija said the flat pack bases could be folded to create a five-sided box with a "refrigerator" door that the "stove" cube could be set on top of. She said the long strips of dark material stacked on the narrower skids just folded into an open-ended duct designed to slide into the outer tapered faces of the cube.

A staging area along the rock wall was full of forklifts plugged up to charge, and stacks of empty pallets left over from deliveries.

The set of windows looking out from the upper level of the rock wall was where the guide binder had indicated the canteen with its dining and lounge areas were located serving those working shifts in the shipping and maintenance areas. They passed through the large rock opening that entered into the Northeast wing and gunned the scooters so that soon the dozens of loading doors gave way to the tunnel leading back to the beltway.

An arc of blue sky appeared through the drop off opening as they came back out into the beltway with its grass medians. They passed the West roadway ramp, with the elevators and parking area for service vehicles, bicycles, and scooters near its bottom. Across from the West elevators was a large maintenance space that was specifically for the robotic loaders that Richard would eventually need to get set up. Just beyond the bay entry they started passing the parking/charging spaces along the outer wall for all the robotic loaders.

Richard mentioned that the five hundred parking/charging spaces for the robotic loaders extended along the entire Southern half of the beltway. The charging spaces were regularly interrupted by a series of large doors marked with giant numbers that would raise to allow entry to and from the cooling and conveyor rooms behind. These were the rooms that had been mocked up in the hangar and that they had been training Khadija's remote operator women to maneuver in.

Richard said the cooling rooms just inside were a bit of a misnomer as, even with blasts of cooled air being circulated, were still projected to be warmed to nearly one hundred degrees. The hotter conveyor rooms further inside could get to nearly two hundred degrees and in the manufacturing facility behind the openings, temperatures were rumored to get as hot as 3000 degrees.

They zipped around the South end and could see the lines of parking/charging spaces coming to an end ahead as they approached the East ramp and elevator entries. Just beyond the last parking/charging space, the entry to the smaller East maintenance bay opened up in the outer wall and Richard motioned Khadija towards it.

A connector tunnel led off the beltway into the high-ceilinged maintenance space. Richard scooted in past a golf cart like service vehicle parked at the entry, over to where dozens of pallets loaded with boxes and equipment were located. A couple of pallets held control chairs like they had installed in the arena.

He hopped off the scooter and checked the boxes on a couple of the pallets making a satisfied sound and said, "This is the stuff for the tech monitoring station that goes in here. And look, they even got my road box sent from the concrete plant, so I'll have the tools to put all this together."

Khadija had stopped by the service vehicle at the entry, set her scooter against the wall, and said, "It looks like they have left us a vehicle for toting things around."

Khadija walked over by the palettes to look at the control chairs saying they would be handy for locally controlling any robotic loaders needing to shift parking spaces or head to the maintenance bays.

They were poking through the boxes on the palettes when the scientist pulled into the bay with the golf cart and trailer. He said, "Glad I ran into the two of you. Ariana and Ahmed would like to meet with you as soon as they wrap up their morning meeting. I told Ahmed I was already on my way here to drop off the communicator cubes and some other stuff for you and would let you know."

The scientist hopped out, dropped the tailgate of the pickup bed and pulled a large case out onto the tailgate. Richard opened it to check that rows of communicator cubes set in foam inserts with their magnetic serial number labels were OK inside the case. He pulled Richard's small tool case out with the communicator cubes he had used at the concrete plant and for running the training loaders. Khadija said they could use these to locally control robotic loaders from the control chairs once they got the chairs set up.

Another box in the trailer turned out to hold the scanning sensor elements that needed to be installed on all the robotic hands, and the last large box held newly made heat resistant enameled versions of the avatar faces Khadija's women had selected and larger printed copies to hang on the charger post upright at each of the assigned loader parking/charging spaces. The scientist and Richard quickly unloaded everything from the trailer and the scientist was closing up the tailgate when a text came in on his phone.

He said, "The control team can dock the containers full of your robotic loaders tonight after the midnight shift change. They have 30 shipping containers of loaders for you and want to know if you would like them all docked for unloading this evening."

Khadija said, "If we could use the loading zone area in front of the exterior docks in the wings for temporary parking, they can bring them all in to the dock."

The scientist said parking there was not a problem and texted the control team with the go ahead. He said he had requested them to text Khadija directly with the arrival dock numbers.

Richard started to ask him some questions about his progress on understanding the communicator cubes, but he quickly hopped back into the driver's seat saying, "Sorry, gotta run. You'll want to head for Ariana's place, as the morning meeting will wrap up there shortly and they'll be expecting you. Her place is the highest house on the hill at the east side of the village. You can't miss it!" he said as he finished turning the golf cart and trailer around and sped out of the space with a grin.

Khadija said wistfully, "Our friend knows we have a lot of questions, and he doesn't seem to want to hang around long enough for us to ask them. Ariana and Ahmed should be able to fill in some of the blanks for us. The scooters are fine on the smooth pavement down here, but we may run into some cobblestone streets heading up through the older village. If you put the scooters back in the bed of this mini version of a pickup truck, I'll get it unplugged so that we can ride in "style" up the village hill."

As he lifted the scooters, Richard said, "If you consider this golf cart of a service vehicle riding in style, you've definitely got to get out more!"

He had barely sat on the bench seat next to her when he was caught off guard by the cart speeding abruptly forward out of the bay and by the sharp turn onto the four-lane beltway outside. Just as he was contemplating what it would be like to land face first on the road stripes flashing by below, Khadija yanked the wheel back around, sitting him back up in the cart.

"Less sass from those riding shotgun would be appreciated," she said with an innocent smile on her face.

Richard started to say something, but the racing turn she took onto the ramp made him think the better of it as they sped up towards the village.

62

Ariana's place, while visible from anywhere in the village, proved a bit more difficult to navigate to through the warren of streets in the lower village. After a winding route, Khadija pulled their cart up next to another four-person cart already parked there and they walked in the front door.

A young woman met them inside and led them into a circular seating area in a large two-story room with floor to ceiling windows looking out the front of the house and said the meeting should be ending soon. She asked if she could get them anything and took their request for some water.

They could see Ariana, Ahmed, Jamal, and a couple of others in the conference room just up the steps at the back of the house. There appeared to be flickering gold-tinged images of the faces of others above some of the seats around the long table. Khadija recognized many of the faces around the table including Jaha's distinctively patterned face and wondered how the tribal leaders were holding up with the fast-track pace of decisions that they were being asked to make and approve.

As they walked around to the circle of chairs, they could see they were a modern steel and black leather design. They were arranged in a somewhat circular arrangement with stove cubes used as side tables between each chair. Rectangular Asian looking planters placed along the rear of each of the stove side table held an elaborate range of bonsai trees that reached about a foot or two above the planter.

In the center of the chairs, a grouping of six of the stove cubes had been moved together to serve as one large center table. An orchid was placed in the center of this grouping and a highly decorated Asian looking wood case sat on the coffee table off to one side. Richard was examining the corner cube of the coffee table grouping but Khadija headed off his questions saying they would have plenty of them to play with now that they were at the manufacturing facility. She was intrigued by the bonsai trees on display, checking out each one in turn, as Richard looked around at the space. The woman arrived with a pitcher and four glasses on tray that she set on the coffee table grouping.

With water in hand, they sauntered back around to the front windows. Looking out over the golf carts in the driveway they could see past the neighboring houses to an expansive overlook of that side of the village. The house was on enough of a hill that they were looking out over the roofs of the village buildings below.

The village buildings were a jumble of architectural styles in periods ranging from the turn of the century to modern. The maze of roads between the old village sections were horse and buggy narrow in places. Old cobblestones sections of road still showed in places, but most of the outer roads had been paved over so that only the old stone curbs still showed.

Even the old village had the smell of fresh paint, so clearly it had been recently spruced up. New construction, like their apartment was shoehorned in among the older buildings in a variety of styles as well. As the village moved out towards the drop off, a ring of parks and bike paths started up. They could see these areas had all been landscaped recently as fresh sod lines could still be seen in the grass, and the flower beds were newly mulched. The trees in the park were small, more ornamental varieties that, judging from the tags still hanging off some, had also been recent additions.

Beyond the ring of parks area was the drop off into the beltway below. They could see how the edge of the drop off was hidden by arrangements of shrubs and rocks so that you would have a tough time telling it was there unless you went climbing up over the rocks to look down. The occasional reflection off of a piece of chrome or mirror on a vehicle travelling below was all that could be seen to mark all the industry going on below.

In contrast to the new landscaping on the village side of the drop off, the outer perimeter area on the far side of the drop off was wild and overgrown. Scrubby trees reached up the rift valley cliff walls. Even from this highest point in the village they still could not see over the top of the cliff walls. The cliff line jagged in to nearly reach the drop off in places, while in other locations it was hundred or so feet back.

The guide binder mentioned that chunks of rock would occasionally fall off the cliff face with some tumbling over the edge of the drop off into the grassy median of the beltway below. The remains of an overgrown dirt road that cut steeply at a right angle through a break in the Eastern cliff, could barely be seen as made its way through the tangle of underbrush in the area below the rift valley cliff. It ended in a pile of rocks at the edge of the drop off. Just before angling up out of sight into the cut through in the cliff, what remained of the road was cut off by a rusty metal barrier with tall heavy steel doors that looked like they hadn't been moved in decades.

The sound of the glass conference room door being opened by the young woman caused them to turn around. The meeting had broken up and the gold-tinged participants had disappeared as she went in to speak to Ariana. Ariana motioned to Ahmed and Jamal and they both looked out at them past the others coming out through the doors. Jamal came out and headed down to meet them as Ariana and Ahmed said goodbyes to a couple of others heading out of the house. Jamal said he was glad they were now in the neighborhood, but things were moving at a crazy pace with the logistics and distribution control centers, so he didn't have much free time to get out and socialize these days. He suggested they get together for lunch, once they had their robotic loader operation up and running, but said he had to dash to put out today's fire. They watched him quickly head down a set of steps at the back of the room as Ariana and Ahmed came down towards the seating area.

Ariana said, "Khadj, great to have you around, and Richard, so good of you to join our operation here."

Ariana warmly took a hand from each of them in hers saying, "I'm glad to have you both join us here. I hope you will get a bit of rest soon to recover from last night's travels."

Ariana looked up into Richard's eyes and then turned towards Khadija. After a beat, she smiled, released her hold. She motioned to the chairs near the oak looking bonsai and they moved to sit.

She said to Richard, "With all the need-to-know secrecy going on, I'm not sure what Khadj has told you about the cubes and their ruwaq origins. Getting up to speed on those aspects may help you better understand why we are suggesting you become extended guests of our secure hospitality. Ahmed, why don't you lay out the "cubic conundrum" as the coalition council has taken to calling it for them.

Ahmed nodded reluctantly and said, "Yes, the conundrum presented by the three types of cubes and their myriad capabilities. Richard, in your time working out the communications protocol and engineering the interface, were you able to determine how the communicator cubes transmit between their twinned pairs?"

Richard blushed slightly. This was the 800-pound bugaboo that still loomed large in the back of his mind after the extensive non-destructive testing he had done. The long pause in his reply and expression on his face must have given away his inner turmoil because Ahmed got up and walked over to the case on the coffee table, opened the lid, and pulled out a communicator cube twisting it in fingers.

Ahmed continued, "The tech at work inside the three types of cubes is so advanced, that our best scientist minds still do not know how they work. The "ruwaq," as our tribal partners call the reclusive creators of the cubes, use an inaccessible manufacturing process that we cannot examine, and build in tamper protection countermeasures that effectively deny us access to the cubes' inner workings. Our science teams have tried every way imaginable to open the cubes up to look inside but entirely without success. The lack of knowledge about the origins of the ruwaq manufacturer has also been the focus of intense scrutiny by our teams since the first appearance of the cubes. Here again, despite continuing intense investigation, we are left with only what we have been able to glean from the native child avatar. The ruwaq intention, as stated by native child avatar, is essentially to gift us the cube technology as a bridge loan to help us get past this climate crisis and the potential civilization ending wars that could result from it. Once the world gets past the crisis, and the risk to civilization is mitigated, the intention is the cube technology would be phased out. Eventually only the stove cubes would remain in use for the lifetime of the stove cube owners.

Ahmed took a sip of water before saying, "Being intentionally denied answers by a technology that is proving to be beyond the understanding of our brightest minds has spawned some rather far out theories as to its origins. I will not burden you with all the theories, but the fact that the cube manufacturing process is effectively hidden from us, and the inner workings of the cubes are intentionally concealed, has presented the coalition council with a hard choice.

Ariana said, " The "cubic conundrum" comes down to this choice. Does the council refuse to use the "gift" of the three cubes and sit by as killer heat waves and extreme weather make the homelands of over a billion people uninhabitable triggering wars and raising the potential for nuclear armageddon? Or does the coalition accept the ruwaq "gift", widely distribute it to mitigate the severe climate change impacts and avert the wars projected to occur?"

Ahmed said, "This conundrum has led to elaborate fail safes being incorporated to ensure the coalition retains entire control over the distribution and use of cubes. To ensure this control, every cube introduced into the world must be individually picked up by human remote operators from the conveyor, scanned by the sensors built into the robotic hands as it is lifted, and have the link to its twinned failsafe particle in the control team stack rooms verified as it is loaded. These twinned particles enable the coalition to be able to remotely disintegrate any cubes we find being used for purposes outside those approved by our tribal partners. This disintegration option also allows the coalition to intervene in case any of the cubes start to behave abnormally or begin to pose an unforeseen threat on their own. Khadj, we will need your remote operators to consistently respond to any alert warnings of a failed scan by immediately placing the cube into one of the containment scanner enclosures in the conveyor room. That way the control team can run a secondary scan of the cube while the remote operator runs a diagnostic on all their robotic hand sensors to check for a failure. Our ability to detect and destroy any cubes with detectable variations from the approved model is the primary key to ensuring the cubes produced remain safe. Having shipping and delivery methods that are fully under the control of the coalition is the second way we retain control over the cubes being introduced to the world."

Ariana said, "The implications of the advanced cube technology for both good and ill is being grasped by corporate and governmental entities. Some have already stolen stove cubes from some of our test communities and have surely been disappointed by the disintegration of those cubes as they have tried to reverse engineer their secrets. Unable to obtain answers themselves, our security team says they are now even more intent on obtaining answers from those with knowledge of the cubes working for or with the coalition. We have given away stove cubes to governments and corporate entities with an interest, but they have not been satisfied with their total inability to find out how they work, or reverse engineer them. The security team has identified a number of nations and corporate entities that would like, in the worst way imaginable, to interrogate our scientists and those having worked with the cubes. We have already had to take extraordinary measures to ensure the safety of the most vulnerable science and NGO leaders. We are now expanding access for other key personnel, like yourselves, to safe spaces in remote locations like this one. After the widespread distribution of the stove cubes has occurred, and they are in common use around the world, we can work to make it safe for those of us in this village to return home. I know this is a lot.   Khadj, you can fill in Richard on the capabilities and some of the origin theories, but are there any other questions Ahmed and I can answer?

Richard asked, "How do you know that the cubes are trying to be reverse engineered?"

Ahmed said, "Every cube we send out into the world contains a form of particle that is, for lack of better description, "entangled" with its twin in the monitored particle stacks of the control team.   Whenever the outer shell of a cube is breached, the disintegration that follows also breaks this entangled connection, and the twinned particle goes "dead" on our end. When this break in connection to a stove cube that has been reported stolen occurs, and a corporate actor specializing in reverse engineering is suspected, it is likely their attempts to break into the cube have triggered the disintegration process."

Richard looked puzzled saying "disintegration process?"

"Better show them, as the same thing can occur if a cube is damaged during the loading or shipping process." said Ariana.

Ahmed walked over to the wall mounted screen and brought up a video. As they watched, a figure dressed in what looked like a bomb protection outfit carried a large drill with a hefty drill bit to the stove cube centered in the view. The figure pointed the drill straight down onto the top of the cube and started it up with a loud hammering sound.

For nearly a minute it seemed to be hardly making a scratch, then suddenly the drill went through the top layer of the cube in a rush. The figure pulled the drill out, hastily setting it on floor and moving quickly out of view. Where the hole had been drilled, sparks as if from a child's sparkler, were starting to appear. A brilliant white fountain of sparks emerged shooting up from the cube while the sparks were starting to spread over and down the sides of the cube.

As the sparkling transition reached the bottom of the cube, the sparkles suddenly shifted to red, and a shock wave appeared to move the cube and the drill laying on the floor next to it. The sparks stopped and the red glow faded leaving just a grayish version of the cube behind. The top of cube, near the hole, then started to collapse inward, and with an empathic whump, the rest of the cube suddenly gave way and collapsed into a pile of ash on the floor.

Ahmed turned off the video and there was a stunned silence. "Well, that's got to ruin someone's day in reverse engineering land," said Khadija wryly.

63

Richard and Khadija had woken late in the evening and taken the service cart with the scooters to head to the loading dock canteen. They left the cart parked in the Northeast wing by the exterior loading docks and took the scooters into the main dock building and down to the pull-in area where the elevators to the canteen were located. They went up and found a table by the windows overlooking the busy dock area below and soon a wait-bot rolled up with their coffee and tea order.

The canteen was a large domed space with the telltale structural pattern of a builder cube constructed space. Its white lit dome made it feel like a daylit space and the mural on the curving surround walls with the small trees and palms planted within the groupings of patio style tables gave the space a park like feel. Along the back curving wall, the tables gave way to seating nook arrangements of outdoor style couches and chairs set under the trees.

The canteen, while able to seat several hundred dock workers at a time, was relatively empty at the moment. A long videow-all was mounted over the long run of windows on the shipping dock end where they were sitting. An image of the full length of the shipping dock looking out to the truck entry doors at the far side of the parking area was shown.

After they had chatted enough for their coffee and tea to fully wake them up, Khadija proposed they just take short trips with the robotic loaders into the wing tunnels and park them in front of the exterior loading doors. Once they had them all out of the containers, they could ferry them down to their parking/charger spaces at their leisure.

The control team had texted Khadija the loading dock location numbers where the shipping containers with their robotic loaders would be docked. Those locations were only now starting to have their filled containers pulled out so the doors could be closed, but many of the locations were still occupied by containers in the process of being loaded by the forklifts. Khadija suggested they order another cup and wait until the forklift activity had died down before trying to get their stuff unloaded.

The number of containers along the dock edge pulling out far enough to have their doors closed suddenly increased as the last of their loads were forked on. The guys on the gyroscopic scooters raced around, closing, and placing seals on the doors. The number of forklifts in action below them started to dwindle as the drivers finished their last loads, parked the forklifts, and plugged them up to charge.

Some of the drivers started to drift into the canteen and take seats on the couches and chairs in the back. The drivers must have ordered ahead, because waitbots appeared the moment they came into the room with their drinks and food and rolled up to meet them as they sat down.

Soon their shipping containers with their back doors open showing the loaders were being backed into the numbered slots they had been keeping an eye on.

There was a last frenzy of forklift movement as the last containers were filled and then all the forklifts were parked and charging a few minutes after midnight. The canteen was filling up with the drivers coming off shift and a lineup of waitbots stood by with trays full of drinks waiting for the workers that had ordered them to arrive.

Khadija and Richard made their way past the waitbots to the exit and decided to take the stairs down rather than fight the crowds of workers coming up the elevators. They could hear music start playing in the canteen to mark the official end of shift as the stair doors shut behind them.

As they rolled their scooters out on the dock level a girl on roller skates wearing brightly colored pads and helmet, was just skating from one container to the next closing doors, putting on seals and giving thumbs ups for the tugs to take them away. She said hi to them as skated by them, but didn't break her pace moving container to container.

There were a couple of other contractors who were apparently also expecting shipments that were sitting in a couple of golf carts farther down the dock, but otherwise they had the place to themselves.

They powered up and backed the first two robotic loaders out of the first shipping container, put their scooters on the loading trays and then drove them out of the main area into to the Northeast exterior dock wing where they parked them in front of the exterior dock doors. They repeated this process for the next couple of hours until all the robotic loaders were out of the shipping containers and lined up along the exterior dock wing walls.

They felt like taking a break to get something to eat and decided to try giving their food orders to the artificial intelligence "village assistant" the guide binder had made them aware of. The scientist had jokingly referred to it as the village "idiot" because it wanted to "wreck a nice beach" instead of being able to "recognize" his "speech" with his Bronx accent. He used "Hey Idiot" as his means of triggering the AI assistant mode on his phone, but Khadija and Richard just used the default "Hey Artie" to place their order. They powered down the last of the loaders parked by the exterior docks and headed for the canteen.

They had no sooner sat in one of the booths that flanked the comfortable couch and chair areas at the back, than a waitbot rolled up with their drinks. "To our first day on the job in lovely wherever this is!" said Richard with a glass raised in his hand.

Khadija clinked her glass against his and drank. Khadija texted the control team to let them know the shipping containers were empty, and soon after, they could see the tugs pulled the empty containers out to park them in the lineup out in the space.

Ariana and Ahmed had never actually said where they were, so Richard scrolled across world maps, and they looked at areas in the world where the climate would match what they had seen of the village's weather so far. Unfortunately, the candidate area for their location was a broad band of South America and they could not see any location on the satellite photos that looked like the rift valley.

A waitbot with their food showed up and as they ate, Richard asked Khadija about the theories of how the cubes worked and their manufacturer origins. She told him no one knew what the actual origin was but shared some of the theories of how they might work that had been bandied about by the science teams. The theories ranged from secret government labs to more esoteric origins that Richard hadn't considered.

Following their conversation, Richard certainly had more to chew on than just their meal as they headed back down to start driving the loaders around to their parking spaces. When they reached the parking/charging spaces with their loaders, they turned and backed them in until the charging connector was docked into the charging ports coupler on the tall safety yellow posts. They would then hop back on their scooters to make the trip back to ferry the next pair of loaders.

As they sped back and forth up the well-lit beltway, the stars in the night sky, barely visible through the drop off opening, were the only reminder that it was the middle of the night in the village above. Richard said the brightly lit nature of all the places they would be working in, while on the midnight shift, would help keep their circadian body clocks from shifting too much. It should make it easy for them to stay on the same schedule as Khadija's women.

They repeated the ferrying process until all the loaders were parked in parking spaces near the first of the giant entry doors leading to the cube conveyor rooms. Dawn was breaking in the sky visible above the low way as they picked up their golf cart and headed back to the apartment. As they drove up the ramp into the park with the sunlit clouds overhead, Khadija said, "We've got three things to decide. What do we want to eat, what do we want to watch, and are sleeping at your place or mine?" Richard, upon hearing the last item, wobbled a bit on his scooter then smiled as they made the turn for their apartment building.

64

Khadija woke with Richard still asleep, comfortably curled beside her in the bed. The orangish glow making it past the edges of the closed drapes told her it was probably about sunset outside in the village, so they had an hour before they would need to get up.

Last night they had agreed they wanted to pursue things further, and while the wine induced weekend fervor had shown there was a powerful undercurrent of attraction operating between them, Khadija felt they really needed to spend time relaxing and getting used to a form of daily normal life with one another. So, they decided evenings together on the couch watching programs would be the norm, just sleeping together when they were not too exhausted would be a more regular occurrence and revisiting that "powerful undercurrent" would be a future option once they were comfortable enough.

The refreshing thing about Richard was he was willing to accept her for the independent woman she was. He did not appear challenged by her strong spirited way and was patient as she found her way in this new landscape of being in a relationship. The warm fuzzy feeling this thought produced made her snuggle in tighter against his body. A tingle was added to the warm fuzzy as she snuggled in. Maybe further exploring those "undercurrents" wasn't as far off as she had imagined.

They woke up and had "breakfast" together on the balcony watching the sunset fade into night. Khadija checked in with her lead women who would be continuing with practice loading runs today back at the hangar. Khadija was telling Richard her women were about ready to start work with the loaders here in the facility when a text came in from the control team. It asked if they could load the stove cubes that were sitting in the conveyor rooms once they had a robotic loader up and running. They said this would save the lab assistants from having to suit up and walk in the hot conveyor rooms to load them out by hand. They said they could dock some shipping containers to receive them whenever they were ready. Khadija, checked with Richard who didn't see any problem. She texted them back to have the shipping containers ready at the dock after the midnight shift change.

They took the cart with their scooters back down to the maintenance bay and settled in to start their day. They dug into the cases the scientist had brought them and found Khadija's enameled and printed avatar face graphics along with a set of hand sensors. The previous day they had brought the last robotic loader into the maintenance bay and docked it in the charger post in there.

They walked over to that loader and Richard showed Khadija how the hand sensors simply clicked onto the "hands" of the robotic loader and plugged into the end of the robotic "arms". He hung the printed version of her avatar face on the charging post behind the loader. He then pointed out the screws that could be used to mount the high temperature compatible enameled metal version of her avatar face on the metal tongue above the cameras.

They installed one of the control chairs and Richard took out a pair of twinned communicator cubes from the tool case for Khadija. Khadija installed the communicator cube inside the cooled electronics enclosure of the maintenance bay robotic loader and powered it up. She walked over to the control chair and installed the twinned communicator cube into it. She told Richard she was going to saddle up and go check out the conveyor rooms.

She got into the chair, did all her checklist moves, and then remotely drove the robotic loader out of the maintenance bay and down to the first giant door leading into the first set of cooling and conveyor rooms. The giant door sensed the loader and raised letting Khadija drive into the cooling room. The door came down quickly behind her loader as she looked around a cooling room space that was the same footprint as had been marked out on the hangar floor for training.

Large openings for the freezing cooled air pumped into the room were cut into the surrounding rock walls just above the safety orange wall base guards. A rime of ice coated the inside of the air openings and extended out across the walls. She followed the walls upward and was surprised at how tall the room was. The walls disappeared into the darkness above so she couldn't tell how high the space was. There were parking space areas to either side of the two-lane drive marked on the floor with one marked as the "on deck" space. The parking spaces were all filled with stacks of stove cubes that had been run during the testing phase of the manufacturing facility.

Word from the control team was the facility was ready to start manufacturing more stove cubes as soon as her remote operators were ready and could clear these cube stacks out of the cooling rooms. She headed for the second door leading into the conveyor room that was ahead. Her cameras started to fog over as she passed the freezing air inlets, but cleared as her loader approached the door. Fogging would not be a problem once production started and hundreds of blazing hot cubes were constantly brought into the cooling room. The second giant door leading to the conveyor room raised as her loader got close to it and she drove in.

The conveyor room footprint was the same as the mockup in the training hangar and again freezing air openings and rock walls extending up out of sight were present. This room, adjacent to the manufacturing facility was plenty warm, even with the small door where the cubes would emerge through the wall on the conveyor fully shut. This door would open and shut quickly to let freshly manufactured stove cubes out on the conveyor while keeping the blast furnace heat behind the door contained.

The conveyor was just a dark surface with safety yellow sides somewhat wider than the stationary line of stove cubes entirely filling it. There did not appear to be any form of belt, so Khadija wondered how it worked. The catch turntable at the end of the conveyor was just a smooth flattened cone of black with safety yellow sides that stuck up high enough to capture the cubes coming off the end of the conveyor. The turntable was also entirely full of "stove" cubes.

Emergency stop buttons were in the familiar places and the safety orange wall protection looked pristine. Two scanning bins were located on the walls to either side of the entry for loaders to place any cubes that the robotic hand sensors set off an alert on. Only if the secondary scan came back with a green indication would the cube be added to the loads being shipped out. A continued red alert following the second bin scan would immediately initiate the disintegration process, leaving nothing but ash remaining in the bin.

The yellow divider lines Khadija had added in the hangar, had also been added to floor to the sides of the conveyor, so she thought her women should be right at home here after their training in the hangar. She positioned the loader next to the catch turntable and then reached out to pick up the stove cubes to start a stack on the loader tray base. She had not taken more than two off when the lineup of cubes on the conveyor started to slide along the black surface with the front two cubes coming off the end of the conveyor and sliding down to take the place of the two that she had just pulled off to place on the loader.

Khadija continued picking a few more cubes off the turntable feeling the magnetic attraction between cubes that allowed them to snap into place against one another to form a secure stack. Long practice in the hangar had made her robotic arm and hand motions fast enough that she could almost keep up with the pace of the cubes sliding off the end of the conveyor.

She mentioned the cubes sliding over the static conveyor surface to Richard and he came over to stand behind her chair and look at what she was seeing on the chair monitor suspended over the front. He was still watching as, with no more cubes coming off the "conveyor" and an open section on the dark cone, the cubes started to slide around to the front of the turntable.

Like the conveyor surface that cubes moved down, the cone of the catch "turntable" did not move, only the cubes moved around on top of its surface until they stopped at the front position. As Khadija picked up cubes from the front, the remainder of the cubes on would slide around on the cone surface so that there were always cubes at the front position of the "turntable" ready to pick up.

She asked Richard, who had been standing behind her chair watching all this on the monitor how in the world the cubes being moved across the surfaces on the "conveyor" and catch "turntable" worked. Richard could only mumble something about possible induced magnetic fields for a bit, before confessing he really had no idea how it was done.

Khadija headed out of the conveyor room and, as the "stove" cubes she had loaded were already relatively cool, she just headed back out the second door leading out into the beltway and headed for the next giant door she could see. The loading in the next conveyor room went quickly, but before she had finished emptying the catch "turntable" in the second conveyor room she had a full load.

She told Richard from the control chair, that she was headed down to the shipping building with a load and asked him to remind her what the number of the dock slot their first container was pulled up at. Richard let her know the number as she used the chair controls to pull the loader out onto the four-lane beltway and head for the shipping area.

The robotic loader covered the distance down past the Northeast dock wing to emerge out into the North central shipping building in less time than she thought was possible. She watched the numbers stenciled on the floor until she reached the dock location where the shipping container waiting for the cubes was at.

She maneuvered around, and just like in practice at the hangar, drove the loader straight into the shipping container. Watching her front proximity read outs carefully she drove slowly forward until the sensors told her the front of the loader was only a finger's width from the front wall of the container.

She engaged the automated unload function that dropped the loader tray onto the floor of the container and started automatically backing up the loader in sync with the automatic push bar moving forward pushing the entire stack of cubes off the tray base. As the last of the cube stack came off the metal thickness of the sheet steel tray base and dropped to the floor, Khadija heard an audible clunk over her headset. The loader stopped as the automated push bar retracted back. Once the push bar was fully retracted, the flashing yellow light in the upper corner of her field of view turned green and she was clear to back the loader out of the shipping container.

As she pivoted around to get back on the road heading out of shipping, she caught sight of the roller-skating girl who had skated up and was leaning her elbow pads and gloves on the edge of the loading dock while looking up at avatar face on Khadija's loader.

Khadija looked down at the girl, keyed the mic and said, "Hey there, it's me, the woman that was working down here last night."

The roller-skating girl said, "Oh hi there" and added, "I'm glad you've got your nifty loaders working. I'd hate to see you two hand loading those "stove" thingies all night long like the lab assistants have had to do since they started production. Well, if you're working midnight shift, I'm sure I'll be seeing you, or at least your loader, around."

"Indeed" said Khadija as turned back to speed out of the shipping area.

Richard's voice came to her saying "Can you stop in the elevator alcove on the way back and borrow the ladder we saw there. Oh, and bring the loader into the bay if you don't mind, to help me move the video wall structure and monitor desk over?" Khadija said sure and asked him to order in some tea for her.

She drove down, nabbed the ladder, and then sped back down to the maintenance bay. Coming into the bay, she saw Richard had the long monitor desk together and the uprights to the video wall structure assembled. She pulled over by the end of the videowall structure and stopped while Richard pulled the ladder off the loader.

The stereo cameras on the loader allowed her to see herself sitting in the control chair across the room with her head in the VR headset. She gave herself a halfhearted wave with one arm from the chair, to make the encounter seem less surreal.

Richard was ready with the videowall structure and had her pull up and just bring the front right rubber bumper in contact with the structure. She then pushed the structure over until it was lined up with the tape marks he had measured out on the floor. She swung the loader back over to the monitor desk and they repeated the process to get it pushed across the room to his tape marked location in front of the videowall frame.

A waitbot, sensing equipment movement came tentatively into the bay asking if someone had ordered drinks. Richard had it drop off the drinks on the monitor desk as he pulled a couple of office chairs off the pallets. Khadija parked the loader, shut down the control chair and climbed out to join him.

They sat sipping on their drinks and discussed what Khadija had seen in the conveyor and cooling rooms. She mentioned the freezing air blasts fogging the loader cameras and wondered what sort of massive air conditioning unit they must have to continually produce that amount of frigid air for the nine conveyor rooms and nine cooling rooms in the warm outdoor environment of the village. Like many of the other aspects of the cube manufacturing puzzle, it only added up to a greater mystery.

After their break, Richard went to work on the ladder installing the top videowall supports, while Khadija climbed back in the control chair. She drove the loader back out of the bay and headed down to the second giant door to enter and pick up where she had left off.

The loading went smoothly, and she soon had all three containers the control team had docked, filled with their stove cubes. She parked the loader back in its charging space in the maintenance bay, powered down the control chair, unstrapped, and got up to stretch while looking for Richard.

She walked over to the monitor desk where Richard was sandwiched down between the desk and panel covered videowall behind making wiring connections.

She asked, "Are you getting hungry? I'm about ready for a lunch break."

She got no response from Richard who still had his earpiece in from his earlier calls. She banged her fist on the end of the metal monitor desk and Richard's head hurriedly appeared.

"Why look who's just popped up ready for lunch," said Khadija loudly pointing to his earpiece.

Richard took the earpiece out and she continued, "As I was saying, why don't we grab our middle of the night lunch in the canteen. I just got a text back from the control team asking if we can pull the control tablet stacks that will be coming out of one of the rock openings in the shipping area and put them on the tail of the containers with the cube shipments. Richard agreed and they drove out in the cart to load the control tablets.

After lunch, Richard helped Khadija load the cases with the communicator cubes, hand sensors, the enameled metal avatar faces for the loaders and the printed avatar faces for the charging posts into the back of the service cart. Richard went back to his wiring on the monitor desk, as Khadija drove out of the bay and down to the first of the robotic loaders that would be controlled by her women back in the control chair arena.

She pulled up her list of women remote operators on her tablet and then pulled out the twinned communicator cube, a set of hand sensors and the avatar faces chosen by that woman. She unlatched the cooling cabinent door to access the receiver for the communicator cube and slid the cube into place. She then in-stalled the hand sensors, powered on the loader and then pushed the self-test diagnostics button.

As the loader ran through its internal checks, she stepped up onto the manual operator platform at the back of the loader with the two avatar faces. She screwed on the enameled avatar face above the stereo cameras used for remote operator vision.

The stylized avatar faces were a means to personalize each ro-botic loader so that loader team members could easily identify the operators of the other loaders in the conveyor and cooling rooms with them. This enabled not only coordinated efforts as they worked in the rooms but gave her women the ability to know who they were chatting with as they worked.

She then reached back to hang the larger printed version of the avatar face onto the upper section of the charger pole above the parking space number. The face on the pole provided an easier way for the remote operators to pick out their assigned parking/charging space from the five hundred spaces that were spread around the manufacturing end of the beltway.

Khadija saw the confirmation of a successful diagnostic with the newly installed hand sensors, powered down the loader and moved on to the next one to repeat the process.

She checked in again with her lead women before heading back to the maintenance bay. They were reporting that they had the practice cube handling down and the women were ready to move on to working actual loading shifts. If Richard could get his monitoring set up together, she now had all the robotic loaders ready for her women to start as soon as tomorrow.

She drove the cart down and into the bay to check in with Richard who was sitting at the lit-up monitor desk switching between the camera feeds showing the interior of the conveyor rooms, cooling rooms, and beltway giant doors entries. He said the emergency stop buttons for the conveyors that were lined up across the back of the monitor desk were the last thing he needed to check out to be ready for her women to start loading.

They checked with the control team to be sure things were good to start the loader shifts up, before Khadija called her lead women and told them they were set to start the women down in the arena operating the facility loaders tomorrow.

It had been a productive but long day, and the morning sun was fully up as they came up the ramp and headed towards the apartments. The beltway, shipping docks, and the maintenance bay were so brightly lit, it was easy to forget the village above had been sleeping while they worked. Khadija said she was tired, and thought they should head to their separate beds. She asked him to leave his balcony door unlocked.

"Who knows, I may come by to visit in the morning," she said.

65

Khadija woke to the smell of steaming tea, opened her eyes, and, yes, there was a cup of tea sitting on the nightstand next to her. The front room of Richard's apartment was lit by the late afternoon sun, and she remembered she had woken refreshed and had decided to come over and join Richard in his bed for a bit before needing to get up. She had slid in under the covers to snuggle in against him, he hugged her back, and soon they were dozing off again.

She turned over to see Richard already sitting up in bed with a cup of coffee in hand.

"Good morning sleepyhead", he said.

She sat up to take sip of her tea and they did their morning chatting as the warm tea woke her. She got up, saying she needed a shower, and suggested he meet her out on the balcony, to map out the day – and, of course, bringing another cup of tea out for her.

Richard was already seated at the balcony table looking at his tablet when she finished dressing and came out. Her tea was waiting for her and as she sipped it, they talked over how the day would shape up for them.

Today was the first day they would have all her women in the arena control chairs to run the loaders. After orientation, they would need to clear out the cooling rooms and yesterday's cube run now waiting on the conveyor and catch turntable. Khadija said she had a call scheduled with her lead women back at the base who would be overseeing the loading shifts today and then starting the next set of trainees on their control chair simulations tomorrow. She reminded Richard that he still had a couple of changes to make to the manufacturing facility simulation that would need to be uploaded to the control chairs in the arena before the new trainees got to the advance simulations later in the week.

A text from the control team said the containers tonight would be only partially filled with "stove" cube quantity orders ranging from 150 to 500 so, Khadija's women should pay special attention to their heads-up display quantity count as some loads would only be partially full.

They said the appropriate quantity of control tablets would come out of the same rock opening at the dock. Khadija reminded Richard that the control tablets were pre-keyed to the community leader the shipment was being sent to, so it was important to get the labeled stacks of tablets into the correct shipping containers.

They had updated the manual before they left, and Khadija's lead women had produced a translation in her home language that she needed to finish checking. She had gone through the selection process for the women who would be included in the next training at the base a while back and was now digging through the hundreds of security team vetted resumes for the candidates to be selected for training at the other facilities.

They had a notification from Jamal's team that the monitor desks videowalls and parts pallets for the other larger maintenance bays would be dropped off in those today. Khadija finished her tea and handed Richard back the cup with a kiss.

She said in a mock American voice, "Bye Honey – have a nice day at work. My little ole self is just going to be sitting around the homestead knitting and waiting for your return." Richard started to smile in an approving manner when she switched to her businesslike tone saying, "Right, like that's going to happen".

She punched him in the shoulder to wipe the smile off his face and strode off into her apartment.

"OK, hon…" Richard started to say playfully but she cut him off chuckling and saying, "Don't make me come out there and punch you again!"

66

Richard finished up the simulation revisions and came out onto balcony into the cool night air with patches of stars showing through the clouds above. He looked in Khadija's balcony door to see her last call had not yet gotten underway and was surprised to see she had her headscarf on.

She said, "I never know who might be sitting in on a video call on the military base end, so I need to be on my best behavior."

He told her he was going down to set things up to monitor the shift and she said she would be down as soon as they wrapped up the call.

He took the scooter around the village under the moonlit clouds, cut across the dimly lit park and headed down the ramp into the brightly lit beltway. He headed past the maintenance bay and went to the parking/charging spaces where the avatar faces of the robotic loaders greeted him. He walked behind them flipping on all their power switches and checked to make sure they all had green operating indications.

Now that he had the loader controls and onboard diagnostics patched into the monitor desk, the loader power switches would just always stay on. He headed back into the maintenance bay, dropped off the scooter, and walked over to pull up a chair at the monitor desk. He checked that all the video feeds from the conveyor, cooling rooms and parking/charging areas were set to monitor the evening work shift.

He set up a headset for Khadija to use to talk to her loader women during the shift and then checked his own headset.

He pulled up the remote operator names with their avatar images and checked that the control team had their loading assignments for the evening ready on the narrow display along the back of the monitor desk.

Each desk and video wall section was designed to monitor up to 50 robotic loaders at a time. There would be two more desks for Richard to set up in this training bay and seven more desks in the larger West maintenance bay. He made sure the remote operator control of the loaders he had powered on were disabled until Khadija could get them set up and checked out at the start of the shift. He set the videowall to display the views of the conveyor rooms, cooling rooms, and parking areas by the giant doors for the nine manufacturing plant entries.

The avatar images of the remote operator women were starting to go from dim to bright as they started taking their places in the arena back at the base and powered on their chairs. Khadija sped into the bay and hopped off her scooter by the end of the monitor desk. She took the wireless headset from Richard's hand, keyed the mic, and started greeting her women as they got into the control chairs in the arena halfway across the world.

She enabled the loaders of those who were ready in their chairs and asked them to pull out and turn towards the right in the striped median to run their startup checklists. She asked the first woman that a green light appeared next to their avatar on the desk display to pull down in the outside lane up by the maintenance bay entry. Khadija enabled the rest of the loaders, asked Richard to monitor the line up, as she took the golf cart out of the bay to pull out in front of the first loader in line.

Once all the loaders had done their checkout and were in line, she asked that they follow the cart, and she started driving down the beltway with the robotic loaders all parading behind her. She acted as a tour guide pointing out only the relevant things they needed to know as they drove along.

She said the East maintenance bay they had started off in front of was primarily for electronics, batteries, and camera repairs on the loaders. They entered the tunnel and as they came out in the

Northeast exterior dock wing, she pointed out the exterior loading doors explaining that these exterior dock would be where they would be loading the cubes in the future. For the present they would be doing traditional dock loading in the vast North shipping building they were now coming out into.

She pointed out the dock location numbers to use to find the container location. She reminded them to pay close attention to the heads-up order info they could see across the top of their virtual reality displays that indicated the number of cubes to load and the dock location that the shipping container to put them in was located.

They headed out of the long continuous dock space with its waiting empty containers, and past the Northwest wing exterior dock doors. They went through the tunnel and came out on the western side of the beltway. The grass median started and Khadija pointed out the night sky visible above, telling them the manufacturing facility was located on a different continent many time zones away from the military base they were working out of.

As they passed the West maintenance bay, she said this was the repair place for any major mechanical or drive issues on the robotic loaders. They reached the start of the parking/charging spaces and Khadija explained they were only the first training group of what would ultimately be hundreds of remote operators running loaders that would be parked in all these spaces.

As they came up on the large door with the giant "9" marking, Khadija split off the first five loaders. She asked them to go in through the cooling room into the conveyor room beyond, take up the positions they had practiced at the hangar, and unload all the "stove" cubes off the conveyor and catch turntable. She said to be prepared for the cubes to move along on the stationary conveyor and around the stationary turntable in a novel manner.

When all the cubes from the warmer conveyor room were grabbed, she said four of the loaders should head into the cooling room while the fifth was to pull under the door leading to the cooling room and park there to let enough heat into the room so that the icy blasts from the wall openings would not fog up the cameras while the others were finishing out loading their order quantities of cubes.

As always, if any cube triggered a red alert, it was to be placed in the scanning bin, and a diagnostic run on the loader's scanning sensors on the hands before continuing with the further loading. After the first loader had its order quantity loaded and had headed out onto the beltway, the loader holding open the conveyor room door could come into the cool room to complete its order quantity.

She reminded them that they could chat normally to those in the same room or nearby out on the beltway without hitting the transmit button, but needed to key the transmit button to talk to her or the lead women at the monitoring station. She said to key the mic to let her and the lead women know when the last of the stove cubes were loaded out of each cooling room.

She continued splitting groups of five loaders off to head into the conveyor room beyond giant doors number "8" through "4" until only she was left driving on the low way in the cart.

She sped back to the maintenance bay, hopped out of the cart, and pulled up a chair next to Richard. She watched the monitors and pushed the talk button under the avatar image on the desk display to give reminders or coaching to specific women as they worked. After a bit, things were running smoothly so Khadija let the lead women back at the monitor desks under the display in the control chair arena, take over and run the show.

Loading the cubes onto the containers was simple for a group this experienced, and only in one case was a load that was starting to go in the wrong container, caught and redirected to the correct container. Richard volunteered to go and add the control tablets to each shipment as they finished loading stove cubes in each container.

The fifty shipping containers with cube loads were done by the end of day prayer time and Khadija let all the women operators go once they had docked their loaders to charge. She had a brief meeting with her lead women to touch base on monitor desk operations and training items for tomorrow's shifts.

She asked Richard to drive by all the containers to check the loads as he finished placing the control tablets in the last containers. The morning crew of forklift drivers would add in the flat pack ducts and bases needed to finish out the loads.

When Richard arrived back at the bay, Khadija said, "The loading should be even quicker when we use the exterior docks for full loads. We should be able to rack up some impressive shipping numbers once we get the next couple of trainings done and those remote operators plugged into the mix. Now let' go get some dinner."

67

The climatologist watched the captain walk in a weaving manner coming back from the cockpit as the military cargo plane bounced in flight. Only the stripes on the jacket he wore over the heavy white snowsuit could pick him out from the other white clad forms strapped into seats down the sides of the cargo hold.

He could see the captain's breath freezing onto the back of his glove as he held up 5 fingers and walked along the group making sure everyone saw him. It was too loud in the cargo bay to be heard so he was just looking for nods from the seated team. The captain had to negotiate around the cargo and the heavy chain tie downs holding the large, tracked vehicle that held his backpack of gas sampling and analysis gear. When the captain reached the climatologist, he leant over and motioned at the seat restraints, pointed at the Climatologist, and wagged his finger in a "no no" fashion.

From the last briefing, the Climatologist had gathered there would be flurry of chain tie-downs being flung off, tractor treads in motion, and the snow tractor being hustled down off the ramp. At the end of the briefing, the captain had said "To keep our mission under wraps, the plane is going to turn at the far end of the runway, drop its tail ramp, and expect us to be off the back and out of sight beyond the ice ridge before anyone at the station is aware we hitched a ride".

Giving a steely look to the Climatologist as the others were filing out of the briefing he had said, "I don't want you to do anything while my team is hustling to get all our equipment off on the ground. Don't even think about unclipping your harness belt until I tell you to. Then I want you to hustle like a jackrabbit down to your place in the sno-T. If you so much as move a muscle before I tell you or are not faster than me getting down to the sno-T, I will be kicking your butt all the way down the plane ramp."

The plane bounced and the captain moved his steely gaze from the Climatologist to give the team a once over before sliding into his seat and snapping his belt harness with single deft movement. The captain looked as if he gave the climatologist's butt so much as a love tap with his boot, he might not be able to sit for a week. He resolved to be fast as the plane's skis touched down hard.

68

Richard left Khadija to sleep, got dressed, and was out on the balcony watching the drizzle of rain from a chair back under the roof overhang. Khadija's women had quickly adjusted to loading the stove cubes and by the end of the week were filling over 50 shipping containers a night entirely with stove cubes.

Her lead women were now running the loader shift leaving Khadija free to focus on the second larger group training back at the base. Richard had finished installing the rest of the control desks in the East maintenance bay that he and Khadija were using. He had three loader maintenance techs arriving on a bus flight coming into the shipping area today. They would set up and staff the other maintenance bays for the expanded operations soon to come.

Like most of the contractors coming to the village, they would be flown on a series of commercial flights through varied routes to bus loading points where they would board one of the autonomous buses with blacked out windows. The buses would drive to remote "ferry" points near the water to ensure they could not be tracked or followed. Builder cube enclosures would form up around each bus until it was ready to take off and be "ferried" to the manufacturing facility.

It was easier for the builder cubes to emulate the engine noises, wave motions, and hydroplaning sensations of a speedy water ferry when flying the enclosed bus at near supersonic speeds for extended periods. It would feel to those traveling inside like the bus was on a water ferry crossing a choppy sea. The change in engine noise and the feel of slowing to come off the "hydro-planes," maneuvering to come into the "dock," and the bump of meeting the "dock" were all emulated convincingly by the flying builder cubes as they arrived at the truck yard. A short drive into entry/exit bays and they were in the facility.

He and Khadija were instructed not to mention to the contractors the actual way that their bus was flown here or share their cover story or latest guess at wherever "here" was.

Richard was thinking through the large maintenance bay set up that the arriving loader techs would be doing, when Khadija emerged with a cup of tea to join him at the other chair under the overhang. She wrapped her robe tight around her to fend off the mist as she sat.

They chatted about the latest news from Miri bemoaning her travels without Jamal now that he was in full control center set up mode. The latest from Xanthe focused on her constant meetings with officials in the countries where they were still working to obtain permissions to do direct "drone" deliveries of the cubes.

They were talking about Ariana and Ahmed's plans for them to remotely supervise the set up of the two additional control chair arenas, when Richard received a text. It had an updated ETA for the loader techs' bus flight that meant he had to go. He kissed her, grabbed his satchel and headed out.

Richard was thankful for the roof over their service cart as he drove through the now pelting rain across the park to head down the ramp. He traded their service cart for a four-seater cart and trailer from the parking area at the bottom of the beltway ramp and headed for the shipping area on the dry beltway pavement.

He pulled the cart up at the end of the outer dock wing and walked out to wait for the bus's arrival. The forklift loading operation for the bases and ducts was still in full swing. The ongoing dance the autonomous trailer tugs were doing to change out filled containers with empty ones was interesting to watch. He wondered how the autonomous system that drove the bus was going to handle navigating the crisscrossing container trailers being "tugged" around.

A text notice told him the bus was arriving, and true to form, one of the heavy truck entry bay doors raised revealing the bus beyond. He watched the bus easily avoid the scrum of moving shipping container trailers in the parking area and pull all the way down to turn his way towards the ramp.

He got back in the cart, brought it out of the wing and immediately turned down the ramp to head down to the parking level. The bus approached the ramp, driving slowly along the wall, but stopped well short of reaching it. Richard pulled the cart up along the side of the bus as the door opened and the three loader techs emerged from the darkened interior of the bus to stand blinking in the brightly lit vast shipping building before them.

Richard said, "Welcome to the rift village" and greeted them personally as they stepped down. They loaded up all their luggage, tools, and stuff from the bus into the trailer, and Richard drove them down to the larger West maintenance bay that they would be working in. He pulled around in a wide circle around the service lifts at the center of the bay.

The lifts were large hydraulic work platforms designed to raise loaders up so that wheels and other undercarriage items could be serviced. The pallets full of monitoring desk and repair part shelving that needed to be installed had been dropped off in the back half of the space. Richard pointed them out as the first things that the guys could dig into when they started on their day shift in the morning. They dropped off their toolboxes and service equipment and then left the bay to drive up the ramp to the village. Richard filled them in on the loading operations but didn't get into detail about the "clean cooking stoves" the robotic loaders were handling.

They came out into the light rain at top of the ramp into the park with the village backed by broken clouds just letting the sunset peek through. Richard ran them around to their apartments, went over the basics in their guide binders and told them to stick to their cover stories when they communicated with the outside world.

He said to enjoy the evening, check out the pubs, and he would meet them in the morning at the West maintenance bay to get them started. He returned the traded out the 4-seater cart and trailer for their service cart and headed then headed down to the East maintenance bay.

Khadija was already at the monitor desk talking on the headset when he drove in. She paused to say she was breaking in some new lead women who were going to be directing the shift tonight from the monitor desks positions arena back at the base. Tonight, they were going to be running the shift while she listened in and watched the proceedings on the videowall.

The forklift drivers were expanding to three full shifts so, the main dock area would become a 24-hour forklift operation. Tonight, the women would start loading into shipping containers at the exterior docks in the Northeast wing so they could keep clear of the forklifts.

Khadija watched as the lead women used their monitor desk back at the base to enable the loaders once the women were "saddled up" in their control chairs. The remote operator women ran through their checklists in the median and then were off to their respective conveyor rooms to start loading. Richard watched for a bit to make sure things were going smoothly, but Khadija and her lead women were on top of the couple of problems that arose.

He pulled out his laptop on the far end of the desk and started working on coordination for the next control chair arena they were scheduled to set up. Before long the women had cleared out yesterday's cubes from all of the conveyor rooms and were taking up their positions inside the conveyor rooms behind giant doors 1, 2, and 3 for the startup of normal cube production. Khadija gave the go ahead to the control team and, one after another, the three conveyor lines were fired up. Fresh out of the manufacturing furnace stove cubes started appearing out of the small door at one end of the conveyor still glowing red. As each cube came through the small door, it flashed white all over for a moment, before moving down the conveyor.

Khadija had asked about this flash that each stove cube was making, but the control team could only say it appeared to be the moment the cube became activated. The women worked smoothly to magnetically snap the stove cubes into layers of stove cubes five cubes high on the loader trays.

It was important to keep the opening in center of each cube aligned vertically for each layer. The openings in the bottom layer of cubes would line up with the square areas of drilled vent holes directly under each vertical stack enabling cool air to circulate up through the centers of every stove cube in the load. Once a full load was stacked, each loader would be driven out to park in the cooling room and be replaced by the loader from the "on deck" parking space.

Even with below freezing air being circulated through the cooling room, it would still take about 15 minutes to cool the load to an acceptable temperature. A green light in the heads-up display would indicate when the load was fully cooled, so it could be driven out onto the beltway for the trip to the exterior docked shipping containers. The shift ended with the women hitting a new high mark, filling 60 shipping containers.

Richard said that he needed to go meet and get the new loader maintenance techs started over in the West maintenance bay. Khadija said, "Well don't be too late. We only have a couple of episodes to finish up for our show, and I will start watching without you if you take too long with them."

69

Each of the days of loading operations went progressively smoother, and the cubes coming off the conveyors were now appearing at full production speed. The lead women had the operation running smoothly so Khadija and Richard were shifting their schedule to overlap with the end of the midnight loader shift and run into the day shift for the Americas control chair arena install and trainings. .

Tonight, they were woken about a quarter after three in the morning by Khadija's phone. She rolled over to answer it and spoke in her native language to someone for a few minutes. She rolled back over by Richard and said that was one of the lead women calling to let her know that there were some rock chunks that had fallen out of one of the cooling vent openings in conveyor room "5." She said they should check it out and clean up the chunks of rock before the control room started up the conveyor and the room was heated beyond accessibility by the red-hot cubes coming into the room for tomorrow's loads.

"Come on, you are helping with this" she said prodding Richard out of bed.

Richard dressed and grabbed a couple of extra sweatshirts, his cowboy hat and his long leather coat. Khadija reappeared with a backpack with extra warm clothes and went down in the cart and headed off towards the ramp. The stars twinkling in the night sky over the village gave way to the brightly lit beltway as they came down the ramp and scooted down to the maintenance bay.

They put brooms, dustpans, some work gloves, and a bucket in the bed of the service cart and she drove them in the cart back down to the beltway to pull up in front of the giant door with the enormous number "5" on it. They got out to dress against the cold and heat that they would face while inside the cooling and conveyor rooms. Richard fastened his long leather coat and put his cowboy hat on. Khadija put a couple of layers of sweatshirts on under a hoodie from out of the backpack. They both put on work gloves before she drove the cart up to the entry sensors.

The giant door raised, and a bitterly cold blast of frigid air hit them. Khadija drove them quickly through the below zero cooling room to trigger the door into the conveyor room. The hot air hit them as she quickly drove inside the second door. Khadija drove them over near the cooling vent where the chunks of rock and spattered gravel lay on the floor below. They got out and walked over towards the vent until the temperature between the incoming cold air and the heat of the room balanced out to a comfortable average.

They could see a track left into the gravel and Khadija said one of the loaders had to back its way out the debris to make it out of the room. They set to work with Richard lifting the larger chunks of rock into the service cart bed, while Khadija gathered up the smaller rock chunks into the bucket. They then both grabbed brooms and dustbins to sweep up the gravel and rock dust remaining.

Satisfied the floor was clean on this side of the conveyor, they got in the cart and Khadija pulled quickly around to park in the goldilocks temperature zone on under the vent on the opposite side of the room to keep from overheating while they looked for any gravel that might have rolled over to this side of the floor.

This side seemed perfectly clean, so Richard was getting in the cart to head out, when Khadija said she thought they should look to see if there was any fallen rock up inside the vent. It would not do to have a partially blocked vent limiting the cold airflow in the vent the chunks had fallen out of.

She got up to stand in the back bed of the service cart, and told

Richard she could see what looked like a goodly pile of fallen rock under a crack in the vent letting in bluish light. She said they ought to clear it before the conveyor room was started up but wasn't sure they could get a manlift back down to get up to opening nearly twice her height off the floor.

Richard looked at the steel supports holding the roof of service cart. They looked strong enough, so he had Khadija pull the cart back around the other side and come up right alongside the outer wall directly under the vent opening. He opened the tailgate and climbed up onto the pickup bed. He then pulled himself up on top of the golf cart roof of the vehicle and stood up to face the blast of frigid air whistling out from the vent opening that was half his height in diameter.

He could see the bluish light coming down through a crack in top of the circular rock duct and goodly amount of rock half blocking the vent duct. He told Khadija that it looked like he could just crawl back quickly and knock the rock pile down to open the shaft back up enough to be workable until they could make arrangements to have it fixed. He ducked down out of the direct air blast, turned to Khadija who was standing back out in the goldilocks temperate zone with her hood down, and said he was going to try it.

Khadija said, "Well I guess I can live with you losing a finger or toe to frostbite, as long as we keep the rest of you intact."

Richard grinned, tipped his hat down to shield his face from the frigid blast of air and pulled himself up into the vent duct. With his head down he crawled the dozen feet in the incredible cold to where the pile of rubble was highlighted by the blue light. He kept his head down so his hat could shield him from the blasting air, as he shoved repeatedly against the freezing rubble. Soon it was knocked down and spread out, so it no longer blocked much of the vent duct.

As the rubble was knocked down and the vent opened up, the force of the breeze dropped. Richard could actually peek beyond the rim of his hat at what had happened to the upper portion of the shaft. The rock that the shaft was tunneled into had cracked and partially caved in at the point lit by the faint bluish light. Richard maneuvered himself around so he could look up into the crack. What he saw surprised him so much that he just lay there unmoving looking up for a time.

A voice calling, "Hey cowboy, it's time for you to get out of the fridge" prompted him to the realization he was losing feeling in his fingers.

He crawled back out of the vent and clumsily made his way down off the cart to come over and join Khadija in the goldilocks area to get the circulation going again in his hands.

Richard said, "I hate to say it, but you have got to climb up and see this!"

He had her put up her hoodie and then strapped his hat on her head to shield her from the wind. They both got up into the back bed area of the pickup and Richard helped Khadija up onto the roof. She was a little short to easily get up into the vent opening, so Richard dumped out the bucket in the pickup bed and handed it to her to set upside down on the roof to use as a step. A boost off the bucket and she was up.

She could actually bend over and squat enough to sort of walk down inside the vent duct cut into the rock. Richard hopped down to watch from the goldilocks zone, as Khadija made her way down to the opening left by the collapse to look up into the bluish light.

"Mother of Allah!" he heard Khadija exclaim and after a minute, he had to shout a reminder to get her to come back out of the vent duct. He helped her down off the roof and over to the goldilocks area to warm up while he pulled the cart around next to her. She was shivering uncontrollably, so they got in the cart headed for the conveyor room door. They had to brave the momentary cold of the cooling room, and then they were back out onto the pleasantly warm beltway.

They sat there in silence while Khadija warmed up looking up through the drop off opening to the starry sky above.

Khadija, finally said, "I need a hot cup of tea, and time to think, before you foist anything out of your engineer brain onto me."

70

Richard sat with Khadija in silence looking at the twinkling stars as she sipped her tea on their balcony back at the apartment. The night air was warm with the smell of freshly cut grass wafting from the darkness of the park out below them. They were both trying to get past the surprise and process what they had seen. The puzzle they were now trying to solve came down to the moment they had looked up through the cracked opening in the rock duct.

Richard recalled that there had been an icy buildup around the cracked opening and initially he had been blinded by the bright bluish light. As his eyes had adjusted, he could see a huge vertical shaft extending up through the rock towards what had to be a sliver of the brightest blue ceiling he had ever seen beyond.

An array of stove cubes was set into the shaft wall just a few feet above the crack opening. He had moved his head to get a wider view around inside the shaft and could see that it was only one of several arrays of stove cubes set into the rock around the bottom of the shaft. Up higher in the shaft were additional levels of cube arrays set into the sides. The cubes seemed to be acting as intake fans for what he assumed had to be other vent ducts, like the one he was in. The other cube arrays must be leading off to the other conveyor and cooling rooms.

A few bits of ice from above seemed to be falling down the shaft and he could see them getting sucked into the upper cube arrays. He stretched to peek farther up the vertical shaft until he could see its perfectly circular blue ceiling far above. He was trying to work out how the ceiling was being lit when a whitish form drifted into view. It was…it was a cloud… yes, a cloud… and if that was cloud then the deep blue circle had to be sky…. and if that was sky… then the icy pieces floating down the shaft and getting sucked into the upper cube arrays had to be snow… and if that was snow being blown over the rim of the shaft, then… yes, the icy buildup around the crack he was looking up through had to be snow. Khadija had called him back out of the vent and then had climbed in to take a look for herself.

And yet, here they were sitting outdoors on their apartment balcony in a warm semi-arid climate half an hour later looking at the starry night that lay over the village.

Khadija, who had been leaning back in her chair moping as she sipped her tea, sat up abruptly. She looked towards the south cliff wall in the direction of where the vertical shaft opening had to be and questions started to bubble out of her.

"How it could be daylight at the surface end of the cooling shaft while it was still nighttime in the village? How could a circular shaft that was easily twice as tall as the cliff, not be clearly visible over the horizon in that direction? How could there be no machinery at the top of the shaft to cool the air to the bitter sub-zero temperatures? How could there be snowflakes drifting down from a blue sky? how….? how….? how….?"

A thought struck Richard as he looked at the moon over the village and he hurriedly went in to get his laptop. Back out at the table he started searching through the files for the drawing sets he had been sent by the architects early on when they were asking for input on the maintenance bays.

They had been trying to work out the placement of the vertical exhaust duct for the welding area in the large maintenance bay. Richard wanted the welding area to be at the farthest back corner of the bay but wasn't sure if the vertical exhaust duct would reach the surface in the outer perimeter area or would come up under the cliff. He had asked the architects for any reference they had on the cliff location, and they had sent him a CAD file with a dashed line representing the location of the cliff face above.

Richard found the file and opened it on the laptop. He zoomed in on the South end, in the direction the shaft had to be located, and found one of the outcrops that had caught his eye at the time. He had noticed that the cliff wall appeared to have several vertical "chimney" crevices occurring where the dashed line representing the cliff face zigged back in on itself before again zagging out again to continue on its way around the village.

His climber instinct had picked these "chimney" locations out as possible routes to practice his free climbing on the cliff, should he find himself with free time at the rift village. The busy schedule and the guide's prohibitions against activities on the outer perimeter had put it out of his mind until now.

He zoomed in on the chimney and measured it where the chimney face inset was cut off by shoulder width straight line. He smiled and interrupted Khadija's verbal "how cans" while turning the laptop screen towards her.

Richard said, "With the level of secrecy going on around this place, I doubt we'll get a straight answer to this particular conundrum out of Ahmed and company. I think we need answers, and I think the simplest way to get them is for me to use one of the "chimney" crevices, like this one, to freeclimb up to top of the cliff.

I can then just take a stroll over to where that shaft has to come out about here," he said zooming out to show a location in the CAD drawing where he had marked up the shaft location in red.

He continued, "There's a chimney opening into the cliff outcrop here, that looks like it could be climbable without too much trouble. I've got all my climbing gear down in my road box of tools. All I need is some way to bridge across the drop off to get me out to the outer perimeter."

The logistical problem seemed to snap Khadija out of her conundrum funk and back into her practical "make it happen" self.

She jumped in saying "You don't have to lower something to bridge across the drop off, you just need to raise yourself up from the beltway below."

Richard looked perplexed as she continued, "You know the big telescoping boom manlifts with the wide work baskets stored in the Northeast wing?"

Richard nodded as she continued, "We just need to borrow the one with the longer arm that's parked there. It will raise us right up to where we can step out of the work platform onto the outer perimeter. If we want to keep from announcing what we are up to, then the boom lift will need to be run back down the beltway to the Southern parking alcove while the climbing and exploring is going on.   So, all we need to do is wake up one of your techs to operate it."

Richard again puzzled said, "Surely you can run a boom lift."

"Oh, I can absolutely run it and get us up to the outer perimeter no problem. It's just we are going after the answers to probably the greatest puzzle I have run across in my life and there is no way I am not coming up that cliff after you,"

Richard objected saying, "Climbing even a small cliff is a dangerous matter, especially if we do it before dawn so we won't be seen by the drone patrols and stopped."

Khadija stood up in front of him, with her hands on her hips, saying, "Bringing me along makes things much safer for you… otherwise, I will be left having to tell the authorities where to find your lifeless body, before we even get up by the cliff."

She was wearing a mischievous grin as she said, "Besides, you get to do the dangerous free climbing. I'm just coming up after you on a rope. If I can't make the climb, I can just go back down and sit patiently until we are ready to be picked up by the boom lift. Surely, we can manage that."

"Well, I guess that could be OK but…"

Khadija cut him off saying, "Good. We still have about 4 hours before the inquisitive eyes of the morning shift start to show up, so we need to move quick. Wake up one of your loader tech guys who can run the boom lift and get him to scoot down to the larger West maintenance bay to meet us.

You can drop me off to snag the boom lift, dig out your climbing rope and stuff out of our East bay and then come around to the West bay where I'll have the boom lift ready to go… OK?"

"Well, I guess OK but…" was all that Richard again got out before Khadija jumped up to head in her apartment and change into climbing wear.

"Here we go again", he thought as he pulled up one of the loader techs numbers to call.

71

Khadija pulled the large boom lift into the larger West maintenance bay and circled the hydraulic work lifts, to park it pointed back towards the entry ready to head back out. She lowered the wide work basket to the ground and opened the side railing to get out.

She had put her hoodie up over her head and averted her face, so she was not recognized by any of her women who were still running loads up to the Northeast wing. They would likely see Richard in the service cart, picking up his climbing gear, but would think that was part of the clean up behind door number 5.

She called her lead women to check in. She let them know everything was cleaned up in 5 , but they had some structural checking to do before she would be letting Jamal's control team know the room was good. She made sure they were all working behind doors 1,2, and 3, where they would be out of sight around the curve from where they would be taking the boom lift. Worst case, if they were discovered, up on the outer perimeter, they could say they were checking to see if there was any sign of an upper collapse that might need to be addressed to prevent further rockfall into the conveyor room.

There were security cameras along the beltway, but all the recorded footage for the entire facility must have been massive, so Khadija was counting on them not bothering to review the footage for any given camera unless something was reported that caused them to go back and look.

Richard drove into the bay in the cart and pulled alongside the work basket. Richard had changed into a form fitting climbing outfit and started transferring his climbing gear into the boom arm basket. Khadija saw a large coil of red climbing rope, a couple of harnesses, and a waistbelt with an assortment of climbing hardware clipped on get transferred to the work basket. Richard fitted her in a climbing harness and then put his own on with the climbing belt.

They were strapping on headlamps when a bleary-eyed loader tech arrived on a scooter. He reported that the coast was clear around the South end of the beltway that Richard had asked him to check out on his way. They all clambered up into the work basket, and Khadija soon had it driving out on the beltway as fast as it would go.

They passed a couple of the giant doors until; just past number 6 she pulled the lift into the center striped median and parked it. Using the lift and telescope controls to extend and raise the boom arm she lifted them up until they were just starting to come through the drop off opening.

They took a moment to allow their eyes to adjust to the night-time dark above before she raised them up further to peek over the shrub border to make sure there was no one nearby in the park. Khadija raised the arm until the bottom of the work basket cleared the outer perimeter and then pivoted them around until the side gate of the work basket was overhanging the scrubby ground.

Richard hopped out and Khadija handed him the coil of rope. Richard headed for the large vertical crack in the cliff that he called a chimney, as Khadija reminded the tech to go back and park in the South elevator parking area and wait for their call. She stepped out of the basket and carefully made her way through the scrub towards the vertical crack in the cliff that was dimly lit against the night sky. She heard the faint whine of hydraulic motors behind her and watched the head of the tech disappear back down through the drop off opening.

The village was cozily lit with a nearly full moon shining brightly in the night. A cool breeze had kicked up, but the cloudless sky said there was little chance of rain. As she reached the trees, Khadija turned on her headlamp to light the way towards the "chimney" as Richard called it.

She had to squeeze between two scrubby trees to get to the vertical crack. As she moved between the trees, she brushed the back of one hand against something hard and sandpapery that scraped some skin off her hand. Looking down, there didn't appear to be anything there to have scraped her hand on but the bark of the scrub tree. Puzzled, she ran her hand cautiously over the tree bark and then pulled it back in surprise.

The bark, instead of being woody was rock hard and abrasive like concrete. She reached out to another tree that had the same feel, before she realized the trees were fakes, albeit very good fakes. As she eased past the tree trunks and walked over into the increasingly strong wind gusts by the cliff face, she ran her hand over the rock face. Instead of feeling like natural rock, the cliff had the same abrasive feel as the tree trunk.

The vertical crack in the cliff face that Richard called a chimney was fairly wide where she entered, but it narrowed as it ran back into the cliff. The stiff breeze coming out of the chimney crack increased in strength dramatically as she made her way in. Richard was standing like a stone facing the far end of the vertical crack with his hair whipping back and Khadija asked him what was wrong. He moved his head up and his headlamp illuminated something that stopped her breath stop for moment.

Even with her eyes squinted in the face of the blasting gusts, she could see the unmistakable shapes of stove cubes stacked in a vertical row disappearing into the darkness above. The gusty wind blasts were coming out of their center openings facing towards them. They both raised their heads to look up the "chimney" crevice, and in their combined headlamp lights, the column of cubes appeared to continue right to the top of the cliff.

Richard turned and motioned to turn off their headlamps, as they went back out of the chimney opening and stood off to one side where the wind was less intense.

Richard blurted out, "That tower of cubes set into the end of the chimney is acting like the cube arrays in the shaft that were blowing air into the rock ducts. Did you notice the trees and this section of the cliff appear to be fake and made out the same abrasive material the village buildings and apartment are made of. I'm not sure I could climb that material without tearing up my hands. I wonder if we could put our arms into the cube openings while they are running as blowers without whatever effect is moving the air damaging us. Do we want to call for the boom lift and…".

Khadija interrupted the stream of thoughts pouring out of Richard saying, "Whoa boy, just hold your horses for a minute". She let Richard settle down for a moment and they both looked back through the trees to the lit village with the moon now higher in the night sky.

Khadija said, "OK, so we are out looking for answers and are running into more things that don't quite make sense. I think the only decision we need to make is whether to continue on our little quest for answers here or give up and go back with only more questions to show for our effort. These appear to be the same size as the stove cubes. If they act in the same way as the stove cubes, the moment you stick your hand in them, the air filtration senses a living body part and shuts down the filtration process. These may react in the same way. I say we check it out and push on if we can."

Richard thought for a moment and then nodded in agreement. Khadija led them both around back into the blasts of wind and focused her headlamp on the lowest stove cube in the column. Khadija stood on one foot with her hands on the rock faces to either to balance her and raised her other foot slowly towards the bottom cube center opening. The forceful airflow coming out of the cube was making her shoelaces dance in the wind. Her shoe just barely reached the front of the center opening when the airflow blowing her shoelaces abruptly stopped and they fell limply down.

Khadija gingerly put her full foot inside the center opening without any effect and then stepped up placing her full weight on the foot in the opening. She propped herself against the side rock face and brought her arm over to slowly move her hand into the center opening of the cube in front of her face. Again, as her hand started into the center opening, the wind coming out of the opening immediately ceased and her hair fell back down around her face.

She reached through the opening and to the meeting of the back tapered faces that provided a good handhold. Khadija pulled herself off the side wall, so she was only supported by her foot in the bottom cube and her grip through the opening in the upper . She stepped up with her other foot into the next cube up and pushed herself up until her hair was again being blown back and then reached her arm in, cutting off the airflow and getting her grip on the tapered faces inside. In this manner she climbed higher learning to reach her arm to get the next grip before raising her head into the force of the wind.

Hanging casually several cubes up from the ground she said, "This is the next best thing to having a ladder."

Richard seeing the ease with which she was able to climb, was relieved and said, "Alright spidergirl, come on down and let's do this climb by the book."

Richard double checked her climbing harness and made some further adjustments to her straps before he was satisfied. He carefully uncoiled the rope and attached it to the back of his waistbelt full of hardware and then started the climb up.

His longer arms and could more easily reach in through the openings in the cubes to get secure handholds. Even though it was ridiculously easy compared to having to use frogging or stemming techniques to freeclimb in a true chimney, Richard kept to his very deliberate climbing routine, testing each handhold and foothold before moving up.

The transition from the cubes to over on top of the cliff was the only slightly difficult maneuver, but Richard managed it in short order and was glad to be up and out of the windy gusts on the clifftop.

He checked the sturdiness of one of the larger fake trees on the cliff top, before wrapping the rope around it to use it as a belay point for Khadija's ascent. He took up the slack and then ran the rope back over to the edge of the chimney. He sat on the ground with the rope run around his back and his feet propped up on a rock outcrop.

He looked down into the chimney to follow the line of the rope to Khadija standing below with an arm in the cube in front of her to cut the wind. Satisfied that the rope was clear, and her harness looked good, he flashed his light three times and started taking up slack in the rope as she started to climb.

She was up the column of stove cubes in just a couple of minutes, and was surprisingly unafraid to wedge herself between the side walls to do the climbing maneuver needed to get herself up over the cliff edge.

Once standing on the moonlit clifftop, they turned off their headlamps to avoid being seen by those in the village. They took off their harnesses and Richard coiled up the rope for the return trip later. He slung the rope and harnesses over his shoulder and led them slowly through the moonlit fake scrub trees and bushes at the top of the cliff.

They were headed in the direction of where they had judged the shaft opening to be but had not gone but a few paces, before Khadija called out, "Stop!" Her headlamp beam came on and showed the scrub abruptly ending about a couple of strides in front of him. A flat area of rock extended another stride out and then there was a sheer drop off into blackness beyond.

Richard turned on his headlamp to carefully make his way through the last of the scrub and onto the rock area that ran like a sidewalk curving out of sight in both directions. Peeking over the sheer edge there was nothing but darkness below and the stars low on the horizon out before him gave the impression of being up on a tall hill or mountain looking down towards a valley.

Khadija, who had thrown headlamp caution to wind, was looking around with her headlamp to check for other drop-offs, when she exclaimed "Are those steps over there?"

She was shining her headlamp down the sidewalk width of clear ground running along the to the left, but he couldn't see anything in the way of handrails to mark the start of a stair.

"Shine your headlamp down there with mine. No one's going to see us from the village this far back," she said.

He turned his headlamp on and swung his head in that direction. He could make out a couple of dark steps now and they turned to start the walk around the upper "sidewalk" to reach it. Khadija's sudden inhalation of breath made him turn back to look out through the scrub towards the village.

The village, visible through the scrub, looked the same, but Khadija was looking up towards the sky. He glanced up and gasped as well. The nearly full moon that had lit their way to the base of the chimney, was now much dimmer and was a narrow oval! How could the moon be a narrow oval less than half as high as it was wide. They both stood frozen gaping at the sight.

"OK, so a fake cliff ends in a sidewalk, the moon's squashed in half, and there are dark steps leading down to who knows where below. What could possibly be giving us pause?" asked Khadija with mock seriousness.

They both broke out laughing at the incongruousness of it all. The moment over, they turned their back on the moon to face the steps ahead.

"Ladies first is what I always say", quipped Richard, but the punch landing on his arm helped push him out onto the landing.

The series of black steps led down along the slight curve of black wall extending down from the sidewalk edge. In their flashlight beams they could just see where the steps met a smooth black floor only about twenty steps down from the cliff level.

As they reached the dark floor, the stars in the distance now ended just above eye level and an odd red glow could be seen reflected in the smooth floor from one direction. Khadija suggested they keep the flashlights focused on the floor in front of them to avoid any further surprises and head in the direction of the red reflected glow. They did not walk far before she mentioned something was very strange in the way the stars seemed to be moving and fading as they walked.

The stars directly ahead remained clear and fixed but all the other stars to their sides were changing position as they walked and were quickly fading in brightness. He was looking sideways watching the odd movement of the stars, when he nearly hit his head on the edge of the sky.

Richard's mind reeled a bit at the concept that a sky could have an edge, but clearly showing in his flashlight beam was an edge at his head height that he had been about to run into. Putting aside the strangeness of what his mind was trying to process, he ducked under the edge, stood up in the space beyond and froze again. Khadija was short enough to walk under without having to duck and she stopped next to him with start.

The stars and sky had disappeared and in his flashlight about 30' ahead he could see the familiar interwoven patterns of a builder cube structure. The support columns were scaled up to massive proportions arching up from the floor to over his head and continuing in the telltale structural pattern out above the blackness of the "sky".

Khadija's voice in his ear shouted "It's like a giant freaking video screen inside a builder cube dome! And I mean a giant, giant, freaking video screen!!!"

They peeked back under the edge to see the stars and then bought their heads on the other side of the "screen" to see them disappear again. Richard was so focused on the "sky" edge, that Khadija had to turn his head back in the direction the red reflection they had been heading towards.

The cause of the red reflection was an ordinary sign with glowing letters that said "EXIT". Her headlamp was showing a door set into the rock wall below just below. Panning back over to their right her headlamp showed a grouping of casual chairs and side tables with lamps in the darkness.

Khadija said, "I know you want to collapse in one of those chairs, but I think we need to see what's behind the door first."

Richard dropped off the climbing gear and rope in one of the chairs and then walked over to join Khadija in front of what appeared to be an ordinary commercial type of steel door. She leaned on the push bar to open it.

The stairwell inside was brightly lit by small glowing white squares on the walls showing staircases going in both up and down directions from the landing they were standing on. The stairs and railings appeared to be made of the same dark polished material the floor had been. Yellow nonskid bands marked the edge of each step.

Khadija said, "I would suggest we try going up first, as that is more likely to lead us towards the top of the shaft we are looking for."

Before letting go of the door, Richard tried the thumb latch to make sure it pulled back the catch so they could not be locked in the stairwell. The latch worked fine, but the handle and latch felt more like a plastic replica of a metal handle than a true metal handle.

They set off up the stairs wondering aloud where they could possibly be leading to. After about a dozen or so flights the stairs ended at a landing with another door like the one below. Richard leaned on the push bar to pop the door open, and they found themselves in a long white tunnel stretching out in both directions lit by more of the square lights. Again, Richard checked the door latch to make sure they could get back in.

The temperature drop was substantial from the cool stairwell to the tunnel which was refrigerator cold. The tunnel ran off in both directions for as far as they could see. Across from the door was a rock alcove with a stair leading up into what looked to be large open space above that their headlamps could not light. The even colder drafts coming down the stairs made their skintight clothing seem unsuitable for further exploration up that way.

Warming up back in the stairwell, they agreed that they could bear with the cold in the tunnel for a bit so, Khadija suggested that they head down the tunnel to the left in the direction of the shaft they were seeking.

They went out, walking quickly down the cold tunnel, and came to where it ended in a flat wall. A two-button control panel was set into the wall at one side. The buttons were engraved with open and shut icons, but there didn't appear to be anything to open or shut.

Khadija suggested they check out the other end, but Richard was already starting to shiver in the more intense cold at the end of the tunnel. He said that crossing the football field length tunnel to get to the other end and exploring up the stairs would have to wait until they could get some proper coats and gear.

Khadija said, "Just for giggles, why don't we press the open button?".

Richard looked around again, but the tunnel seemed to be free of anything that could open so he just shrugged his shoulders. Khadija pressed the button and immediately, in the end wall, a curving crack appeared running around to meet itself in an upright oval shape. As they watched, the oval shape moved out a few inches and then started to pivot. Bright bluish light streamed in through the opening crack followed by the most bitter cold Richard had ever felt.

As the oval rock door swung open, they were momentarily blinded. Richard was shivering violently and Khadija huddled up against for warmth as they squinted to look out. As their eyes adjusted to the bright daylight, they could now see they were up on an icy mountainside with panorama of snow-covered rocky ridges projecting up from the landscape of snow drifts and ice ridges running as far as their snow-blind eyes could make out. This jumble of arctic terrain ran down to a perfectly flat snow-covered expanse bordered by broken sea ice accumulations where a frozen sea met the land under the snow.

Looking around the door to the right, the rocky escarpment they were up on flattened out allowing for large level snowfield to accumulate. In the center of this snowfield, they could see the large circular shaft they had been searching for.

A mock Yoda voice spoke in Richard's ear saying, "Unexpected this is!"

After standing literally frozen for a moment, Khadija dragged them both backwards and punched the "Shut" button. The rock door started to close, and they ran as fast as their frozen feet could take them back down the tunnel to the stairwell.

The stairwell felt blissfully warm after the bitter cold landscape, and they paused to warm their hands and take their shoes off to get circulation going in their blue tinged toes. Once they were warmed up enough to make sure none of their fingers or toes were in danger of frostbite, they put their shoes on and started back down the stairs.

Khadija was listing the number of things that didn't add up as they went down the dozen flights to the landing with the door they had entered. Khadija suggested that they go ahead further down the staircase to see where it went, and Richard now having circulation returning to his extremities agreed. It was another dozen flights down to a landing with a wall that had a lever set into the far end of it with the word "Pull" written above.

Khadija pulled the lever down, but unlike the buttons in the tunnel far above, nothing happened. They continued down another half a dozen flights only to have the stairs end in a slightly larger area. Again, one of the walls that had a lever set into the far end of it with the word "Pull" written above. This time Richard tried pulling the lever down, but with no result. Having come as far as they could go, they turned around and a long discussion started between them on the stairs heading back up.

They reached the landing and opened the door leading from the bright stairwell out into the night on the "sky" level. It took a moment to for Richard's eyes to adjust from the bright stairwell, to be able to make out the edge of the "sky" that he would need to duck under, but as he stepped forward, Khadija elbowed him in the ribs to turn. One of the lamps in the seating area was on and a recognizable figure was sitting there.

Ariana looked up from her tablet and spoke, "Oh, there you both are."

Richard gawked open mouthed as Ariana continued, "I am sure you have a lot of questions, but it is very early, and I still have some sleep coming my way. I will gladly answer them in time, but now that you both are in the know about the snow, I could use your help with an imminent problem about to arrive at our doorstep. If you could both come by my house at 10, I would appreciate it. But for now, I need to return to my home, and you to yours.

She turned on the flashlight app on her tablet, clicked off the lamp and walked over to a 4-seater golf cart parked nearby in the darkness. She turned on the golf cart headlights and beckoned them to get in. Richard piled the climbing gear into one of the backseats and sat next to it, while Khadija sat in the front by Ariana as she started cart in motion.

Ariana said, "Let me take you around the dome road around to the East stairwell like the one you just came out. Taking the stairs back down there would be easier than climbing back down the way you came. When you get to the lowest level, just grab the lever, and pull hard to pivot open the wall far enough to walk through. Once you are through, please grab the sconce uprights and pivot the wall back closed until the latch clicks. You can get to the East maintenance bay easily from there from there."

The curved cliffside wall they were driving along soon showed the red reflection of another exit sign coming into view. Ariana pulled out beyond the edge of the sky up next to the door. Khadija and Richard, loaded with the climbing gear, got out of the cart and headed over to open the door.

Ariana said, "There's nothing like running across something new under the stars to energize you. Be sure to pivot the wall back closed at the bottom and see you at 10."

They heard Ariana faintly singing to herself as she drove out of sight around curve in the night sky.

72

The Climatologist was glad his backside was intact to get him this far. As much as it had ached from the day of non-stop sitting in the cramped sno-T while they skirted the nunatak, his legs now were aching more from the effort of hiking in snow up the last mile to the foot of the ridgeline.

The white world outside was almost too bright to look at, and progress across it in the sno-T had come in fits and starts. The ascent from the snowplowed strip of frozen ocean that served as an airfield here had been slow going. They had been driving up a glacier and alternating team members had to walk out and advance the route before the captain would let the driver proceed.

Once they were around the nunatak mount and down onto the flatlands, the pace picked up and they made good time towards the mountain ridgeline that was their goal. The bouldery snow-covered terrain at the foot of the ridge blocked the sno-T from driving any farther so; to get close enough for accurate readings, the rest of journey would need to be on foot.

What looked like a disconcertingly recent avalanche and series of rock falls off the ridge, left only a narrow winding path that the team was forced to follow. As they came up to the ridge, the Climatologist was focused on watching the windspeed and swirling wind direction on the dials of his handheld anemometer to be sure they would be in good spot for measurements. With his head down over the dials, he bumped hard into the back of the squad member in front of him who had abruptly stopped.

Looking up he realized the captain was holding up a hand

in the air that had stopped everyone. The captain pointed at his eyes and then over at the face of rock just ahead. A ten-foot-high semi-circular crack in the rock was widening with a low rumble in front of their eyes, and sharp cracking sounds of the ice rime on rock face splitting off came to them as the crack widened.

With all the evidence of recent avalanches and rock falls all around them, the Climatologist immediately looked up to be sure nothing was breaking off on the steep rock face of the ridge above them. A ten-foot boulder cleaving off at ground level was not much of a concern. If anything like the giant boulders and fallen snow mounds, they had been wending their way around was dislodged by this tremor from the ridge towering overhead, their day could be ruined in a hurry.

Looking up exposed his full face and neck to the howling wind, and he stamped his feet to keep the circulation going as he examined the cliff face above. The rumbling stopped, and not seeing anything falling towards them, the Climatologist looked down and froze figuratively in his tracks.

The ten-foot boulder had swung open to one side and a tunnel leading into the ridge could be seen. Standing in the opening was a silhouette taken out of a western movie.

The silhouette shouted to be heard over the wind saying, "Hey guys, welcome to the neighborhood! You should be getting a call from your general any time now, but seeing as it's a bit nippy outside, why don't you just come in get out of the wind. Whoever has the phone can wait by the door, but I'd suggest the rest of you come in and warm up. After you hear from your commanding office, we can have a chat to help you understand what's going on around here."

The captain considered it a minute and then asked, "Who are you with and where are you from?"

"I'm working here with a non-governmental coalition of organizations on "clean cooking stove" loading. Me, I'm based out of Austin," said the silhouette and added thoughtfully, "Austin may pride itself on being weird, but it has nothing on the "weird" going on around here."

The expression on the captain's face was looked doubtful and he was looking around as if to make sure they weren't about to be ambushed when his phone rang. He dug it out and talked briefly with someone while he moved to look past the figure to scope out the well-lit tunnel hallway beyond.

He put away the phone and said, "Well, they wanted us to find out what's going on around here. The general seems to think this is as good a way as any to do that."

The captain motioned the team into the tunnel and, once inside the cowboy figure pressed a control button on the wall and the boulder door swung shut behind them.

The cowboy said, "We'll get you something hot to drink, to thaw you guys out on the bus ride back to the village."

To the Climatologist, the captain looked like he was already mad about the appearance of the tunnel in the Antarctic landscape and the orders to go inside. The mention of hot drinks and taking a bus ride made him look like he wanted to kick something. The Climatologist hurried towards the front of the line to keep the temptation of his intact backside from providing an outlet for the captain's bottled-up rage.

73

Khadija was in the kitchenette area of one of the bus-sized rec-reational vehicles, like the one that had brought her and Rich-ard to the South American village…wait… scratch that… to the subterranean sky dome they had been living in with, as it turns out, unlimited air conditioning available just a staircase away.

They had decided Richard, with his multiple sweatshirts under his long rider coat, was the warmer dressed of the two, and he was sent up the exit tunnel from the landing platform they were parked at to meet their arriving guests. She had set out some hot food and drinks for the expected arrival of their expeditionary guests and was now making a cup of tea for herself.

As she waited, sipping her tea, Khadija thought about their early morning escapade with the shock of the winter wonder-land discovery at the surface and the surprise of having Ariana waiting for them when they got back.

She and Richard had entered the stairwell, where Ariana had dropped them, and taken the stairs down to the bottom where the stairs dead ended into the wall with the lever marked "Pull." This time Richard had both pulled the lever out to release the catch and then pulled on the lever to pivot open the wall section for them to walk out.

They had found themselves coming out in one of the fire safety alcoves that were sprinkled around the beltway. They had piv-oted the wall back closed and walked out past the large firehose reels, and trailers of flame suppressing foam out onto the belt-way. They only had to walk a short way down the beltway and then were back in their East maintenance bay.

Richard had called the loader tech to say he didn't need to come after them with the boom lift but did need to bring the service cart around with their clothes and shoes. Khadija had checked in with her lead women at the monitor desk and then contacted the control team to report the vent issue and let them know conveyor room 5 was clear to start filling with hot cubes again.

The tech had pulled into the bay to drop off the cart and then took off with their thanks on his scooter. They had got in the cart, ran back around so Khadija could return the manlift, and then headed back to the apartment. Even though it had seemed like an eternity since they had embarked on the cleanup in 5, and the cliff climbing to frostbite central at the top of the stairwell, the first shades of dawn were just appearing as they got back to the apartments. They had crashed, exhausted from the experience in Khadija's apartment.

Later, they took the cart up to Ariana's house and were greeted by Ariana's husband as they came in. Ariana had seen them from the conference room and had come down to join them.

She had said she hoped they were rested, and started in on the expedition arrival issue, without any further mention of their early morning activities. Richard had given Khadija a look because of this, but she just shrugged slightly as she listened to Ariana describe the expedition, they were tracking coming towards them.

The coalition council had just decided that the expedition should be met, brought into the village, and have the general operations of the facility shown to them. Ariana had said, beyond her Ahmed, Jamal and a few trusted scientists and staff, almost no one else knew the true nature of the village location that the two of them had discovered last night. Since the two of them were now "in the know," she had asked them to act as a welcoming party to go out and meet the expeditionary friends that were headed their way.

Following her instructions they had climbed aboard a bus sized vehicle that, unusually had a roof with several large, arced sections of glass overhead and were driven out of the main loading area into an open entry/exit bay. As the bay door had closed behind the bus, they sat stationary for a minute while the scanning technology in the bay did its thing.

Apparently satisfied, the loading door in front of them had opened and the bus drove out into the massive exterior "truck" yard that spread before them under a vast builder cube structure. The daylight from a series of long openings at the far side lit the interior.

A screen of sparking dust with a projection of ice coated rock appeared to hide the openings from the outside world, but they could see out to the icy landscape beyond. The screen of projection seemed to also seal out the extreme outside cold as there was no ice buildup in the truck yard space.

Trailer tugs were in constant motion bringing full containers out of the bays and taking empty containers back in. As the bus drove, they had watched builder cubes form up around the four sides of one of the nearby shipping containers and lift it up off the trailer so that a base of cubes could form underneath and over the top entirely sealing it inside. They had watched as it joined the parade of containers lifting off other trailers, sailing towards the exterior openings. As each cube surrounded container reached the opening, the cloaking ability of the builder cubes had been turned on, causing them to vanish. The icy rock projection was disrupted for a moment as the cloaked cube wrapped shipping containers flew through it, but the dust soon restored itself and the projection hiding the opening snapped back into place.

They had passed along the wing of exterior docks where Khadija had pointed out that dark shipping container sized shapes on rock bases "docked" at every door were not actual shipping containers. As they had watched, the front wall section of one of the dark container-like shapes ahead of them raised to reveal the full stacks of stove cubes her loader women had put inside during their shift.

A single builder cube had flown over and attached itself to the bottom corner of the stove cube stack. As one, the stove cube stacks had lifted a couple of inches off the floor, and then an entire container length of stove cubes had flown out of the opened end of the faux shipping container. This flight of stove cubes was led by the builder cube towards the daylight openings. As they reached the projection in the opening, the cube cloaking turned on making the entire container long stack of stove cubes disappear in a moment.

Khadija had told Richard that, with the cloaking and energy absorption qualities of the cubes, the multitude of shipments the coalition now had flying around the world were both invisible and undetectable by radar. As they passed by the open end of the container sized shape the cube shipment had just flown out of, they could see the interior looked like a regular corrugated wall shipping container. They watched as the interior "paint" color of the container changed to a different color and floor planking wear pattern shift to a different look. The front end of the faux shipping container was lowered back down into place to close off the container for the next load.

The bus had gone past the end of the outside docked container wing towards the end of series of dark tunnels and one daylit opening with another projection of icy rock across it leading out of the side of the truck yard. Dozens of large bus sized snowcat style vehicles with caterpillar treads were parked near this opening. Richard had figured these were probably a form of lifeboat for those working in the facility in case they ever had to pull the plug on the cube tech and get everyone to safety across the arctic landscape.

The bus had stopped in front of one of the tunnels and a cloud of builder cubes swooped down and started assembling themselves up the sides of the bus stopping as they reached the level of the side windows so only a small portion of the top row of builder cubes on the side was in view. The bus was raised off the ground with a floating motion, turned, and headed forward towards the tunnel.

The bus entered the dark tunnel with walls and ceiling just barely visible flitting by rapidly outside. The bus had headed downhill at a fairly steep angle while gathering speed in the tunnel. After a while, the tunnel had leveled out and joined into a much larger tunnel with the endless piles of black shapes below being conveyed along the 6-lane highway width floor.

They had flown for a time down the wide tunnel over the piles being conveyed below them until daylight appeared ahead and suddenly, they emerged into a long cathedral tall hall with a pattern of square openings "punched" through the walls on either side that daylight was coming through. It had taken a minute for Khadija, looking up through the bus roof glass, to recognize the pattern as endless stacks of stove cubes set into both walls with light coming in through their center openings.

She had told Richard that the council had approved early production runs of stove cubes that they wanted to keep captive while further evaluation was done. She guessed this specialized bus was what the science teams used to monitor these early test runs of the stove cubes.

Richard had been staggered at the enormous quantity of stove cubes and was trying to guess the length and height of the hall to calculate the number of cubes when they were back into another dark tunnel section. Almost immediately were back out in another cathedral hall and Khadija looking closer told Richard the piles moving rapidly down the floor below looked like the filtration "shingles" that she had seen Xanthe's stove cube produce every few days during their testing.

She had guessed that these stove cubes probably had their air filtration set beyond the normal limits to test their ability to filter out carbon and other harmful greenhouse gas elements from the air being moved through the ridge. Based on the highway width of the piles of "shingles" being moved below, the cubes had to be taking out a lot of carbon.

Richard had been briefly concerned about the possibility of these shingles raining down on the glass roof of the bus, but as they looked carefully, the shingles seemed to be sticking to the vertical ridges formed by the tapered faces of the cubes and filing down the towering walls in an orderly fashion. Out the front of the bus, they could see the shingles reaching the bottom and being incorporated into the flow below.

After passing through a couple of dozen of the cathedral halls and doing some up and downhill runs through the "shingle" conveyor tunnels between them, the bus had finally slowed as it came into the next cathedral hall. Every cathedral hall had a large alcove landing space with a corridor running off marked with an exit sign. The bus had turned in the middle of the space and settled on the floor at an angle that filled the width of the landing alcove. The builder cubes to the side of the bus unstacked and scattered away to somewhere before the bus door unlatched.

They had both received a text from Ariana saying the expedition would be forced by recent builder cube terrain adjustments to pass close by the door at the end of the walkway from the alcove they had landed at. Khadija texted back to acknowledge receiving the text from Ariana and had said, "OK, cowboy, you're on." He had headed out the door and down the corridor for the short hike to the ridge exit.

The smell of hot cocoa made the warm bus interior feel homey. She noticed the front and side windows of the bus shift to opaque black while the roof remained clear. Khadija guessed that the coalition didn't want to fully share the builder cube's flying abilities just yet.

It was not long before Richard arrived back with the expedition group, who stripped off their heavy coats and gear, to stow underneath, before stepping up onto the bus. Khadija distributed drinks and encouraged them to take a plate of the hot snacks before taking their seats.

The captain looked suspiciously at the blacked-out windows, but finally took a seat himself and Khadija called the control team to say they were ready to return. As the bus pulled around headed out over the flowing river of shingles, the builder cubes went into their road vibration mimic mode, so, to the expedition group who could not see out the side windows, it felt like the bus was just driving down a paved road.

As the cathedral hall came into view, the climatologist was beside himself with questions, but Khadija could only tell him that the halls of cubes filtered carbon and some other unwanted gases out of the air. She said they would get him in touch with some of the science team when they got back to the village, who could fill him in better.

The captain, already a bit short tempered by having his expedition interrupted, was doubly put off by the unsettling implications of the cathedral hall above him doing carbon capture inside a rock ridge in the middle of nowhere. The captain looked like he had a lot of questions as well but also looked like he wasn't going to believe the answers unless they were extracted under duress.

Khadija said, "Since you boys are clearly not in Kansas anymore, I would just sit back and enjoy the view out the roof, until we can get you settled in amongst us munchkins back at the village."

74

Richard had been amused by how quiet the expedition team had become on the trip back through all the cathedral halls of cubes they could see up through the roof. The climatologist had asked if they would get to tour more of the "direct air capture" facilities. Richard had said he was sure something could be arranged but wasn't sure how much more there was to see beyond what they had just been through.

He got an odd look from climatologist who said, "We've only seen a couple miles so far, and the satellite data shows this operation running along these ridgelines for another nine hundred miles."

He and Khadija looked at each other, before Richard said, "I'm sure much will be explained at dinner and arrangements can be discussed after."

Richard spent the rest of the way back trying to expand his estimate of the number of cubes in use per hall by nine hundred miles and was still working on it as the bus arrived back in the "truck" yard. The group could only see the ceiling as the bus "bumped" along on made its way through the truckyard, so the flying shipments he and Khadija had witnessed on the way out were effectively concealed.

The bus pulled into one of the truck entry bays, was warmed up and then drove around into the main dock building to pull up by the far ramp. They came out of the bus getting their first look at the vast and busy shipping space as they pulled their coats and artic wear out from under the bus.

The day shift forklift scurry could be seen in full swing as they walked up the ramp and piled their coats and artic wear in the back of the trailer hitched to their service cart then took seats in the 8-seater cart. Richard and the captain led out in the service cart with Khadija following in the 8-seater cart with the rest of the expedition guys.

They drove side by side in the lanes so Khadija could give a quick description of the basics of the shipping area and beltway as they passed out of the tunnel. As the "sky" appeared through the drop off opening above, with warm semi-arid setting becoming apparent, Khadija told the group to hang onto their hats and questions.

They turned off on the ramp, and headed up into the park where the expedition guys got their first view of the village. There was a bit of pandemonium with everyone asking awkward questions at the same time, but Khadija said explanations on that front would have to wait until after they had a chance to meet with Ariana that evening.

They took a quick drive around the lower village to give them a sense of what was there and then Khadija had pointed out the pub that Ariana had asked them to meet her at for dinner that evening. They ran them a short way up the street to the construction trades quarters, where a trailer with labeled duffle bags was parked.

Khadija handed out room keys and left the key to the 8-seater golf cart in the hands of the captain. The group was asked to each pick up the duffle bag with their name on it out of the trailer along with a bag containing water and snacks.

They reminded them of their general's promise they would not talk to others in the village about their location or the halls of cubes they had seen on the way back and left them to get settled in their rooms.

Ahead of dinner time, Richard and Khadija had come around to the pub and were taken around to the back into an old looking two-story room by the proprietor. Richard helped Khadija put together a couple of tables and arrange chairs for the evening dinner. He then went out to sit in the pub on the stool closest to the door.

The pub was a reproduction of an existing pub somewhere in the north of England, and the proprietor, who poured him an ale without him asking, had been one of the managers at the original pub for many years. He sipped the ale and pointed the arriving expedition members to a door at the back with the "Glasgow Room" sign overhead. When the last of the expedition arrived clad in shorts and tropical shirts, he texted Ariana and walked to the back room to join them.

The Glasgow room was a reproduction of a library interior that was used as a quiet area to have lunch or a drink, but could be rearranged for meetings, parties, and other events. A couple of the expedition guys were seated along the tables they had pulled together, while others stood around the room talking loudly.

The proprietor was taking drink orders from the recent arrivals and handing them menus to look over. Richard plunked his beer down at one end of the table and grabbed a chair to pull up.

He said, "You guys must be starving, so if you want to order some food, we can go ahead and eat, before Ariana arrives to fill you in."

The proprietor answered some questions about the pub items on menu, but said they could also order anything carried by any of the restaurants in the village. Khadija entered the food orders on her tablet and Richard helped to get another drink round for the guys.

Before long, the waitbots rolled in from the back with the food and the proprietor checked in to make sure everyone was set. The guys seemed to be enjoying themselves as they ate, but the Climatologist, still seemingly affected by what he had seen, just picked absentmindedly at his food.

After a time, the rear door to the room opened and Ariana entered. Richard pulled her up a chair at the far end of the table and she set her tablet down and greeted the guys. She spent some time asking their names and where they were from. Even the climatologist seemed more at ease after 15 minutes of the guys and himself talking about their homes and what they did for fun back there.

She then delved into a brief overview of what was taking place at the production facility and the mountainous carbon filtration halls stretching almost a thousand miles out from where they were.

Her phone beeped with a text. After glancing at it, Ariana propped the tablet up on the table, made a few motions and greeted the someone on the tablet. The voice chatting with her seemed familiar to some of the men, but it was not until, she turned the tablet to face the men at the table did they see the face of the general on the screen.

The general congratulated them on reaching the ridgeline they had been sent to explore, but said their mission was just starting. Before continuing, he told the captain a detail that he had covered in their last private meeting and asked for what the captain had replied at that time.

The captain said, "It was something about not even getting to hang out in McMurdo on the way, because of a fricking strange acting ridge, sir."

The general grinned slightly and seemed satisfied with the reply. He said that Ariana had agreed to allow full and unhindered access to all the production and carbon filtration facilities, in exchange for their promise of secrecy until they fully understood what was taking place there.

Each of the men would be given a secure camera phone and teamed up with a specialty inspection team on the general's end that had experience with nuclear and military facility compliance inspections.

They would spend the next weeks documenting everything about the facilities and conducting interviews with key people at the facility. In the meantime, they were to behave as though they were a contractor team, keep their mission secret, and not let any of the village or production facility staff know about the Antarctic location or other information they would learn.

They were to also use their own camera gear for the daily inspections and make trips at the end of each day back to the surface to independently upload camera footage via satellite, directly back to the military analysts the general would assign for the mission.

It would be a couple of days, before the full inspection and analyst support team would be in place, so they were to be free to relax and explore around the village and manufacturing facility for the next couple of days to get their bearings before starting on the more thorough inspection the next week. The general wished them a good evening and asked the captain to contact him separately via satellite phone from the surface in the morning to get detailed orders.

Ariana thanked the guys in advance for their cooperation and hoped they would have a more pleasant time in the village environs than they would be having on up on the surface before she left. The captain grudgingly thanked her, but the rest of the guys reacted to the couple of days of leave by ordering another round of drinks.

Richard and Khadija left the guys to their partying and exhausted from all that had taken place decided they should turn in early. As they got into bed, Khadija asked why Richard was so distracted and he confessed that all he could think of was Ariana confirming hundreds of miles of cube lined halls. He said that his back of the envelope calculation of nearly half a billion "stove" cubes in the cathedral halls might be on the low end.

She pulled him over and gave him a long kiss before saying, "Well, let's see if we can find something else to distract you so you can get to sleep."

75

Xanthe wrapped up the video call with the government officials and her two regional coordinators, and sat back in workstation chair, relieved that they had finally obtained approval for drone delivery of the stove cubes in that country.

She looked up at the wooden shade structure/sky image created by the builder cubes enclosing Jamal and Miri's beach place that the security team had her hiding out in. While Miri would still fly her into locations for few hours of critical meetings, the security team always wanted her safely back at the beach place by nightfall.

As she watched the movement of the clouds in the sky above the overhead gazebo "wood beams" she thought about how the pace and reach of coalition efforts had rapidly expanded around the world to set the stage for the massive "drone" delivery roll out of stove cubes.

Her regional coordinators had been working with the governments and her organizer teams had been building support on the ground in the communities projected to have the most severe climate crisis impacts. Widespread distribution of millions of bases, ducts, and control tablets in those countries had already taken place, but the distribution of the now highly valued stove cubes had become increasingly problematic.

Today's videoconference meeting with government officials was focused on those stove cube distribution problems. While the national government had been glad to have their populations receive the "clean cooking stoves," their governance in the poorer and more remote regions of their country was weak.

The corrupt regional officials that held sway in these areas were holding container shipments of stove cubes ransom until the coalition would send money to get the shipping containers released. The coalition would not pay, and the national forces were too weak to help, so the stove cubes were not getting through.

The militias operating in other areas of the country were the second problem. There had been attempts by the militias to simply steal stove cubes directly from the new owners. As soon as the owner notified the community leader and had a new control tablet keyed to them by the community leader for a replacement stove cube delivery, an automated disintegration command would be triggered by Jamal's failsafe program. Militia leaders had learned that stove cubes stolen from owners would simply turn into ash piles before they could get them sold.

The militias had taken to intercepting the stove cube shipments before they reached the community and were keyed to owners. It might take Jamal's failsafe system a couple of weeks to realize a shipment had been stolen, so the militias could sell them "fresh" on the black market, giving any buyer seeking to try and reverse engineer the technology a couple of weeks to probe them before the Jamal's failsafe system would disintegrate them.

Having exhausted all outside means to tell how the stove cubes functioned, the buyers started trying a multitude of ways to get inside. The tamper proof nature of the stove cubes would quickly turn the point of intrusion into a fountain of sparks followed by the collapse of the cube into an ash pile.

These constant attempts by the growing number of those trying to get inside the cubes had already triggered the disintegration of tens of thousands of the stove cubes from intercepted shipments.

These reverse engineering diversion efforts had been foreseen by Xanthe, Ahmed, and the coalition security team. The coalition had made it an early priority for Jamal's team to develop a global logistics system that would enable nighttime "drone" deliveries of stove cubes directly to the new owners. By encouraging the keying process of these individual "drone" delivered stove cubes soon after the delivery to each new owner, these growing thefts could be circumvented.

Xanthe and her community organizers had refined the distribution process for those bases, ducts, and control tablet accessories. Fortunately, the bases, ducts and control tablet accessories had little value, so shipments of just those were not held for ransom or stolen on their way to the communities.

The process started with community leaders hiring local community members to staff community centers or distribution locations using coalition funds. A typical community center distribution set up would start with ongoing demonstrations of a stove cube to community members coming in. The majority of those, having seen the demonstration, would want to receive a stove cube and would be directed to the roomful of tables staffed by those hired locally for the process by the community leader.

They would be handed an assembled 5 side folded "refrigerator" base, the duct accessory, and walked through how they would attach to a demonstration stove cube. The locally hired staff would then walk through the step-by-step graphics printed on the inside of the base on how to send a request for the delivery of their "clean cooking stove" cube. The assistants would point to the graphics, reminding the new owners to place their base at an outside location, free of people, at least 10 paces away from any house, trees, or other obstruction by sunset. The owners were told the stove cube would be delivered by drone at some point during the night.

The staff member would quickly bring the demonstration stove cube down on top the "refrigerator" base to illustrate how sudden the delivery would be. A community "trustee," given the power, would do the "hand jive" procedure to individually "key" the control tablets to each of the soon to be stove cube owners.

When Miri had flown back to Athens to pick up Xanthe, she had encouraged Eleni to join them. They had loaded a bunch of Eleni's painting supplies in the plane to bring with them to the container hangar/living quarters Xanthe would be using as a base of operations for the near future.

Eleni had been enjoying using the back end of the living quarters as studio space while Xanthe was on video calls or flying off with Miri during the day. Some of the art Eleni had recently done was to be featured in an upcoming show.

Miri seemed to be settling in nicely with Jamal during his frequent trips out to join them. Jamal's ability to get away for even a day was becoming increasingly limited as the date for the logistics system roll out to make drone deliveries approached.

Xanthe made her way into the living room area and could look out and see Eleni already down on the beach with a drink in hand. She put on her beach wrap, made a drink, and went down in the elevator.

She popped her head out into the hangar where Miri was working and said, "I'm heading out on the beach to get a swim in. I'd suggest you get a drink and join us, so we can watch the sunset before dinner."

76

Khadija and Richard were getting up earlier in the day now that the night shift was running smoothly, and their focus was shifting to working on the other two control chair arenas in other time zones. Khadija was spending more time on conferences with the training leads in these other locations, while Richard worked remotely with those who were installing all the control chairs, racks, and monitor walls in the spaces.

They took a pause in their online conferences to head up into the village to meet Jamal for lunch and for a promised show and tell of his super-secret control area after they had eaten. They took the service cart up the hill to where Jamal and his team were housed and one of Jamal's team met them at the door. He led them around the outside up a ramped walkway and out onto a back patio that looked out towards the cliff to the North. He said their food orders should be arriving soon and hoped Jamal could join them before long.

Richard said that it was odd that after weeks of living in the "village", they still did not know where Jamal's control room was located. Khadija said that was nothing compared to virtually the entire workforce thinking they were somewhere in South America, when they were all living under a gigantic dome in the Antarctic.

The expedition captain, who regularly went up to the icy surface for his daily check in, shared the latitude and longitude of the door location off his GPS. Richard looked up the location and it appeared the village and sky dome was built into the side of a volcano. The manufacturing side was close to the magma tube of the volcano while the shipping area and truck yard was located on the rocky escarpment side of the snow-covered mount over a mile up in the air. One of the major Antarctic stations turned out to only be about a day's drive away using the bus sized snowcats they had seen in the truckyard.

The waitbots with the drinks and food rolled up around the side of the balcony and, as they were setting things out on the table, Jamal came striding out from the living space to greet them. Jamal apologized for not getting out to see them earlier, but he said the schedule moving up meant that his teams were jammed trying get it all done.

They sat down to eat, and Jamal caught them up on his escapades around the desert with Miri followed by their tour of all the control centers to bring them online. Khadija asked him how they were getting along together, and it sounded like he and Miri had really hit it off. He had not been able to visit Miri for a while now. With the rollout of the logistics and drone delivery system, he would be able to get away and have some fun again with Miri soon. At least today he had some breathing room to have lunch.

Jamal said, "Speaking of fun, the monitoring team, had an entertaining evening watching your climbing exploits on your way to visit the cooler weather upstairs. Tell me what you have been up to since then."

They filled him in on loader operations, what they now knew about their location, and what was going on with the cloaked shipments flying out of the truckyard tucked inside a cliff a mile up in the air. Richard said that was nothing compared to his recent overlay of the facility plans on the satellite maps that showed the manufacturing end of the facility backed directly under the cone of the volcano. This had to mean the stove cubes were being manufactured in an area where there was still molten magma occurring.

"Yeah, pretty wild hey," Jamal said between bites and continued, "My mind was already blown when I realized the communicator cube server capabilities were way beyond anything the tech world had even dreamed of. I can't really tell you a whole lot more about the manufacturing process, cause even our science teams that have been tearing their hair out since the start don't really know how it is done. All they can tell me is a butt load of carbon coming out the filtration halls, is funneled into the magma chamber below the volcano and that the ready to use cubes and other carbon-based pieces parts show up on demand at doors coming out that molten rock furnace."

One of Jamal's team came out to check in with him and Jamal said, "Well recess is over. Ariana has invited you to sit in on our latest "stove" cube delivery roll out so, let's head into the central control space."

Jamal led them inside across the common space, to a door he opened with his palm on a dark pad. The door opened into a tunnel walkway running into the hill behind. Jamal unlocked a door at the far end and as he opened it, he saw their eyes widen.

He said, "Welcome to the nerve center of our control operations".

77

The door Jamal was holding open led into a large space, at least three times the size of the basketball court control room back at the base. The walls had the telltale structure pattern of a builder cube construction with a domed ceiling and white square lights spaced to dimly light the room. They came out onto a walkway that curved around to follow the dome wall around the upper third of the space.

The video wall stretching across the front was vast and the number of control desks spread across the floor below held a small army of controllers. The room was filled with the buzz of conversations coming from below as Jamal led them towards what he called the situation theater that was carved into the builder cube dome at the midpoint of the dome walkway. The situation theater had steeply tiered seating and a continuous glass front and sides that looked out at the video wall and floor operations below.

As they walked, they could see multiple entrances out onto the walkway, that Jamal said came from some of the other houses and buildings on the hill. Jamal pointed out the monitor desks behind glass windows on a level below and said that was where all the manufacturing operations were controlled and monitored. Jamal said while the actual cube and pieces parts creation process taking place in the depths of the volcano was hidden from them, everything from the conveyor rooms to the truckyard was monitored and controlled here.

They arrived at the situation theater and went in through the glass door leading in from the walkway. The situation theater had a three-story glass front wall and side glass returns that extended back across the walkway to the dome wall. As soon as the door shut behind them, the hubbub from the control floor below was cut off and there was quiet inside.

Another glass door, like the one they had come in, led out to the continuation of the walkway on the opposite side and they could see an elevator set into the wall not far away. Two guys and a girl were looking over the walkway railing just in front of the elevator.

There was a ledge around the inside of the front window with an array of communicator cubes set out on it. The seating stepped up steeply to a railed alcove area at the top of the theater with more doorways just visible in the alcove beyond. The guys and the girl out by the elevator caught sight of Jamal and made some urgent motions to him. Jamal looked rueful and said he needed to go, but that they should hang out here in the theater and Ariana and company would be along shortly.

Richard and Khadija climbed up a couple of rows and took the end seats to look out the front windows. They could see the entire expanse of the video wall with all its colored dots, dashed arcs, and white numbers. The video wall showed a slowly spinning world globe in the center with regional area maps flanking it and an inset map of Antarctica to one side on the bottom. Beyond the maps several columns of aerial views of locations were arranged that switched views from time to time.

A couple of the science staff started to drift into the situation theater from the door by the elevator. One of them went along the communicator cubes on the rail and made finger motions to start the projections. Projections of several of the coalition council heads started to appear as others started to arrive by elevator and file into the situation theater from the walkway outside. Several of those appearing, including Jaha recognized Khadija and said they were happy to see her again.

They heard the sound of conversation up behind them, and a small gathering seemed to be starting down the steps from the alcove above. Ariana greeted them on her way down and said she was glad they could join them. She made her way down to the front to greet those joining remotely and coming in the door from the elevator. A voice from behind them spoke and they turned as Ahmed greeted them from the seat he had taken just behind them.

He regretted it had been a while since he had seen them but said that he and other council members had been in almost constant negotiations with the countries they hoped to distribute the stove cubes in.

He said with a smile that their cliff climbing exploit had caused a bit of a stir. They had not been noticed until they were halfway up the wind vent, and the monitoring team had woken Ariana with concerns about them injuring themselves. He said that Ariana had vouched for Richard's climbing experience and said to let them go. Word had it that there was a round of applause in the monitoring room once Khadija made it safely over the top.

Ahmed pointed out the shadow of night that was slowly moving across the globe display on. He said that once night fell in the country they were delivering to, shipments of stove cubes flying in could be met in over the delivery area by builder cubes stationed there. He said that the stacked container sized stove cube shipments would start to break up as the builder cubes swooped up to meet them. A builder cube would snap on the top of each stove cube and guide it down. In a blink they would land on the base units with the activated control tablets that were being put out by the new owners.

They could see Ariana smile as the band of darkness crawling across the immense video wall was starting to show a display of yellow dots appearing with popcorn frequency. Ahmed said these were all the locations where the new owners were placing their cube base units out and swiping on their control tablets to activate and request a stove cube delivery before setting them down inside the base unit.

Ahmed said that the algorithm Jamal had developed, broke the deliveries down into districts, and tried not to have too many simultaneous deliveries in any one district at the same time. He said that the clustered blue dots on the screen represented the propeller driven drones with stove cubes loaded that were ready to fly for twilight deliveries. The green clusters along the top of the map represented the container sized stacks of cubes that were activated and waiting at their storage location on the bottom of the Mediterranean. White numbers moving across the map represented airline or military aircraft in flight. A number of lavender lines represented shipping container shipments from the truckyard in flight.

As the band of darkness was reaching their time of deployment, the controller lead's voice came over speakers in situation theater. They heard him check with all his delivery controllers to make sure everything was looking good on the actual number of tablets activated for deliveries verses the night's projected deliveries. The numbers matched close enough that everything was a go, and the control lead said to launch the undersea cube stacks.

Immediately, the green colored shapes showing cubes on the sea bottom turned to lines as the container-sized stacks of stove cubes launched out of the sea and arced up into the stratosphere towards their assigned delivery areas. The lines changed into blue dot clusters as the groupings broke up into individual cubes.

As they waited for the cube stacks to reach their drop zones, Ahmed filled them in on the delivery process. He said that the stove cube delivery was demonstrated to government and community leaders using custom propeller driven drones that the coalition had commissioned to carry and deliver a single stove cube at a time. Governments were told that deliveries had to be made after dark to prevent militias from shooting down drones to sell the stove cubes on the black market. A fleet of these propeller drones was shipped into each country and was used to make twilight deliveries, overnight deliveries to brightly lit locations, and dawn deliveries.

These propeller driven drones provided a visible cover explanation for the government and population that was actually contrary to the way the majority of stove cube were deliveries were actually made after nightfall. Once full darkness had fallen, the container sized stacks of stove cubes in the stratosphere would break apart into a spread out swarm. Individual stove cubes would each have a builder cube fly up to meet it in midflight and attach onto to its upper edge to guide it down to the activated control tablet destination miles below. As these paired up cubes approached the ground the builder cube would start producing a sound identical to the whine of the propeller driven drones. Both the stove cube and builder cube were fully cloaked to be invisible to both eyes and radar as they descended.

Approaching treetop level, and upper corner of the builder cube would glow with a drone "navigation" light as the pair of cubes rocketed towards the ground. A nearby cube recipient watching the delivery would hear the propeller whine, see the "navigation" light streak down and hear the impact of the stove cube dropping onto the base unit. The builder cube with only its navigation light visible would immediately streak back up into the sky mimicking the higher pitched whine of gunned propellers, turn off its light, and be immediately lost in the night sky. The decloaked stove cube that appeared in this instant would be left sitting atop the base unit that the activated control tablet had been placed within.

In this manner each stove cube delivery could take place at lightning speed with only the audible whine and streak of the navigation light left burnt on the retinas of the recipients to provide an explanation.

They watched as colors start to shift as each delivery was made and the yellow dot changed to green on the videowall displays. With a board full of color changing dots and branching lines lighting it up brightly, Jamal came back into the situation theater. He reported that the logistics system was up and running and that several thousand stove cubes had already been successfully delivered in just the brief time everyone had been watching.

Ariana started clapping her hands and soon the entire situation theater was clapping, while Jamal made a gesture out the window to include his team in the control center below. Ariana took a moment to thank Jamal and his team for their incredible work leading to the deliveries that they had witnessed today.

She also thanked the council for all their hard work as well to get all the government approvals and clearances. And lastly, she thanked Khadija and Richard for their efforts to get the facilities and remote operator training on a path to enable them to soon meet their million stove cube deliveries a day goal.

78

After Ariana's thankful words, the gathering in the situation theater broke up. Ahmed asked Khadija and Richard to head up the steps to the top of the seating area and back into the upper entry alcove. They went up and Ariana's husband met them there at one of the alcove's doors, took them inside, and up a set of stairs that led right into Ariana's house. He took them out into the side garden, sat with them at the patio table there and ordered refreshments.

Khadija mentioned how easy it was to forget that this pleasant sunny day they were experiencing in the village, was being created for them under a dome of rock inside a volcano mount in Antarctica.

Ariana's husband chuckled at the incongruity and said, "Yet, even for those in the know, what is amazing is how quickly this environment gets taken for granted, while we are all focused on our portion of the coalition efforts. Speaking of which, how are you both doing with your current projects?"

Richard said they now had the full complement of 500 robotic loaders in the facility ready to go and the maintenance areas set up. The techs he had been supervising remotely had completed the set up for the other two control chair arenas that Khadija now had in use.

With the assistance of "baby Einstein" and Jamal's processing power, the training simulations had been upgraded to realistic representations of the actual manufacturing facility. Those in training could now go straight from the simulations

to working shifts using alongside experienced remote operators to load real cubes here in the facility.

Khadija told him they already had completed the first training
in the new arenas and the new shifts were enabling round the
clock loading operations here in the manufacturing facility. Her
training leads at the new control chair arenas were already working with their second trainee groups, while her women back at
the military airfield had completed their last training and were
now fully staffed.

Those already trained had been offered more overtime in the
near term to help boost the number of stove cubes getting out
until the newer trainees rotated into the mix. She said by the
end of the month, they should have three fully staffed shifts in
three time zones to operate the facility at full capacity round the
clock. At full capacity they should easily be able to meet the
million stove cubes per day shipping and delivery goal.

Richard said that his projects were largely on cruise control
at this point, and Khadija said she her training leads had things
well in hand she was just doing a last edit of the training manual.
She said, since the security team thought it could be another year
before it would be safe enough for the two of them to return to
normal lives in the "outside" world, they were wondering what
they would do in the meantime.

Ariana's husband said, "Glad to hear things are moving so
quickly, but sorry to hear about the security team's forecast. A
number of us are in that same situation. Ariana and Ahmed do
have some thoughts about how you might occupy yourselves in
the meantime."

He paused for a moment to look at them, then continued, "You
may not be aware, but the coalition has had me working with engineering firms around the globe to develop detailed plans on a
range of climate resilience infrastructure projects. In addition to
building code approvals for some new carbon-based structures,
the NGO coalition has received approvals from the national level down to local governments and communities to proceed with
project implementation in the event the coalition can come up

with the funding and manufacturing capability to make them happen. Putting in place this scale of mitigation infrastructure and buildings has been regarded by many officials and critics as pie in the sky. This perception of impracticality has made it easier for the coalition to get the essential people in each locality to the table, the detailed plans developed, and agreements signed off by skeptical officials. Using ruwaq technology, and the income provided from our clean transition minerals mining, we will soon have both the capacity and the funding to deliver on these plans.

He paused again to let them take in what he had said before continuing, "The coalition council and tribal elders plan to meet as soon as we can produce examples of these "pie in the sky" structures and systems. As with the stove cubes, we are trying to move forward with laying all the groundwork and putting the logistics systems in place ahead of time, so we will be ready to move forward should the recommendation from the council and approval by the tribal elders occur. I'm glad to hear your schedules are freeing up, because I think there will be more than enough opportunity for you to help us out with some of these efforts."

Khadija and Richard were considering what they had been told when Ariana and Ahmed arrived in the garden to join them. Ariana's assistant appeared with drinks for the five of them as they scooted around chairs so everyone could sit at the table.

Ariana took a moment while they were sipping their drinks to check in on the budding relationship between the two of them and if they were still happy working together. Khadija and Richard answered that they were and after some probing, Ariana seemed pleased with their progress as a couple and satisfied with their responses regarding working together.

She nodded at Ahmed who said, "Let me fill you in on some other developments and mitigation efforts that the tribal leaders and coalition have decided are necessary considerations for meeting the larger goal of preventing mass migrations."

Ahmed said they had been installing other filtration "cathedral" halls of stove cubes to capture carbon in other remote mountain ranges from the Himalaya's to the Andes. While these would help counteract the worsening buildup of greenhouse gases, they could not avert the imminent killer heat waves and extreme weather projected in the coming decades.

The output of solid carbon coming off those installations was going to be as enormous, so additional underground manufacturing facilities were being constructed to turn that carbon into massive numbers of cooling center buildings, resilient housing, and other mitigation infrastructure.

Ahmed outlined how they also had to be sure the overall food and economic infrastructure continued to work despite extremes of heat and weather that would lower crop yields and dry up water sources. Using techniques like cropland mirroring to maintain yields and desalinization of sea water to bring fresh water for irrigation far inland to the fields would avoid famines.

He said modifications to boost the insulative and reflective qualities of urban buildings would mitigate heat island effects in the poorest sections of the cities. By starting stove cube deliveries and mitigation projects in the poorest and most vulnerable areas and finding equitable ways to provide resiliency against the projected impacts was a central tenet of the coalition mission.

Ahmed thought Richard's help would be needed to integrate the underground manufacturing facilities, with the shipping, storage, and control room areas laid out by the architects. He thought Khadija could help with implementing a version of the coalition's inventory and logistics system to monitor stocks, fill orders, and send delivery requests to the control team.

Ariana's husband said he would send them the underground facility plans and details on the thousands of infrastructure related projects they had plans approved and ready to move forward on. Ariana said to look the plans over, check in with Xanthe on the implementation, and take some time to think it over.

Khadija looked over at Richard who shrugged and nodded and then said, "It sounded like something they would up for, but they would again need to build out significant staffing and hire extensively in each project locality to make it all happen.

Ariana said with a grin, "Well Khadj, you've never been shy about making a case for more help, even in tight times when we had difficulty funding your requests. With our growing mineral sales income, I can say that funding the additional workforce needed will not be a problem."

"One other thing," Richard added, "We made ourselves a promise to visit our families once the loader program was up and running. It feels like this would be a good time to do that, before we get too involved in this next phase of projects."

Ariana gave them both an apprising look, smiled and said, "Of course, just let Jamal's control team know when and where so they can arrange transport for you both."

79

Xanthe was tired from the recent long days of flying around this region of the country. The coalition had been working at a frenetic pace with community leaders to get as many control tablets distributed ahead of the likely drone delivery ban that would be put into effect in the region tomorrow.

The politician in authority with the help of the Chief of Police had been behind early seizures of shipping containers with stove cubes, impounding them until "appropriate donations" could be extracted from the NGO coalition to the politician. Xanthe, early on, had been sent to meet with the politician and chief of police to try and work through this literal "hold up." As the coalition had steadfastly refused to pay, her entreaties fell on deaf ears, and the shipments remained impounded

The politician and chief of police soon discovered the lucrative returns to be had selling the impounded stove cubes on the black market. The coalition had continued the ground shipments of stove cubes to get the populace supplied, but a large percentage were being intercepted by the regional police and sold on the black market to line the pockets of the politician and chief of police.

Following a recent heat wave that had killed hundreds but left everyone who had already received a stove cube alive, the reluctant national legislature had finally approved the coalition's request to deliver stove cubes more quickly by "drone". With stove cubes now being delivered by drones in the air, they could no longer be intercepted causing the politician some consternation.

To restore their ill-gotten gains the politician and the chief of police had managed get a local judge to hold a hearing intended to block the deliveries by drone in their region. The local judge was rumored to be in the pocket of the politician so a cease-and-desist order for drone flights was expected immediately following the hearing.

The coalition had predicted further severe heat waves in the coming weeks and wanted to be sure the cubes got out to the poorer population, especially the elderly and those with children who would be most at risk. Xanthe had an enormous number of control tablet deliveries sent directly to trusted community leaders who secretly worked to get them widely distributed and keyed to the local at risk population without the politician and chief of police being aware.

Xanthe had worked overnight and all through today with community volunteers to get as many control tablets as possible handed off to the remaining population ahead of tomorrow's deadline. They still had permission for one more evening of drone deliveries and the large population secretly provided with control tablets was under instructions to activate their tablet's delivery function no later than 8 PM that evening.

Xanthe had been invited over to the home of the politician to revisit the terms of ransom in light of the expected judgement banning drone deliveries expected the next day. It was an evening meeting that Xanthe was sure the politician had scheduled so he and the chief of police could show her that even the few drone deliveries they were still attempting to make after dark could be intercepted by the waiting police in their cars below.

Xanthe showed up tired and frazzled at the rear entrance of the politician's house half an hour early. The politician's housekeeper, who was in favor of the stove cube effort, met her at the back door and ushered her up a back stairway to the second floor. She sat Xanthe in an alcove on the second floor by the top of the main staircase so she could be out of sight but still ready to make her appearance for the meeting, exactly 5 minutes before the 8 PM target for all control tablets to be activated and awaiting a stove cube delivery by drone.

Xanthe could peek out and see the politician and the police chief sitting out on the politician's balcony with the last bits of sunset fading into the stars overhead. The politician was saying the whole drone delivery approach had put a dent in his bank accounts and he hated things that put a dent in his offshore accounts.

The Chief of Police said that they had been intercepting a fair number of the daytime food drone deliveries, though they could never seem to nab the drones themselves, and tonight his men would be intercepting the "stove" deliveries by following the blinking lights on the nighttime drones to the locations of the deliveries.

Xanthe looked at the time, and right on the dot the housekeeper rang the front doorbell, said something out the door and then came up the stairway. Xanthe waited in the alcove as the housekeeper came up the stairs, walked through the front room and politely interrupted the politician on the balcony to say that their guest had arrived.

The politician and Chief of Police chuckled and then the politician asked the housekeeper to show her up. "We'll see if little miss Xanthe will be singing a different song, now that her relief supplies are being rounded up and her precious stoves are about to be nabbed as well."

The housekeeper waited for an appropriate time in the stairwell then led Xanthe into the room. The housekeeper asked Xanthe if she could get her anything and headed off with her drink preference. As she strode out onto the balcony where the two men were sitting, they saw she was sweaty and dirty, and her boots were tracking bits of mud across the rich rugs and floors of the politician's villa.

"What, may I ask, are these recent reports of your police officers impounding our relief supplies?" she demanded of the chief of police.

He smiled and looked over at the politician, who said chuckling "Well, as of tomorrow's judgement my dear, all deliveries will have to be done by ground and inspected by our local authorities before they are released. Surely, we can overlook a few impetuous officers in the meantime."

"So, your force is getting a head start today illegally diverting relief, so you can have it held it hostage after tomorrow's judgement," Xanthe said shaking her head in disgust at the chief of police.

The politician said, "All we want is a return to the proper channels where all of us can truly benefit from your organization's largesse."

The chief of police chortled at this and raised his glass to the politician. They paused to watch as the first of the night drone deliveries appeared blinking against the sky. Headlights appeared on the mountain road below and flashing lights were turned on as the police cars followed the slow-moving drones into town.

"Just to be clear, we do have until the judge rules tomorrow to continue legally delivering our supplies and stoves?" said Xanthe. The politician watched the headlights turn to follow the blinking drone's lights as it came down into the city.

"Of course, of course my dear, your drones remain legal for tonight. Deliver, all you want." He and the chief finished watching the police car pull up where the drone had landed to commandeer the supplies it was bringing in.

He added, "Please give our regards to your fellow leaders and let them know we will want to start a new, more expensive conversation after tomorrow's judgement."

"Well, let me just pass on your regards," Xanthe said texting something on her phone, "and I think our business here is about done."

The housekeeper came out to hand Xanthe her drink off the tray.

"You know I think I will join you in your celebrating our last night of drone deliveries here." she said, raising her glass.

The politician and chief looked at one another perplexed before turning to look back at Xanthe standing behind.

"To new conversations." she said holding her glass out at then in a toast.

The politician and chief were looking somewhat unsure as they reluctantly clinked glasses with her and watched her take a satisfying sip. A small gasp escaped the lips of the housekeeper who was looking out past them towards the city, and the two men turned to see what had caused it.

The night sky was starting to light up with flashing drone lights appearing everywhere in the night sky crossing one another in zigs and zags at lighting speed. The flashing police cars lights came on in the foothills on the far side of the city where they were waiting, but they didn't move. Clearly the impetuous officers scattered across the hills were having trouble deciding which of the multitude of lights to follow. Every second a drone was streaking down to make a delivery and the lights in the sky had expanded to tens of thousands.

The politician and police chief were still staring open mouthed at the delivery light show as Xanthe finished her drink.

"I think I will leave you to your thoughts. You clearly have a lot to consider before tomorrow's conversation" she said placing her empty glass on the tray still held by the smiling housekeeper and showed herself out.

80

Their time together since they had watched the stove cube deliveries in the situation theater and been breifed on the mitigation projects had flown by. Khadija and Richard had grown closer and taken over one of the bus/RV units with a bedroom built in the back to adapt into their home away from home for all the traveling they were doing.

They had done a checkout of the Asian underground manufacturing facility in the Himalayas and then had the bus flown to a secluded place near Khadija's parent's home outside Glasgow. They got to spend a couple of days with her mom and dad there before they were joined by some of Khadija's extended family that were flown in to meet Richard.

After days of interesting conversation and even more interesting food, they were back their bus/RV and being taken to the American Rockies underground manufacturing facility for its check out. Khadija had recruited some of her lead women to help with new logistics and inventory system and the initial cataloging of parts had been completed. With the help of "baby Einstein" they now had an automated way of tracking every item added to inventory and every item shipped out.

Having some days before they needed to travel to the mitigation measures approval meeting with the tribe, they headed up to visit Richard's parents and spend some time on the Montana ranch where Richard had grown up. They spent their days riding horses and hiking in the wide-open country around the ranch and enjoying meals with Richard's parents and nearby family.

On their last morning, they got up before dawn and rode the horses up to the top of a mesa behind the ranch, with a view for dozens of miles in all directions. The rising sun was starting to paint the tops of surrounding mesas in a warm light as they got down off the horses to look at the view. They stood there together with Khadija resting her head on Richard's shoulder as clouds were turning brilliant sunrise colors and the sunlight was now reaching down the sides of the nearby mesas.

Richard broke their reverie by kneeling and eloquently asking for Khadija's hand in marriage. Khadija, touched, said yes and leant over to kiss him. On the ride down they talked about what their future together might hold for them once this rush of coalition work was done.

As they approached the stables, Khadija was wondering how to tell her family. Richard confessed he had already talked to Khadija's dad and mom to get their permission when they had been in Glasgow. He said one condition her mom had insisted on was that her daughter have a proper Pakistani style wedding, so they would need to let Richard's folks know about that when they told them.

Richard's parents loved Khadija, were delighted at the news. They said they would be happy to travel to the wedding. Khadija called her dad and mom and unusually found them at home outside Glasgow. Richard's parents waved in the background of the call and introductions were made all around.

The next day when Richard and Khadija were ready to hike back out to the concealed bus location to head off for their council meeting, there were tearful hugs and well wishes all around from his parents.

The builder cube enclosed bus lifted out of the steep sided canyon and Khadija and Richard looked out the windows from the front seats of the bus through the "transparent" builder cubes. The rolling Montana hills and mesas could be seen for dozens of miles in each direction before they were hidden by the screen of thin clouds the bus rocketed up through.

The native child avatar had learned how to pressurize and

heat the interior of the builder cube shell, so that they could now reach heights where the sky started to turn from indigo blue to black to enable supersonic travel speeds.

They settled back in on the couch to review the latest plans that Ariana's husband had sent them to prepare for the meeting. The three-day meeting they were headed towards was intended for the tribal leaders and coalition council to review and consider mitigation measures and planned infrastructure projects for implementation. Even at supersonic speeds it would still take hours for them travel between continents, so they settled in for the trip.

The bus landed in the rainforest next to several other buses already on the ground in the clearing. After the builder cubes cleared off, they could see a figure walk into the clearing heading towards them.

"Jaha", Khadija exclaimed as she jumped out the bus door and ran across to meet and hug him.

Richard followed at a more dignified pace and was introduced to Jaha, the native man with the patterned tattoo on his face he had seen in many of the meetings.

Jaha, took Richard and Khadija's hands in his, closed his eyes and said ceremoniously , "I see you are… in love…, and will… marry."

Khadija said a surprised, "Yes," and then asked incredulously, "Did you see that in a vision?"

Jaha's eyes opened and the stoic expression was broken by a grin as he said, "No… you dad say…to some in medical… and saying fly here… ahead of you. Get things…long walk to tribe and tents."

They got their packs and followed Jaha as he picked his way through the rainforest. It was nearly an hour later when they emerged out of the trees to see standard coalition issue relief tents appearing to surround a modern looking glass wrapped building incongruously set in the rainforest clearing.

Jaha said the building was an example community/cooling center that the builder cubes had plunked down wholesale in the clearing the other night. Richard could see it was a simple square plan form with identically sized foundation and flat roof slabs separated by 12-foot-high square columns spaced around the very outer edge. A floor to ceiling glass-like unbroken window wall ran just behind columns on the sides but angled in to leave a 10-foot-deep covered entry area on the front and back where large glass-like double door entries were located.

Jaha took them inside where the warm humid rainforest air changed to cool dry air-conditioned air. Wide stairways led up to an opening in the roof along the side walls that had been covered over. In the very center, a square opening about 10 feet across was punched through the roof and floor in the center and a second window wall was set back about a foot from its edge to wrap around letting light into the center of the building.

The entire upper section of the window wall had stove cubes arrayed projecting through the window wall. Additional frosted "glass" walls inside the building defined some smaller rooms.

Kitchen style counters were set out in front of this central window wall, and the rest of the space was tastefully furnished with modern furniture. The overall width of the cooling center had to be a hundred feet on a side.

Looking out the side windows they saw what looked to be three housing units built in a similar style stacked up in a staggered arrangement with a stair access up the side. Jaha led them around towards the back they could see those gathered inside.

The tribal leaders were there along with members of the coalition council. Richard could see Ariana and her husband, Xanthe and Eleni, Miri and Jamal, and Ahmed who caught sight of them coming in the door. Ahmed said overly formally, "Greetings and salutations on your engagement!" getting the attention of the rest who then greeted and congratulated them on taking the plunge.

Eleni immediately uncorked a couple of bottles of champagne taken from behind the counter and was filling clear compostable cups with what Khadija considered an uncharacteristically modest amount per glass. Jaha was explaining what was taking place to the tribal leaders who smiled, while Miri and Jamal helped hand everyone a cup.

Ariana had them all gather in a circle to make a toast to the happy couple and asked those gathered to each say a few brief words.

When it finally came around to Eleni, she said, "My wish is… the next time either of you decide to get engaged, you give me time to scrounge more than just a couple of bottles of dusty bubbly!"

They did not have anything scheduled for the evening, so they just hung around talking in the coolness of the community center. Dinner was brought in and set up on the counters. They all made up plates and took them over to sit and eat at the long conference table.

They spent the rest of the evening sitting around on the sofas and chairs catching up. Xanthe related her experience of the massive overnight delivery of every "stove" cube in the city while the politician and police chief helplessly watched.

At last, Richard and Khadija finally wished everyone a good night, were pointed in the direction of their tent and were soon tucked in asleep.

81

The next day the conference table had extra folding tables added to it to form a long U-shape with the oversize monitor that had been left at the eco lodge brought in to show the presentations on. Gold-tinged projections of the expanded council, science team, and others unable to travel in were already appearing, and Ariana was already greeting and talking with them.

Khadija and Richard got their hot drinks and something to eat from the counter and wandered in to sit in chairs at one end of the conference table where their name placards were located. Eleni was serving in a hostess role seeing that everyone had something to eat, and their cups of coffee and tea were topped up.

Jaha led the tribal leaders in to places at the center of the conference table. Jamal finished getting Miri set up to run the slideshow of images up on the oversize monitor and came up to sit at the front table next to Xanthe. The lineup of gold-tinged faces down the side tables was just about complete when Ariana called for the meeting to start. A blessing from the tribal leaders for wisdom and beneficial intentions to guide the meeting was voiced in their native language which Jaha translated.

Ahmed was the first on the agenda, giving an update on the latest climate model projections. The areas of extreme heat red zones they were seeing highlighted on the monitor, combined with a high likelihood of prolonged drought was the central threat in the regions Miri was now showing on the monitor. Ahmed recommended that in addition to the cooling center distribution, the farmland irrigation and mirroring contingencies for those regions be put into effect when those projects came up on the agenda.

The baton passed to Jamal, who outlined the successful deliveries of enough cubes to the extreme heat impacted regions, that fatalities from the deadly combination of high heat and high humidity the region had seen for a day, had been minimal. He said they had now delivered over 100 million "stove" cubes across the high-risk areas and were now delivering a million stove cubes a day.

Jamal said the next challenge was going to be delivering on whatever the tribal leaders approved in the way of mitigation infrastructure and buildings. Ariana thanked Ahmed and Jamal for working together on the targeted distribution done to date that had already saved lives.

She asked one of the science team standing outside dressed in what looked to be a reinforced paper coverall with a hood to come in. As he entered through the rear doors, they could see there was a connection between the suit and a stove cube mounted on a simple backpack support. As the dressed figure turned on the cube cooling, the incoming cool air coming out of the backpack vents inside the suit, slightly ballooned out the suit. The scientist said it wasn't fashionable, but it should allow those in red zones to keep cool when venturing outdoors to work or shop.

Ahmed said, based on their projections, at least a billion people would be affected by extreme heat and would each need a few of these inexpensive suits to wear. The scientist recommended that 5 billion suits be initially produced and distributed. Ariana asked for a recommendation from the council, and then an approval from the tribal leaders which she received.

Ariana pointed out while the "stove" cubes provided an immediate solution for short-term sheltering in place at home, the suits a bit more freedom of movement outside the home, and the relief tents temporary cool shelters, longer term solutions would be needed as extreme conditions worsened in coming years.

Ariana pointed out that cooling centers, like this building they were in, and the stackable housing outside could be built out the massive amounts of carbon coming from the mountain ridge air filtration halls. This incredibly strong construction similar to carbon fiber and clear sheet diamond could not only cool, but provide protection from the strongest hurricanes, or hottest wildfires. She asked Xanthe to speak to the willingness of the ruwaq to manufacture and provide these infrastructure items.

Xanthe had Miri bring up a slide that said, "If it exists and aligns with the mission, the ruwaq will build it."

Xanthe explained saying, "If we can show the native child avatar, and by extension the ruwaq, that a construction technique or technology has already been developed and piloted in the world, then the ruwaq are willing to use their equivalent of the technology to produce similar items at the scale and speed needed, should the council and tribal leaders recommend and approve it."

She waited a moment while Jaha translated for the tribal leaders and made sure they understood, before continuing, "Long term, this can be a gamechanger in our efforts to ensure populations can continue to remain in place in their home countries."

Xanthe had Miri skip to the potable water and irrigation contingency slides and ran through them to recap saying, "As you know, the need for new sources for drinking and irrigation water was one of the projected crises Ahmed's modeling team identified early on. At the time, the coalition council had recommended, and the tribal leaders approved, forming up the cube-based desalinization nodes on the bottom of the Mediterranean and having the builder cubes proceed with excavation of the fresh water carrying tunnels running inland a thousand miles or more in many cases to reach sub-Saharan areas where the droughts were predicted to hit. The tunnels along with the approved distribution trunks are all dug and in place awaiting activation should the council recommend, and the tribal leaders approve its use."

Xanthe motioned to Miri who brought up a map of North Africa with the projected drought areas highlighted and the underground tunnel feeders to those regions shown. She continued, "Based on what Ahmed's weather forecasting group is seeing in the data, droughts will cause crops to fail and existing drinking water sources to run dry in the red highlighted areas. Ahmed's team recommends activating the desalinization nodes to remove salt from the Mediterranean water pumped into the tunnels leading to the freshwater distribution network in these four zones. When activated, builder cubes will finish digging the vertical pipelines to the surface, with connectors for irrigation system attachment and faucets for drinking water. We have all these plumbing fittings in our stockpiles and can have the builder cubes plumb them in many areas virtually overnight. We already have buy-in from the governments and communities to provide water in time of drought. I would second Ahmed's recommendation that the irrigation contingency be put into effect."

Ariana paused things to make sure Jaha had caught up with the translation and explanation for the tribal leaders before asking for the council to vote to recommend the activation. The council voted to recommend the irrigation contingency be put into operation and after some discussion the tribal leaders approved moving forward.

Xanthe moved on to review the mirror contingency that Ahmed's climate folks were also recommending be activated in the red zone areas and Miri brought up those slides. Xanthe explained the mirror contingency was based on a piloted program that had shown the benefits of using thin film mirror to simply reflect enough of the incoming sunlight back out into space to reduce heat levels forecast in the red zone cities, towns, and croplands.

The builder cubes had been turned loose under landfills in the developed world to mine out the aluminum, glass, and plastics from the cans and bottles that had accumulated there. The ruwaq could produce mirror finish coatings of aluminum on an incredibly strong carbon fiber backing and encapsulate it with a clear durable top coating made from the bottles.

The mirror contingency for crops involved the simple suspension of North to South separated runs of mirrored sheeting over the fields on carbon support frames. By reflecting a portion of the sunlight hitting the field back up into space and providing a moving band of shadow during the day to keep the ground sufficiently cool, crops could still grow and deliver the full yields the population relied on. These methods had already been demonstrated to governments and local communities and the coalition had obtained the approval from many farmers to install these.

Xanthe talked about plans to also reclaim cropland that had been turned into desert by utilizing the irrigation water now available there with the mirror sheeting panels and inputs of topsoil shipped in by builder cubes.

She said that in cities and towns this material could be used to mirror building roofs and used in mirrored shade structures over open air markets, parking lots and other places where people needed to walk or congregate outside. This mirroring could reduce the temperature up to 10 degrees allowing a more normal life and commerce to continue.

When used for floating mirror coverings over canals and holding ponds, evaporation of the precious water held in those was also reduced. Ariana spoke to the tribal leaders saying you have seen the demonstrations from the mirrored roofs on the housing units, and the crop row and canal covering demonstrations at the end of the clearing. Getting nods and a reply in the affirmative from Jaha, she again called for a vote to recommend implementation of the mirror contingency in the regions highlighted.

The council made a recommendation quickly followed by the tribal leaders giving approval to move forward. Ariana looked over at Khadija and said, "Khadj, we're going to need your help wrangling all these mirror deliveries and coordinating with the local community leaders for install labor. Alright Xanthe, why don't we move on to community cooling centers like the one we are seated in now."

Xanthe explained that the fantastic amounts of carbon being taken out by the air by the halls of "stove" cubes in the could be repurposed into lightweight, but incredibly strong structures like the community center they were seated in. The community cooling centers were built as a whole unit that could be flown into place by builder cubes to provide centrally located cooling and storm/fire shelter complexes where populations could come to shelter.

The community cooling centers could be adjoined and/or stacked up to 7 floors high depending on the needs of the population. The construction was so fantastically strong the building type had already been approved in nearly 150 countries.

Approval of plans by localities and communities had been obtained for a mix of community cooling centers and housing. Land rights had been acquired, and scaffold surrounds with opaque fabric had been erected by local labor to screen the sites from view. The builder cubes had already done the grading and compacting of the site soil.

The community leaders in each region had staff already hired to manage the facilities and see to the equitable housing of the homeless and rehousing of those at risk in the slums and poor areas. All that remained was to approve the deployment of the housing and community cooling centers into the red zone areas.

Ahmed asked Miri to bring up the slide showing the priority areas and suggested the council recommend and the tribal leaders approve the first 50,000 of these centers be produced and installed as quickly as possible. The recommendation/approval for the centers was soon given and Jamal was given the go ahead to have the builder cubes start the foundation work at the graded sites while the production facilities making the cooling centers were finished and production geared up.

Housing was next on the agenda and Ariana said that while relief tents could provide temporary cooled shelter, the housing units, like the demonstration ones stacked in the clearing outside, were needed for the decades of extreme weather sheltering projected. The efficient compact building type using the same carbon materials as the cooling centers had also met code and was approved for building type usage in a variety of configurations up to twelve stories in height.

The goal was to quickly provide housing for those presently living in shanty conditions that would not protect them sufficiently in the event of heat waves or extreme weather. The architectural configurations allowed for lots of daylight, common green spaces and green roofs for gardens. They could be flown in and placed by builder cubes to be ready at each site for residents in a couple of weeks.

Again, sites had been acquired and building permits obtained, and grading work done for the first ten million units in the projected red zone areas. Ahmed suggested that the council recommend, and the tribal leaders approve, the production and installation of this first ten million as a starting point, with the understanding this was just a drop in the bucket of what would likely be needed. After questions, Ariana again asked the coalition council for a recommendation and then looked to Jaha for approval by the tribal leaders.

Xanthe moved on to report that contingency infrastructure projects were already underway to prevent bad actors from causing harm to better off, but still potentially impactable populations. She highlighted a scenario where bad actors might blow up existing high voltage line towers, crippling electric grids and knocking out air conditioning during a killer heat event.

Because stove cube distribution was prioritized to the poorest and most vulnerable populations, those already having air-conditioning would not be given stove cubes. A sustained power outage would strip them of their means of cooling leading to deaths.

The science team had shown the native child avatar examples of high-capacity superconductors. The child, once it understood what they were trying to do, showed them how builder cubes could tunnel and extrude room temperature capable superconductor runs nearly as easily as the structural rebar for the underground facilities.

Backup underground high voltage direct current superconductor lines had been tunneled under what the planning teams considered essential high voltage tower supported runs. In the event of a weather-related disaster or actions by a bad actor taking down transmission lines or towers, the builder cubes could fly in large in the large DC inverters that could be tied in enabling the damaged line power lines to be quickly bypassed and power quickly restored. Ariana reminded the coalition and tribal leaders that conditions for activation of these contingency measures had already been pre-determined and approval for these contingency measures had already been given.

Xanthe moved on to the infrastructure modification projects needed to slow, stop, and turn around the emissions leading to the extreme weather and heat related harms they were dealing with. Xanthe had Miri flip through a number of slides to remind them of all the efforts underway. As an example, she focused on the deep geothermal wells the builder cubes were drilling at existing coal and gas fired power plants as the poster child for what they were trying to accomplish.

She reminded them that the rock at 20-kilometer depths anywhere in the world was hot enough to create super-critical steam suitable to replace that produced by coal and gas boilers at existing power plants. The coalition wanted to focus on the US as a way to demonstrate to the world the workability of these deep geothermal systems and had identified 1200 coal and gas fired electrical generation plants they wanted to start with.

Again, the work and planning had been done, political arms twisted, land leased, and approvals given by doubting public officials and by even more dubious utility executives for the coalition to put in geothermal wells next to all their plants. The council had recommended, and the tribal leaders had approved, the drilling of the wells and the manufacturing of the wellheads and steam connector pipes. All that remained was for the council and tribal leaders to approve the final installation of the wellheads and the simultaneous reveal of the working wells to the world.

There was some extended discussion and debate on the merits of suddenly revealing the deep thermal well digging capability in this way, but in the end the council came together to recommend this course of action. There were smiles on the faces of the tribal elders who Jaha said approved of moving forward.

Ariana looked over at Richard and said, "We are going to need your help with coordinating this rollout."

Richard asked, "Is the plant with the smokestack I did some recreational climbing on by chance on the list?"

Ariana smiled knowingly and said, "Absolutely."

82

The coal fired plant manager had a fraught couple of years following the press conference where he and the utility had been given credit for discovering how bad the pollution coming out of the new plant was. Being forced to follow through with the expense and hassle of adding the pollution controls needed to meet regulations had not been pleasant and the wrangling had made him highly unpopular with those turbine generation degeneratetes on the other end of the steam pipes that he was always feuding with. With their total dependency on the steam his coal-fired boilers sent their way, he could and frequently did make life difficult for them whenever they made noises about complaining to the suits. Things had settled down over the years and he figured he could ride his coal fired gravy train right up until he was ready to retire.

The only problem in recent years was the continued noises from the same coalition of groups that had railroaded him and the utility into installing pollution controls, that now had their sights set on reducing carbon. Coal was carbon at its heart, and it was a just a fact of the plant manager's life that burning it at the coal-fired power plant dumped millions of tons of carbon dioxide out into the air.

The heat trapping potential of all this carbon dioxide being emitted and hanging around in the atmosphere for like a hundred years to melt ice caps and frozen tundra on the far side of the world had the coalition in a tizzy. He had to admit it was an effective tizzy as these coalition groups had made headway getting regulations in place that mandated ever stricter limits on carbon emissions for plants like his.

Installing expensive carbon capture equipment on top of the pollution controls to take the majority of that carbon out of the stack emissions had to be paired with an expensive means of piping and storing those millions of tons of captured carbon somewhere underground for the rest of eternity. Saddling his smokestack with the added expense of this carbon capture stuff was still years off, but his utility bigwigs were worried that the new climate reports these groups were waving around would get the regulations moved up or further tightened. Any tighter and there would be no coal plants left period.

When that NGO coalition had been formed, the ringleader woman, who was behind the press conference debacle that had shoved the pollution controls down his throat, had taken the reins. That woman had been fed some science fiction hokum and gone off the futuristic rails recently. She had finagled a presentation at last year's utility trade show and had gotten nearly all the influential utility CEOs and COOs in a room for it. This was where the coalition team had handed out overview binders for their fossil fuel plants and pitched them with the total "pie" idea.

The total "pie in the sky" idea was based on the fact that if you drill down a dozen miles anywhere on the planet the underground temperatures become so hot, they cannot only produce steam but achieve the higher temperatures for the supercritical steam needed to power the steam turbines that produce electricity at many coal and gas fired generating plants. Once you could use the underground temperatures to produce supercritical steam in a heat exchanger at the surface it was just a matter of feeding it into the plant and tying it into the turbines to produce zero carbon power.

The deal the NGO coalition was offering the CEOs was basically a boatload of money to lease the coalition a small plot of land directly adjacent to their turbine buildings for the drilling and installation of a geothermal wellhead. The NGO coalition would underwrite the cost of hiring the engineering firms, producing stamped drawings, and obtaining permits for a potential geothermal wellhead.

They would also pay the full salaries for the year for the plant managers and staff that would need to work with the engineering firms to fully plan and permit the construction. An additional year of salaries would be picked up once the wellhead was in place to facilitate the tie in, to their existing electrical generation turbines, using the coalition provided piping. At the time a working geothermal wellhead was installed, the utility was obliged to hook up at least one turbine, for initial testing and for electricity production if tests proved out.

A budget page for each CEO's coal and gas fired facilities included the binders, and the generous upfront payment for the land lease, and money the utilities would make off hiring out their staff was impressive enough. The kicker was the amount of money that would be placed into escrow and forfeited to the utility in the event that a producing geothermal well was not installed and ready for piping to the turbines within a three-year period following a mandated nationwide simultaneous press announcement event.

In exchange for leasing the land and allowing the construction, the NGO coalition also offered to back off pushing for stricter requirements that would force the early adoption of carbon capture technologies. By the end of the meeting the CEOs were sitting pretty with a proposal that would not only limit the potential downside of costly carbon capture and underground storage, but could make them a fair amount of in the near term, and potentially rake in a ton of money after three years when the coalition failed to install any of these sci-fi wells.

The plant manager knew there was no way existing drilling tech could reach down that deep and the millimeter wave futuristic stuff that some university geeks were using to burn holes in lab rocks was so far off, he planned to be long retired before any of it could ever see the light of day. The turbine turds, being preoccupied the past year with the all the engineering and planning being done on the coalition's dime, had kept them out of his hair.

The completion guarantee funds from the coalition had been scraped together and deposited, so the plant manager figured the coalition budget had to be running on fumes. He was so looking forward to that woman having to eat crow when they failed to get the wells installed and the NGO coalition being bankrupted by her failure.

He was surprised to see the turbine turds produce a stamped engineering plan set at one of their staff meetings and announce that the construction and drilling permits were all obtained. He was even more surprised to see the nationwide simultaneous press announcement date be set, and his attendance requested. The plant manager didn't know what the coalition was up to with all this shooting for the stars stuff, but there was no way was he going to let some "well to clean power hell" replace his coal fired gravy train.

83

Khadija and Richard unbuckled, after the seat belt warning had dinged to tell them the bus was at cruising altitude, went to the back and half collapsed onto the couch for the ride back to Glasgow for their wedding.

They had been rushing to keep up with the pace of infrastructure rollouts in the months since the coalition confab with the tribal leaders in the rainforest. The fast-moving pace had left them little time to think about the wedding in the meantime. Thankfully, their parents had largely taken on the planning for the wedding, with Khadija's mom and aunts being instrumental in getting the traditional wedding preparations done.

Khadija had worked with Jamal's team and the native child avatar to expand the coalition's inventory and logistics systems to include items from entire community cooling centers, down to the stakes used for mirrored drip irrigated row coverings. She then taught the native child avatar to automate filling orders placed by the community leaders and the on the ground staff, with all the accessories and supplemental supplies needed for shipment.

The items were frequently pulled from various manufacturing locations, added to transports running out to the regional underground distribution centers, and then consolidated into individualized builder cube shipments sent out for each specific site. The bulk of this could be done by the native child avatar, but there were enough hiccups that Khadija had the logistics women back at the base expand their ranks to handle the problematic orders and deliveries.

She was amazed that the thousands of infrastructure deliveries added onto the approaching goal of reaching the first billion stove cubes delivered was shrugged off by Jamal. He said as long as they used standardized builder cube delivery "box" configurations, and the automated delivery interface, they easily had the bandwidth for the millions of deliveries being made each day.

There were increasing extreme weather-related incidents that were putting Khadija and her logistics' women into disaster relief mode on a more frequent basis. They had been scrambling the past week when an unexpectedly severe heat wave affected densely populated areas of the Indian subcontinent.

There was still a good percentage of the population in that region that had been unwilling or unable to sign up for stove cubes, so the coalition had installed thousands of single-story community cooling centers for the use of those without a stove cube or air conditioning to use in a heat wave. The day the heat wave hit, these cooling centers had been instantly overwhelmed, hospitals were packed, and deaths were mounting so the coalition contingency plans were triggered.

Just after dark, thousands, still standing out in front of the cooling centers in the heat hoping to be let in to, had heard repeated loud whooshes and downward air blasts that buffeted the mirrored shade structures above them in the entry plazas. The onsite facility managers felt repeated rumbles shake the structure.

When the rumbling had subsided, the managers received a text from Khadija's women telling them to take the side stair roof inserts out and walk up to confirm the cooling, water, bathrooms, and electrical outlets were working on the upper floors. They were initially perplexed by the upper floors reference but, as they climbed, it became clear that their single-story cooling center had been expanded with upper floors into a seven-story high shelter. Once they reported the upper floors were cool and everything was working, Khadija's team had instructed them to let in another three thousand people in from the street below.

The following day shipping containers of "stove" cubes, bases, ducts, cooling suits, and packaged ready to eat food were dropped on the cooling center roofs, Once those with suitable homes had recovered and willing to return home, they had a stove cube keyed to them, were bundled up in cooling suits, and sent off home with as much ready to eat food as they could carry.

Food preparation and local food and supply deliveries to the cooling centers were expanded to meet the increased needs. Thousands of disaster tent cooling stations with running stove cubes were set up throughout the cities and towns to provide cool places for anyone trying to move about in the heat and feeling the effects of heat exhaustion or heat stroke coming on.

Teams in cooling suits were dispatched to check on vulnerable populations and make sure all those sheltering in place without air conditioning were set up with stove cubes for cooling. Soon even these tents were packed full of those with nowhere cool to go. For a couple of days, the combination of feverish temperatures combined with high humidity made portions of the red zone region literally unlivable without some form of cooling.

Despite the coalition's best efforts, tens of thousands succumbed to the heat and died over those days, their bodies just left lying in their homes or on the streets until the heat wave had passed. In the end the death toll across the region was over 100,000, but the governments acknowledged that without the planning and preparedness efforts of the coalition, that death toll figure could have easily had another zero or two added to it.

The demand for the stove cubes skyrocketed following the heatwave and the million a day that were now being shipped was not keeping up. Khadija's women and the other remote operator teams had been working overtime as Khadija set up added trainings to be able to double the numbers of remote operators at all the facilities.

To make things worse, following the heat wave a drought set in, and crops in fields without irrigation and overhead mirrored sheeting protection to keep the ground cool started to fail. A famine started to break out in the region, and it was soon clear existing food stocks and relief food shipments were not going be nearly enough to avoid widespread starvation.

A council meeting was convened where Ahmed pointed out that cube ownership was now almost universal in the populations that were most likely to face starvation, and he recommended activating the food contingency for the stove cubes to provide relief and prevent food scarcity migration from occurring. The council, after some consideration, made the recommendation and the tribal leaders approved the activation.

Jamal's control team soon had the food generation capability enabled and immediately across the world, every control tablet had another control line on it defaulting to "on" and every stove cube lit up with an animated graphic. The graphic showed how to take spadefuls of soil and simply place them in the center stove cube opening to give the stove cube something to work with.

Over a couple of hours, the necessary elements would migrate out of the placed soil up onto the interior opening sides to form the "lembas" food. These domed biscuits of food could be released by the owner putting their hand on the cube and gently pulling on the "lembas" biscuit to snap it away from the side face. Any unusable soil material left would be incorporated into the carbon "shingle" that was regularly discarded.

More soil could be placed inside the opening and the process repeated to provide enough nutrition for up to two adults or three to four children per cube, per day. Overnight the famine was alleviated as word spread quickly through communities of the food generating feature.

Richard, on the other hand, had been coordinating the geo-thermal wellhead deployment and scaffold surrounds with graphics at all the geothermal wellhead locations across the US. It was tricky because the visual screens of the scaffold graphics showing life size photos of the wellheads had to conceal the 1200 actual wellheads being installed and cloaked by builder cubes inside. Things needed to be coordinated and on track across all the sites for the simultaneous press announcements taking place across the US.

Since he was going to be back in his college town soon after the wedding for the press event there, Richard was also arranging a tent to hold a reception at with his friends there. They planned to hold their own reception so his friends could meet Khadija and then be on hand for the press event.

Khadija broke his train of thought by bringing up a program on the bus video screen and handing him a beer as she snuggled up against him to forget about things for a while as they flew back to his college town.

84

Richard and Khadija were gathered with Richard's family, friends, and activist allies, in the party tent pitched on the large grass field. The grass field was part of coalition leased property at the coal fired plant site where Richard had done his evening smokestack climbing adventure years before. Khadija was recounting and showing photos of the wedding and the several days they had spent with her family.

Khadija's relations and Richard's parents had flown in to gather at a grouping of houses around an event pavilion on the coast near Glasgow. Richard had soon learned that a traditional wedding that met with Khadija's mom's approval was a colorful and somewhat chaotic affair as the photos showed. Khadija's wedding dress was both colorful and ornate with a very fancy headscarf. Richard had been willing to wear the traditional silk leggings with a long Nehru jacket and the over the shoulder sash, but he had drawn the line at wearing the traditional turban.

The photos of the wedding service showed him dressed that way, but one of Khadija's aunts, somewhat miffed by his refusal to wear the turban, nabbed his western hat and dressed it up in gold fabric with an ornamental hatband. It was placed on his head from behind just as one of the group photos was snapped. He was made to wear it as a penance during a part of the reception that seemed to be unusually well documented in the photos Khadija was showing.

They were joined by Miri, Jamal, and Eleni who said Xanthe was going to be speaking and was stuck back with Ariana and some of the other national and regional leaders in the green room tent up by the stage.

The reception wound down as the time approached for the press conference and they said goodbye to family and a few friends who would be leaving them. Most of Richard's friends and all his activist allies were sticking around to see the big announcement so Richard and Khadija walked out of the tent with them to get a good viewing position for the proceedings.

A small stage with a podium had been set up in front of the fenced off area where the wellhead was meant to be installed. A green room tent was off to one side of the fenced area where Xanthe, Ariana and the mucky mucks were hanging out.

A graphic wrapped scaffold structure was positioned inside the fence exactly in the space where the geothermal wellhead was supposed to be installed. The scaffolds were wrapped on all four sides in large, printed graphics showing various illustrations of how geothermal wells work and how deep this well would be.

Spanning between the scaffold towers at the top were runs of horizontal truss supporting a large center graphic with a full-size view of the geothermal wellhead that would be located at the site. A banner across the top of the backdrops billowed a bit in the wind as it proclaimed the advance in technology the geothermal well would provide.

The press turnout was fairly impressive and the podium on the stage bristled with microphones. A tanker truck with a water tank marked "Distilled" was pulled up along the other side of the fence and a firehose was run from the truck under the fence and into the wrapped scaffold structure.

A significant crowd was assembling, and Richard recognized and said hi to some of the local leaders as they entered. He introduced Khadija to a late arriving group of his friends, as they arrived and joined the group from the reception party.

As the press announcement time approached. Richard caught a glimpse of the utility CEO and the plant manager heading into the green room tent but could not see Ariana or Xanthe. His late arriving activist friends were wondering what the couple of semi-trailers of large black pipes being backed into the parking lot were for.

Miri, Jamal, and Eleni who were in the know, kept quiet and only occasionally let slip a knowing smile. The chatter in the crowd quieted down as they watched Ariana, Xanthe, the utility CEO and plant manager and a mix of local environmental, social justice and faith leaders step up on the stage.

After introductory remarks by the local and regional coalition leaders thanking all of those whose efforts had contributed to getting to this day, Xanthe was up next. She spoke about the promise of many newly developing technologies and outlined how the geothermal well worked pointing to the illustrations wrapping the scaffold towers at the sides.

She pointed to the large heat exchanger enclosure shown in the full-size wellhead illustration on the backdrop behind her and noted where cool water would enter the heat exchanger. That water would flash instantly into superheated steam which would be piped into the nearby building to run the turbines inside. Done, she introduced Ariana and came out to join their group standing in the crowd.

Ariana spoke about the productive relationship the project had created between the coalition organizations and the utility companies after long years of "frankly butting heads", a comment that produced a titter of laughter in the crowd. She said she looked forward to the near future when they could move projects like this one forward across the world at a rapid pace to speed the transition away from fossil fuels.

The utility CEO was introduced, and Xanthe said, "This ought to be interesting."

The CEO spoke echoing Ariana's positive sentiments, and then focused on the potential that this new technology might provide to utility ratepayers and shareholder profits in the long term. After droning on a bit about continued coal use maintaining share price stability for what were surely years to come, he introduced the plant manager he said would oversee that coal use for the foreseeable future.

The plant manager stepped up to the mics, saying he was under instruction to work with the coalition hired engineers for however many years it took to accomplish the drilling.

He added perking up, "but until that year comes around, he would see to it that the plant would continue to provide the coal-fired steam he was known for ..." He was interrupted by a loud hissing sound that was coming from behind the graphic-wrapped scaffold structure. With a whoosh an enormous column of steam shot skywards, while the front graphic dropped to the ground. Revealed in an instant was the real geothermal wellhead being fed water from the "distilled" water truck and jetting the tower of steam out that was now billowing up nearly a thousand feet into the air above the crowd.

The plant manager had staggered back to one side of the podium and was left with his head craned back and his mouth open making gurgling noises as Ariana stepped up to podium microphone saying, "The NGO coalition and utility are proud to present to you this fully working geothermal well. This is just one of the several thousand across the country being revealed to the public today. I think if you look back towards the city, you can see the steam vapor rising from a couple of the other geothermal wells at the other coal plants."

The plant manager whirled and rocked back on his heels as he caught sight of the other plumes of steam rising clearly into sight in the distance. Ariana took the plant manager's hand and started shaking it while pulling him back over to the podium,

"We appreciate the sincere offer of cooperation just expressed here, but we in the coalition feel there is no time like the present, when it comes to moving to clean, zero emission energy."

She released the plant manager's limp arm and strode back over to the stunned CEO who reflexively managed to pose with a half-smile and a handshake with Ariana for the press photographers. Ariana brought up all the regional and local coalition leaders to the stage, giving hugs to each one and had them pose for a group photo with the geothermal well shooting steam up in the air behind them.

With the event over, they all then came off the stage, past the reporters asking for interviews and out to where Khadija and Richard were standing. Ariana's husband and Eleni appeared with baskets of miniature castings of the wellhead with large feathery "steam" plumes attached to commemorate the event. Eleni handed off baskets to the various leaders to give out to their key people while Ariana's husband stood by Ariana who handed them to Miri, Xanthe, and the science team there. Lastly, he handed one to Richard and Khadija. Ariana thanked them individually and then collectively from the bottom of her heart for all their work and efforts. She called for a round of applause for the newlyweds and wished them well on their honeymoon.

With the steam plume now arching thousands of feet in the air overhead, Richard and Khadija headed over towards the parking lot where their bus was parked. "Just Married" had painted in large letters across the back with streamers hanging off.

Everyone was gathered waiting to send them off. After a series of hugs and well wishes, they ran the gauntlet between the lines of birdseed throwing well wishers and boarded the bus. Khadija, put the bus in drive and they could hear the cheers and the last of the birdseed hitting the windows as they pulled around.

Waving out the windows, they got a last look at the gathering with the brilliantly lit white column of steam eclipsing the gray smoke from the smokestack that now seemed small by comparison.

Khadija drove up on a side road leading up the mountain and pulled into a secluded spot overlooking the city where she parked the bus. Richard went out to check the streamers so they would be out of the way of the builder cubes.

Khadija caught him from behind, put her hands over his eyes, and walked him away from the bus towards the overlook. Releasing his eyes and wrapping her arms around his chest to hug him, he could now look back towards the city where towers of steam coming up from the other power plants could be clearly seen stretching a mile or more up into the sky.

Khadija said, "Well, that something I'm happy to see finished, but I'm pretty worn out from all this wedding hoopla. So, husband mine, what do you say we get this puppy in the air and on the way to a secluded beach place that comes highly recommended by some of our compatriots. Richard said nothing but smiled, drew her close, and kissed her passionately.

531